D0729815

CAT CORE

2

LICH'S BARGAIN

A LITRPG DUNEGON CORE ADVENTURE

CAT CORE

LICH'S BARGAIN

DEAN HENEGAR

Recap

If you haven't read Book 1, I highly recommend you do so before starting Book 2. You can find the first book here on Amazon:

https://www.amazon.com/dp/Bo8WQ5VFLC

Here's a brief recap if it's been a while since you've read Book 1. The book starts with Florence Valentine going out on a simple trip to purchase some cat food. She lives at home with far too many cats and has little use for other people. Florence is shocked to see that the usual pet store she shops at is gone, replaced with a gaming and vape shop. In a tizzy, Florence storms out of the store and directly into the path of a delivery truck, ending her life.

The afterlife and an eternal reward should have been waiting for Florence, but instead, she finds herself transformed into something called a core gem. This must have been a mistake, and just like she normally does, Florence asks to speak to the manager. But it turns out she isn't the soul they were trying to capture. Unfortunately for Florence, she has no choice in the matter and is sent to a world called Aerkon to live the life of a dungeon core.

Florence isn't going to have any of this nonsense, so she sets out to create a home, not a filthy dungeon. Ignoring the advice of the advisor sent to assist her, Florence does things her way. The advisor is none other than the entity "Doug," who was responsible for collecting the wrong soul in the first place. Doug is given the form of a tiny white kitten by Florence, and the two bicker constantly.

Instead of monsters to defend her, Florence decides that she wants cats, lots and lots of cats, for her new home.

The home grows in power as adventurers start to turn up and begin their delves. Florence reluctantly steps into her new role, finding she enjoys many aspects of this new life and going so far as to make friends with a party of adventurers, much to Doug's horror. Trouble begins when cultists that follow the minor deity Kunrax show up. Kunrax takes the form of a hound, and his followers think a dungeon dedicated to cats is an abomination that must be destroyed.

The cultists attack the dungeon and the burgeoning town growing just outside it. A long battle ensues, and the cultists unleash a three-headed monster dog avatar that tears its way through Florence's cat defenders. The avatar is stopped in her core room, but it has seized Florence's core gem, which is shattered in the monster's death throes.

Instead of being destroyed, Florence finds herself in a hospital back on Earth. Believing that the whole experience had just been a hallucination due to the injuries she sustained in the truck accident, Florence goes about her life with new zeal. She makes friends and finds new homes for her cats, homes that can take better care of them. One night, a meow at her door reveals a small white kitten. That kitten is Doug, and he has been sent to tell her that she has been granted a chance to live out the remainder of her life here on Earth as recompense for the mistakes made after her initial death.

Doug joins Florence for this second lease on life but does mention that when her life on Earth ends, she will have to return to Aerkon and resume her duties as a dungeon core. There has also been a deal struck with the lich Berikoz, a deal to keep Florence's memories intact when she returns, a deal with unexpected demands that will soon be made known.

Introduction

"MY MASTER, THE ADVENTURERS DRAW CLOSE," A VOICE HISSED INTO the darkness.

"They are of no consequence, a minor disturbance that I will deal with should they make it past my defenses. On to more important matters than witless adventuring parties. It is time that I send you to your new home. Work hard and teach your charge so that you both may become more powerful and thus serve me better," Berikoz ordered.

"As you command, so shall it be done, Master," the voice replied. A sickly green glow penetrated the darkness, revealing a cloaked figure. A portal opened, and once the figure stepped through, it snapped shut, returning the chamber to darkness. The darkness didn't matter to Berikoz. He was no longer constrained by things such as vision. Mana flowed through his body, allowing him perfect awareness of everything nearby. That awareness could focus on more than just this deep outpost. He could see through his other agents, those that went about the world and did his bidding.

The chamber shook as something exploded nearby. With a sigh of annoyance, Berikoz released a bit of his power, and torches burning with green flame ignited around the chamber. In the growing light, Berikoz continued his latest experiment. There had been many failures but also the occasional success in his work.

When you had the potential to live forever, a few minor setbacks no longer mattered in the grand scheme of things.

The subject of his experiment whimpered. It was a simple human, one abducted for this purpose by a spell he had crafted. His spell had sought out a viable candidate for the experiment, but in hindsight, he should have spent more time narrowing down the spell's parameters. If he had the chance to do things over, he would have excluded any personages of high standing from the list of potential candidates. Alas, this young lady was a princess or some such. The mortal powers that controlled this world rarely troubled him or even knew of his existence, but upon capturing this young maiden, he had brought the wrath of a powerful kingdom down upon himself.

Normally, when a powerful mortal had cause to pursue Berikoz, he would find their pitiful actions amusing, but his work was at a critical juncture and he couldn't be bothered with the constant intrusions of adventurers hired by his captive's father. To make matters worse, this king's pockets were deep enough that he could hire somewhat competent adventuring parties. This latest group had tracked Berikoz to this redoubt, a long-abandoned fortress that sported a surprisingly vast underground complex.

When he had taken over this complex as one of his workshops, Berikoz found it swarming with various creatures that loved to call the dark places of the world their home. He slaughtered some but kept the more powerful ones as slaves to defend his work. The enslaved creatures had been reinforced by several of his undead minions. Up until now, the combination of defenders had been enough to keep explorers and the like away. Normally, the more powerful adventuring groups focused on dungeons they could exploit over and over again, not a single location full of dangerous creatures and traps that might or might not have any treasure for them.

"My father will kill you for what you've done to me," the girl squealed.

"None of that. I have no time for another of your rants. We had a deal, didn't we? I would prevent my experiments from causing you pain, and you would refrain from your mindless banter. Do you wish to renegotiate our deal?" Berikoz replied, dispelling the magic that kept her from feeling the pain his work inflicted.

She screamed louder than before as the pain wracked her body. Berikoz let this go on for a bit to reinforce his argument. He knew that lesser beings would see this action as cruel and evil, but it was solely a means to an end. The feelings of this girl were of no more consequence to him than the feelings of a dying ant were to the simple human who stepped on it. After an appropriate amount of time had passed, he reinstated his enchantment, granting the young lady respite from her torment.

"There. Now, I suggest you remain quiet unless you wish me to reverse the enchantment permanently. We will continue once I've dealt with this latest batch of your father's minions," Berikoz said as the wall to his chamber shattered, allowing water to flood in, along with the body of the creature that resided in the nearby underground lake.

"That was a shame. I had plans for the deep fiend," Berikoz lamented. Rare creatures such as that beast were difficult to find and even more difficult to bend to his will. It was a powerful monster, and the fact that the adventuring party had defeated it meant they were more dangerous than he initially believed. It was time to activate a contingency while battling them directly.

Magic tried to repulse his attempt; the adventurers were using a spell to prevent him from connecting to his phylactery. But Berikoz had planned for this: his connection was instead directed to one of the new vessels. These new vessels were perfect for the task; their inherent magic force prevented his phylactery from being detected. A heavily armored man entered through the shattered wall. A golden glow surrounded him as several enchantments enhanced his armor. In one hand, he held a broadsword with a blade of black light, while a heavy golden shield fashioned as the mouth of a lion was in the other.

Thankfully, the adventurer didn't spout threats or condemnations; those were so tiresome. He simply attacked the moment he spotted Berikoz. Contingency spells activated now that Berikoz was under direct attack. Shields protecting him from various forms of energy snapped into place even as a barrage of battle spells flowed forth from his hand. There were the usual suspects: magic missiles, magic arrows created from acid or poison, a traditional fireball, a cone of cold, and, finally, a bolt of pure necromantic energy.

All his attacks splashed off the adventurer's defenses. While none had penetrated, Berikoz could feel the enchantments around the human wavering. Before he could expend another multi-cast spell, Berikoz was blasted by magical attacks from a new pair of adventurers entering his domain. One was completely covered in robes, and only a pair of bright white glowing eyes were visible behind his dark garb. The other wore armor that was almost as heavy as the gear worn by the first adventurer. A mage and a divine caster had entered the fight. The divine caster no doubt belonged to one of the many good-aligned deities that had proven so troublesome in the past.

If there were these three, that meant there was likely one more Berikoz couldn't see. Given the lack of ranged firepower pelting him, aside from the spells, he assumed that meant a rogue or assassin of some type. He heard the screech of a blade dragging over his magical barriers as the assassin made herself known. With powerful enchantments woven into them, the assassin's blades stripped away several of Berikoz's magical protections, so he unleashed a concussive wave from his body, causing the assassin to stumble back as the power slammed into her. Even his mana-enhanced vision had trouble keeping track of the assassin; her form became just a blur of darkness that his focus refused to latch onto.

The warrior had reached him now. Flames poured from the mouth of his lion shield as the black energy of his blade hacked through Berikoz's final protective barriers. Contingency spells activated, replacing some, but not all, of his protections, and he fired off a wilting death spell. The warrior gurgled in pain and collapsed to the ground as all the fluid was pulled from his body. It was a messy but effective spell, one that penetrated through most magical protections.

While he had been dealing with the warrior, the mage continued to pepper him with various spells designed to negate magic. The assassin recovered and drove her blades deep into his back. Being undead meant that Berikoz couldn't feel pain, but he could feel large portions of his health being sucked into the weapons, the blades draining away his dark energy. With a thought, he summoned the last of his minions. A half dozen enhanced ghouls appeared around him and immediately piled onto the assassin, claws and teeth seeking the tender flesh beneath the attacker's limited armor.

A pillar of light summoned by divine magic dropped down on them all, causing his ghouls to erupt in flame and even burning away what flesh still covered Berikoz's form. He had underestimated this group. They had prepared well to defeat him, and if his phylactery had been of the normal variety, he would be doomed. Instead, he would just face a bit of a delay and, sadly, lose his latest experiment in the process. With a thought, Berikoz sent out a series of instructions to his minions around the world and at the same time woke the mountain beneath him.

He had chosen this ancient fortress as his workshop for good reason; it had inadvertently been built upon the surface of a dormant volcano. While the mountain slept with only the occasional rumble, Berikoz had been able to tap into its power—a power he now woke to full effect. He watched the last of his health get blasted and hacked away by the adventurers even as the hot lava began to burst through the floor. His soul was pulled toward the designated phylactery, but the process took just long enough to grant him the satisfaction of watching the party of adventurers become consumed by the molten rock filling the chamber. They were powerful and prepared for a lich, but they hadn't even considered the need to also be prepared for a volcano.

***

Deep inside another mountain, a dungeon core prepared for a fresh group of adventurers to enter. It was a vermin core, and having just gained level 20, it was excited to show off its latest floor. Before it could remove the stone covering its entrance and welcome in the waiting parties of adventurers, it began to feel pain deep inside its gem. At first, it was almost like a tiny itch in the center of its core, but as the seconds passed, the pain became more and more intense as a second presence asserted itself inside the cramped confines of the core gem.

The dungeon core panicked, remembering its pact with the lich, one in which it had been granted several resources it desperately needed, as well as some new defenders for its dungeon. Now the lich's side of the bargain was coming into play as he began to rebuild himself in the core-turned-phylactery. The process would be a slow and drawn-out one; the rebuilding of a being as powerful as Berikoz took time. Fear gripped the dungeon core as the power of the lich grew and its own faded, being slowly consumed to help bring the undead abomination back into existence.

Chapter 1

"Pairings are up. This is the final round of the tournament," Bobby shouted across the crowded store. Florence thought the young man looked a bit frazzled, but she decided to cut him some slack. There had been a bigger-than-ever turnout for the event since the winner of the tournament would be invited to the Dungeon Delve regional championships.

"Who are we up against?" Doug asked. To the others around them, the cat gave a little meow, but Florence could understand her friend as clear as day.

"I don't know, and I sure don't want to get in the middle of all those people. Look at them," Florence replied.

Since the rounds were timed, many of the players would rush the counter, where the pairings for the next match were posted. Florence might have liked playing Dungeon Delve, but that didn't mean she wanted to fight off a crowd of young people just to find out who she was going to be playing against. She also didn't have any desire to get within sniffing distance of several of them. Lord only knew when some of them had last bathed. It was almost like she was in France or something, given how many of them didn't seem to know what deodorant was.

The crowd began to die down, only the last few going over the pairing lists. Eventually, there was just one kid holding the parings sheet, and even though her hearing weren't too good these days,

Florence could hear the young man curse when he saw whom he was paired with. Bobby tried to get him to tone it down; there were several younger kids in the store, and the frazzled manager also knew that Florence didn't approve of inappropriate behavior or language in her presence.

"That must be our opponent," Doug said as the kid stopped cursing and looked over at Florence.

"Hey, lady, come over here. I've got my stuff set up already." The kid gestured toward a table in the back corner of the store, where his jacket, backpack, playmat, and what have you were spread out.

"Not a chance," Florence replied. "Were you raised by wolves? You're young. You can come over here. I've got bad knees, as everyone knows, and I'm not going to be galivanting around the store just because you're too lazy to get your stuff and walk over here."

"Oh, that touched a nerve. This is going to get good," Doug said as the kid started hollering at Bobby over the situation.

"Why do I have to play the old bag? I'm one win away from regionals and you have to pair me with her? She takes too long to play, and I need a win, not a draw due to time running out," the kid complained loud enough for Florence to hear.

"Dude, the pairings are done automatically by the computer system. I don't pick them. If you don't want to waste time, then stop complaining and get over there and play," Bobby said. Florence could see he was starting to lose his patience after a long and stressful day of running the tournament.

"Fine, but see if I come here to this crappy store to play again. I'll take my money elsewhere," the kid replied. Bobby shrugged him off and helped another customer. The grumpy kid stomped over to gather his possessions, glaring occasionally at Florence while muttering under his breath.

Florence had been playing at Mad Dog's Games and Vape for

nearly four years now and got along well enough with just about all the regulars here, except for that one guy Dave. Nobody liked him. This grumpy kid wasn't a regular, but she knew his type. They would only show up at the store for the big events that offered a good prize pool. To make matters worse, they bought all their cards online and didn't spend any money to support their local gaming store.

"How much do you wish to wager that he's playing four pally?" Doug asked. It was a bet Florence wouldn't take. Dungeon Delve was a surprisingly complex yet balanced game. The developers did a good job at making sure each expansion was fun and didn't favor one playstyle over another. Sadly, even a good gaming company could make a mistake, and their last expansion, Holy vs. Infernal, had seen a clear build emerge as the best, skewing the game toward favoring the adventurers over the dungeon keeper.

Normally, a party consisted of between four and six characters, the characters chosen from among a dizzying array of classes to build a balanced group. Now a party of four paladins was almost unbeatable due to their new healing link ability. They could just about shrug off any amount of damage that a dungeon could dish out, and barring a string of bad draws from their deck, the paladins would emerge victorious over the dungeon about seventy percent of the time. Rumor had it there were some card bannings on the horizon, but nothing official had been announced. Florence even had a version of the four pally deck in her bag for when she played as adventurers, but her real love was for playing as the dungeon.

"Fine, I'm here. Let's not waste any more time," the kid said rudely as he sat down and spread out his gaming mat. "Roll for priority?" A simple dice roll allowed the winner to choose whether to start as the adventurers or the dungeon, with the roles switching for each game of the three-game match. Winning the roll and choosing adventurer would give the winner a decided advantage, given the current meta.

"Sure. I'm Miss Florence Valentine, by the way. It's only polite to introduce yourself," Florence said as she rolled her d20, getting a miserable six.

"Yeah, whatever. I'm Shane, and I'm choosing adventurer," the kid said as he rolled, getting an eighteen.

"Of course you are. What party size? I suppose you want four, don't you? You strike me as a net-decker that would run four pally," Florence said. The player got to choose the size of their party, and the party size determined the size of the dungeon that Florence could build, giving her two tiles for each party member.

"Net deck or whatever. It's the best build and I'm here to win."

"You keep telling yourself that, dearie," Florence said in her sweetest, most insincere grandma's voice as she pulled out the eight tiles she wanted for her dungeon, placing the first tile on the table and drawing her hand of seven cards to start with.

"Turn one. I'm holding the party to prepare, and I'll play life bond." Shane dropped down the life bond card, the main piece that made the build so powerful. He had delayed going into the dungeon to get the buff on his party, allowing Florence time to place another tile and play one of her cards. It was a creature card, a starving cheetah she placed face-down on the first room of the dungeon.

The game progressed, with Florence fighting a losing battle against the broken combination of cards her opponent was playing. When it was her turn to be the adventuring party, she played her version of four pally against Shane's dragonkin dungeon, the dungeon said to have the best chance against the current adventurer meta. She won the game, but it did get close a few times.

"One and one, and I'm on adventurers. You going to throw your cats at me again?" Shane said with a confident smile plastered on his face.

"Of course. Cats are best, aren't they, Doug?" she asked, giving Doug a scratch behind his ear through the bars of the cat carrier.

"No, they're not. We would have been much better off with some other dungeon type," Doug replied, still all angry about her choice to go with cats in both their real and game dungeons. His response came out as a long meow to everyone who was listening.

Shane made sideboard changes to his deck. "You should play dragons if you want to have any chance to win at all."

"Cats are all I need." Florence made a couple of substitutions to her deck as well. Between games, they could replace up to ten of their cards with others drawn from their sideboard. Doug meowed again, loudly.

"Can't you shut that cat up? Really, I've already got to play against you with my allergies. I don't need to also have to listen to the stupid thing," Shane whined, looking for Bobby so he could complain again.

"Oh, little Dougie wants out. Can I take him for a walk, Miss Florence?" one of the regulars asked, walking over after hearing Doug.

"He'd love that, Deb. Just don't go too far," Florence said as she opened the carrier so Deb could grab Doug. For his part, Doug let the girl coo and baby-talk at him, eating up the attention.

"He's subbing out counterspells and single-target damage spells for area-of-effect and cleave cards," Doug meowed to Florence as he was carried past Shane, who had resumed his deck-building. It wasn't exactly a big revelation. In fact, Florence was counting on her opponent to do just that. Still, she gave Doug a stern look. She didn't think it very sporting for him to try and spy on the opponent's hand, so she would give Shane a chance to fix it.

"Oh, young man, I have to tell you that Doug just saw some of your substitutions," Florence said, finishing up the changes to her deck.

"Really? The *cat* saw my sideboard choices? Well, even if it was you that saw them, it's not going to matter. Let's get started. Time's running out," Shane said. She'd given him the chance; now he was going to pay the price.

The game progressed much like the first one had, Florence's early dungeon rooms and defenders doing little to stop the four paladins that progressed tile by tile toward her boss creature. Like before, she threw large numbers of fairly weak cat creatures at the party, which Shane countered easily with his changes to the deck. The area-of-effect (AOE) and cleave cards allowed him to take out several of the low-health defenders at a time, despite the fact those abilities did less damage to each target. By using weaker defenders earlier in the game, she was able to reserve a place for a few extra defenders in the boss room.

"All right, lady, it's the final room. Let's see your boss and your minions. Let me guess, the cat swarm is back," Shane said as the party entered the last tile. Should he win this fight, he would win the game—and the tournament as well. In her previous matches, Florence had used a swarm host final boss. The swarm host allowed her to select a specific creature to populate the swarm, and she selected cats, which were the best things ever. This time, she really wanted to win the tournament, so she had changed her final boss to something unexpected.

"Nope, I decided to change things up a bit," she said with a smile as she revealed the boss and the three other minions inside the room.

"No way. You cheated after seeing my cards," Shane complained as he saw what she had turned over.

"Quit your whining, junior. I told you what happened and gave you a chance to change things. It's not my fault you were too dense to do so," Florence said.

"Judge!" Shane bellowed out, and Bobby showed up a minute later.

"What's going on?" Bobby asked. The store manager was also an official game judge. His decision would be final and binding.

"The old lady cheated. She saw my sideboard cards and even admitted it," Shane accused.

"Is that right, Miss Florence?" Bobby asked.

"Not quite. Doug happened to see some of his sideboard changes. I told him at the time and gave him the option to make more changes, but he declined." Florence sat there quietly after having said her piece, enjoying the confused look on Bobby's face as he tried to tell if she was messing with him or if she was genuinely crazy enough to believe her own words.

"Dude, see? She totally cheated," Shane replied.

"Sorry, if you were careless with your card-handling and Florence happened to see them, she did the right thing and let you have a chance to fix it. You declined, so you can't complain now," Bobby said.

"No way. She cheated and needs to be disqualified."

"You had your chance to change things, but it's not her fault if you flash your cards in front of her," Bobby replied.

"I know how to handle cards. There's no way she could have seen them 'accidentally.' She had to try and look."

"I didn't say I saw them, and in fact, I didn't. It was Doug that saw them, and you can tell how sorry he is. Just look," Florence said. Nobody bothered to look over at Doug, who Florence thought was doing a great job of looking cute and innocent.

"See? She's totally crazy and even talks to that mangy cat like it's a real person," Shane said.

"You're crossing the line. Make one more personal insult toward another player and I'll disqualify you from the event and ban you from the store. Play the game or scoop up your cards and leave," Bobby ordered. The store owner was normally mild-mannered, but he wouldn't abide by someone causing trouble with his regulars.

Heavens only knew how much money Florence had spent in there over the last few years. Gathering the right cards and dungeon tiles when each new set released was a durned pain in the rear.

"Fine," Shane mumbled as he announced his next moves. Bobby and several of the others who had already finished their matches came over to watch. Normally, Florence wasn't too keen on a crowd, but this time, she kind of enjoyed being in the spotlight.

The final battle turned out as she had planned; the three minions supporting her boss were blink dogs, a kind of dog that could phase an adventurer out of the fight for a turn. She used them to break up the party, leaving only one or two at a time to face the boss and diluting all the buffs on each character. Shane's damage cards were mostly AOE effects and didn't put out enough damage to take down the boss quickly. Her final boss was some creepy-looking thing called an ancient one. It looked like a squid monster, but it did really good at single-target damage. One by one, Shane's paladins fell, and with a final huff of indignation, the kid scooped up his cards and left the store in defeat.

"Ladies and gentlemen, let me present to you the Mad Dog's Games and Vapes tournament champion, Florence Valentine," Bobby started to announce.

"And Doug. Don't forget Doug," Florence interjected, holding up her cat carrier, where Doug had been re-deposited after his walk around the store.

"Fine, Florence Valentine and Doug are the store tournament champions and will go on to compete in the regionals next month!" Bobby said over the din of gamers chatting about the accomplishments and defeats.

Florence and Doug stayed at the store for a few minutes after gathering their prize packs, but she was getting to the end of her energy. Now that the adrenaline from the game was gone, her pain had returned. It was not only in her knees and back, but also in her

chest, an ominous sign of something the doctors had tried to prepare her for. The ride home was quiet, Doug taking a nap on the
passenger seat, worn out after all the day's excitement. Florence
didn't feel well, and she had a sneaking suspicion her second and
final time on Earth was coming to an end.

She knew they wouldn't be here all that long. After all, she
wasn't getting any younger, and when she returned to her body, it
was the same old worn-out one she had lived her life in. Over three
years had passed since she returned from her dungeon on Aerkon,
and she and Doug had tried to make the best of it. They joined
most of the seniors center's activities and get-togethers; Florence
enjoyed the company of the folks there more than Doug did. Old
Doug never did complain about the potluck gatherings, though.
He was spoiled by some of the other ladies, especially Tabitha
Long, who would slip him treats that weren't none too good for a
kitty's tummy.

Every Friday, without fail, Doug and Florence would head
to the game shop to play Dungeon Delve. They also spent a lot
of time talking about and planning what to do with their home
once Florence was back in her gem. They couldn't be too sure what
would await them when she passed away and returned to her gem,
but no stupid dog monster was going to crush it again this time, no
siree. They were going to be prepared.

"What should we watch tonight?" Florence asked as she unlocked the door to their house. She really didn't want Doug's opinion, but it was only polite to ask.

"Hmm, my personal favorite has to be *Big Trouble in Little
China*. Can we watch that again?" Doug asked. For some reason,
the little critter had a fascination with 1980s movies, but Florence
wasn't going to have none of it.

"No, I think I'll watch one of my shows." Florence pulled up the
menu on the television while she tried to remember how to get to

the recorded shows Tabitha's grandson had set up for her. Picking out the latest episode, she tried to focus on the show, but the pain was getting worse.

"Hey, Doug," Florence said.

"No, I do not want to watch your 'shows.' I'll just take a nap," Doug replied.

"No, this ain't about my shows. I just . . . Well, I think it's about that time." Florence cringed as the pain gripping her chest intensified.

"Oh dear. Is there anything I can do to help?" Doug asked, swishing his tail back and forth with concern.

"No, I'll just try to relax and see what happens." Florence rested her head back against her favorite recliner chair. Doug climbed up in her lap and started purring to help her feel better. He could be a sweet little kitty when he tried, but it was getting hard to think and she wanted to say something to him but couldn't. Just like after the delivery truck hit her, Florence felt herself being drawn somewhere else. At least this time she knew what awaited her.

Chapter 2

WELCOME, HUMAN! YOU HAVE BEEN SELECTED AMONG THE billions of your kind to be granted a great honor.

"Just hush with all that nonsense. I know what's a-going on and you can just go ahead and send me to my gem," Florence called out, noting that it was the same prompt that had appeared the first time she died. As far as she was concerned, these here administration folks were just getting lazy. She surely didn't like floating here without a body, waiting for someone to do their job.

The natural life of this core has been completed. Please wait while you are connected with your core gem.

"Hey there, system prompt guy, how long is this process supposed to take?" Florence asked as more time passed and nothing happened.

"Please refrain from interruptions. I am endeavoring to complete your transfer," a voice called out.

"How about you also transfer some manners into yourself while you're at it? Don't you know it's rude to not introduce yourself?" Florence chided. Her friend Tabitha Long might have said that Florence had become downright pleasant to be around these last few years, but pleasant or not, she wasn't going to put up with rude behavior from anyone.

"Introductions are not required. Please cease any further interruptions."

"What is with you people? This is the second time I've died, and both times the service has been terrible. What's your name? I'm going to report you to the manager if you don't get on with this transfer process thingy and apologize for your rudeness while you're at it." Florence had been down this road before and wasn't afraid to tangle with disembodied voice guy. After all, she sure set Doug straight when they first met, didn't she?

"I do not have a name. My kind has been elevated above such petty things," the voice said.

"Ha! Tell that to Doug. You know, he said the same thing when I died the first time, and he created my core. Now, unless you want to end up as a kitten-sized dungeon assistant, I suggest you get on with this, *Charlie*," Florence said. If the voice wasn't going to tell her his name, she was just going to go ahead and give him one of her own. Just to spite the voice, she named him after her crazy old uncle, Charlie Valentine, who believed the Russians were trying to tunnel under his house in order to start their invasion.

"I have heard rumors of this Doug. His is a cautionary tale told among my kind. You are the catalyst mentioned in the tale, are you not? I have no desire to be this Charlie. Please refrain from any escalation and I shall see about expediting your return to Aerkon."

"Guess good news travels fast. Glad to see you disembodied voice guys got the message to not hassle Florence Valentine," Florence said, pleased with herself and the notoriety she had gained with these weirdos. In what only seemed like a short time, although she had no way to really gauge how long had passed, a system prompt appeared.

Abnormality in the subject core gem has been detected. Analyzing the cause.

"Oh, no, I ain't waiting any longer, Charlie. Get on with this. No system jibber-jabber is going to keep me floating around like a ghost, no siree. Get me back in my gem or I'm going to escalate. I got a dungeon to build."

"Oh, rest assured, there is no escalation necessary," Charlie said. "I'll send you to your gem presently. Just understand neither I nor the powers that control the system can be held responsible for any problems due to the hasty transfer."

"Yeah, yeah, just get a move on," Florence replied.

Analysis of gem abnormality overridden. Transferring the entity known as Florence Valentine to the aforementioned core gem.

Florence felt her mind being drawn away from Charlie and his gem-making place. Darkness engulfed her, and after a short time— at least she thought it was a short time since the people in charge didn't even give her a watch or a clock or anything—tiny pinpricks of light appeared. She could see the darkness being pierced by the faint red glow of her gem. Of course, she liked to think of the glow as a happy rosy color, but Doug insisted it was just plain old red. What did he know? Cats were colorblind, weren't they? The glow revealed she was enclosed in a container of some sort. If she had to guess, it was a crate or wooden box.

The licking skeleton guy was supposed to make sure her gem was safe and that she didn't forget her memories and whatnot. Well, she remembered everything, or at least she thought she did. If this lich expected Florence to owe him a favor, he better not just leave her in a stupid box. She was back and had lots to do if she wanted her home back in order. Why, even for a storage box, this was a dingy-looking container. For all she knew, her beautiful gem was going to get splinters. Could a gem get splinters? Well, she sure as shootin' didn't want to find out. Despite all her power as a core, she was unable to get herself out of her box. Better call in some backup.

"Hey, Doug! Get over here and open this box up," she called out.

Silence met her request, and she began to fear her friend hadn't joined her. Was Doug just taking his sweet time in getting back, or had something else happened to him? She began to worry, not liking being trapped in a box one bit. To make matters worse, the enclosed space made her gem feel tight, as if she was wearing a dress that was a half size too small. Of course, Florence Valentine would never try to wear the wrong size, not at all like Cindy Klineman, who always tried to insist she was two sizes smaller than she really was. Florence could hear Cindy's complaints now; she was always whining that the clothing companies were sizing their stuff wrong. It never occurred to her that the problem was the seconds on dessert she always seemed to take at the seniors center potluck.

Well, if Doug weren't here, she'd just have to take matters into her own hands. She was a core, after all, so she pulled up her status screen.

Florence Valentine

Cat core, level 4

Experience: 1/1500

Funds: $0/$350

Defender expense: $0/$350

"Hey, I've been robbed! Where's my money?" Florence shouted. It didn't seem like there was anyone there to hear her. Her voice wasn't even projecting from her gem at all. She distinctly remembered that while her account wasn't full when she died, there was some money in it. Did everything drain away while she was gone? Now, that just wasn't fair, taking a senior citizen's money just because she died.

Fine, she knew what to do. She and Doug even had a plan for starting from scratch again. Florence just had to wait for funds to start trickling in naturally. When she had enough, she would take control of the room she was in and dissolve the box around her. What really irked her was that she was going to have to rebuild her rocking chair. Why didn't that licking skeleton at least keep that here for her to sit on? Rude, that was what he was. A rude undead skeleton guy. From everything Doug had her read to prepare for her return, these liches were supposed to be super smart and whatnot, but this one wasn't impressing her at all.

Her plan to start from scratch was solid, but there was only one problem: no money was coming in. It was that durned box; it was blocking her abilities somehow. No matter how hard she tried, she couldn't exert her influence past it. She sat there inside her stupid box, wondering how long it would take that skeleton to come get her out. To pass the time, she composed quite the scathing speech she was going to give once she was free. Both that Berikoz—that was the skeleton guy's name, she remembered—and Doug were going to get it. And to think, Doug wanted her to create his avatar as a giant tiger-sized cat this time. Nope, it was back in the kitten form for him. If he didn't show up soon, she would make his kitten form one of them creepy hairless cat things. That should teach him to not keep a lady waiting.

Florence tried to access her interface, but other than the same limited data it had shown her earlier, nothing else could be accessed. She kept getting an error requesting she find a suitable location for her core to control. Why didn't they just leave her in the home she had already built? She had big plans for that place. Of course, she and Doug had plans in place if she was located somewhere else, a possibility that Doug had warned her about. They had looked at everything from volcanos to underwater locations, but never did they consider a box.

She was beginning to worry about Doug, realizing how much she missed his company. They had been working together as a team for years now, and it was strange to be alone. Even worse, she was without all the kitties. Her little babies had such interesting personalities and powers, and she couldn't wait to bring them back. Why, they must be as lonely as lonely could be since Florence had been gone for so long.

Her thoughts and concerns were interrupted by the sound of someone banging on metal. Dull thumps reverberated through the box she was locked inside as the sounds increased in volume. Finally, Florence heard a small pop, and she thought she detected the sweet scent of mana being expended. It had been too long since she had controlled and tasted it. Of course, she would still think of it as money since that seemed to irk Doug to no end. Playing Dungeon Delve had taught her a lot, but she still preferred things to be labeled the way they used to be.

Voices broke the silence.

"Why didn't you just do that earlier?" a gravelly voice demanded.

"I didn't know I could," the voice of an elderly man replied. "The compulsion of the geas we are under doesn't manifest until something triggers it. It is a true testament to the power of the caster that the lich was able to weave such intricate instructions into the spell. I sincerely hope he will hold up his end of the bargain and impart some of that knowledge to me."

"Mages, always using fifty words when one will do. Now, everyone, quiet down. I have to read this, and then whatever it is that we're supposed to grab will be revealed," the first man replied. Florence could hear paper being crinkled as the man cleared his throat and began reading. Bless his heart, he sure had trouble sounding out the big words. He should have given the paper to the old fart, but that guy might have taken too long to read it; he sounded like kind of a know-it-all.

"Dear Florence Valentine. I issue you my sincerest apologies for not being here when you returned to this world. I intended to greet you personally and take you to the perfect location for your new dungeon. Strike that. I recall that you prefer to call your abode a home rather than the common designation of a dungeon.

"Unfortunately, events have transpired, and I shall be occupied with other endeavors for quite some time. Rest assured that your gem is in perfect condition, and as you obviously can tell, your memories are intact. My requirements from you will be made known in the future. Should things go well in my current task, I may never need to call upon that favor.

"These people that are currently in the vault with you are under my employ. A bigger collection of deviants, cutthroats, and villains of all sorts you will not find anywhere else on Aerkon. Do not fear them. They are under my control and will die to protect you until you can be situated in your new home. Depending on how frugal the party is with the advance payment that I've provided them, the journey may take some time unless they spent at least some of their coin on a teleportation scroll. Have no worries. You will be in capable hands during your travels, however long those travels may be.

"Once more, welcome back to Aerkon, Florence Valentine.

"It's signed by the lich, and the signature reads, 'Berikoz the lich, not a licking skeleton,'" the gravelly voiced man said.

"Oy, look on the shelf. We's got a glowing thing," a new and screechy voice called out. The accent was familiar, but Florence couldn't quite place it. According to Berikoz's note, she was going to be taken to a new home by these hooligans. While she was grateful for the skeleton guy keeping his end of the deal, he was in for a piece of her mind when they met again. How dare he saddle her with scoundrels during the relocation to her new home. She supposed creepy liches and the like couldn't exactly walk into town and hire a reputable party, but it would have been really nice to have been met by Shara and her friends.

"I's takes a peek," the screechy voice called.

"I wouldn't do that, Blivix. We weren't instructed to tamper with the package," the old man said.

"I's not scaredy likes youse are," said the person that seemed to be called Blivix, as stupid a name as Florence had ever heard.

With a creak, the lid of the box was opened, and a face peered down at her in the faint torchlight. The green skin and red eyes of a goblin gleamed with greed as he looked at Florence. Unlike the delightful little scamps that lived in her home, this one looked like trouble. A deep scar ran across his face, and one of his pointed ears had been clipped off as well. Grubby hands that looked like they hadn't ever seen a bar of soap reached down and lifted her from the box.

"Oh, a shiny one, this is," Blivix said.

"Leave it be. We're here to protect it, not ogle it," the burly human with the gravelly voice grunted out.

"I wasn't going to takes it. I was just having me a look-see, Kam," Blivix replied. This Kam was the gravelly voiced guy, and as she watched, his hands strayed to the hilts of the two curved swords at his waist. The man was armored in chainmail, and if Florence was any judge, the gear was well made and gave off the feeling of something that was enchanted.

The goblin wasn't any slouch in the gear department, either. Despite his obvious lack of hygiene, the goblin sported well-cared-for studded leather armor, and a whole passel of knives were strapped all over him. His gear also gave off the faint aura of enchantment. Behind the pair was the old guy, and instead of a wizard's robes and the staff she expected, he was dressed like a commoner and had no visible weapons on his person. With them there magic-slinging types, you could never tell, and for all Florence knew, this guy was all decked out in the good stuff and was keeping up an illusion to appear poorly equipped.

One final member rounded out this party of ne'er-do-wells, a massive orc in heavy plate armor. His armor and weapons were as black as night, and a massive shield festooned with spikes was resting on the ground while an axe with a visible red glow was clenched in his beefy fist. If these folks were going for the ugliest adventuring party award, Florence believed they would win it easy. Tearing her eyes from the ugly party, Florence got her first look at the chamber she had been trapped in. It was kind of like she had figured: a storage room of some sort, lots of dusty boxes and chests. The only exit was an imposing door made of metal with no visible handle or latch. These clowns must have been trying to force it open, making all that noise she heard earlier, before they had finally just teleported inside.

"Let's all proceed with the task given to us. That way, we can reap our rewards and go our separate ways," the old man said. With a grunt, Kam moved his hands away from his blades, and Florence could see Blivix visibly relax. Instead of dropping her back into her box, the goblin tied a length of cord around her gem and proceeded to wear it as a necklace. That almost caused another fight among them, but whatever hocus pocus the skeleton guy had put on them must have prevented them from hurting each other, no matter how much they seemed to want to. Whether they were scumbags or saints, Florence didn't care as long as they got her to her new home quickly.

Chapter 3

THE OLD MAN PULLED OUT A SCROLL AND STARTED CHANTING AS he cast the spell written upon it. With a flash of light, Florence found herself and the adventurers suddenly outside and under the night sky. They were near a road that cut through rolling hills and stretched as far as she could see. Florence looked around, but her whole experience in this world had consisted of the view from the front door of her home, and this place sure didn't look anything like it. She weren't none too happy to have her gem carried around by some stinky goblin, but at least they were supposed to be hauling her someplace where she could build her new home.

"Good, let's get moving. That scroll shaved a lot of time off our journey, but we still have a ways to go. Don't forget you all owe me for casting that. I expect to be paid once we've completed our task," the old man said.

"Yeah, yeah, Harmon, you'll get your share when we're done. Remind me to never take a job that requires a geas again. Half the time, I'm not sure if my decisions are my own or if it's the lich's spell popping them into my brain," Kam replied.

The big orc just grunted his agreement, and the stupid goblin was too busy staring at Florence, something she could have done without. She knew goblins weren't like normal folks, but you would think that one galivanting around with adventuring parties would have picked up some manners. To make things worse, she couldn't even properly chastise anyone. Without a home, her gem had no way to speak.

The party didn't stop for the night and journeyed down the road for a bit. Florence had no idea what direction they were heading, but the terrain they passed seemed like more of the same. Given the well-traveled nature of the road, it was no surprise when they happened upon a small caravan setting up camp for the night. A cheerful fire was blazing, and several people were cooking or seeing to the animals. Workers moved about the half dozen wagons laden with various types of produce and bulk goods.

"Ahh, now that is a cheerful sight. What say you, gentlemen? Do we ply our trade this evening or leave it be?" Harmon said.

"Leave them be. Look at their cargo. It's just bulk goods we can't turn into coin easily and I don't want to drive wagons all over the land looking for a buyer," Kam said.

"It's a bad target, but I needses me some stabbing. Been too long without any killin'," the goblin said, licking his lips at the thought of battle.

"What about you, Durg?" Kam asked the hulking orc. The orc said nothing and instead readied his shield and axe, stomping his way toward the fire. With a gleeful giggle, the goblin slipped away from the rest of the party, and Florence was along for the ride whether she wanted to be or not.

Her vision blurred as the goblin activated some ability just like them there rogues who used to explore her home. If she had to guess, she would say the little creep was now invisible. The heavily armored orc was not exactly stealthy, and the man on watch called out as he heard their approach. Kam and the old man followed slightly behind their bulky friend. The warrior had already his weapons, and spells were already glowing on the fingers of the mage.

"Who's out there?" the caravan guard shouted into the night, his hand tightly gripping his spear. His call alerted the other caravan members, and those without weapons on their belts moved toward the wagons, where they likely had something stored to defend themselves with.

"Ho the fire. We're just some adventurers looking for a place to rest. May we join you and borrow your fire to cook our supper?" the old man called. The sound of an elderly person just outside the firelight seemed to relax the caravan members. Florence tried to shout, tried to do something to warn these people. They were just minding their own business, and now the group tasked with getting her home were a-fixing to rob them.

"Sure, come on in and make yourself comfortable. We're glad to have the company," the man on watch told them.

"Thank you, but I doubt you'll enjoy our company all that much," the old mage said, then released the magic of a spell he had held in check this whole time. A black cloud of insects flew from his hand and covered the watchman and two nearby caravan drivers in stinging and biting critters. Florence hated bugs, and these poor men that were afflicted by the spell were being given a horrible way to die.

The goblin had made his way to the back of the wagons, and when the spell went off and the screaming began, a flick of his wrists sent two blades spinning into the back of a man just now pulling a short spear from inside the wagon. Going down with hardly a sound, the others nearby didn't see the little green death machine bearing down on them. With a pair of larger knives in hand, the goblin activated some ability. He magically hurled himself forward, driving the blades into the back of his victim, only to have the ability activate a second time and repeat the attack on another target.

A roar erupted from the orc, who charged into the largest group of defenders, scattering the poorly armed and unarmored caravan members with ease. The orc's axe lashed out in a blur of strokes, each swipe taking down a victim. Florence wished she could close her eyes, but being in her gem meant she could see everything around her at once and was unable to avert her gaze. If she had been in her home, she could focus on one room or one defender to prevent seeing what she was seeing, but now she was nothing but a helpless spectator.

It didn't take long for the experienced party to take down all but two of the caravan crew. That was when the goblin got to work, and Florence would try her best to forget the things that little monster did with his daggers to those poor men. By the time the screams were over and the final victim had expired, the adventurers had found the location of the only real valuable item aboard the caravan: the pay chest. It must not have been all that much in the way of coin, given their reactions, but she knew they had committed their heinous crimes not for the profit but instead for their twisted version of entertainment.

"Now, that was rather invigorating. I suggest we continue on our course and leave this area. Who knows what might show up, drawn to the scent of blood and carnage?" Harmon said. Nobody asked Florence her opinion, but she was all for leaving this horrible scene behind her. They continued at a brisk pace, eventually taking a side road that appeared to have seen little use. That was all well and good for Florence; she had no desire to watch these bloodthirsty monsters harm anyone else.

The mage, Harmon, passed out potions to everyone when they started to run out of steam. After drinking them, they all had a pep in their step once more, enabling them to keep up the impressive pace they were maintaining. Eventually, the small road they were on became a faint game trail until that gave way to nothing but rough underbrush and rock-covered hills. Florence didn't like the lack of trees and hoped they weren't going to leave her somewhere out here. She wanted a pretty backdrop for her new home, not some boring-looking wasteland.

It turned out that licking skeletons weren't too good at picking places for a home, as the group led Florence toward a small, rock-covered hill. At first, there didn't appear to be an entrance, but one of the boulders at the base of the hill had a large crack in the center, just wide enough for Blivix to slip inside. The goblin sniffed at the entrance, none too happy to go inside alone.

"Youse use magic, old hooman. Teleport gem inside. Thingses I smells in there, thingses I don't want to have to stabs on my own," Blivix complained.

"This is your task alone, one particularly suited to your kind, I must say. My powers are not needed here, and I'll not waste my mana on your comfort. Go, complete our quest so that we may reap our just rewards and be free of this geas that so compels us," Harmon said. The goblin didn't look none too happy with the old man's reply; his hands strayed toward the daggers at his waist.

Just when Florence thought that Blivix was going to go all stabby on the old man, the goblin started to shudder in pain. The shaking stopped as soon as he turned and started to squeeze his way inside the narrow opening. That must be that there geas thingy they kept talking about; it prevented them from hurting each other and made them do what the lich wanted. A handy spell, if you asked Florence.

Once past the boulder, she found herself inside a narrow passageway leading downward. Being a core, she could see in the dark just as well as in the light, but being able to see didn't make the place look any less creepy, given how filthy it was, not to mention the bugs that were scuttling around all gross-like. Nope, she wasn't going to live in some filthy pit. This place was getting a top-to-bottom scrubbing once she was back in charge. That skeleton was going to get a piece of her mind once she saw him again. How dare he stick her in some run-down pit.

The goblin blurred out his form, hiding from whatever might be down here. Florence had to give him credit; the little critter sure could move quietly when he wanted to. Before too long, they reached the end of their journey, the narrow passage ending inside a larger chamber. In the center of the chamber stood an ancient stone pedestal, the surface pitted and worn down by time. The top of the pedestal had a small indentation just large enough for her gem to be placed inside.

"Maybes I's come back sometime to take you again, shiny gem. When the lich's magic is gone, I can do whatses I wants, and I think I wantses your power," Blivix said, a disgusting strand of drool hanging from his mouth as his grubby hands placed her on the pedestal. The little guy might have scared her with his threats back when she was just starting out, but now, she would love to have a crack at Blivix and the rest of his companions once her new home was up and running. Oh yes, there were some kitty cat claws with that goblin's name on them.

When the green guy gave another shudder of pain, Florence knew the geas stopped him from doing something he shouldn't. Giving her a final leer, Blivix left the small chamber. She waited to see if he or any of the others would come back, but thankfully, it seemed that they had moved on now that their task was complete.

A welcome prompt appeared in front of her. Florence Valentine was back in business.

This area is suitable for the formation of your dungeon. Do you wish to claim this chamber as your core room: Y/N?

Florence selected *yes* and could finally feel her power expand from the gem. She watched as the first few cents of income trickled in. Relief flooded her as each penny was absorbed by her core.

While Florence still felt a little strange, she would get back into the swing of things in no time. With nothing else to do but wait, she reviewed her core information. She had come a long way since that level 0 core she had been back on her first day in this strange world. Thankfully, she started over again at her old level and with all the benefits she had unlocked through her earlier efforts.

Florence Valentine

Cat core, level 4

Experience: 0/1500

Funds: $0.02/$350

Defender expense: $0/$350

Current Core Upgrades:

Core Housing: Core housing creates a protective barrier around your core, enabling it to withstand much more damage. The core housing will self-repair over time and can be further upgraded at level 5 and every 5 levels thereafter. The core housing can take on the appearance of something comforting and safe that the dungeon core is familiar with, or it can be designed in a manner that will intimidate your foes. Your core housing is currently destroyed. A replacement will craft itself over time. To fund its creation, a small percentage of all income will be redirected to this task.

Protective Avatar with Level 1 Upgrade: The dungeon avatar is a construct that provides a final layer of defense for the core. Able to attack autonomously or under the core's direct control, the avatar can be upgraded into a fearsome defender. Your avatar has already been upgraded with the skill Shake the Cane. Every 30 seconds, the dungeon core's avatar can now shake her cane at approaching foes. This ability unleashes a flurry of 5 blows on any enemies within a small area of effect. Targets are

selected at random. Another avatar ability will be unlocked once the dungeon core reaches level 5. Your avatar has been destroyed. A replacement will craft itself over time, and to fund its creation, a small percentage of all income will be redirected to this task.

Deadly Doug: When your core is threatened, you can push funds into your assistant, granting him more strength and power to defend your home. This ability is only useable when invaders are in your core room and can only be activated once per week. The Deadly Doug ability lasts for 30 seconds and requires $25 to activate. Once the ability is activated, your assistant will grow and become empowered as if he were a champion. This ability will improve as you level.

Summoner: This upgrade allows you to spawn temporary defenders once every 24 hours. The spawned units will be random duplicates of named defenders inside your dungeon. Champions and minor champions will not be summoned by this ability. This ability will improve as you level.

Defender Upgrades:

Individuality: This upgrade allows your defenders to develop new abilities based on their individual preferences. The core has no control over what the defenders select.

Named Defenders: The cost for each of your defenders is increased, but named defenders will respawn with any memories they have previously accumulated and often develop combat abilities beyond what their levels would suggest.

Defender subtypes have been unlocked. The following subtypes are available.

Brawler: The brawler subtype gives your defenders enhanced strength and stamina, their natural defenses are enhanced, and they can take and give more punishment in a fight. Brawlers are melee-focused, lose some of their natural agility, and have enhanced vulnerability to magic.

Commando: The commando subtype focuses on stealth and agility. They strike from the shadows, deal damage to their foes, and then retreat from view. Commandos have average strength and stamina, along with a higher chance of landing a critical strike against an unwary foe. They have enhanced reflexes and will take less damage from area-of-effect attacks.

Mage: The mage subtype focuses on using magic power to destroy enemies, control the battlefield, or support allies. There is a wide variety of magic types, and since your dungeon does not have a specific elemental affinity, a random magic type will be assigned when you create your defenders. Mages are physically weaker than other classes and should be protected to maximize their effectiveness.

Plague Mount: The plague mount works in tandem with another dungeon inhabitant to enhance the combat prowess of both. The plague mount gives off noxious fumes that weaken enemies within 5 feet of the defender. A plague mount can activate the charge ability every 30 seconds, giving its rider a higher hit, damage, and critical chance on its next blow. This subtype can only be chosen by the defender itself and cannot be selected at creation by the core.

You need to set the reward level for your dungeon. Please choose a reward percentage from the options

**below. Note that reward levels can only be changed once
every 7 days and are the same throughout your dungeon.**

    1. Miserly: 5%

    2. Poor: 10%

    3. Average: 15%

    4. Fair: 20%

    5. Generous: 25%

    6. Extravagant: 50%

It appeared everything was right where it was supposed to be. Well, except for all her money being missing. Imagine that: bringing a poor old woman back from the dead while at the same time emptying her bank account.

Chapter 4

FLORENCE SET HER REWARDS LEVELS TO AVERAGE. SHE STILL FELT that they were far too generous to be called average, but Doug had finally convinced her that it was the best level to keep adventurers happy. Happy adventurers were much less inclined to try and destroy her core. She had also forgotten how slow the income for her home accumulated without adventurers inside. At least the passive income would improve as she expanded, a task she wanted to start as soon as she gathered enough coins.

"Oh dear, given all our planning back on Earth, I would have hoped our home would start out much further along than this, Florence. You've been here nearly a week already," an annoying if welcome voice said.

"Doug! What in tarnation took you so long? We had a plan and you're supposed to be here advisin' and helping me," Florence said. She tried hard but didn't quite manage to pull off being angry. Doug was here, and she wasn't alone anymore.

"My delay was not due to any fault of my own. I was hung up in an administrative dispute. You see, they wanted to reassign me, and it took some time to sort things out," Doug replied.

"Yeah, I suppose I had a bit of a problem with Chuck as well. Thankfully, he weren't nearly as hard-headed as you were."

"Ah, that was you. I wondered why such an accomplished core gem creator was sporting a human moniker. It appears your reputation has preceded this death. You have the staff terrified that they will face the same humiliating fate I have," Doug replied with an indifferent air.

"Don't you start acting up again. You know as well as I do, Doug, that you enjoy every minute of being in a real body," Florence retorted.

"Granted, this form does lend itself to certain amusements, but there are so many drawbacks as well."

"Like what? Getting attention and delicious food every day?" Florence asked, upset at the ingrateful little ball of fluff that was wandering around her core room like he owned the place.

"Well, though I continuously endeavor to have that memory removed from my mind, there was that one visit to the veterinarian."

"Bah, everybody knows you have to get a stray fixed. Can't have you gallivanting around the neighborhood, entertaining the ladies," Florence replied.

"Fixed! What they did was far from 'fixing' me. It was an affront against my person, one which I most certainly did not consent to," Doug spat. His little fluffy kitten body had its fur all bristling out in anger. While he probably thought he looked intimidating, Florence thought it just made him fluffier and even more darling than normal.

"Arguing about it isn't going to help either of us. You're in a new body now, so no harm done," Florence said, ready to change the subject back to their home.

"Very well, though I must protest your insistence that no harm was done. Let's get on with things, and first off, where are we?"

"I guess they didn't tell you about what happened to me after I was shoved back in my gem?" Florence asked. Doug shook his head and curled up next to the pedestal, listening to what she had to say. She tried to include as much detail as she could, bringing

Doug up to speed and letting him know about the hooligans that brought her here.

"Well, despite our inauspicious start, I suppose we should follow our plan," Doug said. "I have no more insight than yourself as far as our location is concerned, but thankfully, it doesn't seem like we were dropped into the middle of a high-population area. How do you want to proceed, Florence?"

"I was a-thinking that we rebuild what we had, but with a second story, and add either a basement or a backyard. We'll take things slow and steady, adding rooms and defenders as we go."

"Good enough. We'll give that a whirl. You've only got the core room so far, so let's make the champion room and work our way out from there. Build defenders after each room is complete. That way, we'll have some protection if we get unwelcome guests like last time," Doug offered. He was right; last time, she had to fend off dire rats with only her cane, a cane that hadn't been rebuilt yet.

Florence concentrated and began to expand her home. The construction went at a slow pace; she was out of practice. At least by taking it slow, enough money trickled in to keep pace with her efforts. The first room would be the master bedroom, and she was going to expand it a bit from the previous design. Zork and Chubbs—well, really just Chubbs—seemed to get bigger each time she leveled. They needed some fighting room inside there. Once the overall dimensions were complete, Doug interrupted her.

"Might I make a suggestion?"

"What? You're messing up my concentration," Florence shot back.

"Why don't you stop with just the basics of each room and then summon our defenders? Before we reopen to the public, you can add all the decorations and frills your dubious taste desires."

"Well, despite the fact you're a sarcastic and rude little kitten, that's not a bad idea. We are a little exposed here."

"Wait, what do you mean?" Doug asked, concern etched on his little kitten face.

"Them good-for-nothing adventurers dropped me in here and we came in through some cave entrance. That means we're open to the outside world already, doesn't it?"

"Oh, dear me, I didn't even think of that. I'm so used to new dungeons being dropped into inaccessible areas. That means your core could be calling hostile native inhabitants, well, at this very minute. I suggest we build defenders posthaste."

"As soon as we save up $10, it'll go right into our first kitty," Florence said.

"Yes, that would be wise, though I fear our ambient mana—I mean cash—flow is much below normal for an area that is supposedly suitable for a dungeon or home," Doug said, confirming that things were going slower than before.

"Not much we can do about our income, except get our home open as soon as we are able," Florence replied.

"Maybe we can spare enough resources to create that special item I requested?" Doug said.

With a sigh, Florence made him a ball of yarn. The penny it cost wouldn't delay them for too long. Keeping Doug out of her hair while they waited was more than worth the price. She was thinking about printing up a set of Dungeon Delve cards, but without hands, neither of them could play.

"All right, Doug, here we go," Florence said after her balance finally hit $10.

It was just like riding a bike. Florence pushed money into the glowing ball of light on the floor that would become her defender, attempting to re-create the first cat she had made. Just as she had hoped, the glowing ball coalesced into a fur baby. The shorthair gray cat with a white bib and paws was standing there looking up at her. It was her precious Tater.

"Welcome home, little guy. Keep an eye on things while momma works," Florence told the kitty. Tater walked up to Doug and gave him a curious sniff before walking about the room, exploring his new surroundings.

Turning her attention back to their home, Florence kept an eye on the small tunnel passage connected to what would become the master bedroom. Of course, she could close things off to see what would happen. It didn't take much effort, or money, to push a layer of stone over the entryway. Just as she suspected, a system prompt appeared once she had done so.

Your dungeon has been cut off from the outside world. Reopen the entrance to adventurers within the next 24 hours or face a permanent reduction in mana generation.

"Hey, Doug, why am I getting hassled over closing off our home? We did that all the time when adventurers were inside. In fact, it was closed down for quite a while when we were upgrading things."

"I believe it has to do with the lack of adventurers," Doug suggested. "Cores undergoing leveling activities, hosting a steady stream of adventurers, or recovering from core damage often have an extended time they can remain cut off from the surface. We never abused that feature, and subsequently, we were never given a warning prompt. Since we haven't really done much yet, the system is a bit stricter on us. In this case, I say we exploit whatever time we can. They've given us twenty-four hours. Let's remain closed until the time is nearly expired. That should give us some safety as we start to develop our home."

"Sounds good to me. The more kitties we have when some critter shows up, the better." The system gave Florence an update announcement every hour. It was annoying, but since she didn't have a clock, it was necessary.

With her home cut off from attack, Florence had time to build two new rooms: the living room and the front porch. She would put off decorations until there were more defenders. It seemed that old Tater had retained his previous knowledge and parked himself in the living room. Florence couldn't decorate the way she wanted just yet, but she could make sure her kitties had every advantage she could give them, opting to re-create the ceiling-mounted walkways to allow her babies to leap down on their victims.

After making the kitty-sized passages between each room, Florence held off on any further construction. She needed every penny she had for more cats. Time was nearly up when she gathered enough funds to create her second cat. A new ball of light pulled money into it, eventually revealing precious little Midnight. The cat mewed with joy as it greeted Florence with a kitty hug. The sleek black brawler kitty rubbed against the pedestal and Tater as she made the rounds.

"Well, it does appear that our previous denizens are being recalled accurately," Doug said. He tried to sound all proper, but it was hard to take him seriously when he was wrestling with the other kitties. The defenders seemed to enjoy playing with Doug and were surprisingly gentle with the little guy. Her kitties were both brawlers and could shred their way through an armored adventurer, but they left nary a scratch on old Doug.

"I guess it's time to open for business, even if I am a bit embarrassed over the state of things in here," Florence said, dissolving the stone that covered the tunnel opening. Thankfully, there wasn't some horde of bloodthirsty—or would it be gemthirsty?—creatures waiting to charge inside. Only a few bugs and the like, which her cats took the opportunity to chase.

"I find it rather enjoyable to have prey that is just right for my size," Doug said, his little kitty jaws closing on a beetle that he had cornered.

"All of you better make sure to catch them bugs. Some of them there beetles look a little too much like cockroaches. I won't have anybody saying that Florence Valentine's home is infested with creepy-crawlies." Florence didn't like bugs, didn't like them one bit.

"We shall endeavor to keep the premises safe," Doug said, moving after his next victim. It was too bad that killing the bugs didn't give them any cash. That would have made them almost welcome.

Florence finally reached her limit. As much as she wanted to save up for another kitty defender, there was no way she could stand looking at plain stone walls and dirt floors any longer. She took what funds had already accumulated and went to work on the living room, re-creating it exactly the way it had been previously. As soon as the sofa was created, her kitties left their bug-catching duties and curled up for a little nap.

"No, this is not what we have agreed upon. Defenders before decorations!" Doug insisted.

"Oh, shush up, Mr. Grumpy Pants. I won't have to deal with the tunnel bugs if the rooms are built out. Just look at Tater and Midnight. They're enjoying the sofa, and my babies deserve to be comfortable." Florence knew it was a risk, but gall durn it, she was going to do things her way, and her way was a clean and proper home.

"Insects are unable to do anything to you, but things more dangerous than tiny bugs will be drawn to your core, things that can hurt us both," Doug argued.

"I'm a-going to finish decorating the three rooms we have. Then we'll build up our defender count." It took Florence a while to get the room just the way she wanted it, and while she made some small tweaks, the funds built up enough for her to get a good start on the front yard. The porch was built up next, but the money ran out before she could put the plants and rocking chairs in place. Her lawn was also just an open patch of dirt and rocks, not at all the clean-and-tidy look she was going for.

"And just as I predicted, our doom approaches. We should have been better prepared," Doug said. The little guy crouched behind Florence's pedestal as something horrible skittered across the barren lawn, heading toward her front door.

Chapter 5

"STOP YOUR FUSSING, DOUG. TATER AND MIDNIGHT CAN TAKE CARE of that critter."

Florence was frankly terrified but didn't want to let Doug know it. Hacking away at her front door was a spider the size of a refrigerator. Now, not one of them little fridges that folks put in their rooms and offices and whatnot, but a good-sized kitchen one. Florence hated spiders and had always been most terrified of black widows. The creature at her door had the same black carapace and red markings she knew to fear. Unlike a regular spider, this one had two sets of fangs, giving it double the damage output and the chance to clamp on good to its victim. To make matters even worse, she could see a stinger dripping venom at the back of the abdomen.

"Why isn't the door keeping that thing out?" Florence asked as one of the spiky legs of the spider pierced through. Tater was waiting just inside the door and took a swipe at the leg, but he was too slow to catch it this time.

"We've gone over this before. Interior spaces can be separated by a doorway, but that doorway cannot be locked or reinforced unless it's part of a side passage or puzzle trap. The system will report any violation, even a minor or temporary one, to the appropriate authorities, and that, my dear, is a good way to get the adventuring guild to destroy your core as an aberration," Doug replied. Yeah, she knew that, but it didn't mean she couldn't complain about it.

"That's a stupid rule, and when them there adventuring guild folks show up to give me a perfect grade again, they're going to get a piece of my mind," Florence said.

The spider's legs lashed out again, and this time, the spear-like appendages finally ripped the door from its hinges.

Tater wasted no time, and with a yowl of righteous kitty anger, he pounced on the spider. All her babies were quick and agile, but the brawler types, like Tater, were a bit slower than the rest, slow enough to let the spider react to the attack. Its fangs dripped with venom in anticipation of a fresh meal as the front pair of spiky legs shot forward. Tater's paws skidded on the wooden floors, his claws tearing gouges in the wood as he stopped himself from being impaled on the spider's legs. It turned out to be just what the spider wanted him to do, and once he stopped, the other six legs flexed, causing the spider to leap onto her poor baby.

The kitty gave a mew of pain as all four fangs sank into his back. Before Tater could respond, the spider curled around him, bringing its stinger into his soft, fluffy belly. Her defender had no chance; the venom being pumped into the cat rendered him immobile. The spider had made its kill, but it didn't seem to know that a core defender would just disappear when defeated. It also didn't appear to notice Midnight leaping off the ledge over the doorway, ready to get some revenge for her brother.

Midnight landed on the back of the spider, and though its exoskeleton was as hard as bone, it didn't stop the kitty's claws from piercing through. Enhanced by her core, Florence's defenders could cut through armor with their teeth and claws, and the spider's shell was nowhere near that tough. The spider tried to roll onto its back in an effort to dislodge the cat digging into it, but Midnight held firm.

With the spider in the firm grip of her front claws, Midnight began to give the monster rabbit kicks from her rear legs. With each kick, the claws sheared off chunks of the spider's armored shell, and soon she was digging into the soft flesh beneath. Florence didn't know if a normal spider could squeal, but this creepy giant one invading her home sure did. Midnight wasn't giving it any quarter, biting at and latching onto one of its legs, which were flailing around as it tried to stab its attacker. With a crunch, Midnight bit through the leg and tore it from the spider's body, making it screech even louder than before.

"That thing sure won't shut up, will it?" Florence said to Doug.

"No, and that worries me. It's almost as if it's trying to call for help. Oh, there we go. Quiet at last," Doug replied, both of them happy when the spider went silent as Midnight finished it off. Wasting no time, Florence respawned Tater and took another look at her stats.

Florence Valentine
Cat core, level 4
Experience: 15/1500
Funds: $44.86/$350
Defender expense: $20/$350

"Hey, what gives with the experience? Fifteen seems kind of cheap for a critter that big," Florence complained.

"I have no idea, but at least it gave us some decent funds, likely a first-kill bonus for our new dungeon," Doug replied. It was true; she had enough to bring back Tater, create a few more kitties, and finish up the front yard.

First, she created more defenders, and in her core room, another ball of cash coalesced into a black shorthaired cat with a white bib and belly. It was her poorly named kitty Obiluxnerance. The stealthy little guy wandered the living room, greeting the others before sauntering out to the front yard, where he used to like to hang out. Cash flowed into the second ball of light, and when it was done, a sleek longhaired black cat sat there, grooming one of her paws. It was her little commando kitty Shadow. After cleaning up, Shadow made her rounds through the home and eventually plopped down on the front porch for a nap. For her last cat, Florence summoned Bhargath the Foe Render, reinforcing the living room defenders.

"It seems like they are gravitating toward their old locations. Some residual memory of the rooms you assigned them to," Doug observed.

"Well, of course. My little darlings are smart and remember where they were assigned. Well, everyone but Spud, whenever he shows up again," Florence replied. Spud was now a minor champion, and it might be a while before she had enough money to make him or the main champions of her home. For now, the regular defenders would have to do it on their own.

The front porch and lawn were complete, and Florence was left with $2 after she placed the finishing touches, their mailbox in particular.

"Do you want me to re-create our crossbow trap?" Doug asked.

"Sure, but why don't you wait until we have $5 so it can be a good one, not the cheapo $2 one you used before," Florence said. To be honest, she wasn't all that interested in traps and couldn't remember if Doug had upgraded it in their old home or not. Five dollars wouldn't be too much of a drain on their defender expense limit, and it would be some time before she got anywhere close to the cap. Right now, income was more of a bottleneck than defender expense.

Her home now consisted of the front porch, which was connected to the dark tunnels, the living room, the master bedroom, and, finally, her core room. The master bedroom hadn't been touched yet, and Florence had a lot to do in there to make it ready for Zork and Chubbs. As soon as Doug created his trap, she would get the room decorated and then start saving up for her champions.

They didn't get a chance to save up enough for Doug's trap before some movement was seen in the darkened tunnel. A normal person might not have seen anything, but Florence had no trouble spotting anything in or around her home. There, in the dark, were three more of the creepy spiders. They were hovering just outside the front lawn, not quite ready to charge in and attack.

Obi and Shadow sensed the threat, both of them slinking through the tall grass as they set up to ambush the first intruders that made it into range. A fourth spider joined the other three, and as if that was their signal, the four charged across the lawn, oblivious to the cats lying in wait. Florence watched as her kitties let the first pair of spiders make it onto the porch, the two of them already poking at the door with their sharp legs. The other two were on the steps leading to the front door when the cats attacked. Shadow and Obi were both commando kitties, and their initial attack from stealth was a devastating one.

"My, that was quite the initial strike. A critical hit for certain," Doug said as Shadow landed on her target. Her teeth latched onto the head of the spider and crushed it, killing the monster instantly. Obi didn't fare quite so well; his attack tore a chunk out of the back of his foe and sheared off a leg, but he left the monstrous spider still able to defend itself.

Her commando kitties were great ambush hunters, but once exposed, they were much less powerful than her brawlers. The spiders bashing open the front door turned as soon as they heard the commotion behind them, both moving to counterattack Florence's babies. Shadow almost made it off the corpse of the spider she had killed, but one of the legs of the spider that Obi was still attacking managed to spear her in the side, holding her still long enough for a spider from the doorway to reach her. Venom-filled fangs latched onto Shadow as she raked her claws across the attacker's carapace.

Obi was in even worse shape, still fighting with his initial target.

He couldn't get away when the reinforcing spider arrived and immediately stung the poor kitty. Venom already slowing him down, Obi made a futile last stand, unable to land a blow and finish off the wounded spider before he succumbed to his injuries. With a pitiful little mew, her kitty collapsed on the lawn.

Shadow was also not long for this world, her attacks getting weaker and weaker as the spiders continued to bite and sting her. As soon as Shadow fell, the spiders resumed their attack on the front door. Within moments, the door gave way and the spiders poured inside. Tooth and claw met fangs and stingers as the two groups engaged each other. Florence's brawler kitties were pretty tough, but even they were having trouble once a spider managed to land a sting or bite. It seemed that even a small amount of venom was enough to slow her babies, even if it didn't kill them.

Neither side gave any ground, and the spider wounded by Obi was taken down first. The remaining pair of spiders managed to bite both Tater and Midnight, who didn't give up. Bhargath tore into one of the spiders as it paused to land a sting into a slowed Midnight. The added venom from the sting finished off the kitty, but Bhargath's attack avenged his sister. Tater went down next, a pair of spider legs impaling him even as Bhargath moved to attack. The final spider got a lucky nip on Bhargath, the venom slowing him down just enough for it to land a sting. Once hit by the added damage from the sting, Bhargath was on borrowed time as his kitty body began to shut down. He did manage to at least injure the spider that had hurt him, but even with a missing leg and goopy blood pouring out from a cracked carapace, the spider made its way toward the core room.

"Oh, no you don't. Doug, take care of this pest," Florence said as the spider skittered its way toward her gem. Deadly Doug activated, and her diminutive little kitten assistant instantly grew into a tiger-sized kitty. With longer reach and without wounds to slow him down, Doug went to town on the spider, swatting off its legs, then crushing its body with a powerful bite.

"Have at you, fiend. You shall not dine upon Florence's gem this day. I put too much work into that to have it become some overgrown arachnid's lunch," Doug said, really getting into his role as her defender.

"Not bad there, Dougie. You done good," Florence said as Deadly Doug wore off and he returned to his cute kitten-sized self.

"I'd prefer you not call me Dougie. I go by Doug, or if you prefer, you may call me Douglas."

"There's no way I'm calling you Douglas. You were named Doug, so no going on and getting highfalutin ideas about making your name sound more fancy," Florence replied as she re-created her defenders.

"Sadly, that rather impressive ability will be on cooldown for a while, so you may want to think about using your summoner ability before activating Deadly Doug. We should also focus on purchasing our champions before you begin to decorate the master bedroom."

She hated to admit it, but Doug was right. At least until Deadly Doug reset, or her cane finally regenerated, Florence needed more defenders. Her champions would have made short work of all four spiders on their own, and given the way them four critters were a-squalling, Florence would be willing to bet there would be more of them creeping into her home before too long. The attack of four of the creatures had left her with enough to resummon her defenders and then have just under $50 remaining. It didn't take too long for the last of the needed funds to trickle in, and Florence summoned her champions.

A much larger ball of glowing money was created, the light turning into the two precious kitties that were her champions. Zork looked like a tired old tabby cat, with a clipped ear and what

Florence thought was a wise and regal gaze. Chubbs was a huge ball of fur, fat, and muscle that was ready to take on all comers. Unlike when the other cats had been summoned, the pair didn't go out and greet everyone else. This time, everyone else came to greet them, perhaps in deference to their status as champions.

"Welcome back, Zork and Chubbs. Don't let the attention go to your heads, though. I'm going to get to work on your room as soon as I have the money, so until then, you're going to be stuck with what you got," Florence said. The two didn't seem to mind that their room was completely empty, and they still did their duty by standing watch against any attackers that might make it past the other kitty defenders.

With the return of her champions, Florence felt that her home was coming together rather nicely. If only she could get rid of all these creepy-crawlies, then things would be perfect.

Chapter 6

FLORENCE DECORATED HER MASTER BEDROOM JUST LIKE SHE HAD before. The oversized bed with a frilly dust ruffle hid Chubbs from sight, while Zork preferred to sleep among the plush animals and pillows that covered the head of the bed. Side tables with lamps and a dresser were created, and a large mirror finished the room. Florence then pushed out her home to make room for the hallway that led from the living room to the master bedroom. There was a long way to go, but she would get there and make her home even better than it had been in the past.

"Oh, look at this, Florence. It looks like we've got the first visitors that aren't swarms of arachnids," Doug said as a flash of light burst on their doorstep, revealing two humanoids standing near her front lawn.

"What do you think? Are these them there dungeon guild folks?" Florence asked.

"Quiet. I think they're about to tell us," Doug said.

With the light show over, she could finally get a good look at the two. One was armored in a set of light chainmail with a breastplate and no helm. He was human and well-groomed, not like some of them scruffy folks that would sometimes explore her home or them hooligans that brought her here. The man's gear was of the highest quality, and she could see the waves of power radiating off it. As far as the second guy went, he was wearing some fancy-guy robes, and the only visible weapon was a dagger strapped to his waist. He was a mage of some sort, and given the pointy ears and "I'm better than you" attitude plastered on his face, Florence assumed he was an elf.

The elf raised a scroll and began to read. "Attention, dungeon core. We are representatives of the adventurers guild and are here to categorize and rate your dungeon. Deactivate your traps, set your defenders to passive, and open any hidden passageways. Attempts to hinder our examination will be met with deadly force," the elf said in the bored voice of someone who had given this same demand far too many times.

"Well, I guess we'll do what they ask, but when they're done, I'm giving them a piece of my mind about the whole closing-off-the-door thing," Florence told Doug as she complied with the guild's demands.

"No, do not interact with them at all. We're odd enough as it is, and I don't think it wise to draw any unnecessary attention to ourselves. Say nothing unless they ask you a question directly, and if they do ask you a question, try not to respond in your normal manner," Doug warned.

"And just what is my normal manner?" Florence snapped at the rude little kitty.

"Acerbic, overbearing, prideful, self-important, rude, and generally unpleasant to those around you," Doug said flatly.

"Oh, is that what you think? See if you get any yarn from here on out." Florence reabsorbed Doug's growing collection of yarn balls.

"There you go, proving my perfectly argued point," Doug said. It was hard to stay mad at the little guy. He looked so cute when he was trying to be angry at her. Still, Doug had a point about these guild folks, so she would hold her tongue for now. If she were honest with herself, and Florence Valentine was a woman who prided herself on honesty, she was a bit intimidated by the pair. The power coming off them was incredible, and she figured that either one of them could take on her entire dungeon without breaking a sweat.

"The core has complied with our demands. Begin noting traps and defenders as we move forward. This dungeon is most odd. We'll have to examine the archives, but I do recall something similar cropping up years ago," the elf said.

The armored guy nodded and pulled out a quill and paper to begin noting her traps, defenders, and the like. Florence wasn't exactly pleased with them rudely not introducing themselves before entering her home, but she didn't want to rile them up by correcting their behavior.

"Yes, the pictures of the defenders, I remember something similar noted in a dungeon over in Haverston, a place that was also entirely populated by felines, just like here," the elf said.

"Do you suppose it's the same one? It's not unheard of for a core to relocate," the armored guy said.

"No, that core was destroyed by the followers of Kunrax. It was before your time, but I remember there were several requests for retaliation on the cult for the destruction of a new core so soon in its life cycle," the elf replied.

With her home only having four rooms, it didn't take them too long to complete their inspection.

"Any final observations?" the elf asked his companion when they finished at her core room, giving her core only a cursory inspection and completely ignoring poor Doug, who looked a little upset over the slight.

"Yes, it's odd that this place only has four chambers," the armored guy replied. "Granted, they are more highly detailed than most, but a dungeon that has been around long enough to achieve level 4 should have expanded further than this one has. I'm inclined to believe that the higher-than-average core level for such a new core must be due to a higher-than-normal incursion rate from local wildlife."

"Very well. This warrants further investigation. Let me try to engage the core directly. Core, can you tell us how you chose your core type?" the elf said, talking loudly and slowly. Florence almost laughed. The guy was doing the same thing folks tended to do when they were talking with someone who didn't know their language.

"I can hear you just fine. No need to raise your voice. As far as why I chose kitties for my home, well, they're the best things ever. I'll also have you know that this is my home, not some creepy dungeon, so please refer to it as such," Florence replied.

"Sir, I think perhaps this core is flawed in some way. Its speech patterns are . . . unusual," the armored guy said.

"How dare you come into my home and insult me. I'm not unusual. I'm eccentric, and that's a whole different bag of marbles, let me tell you. Did your mama not raise you right? Did she teach you to go around insulting people in their own home?" Florence was losing her patience with these two, and it had been a good long while since she had someone proper to complain about.

"I apologize for any misunderstanding. We are only performing the tasks assigned to us," the elf said.

"Oh, that just makes it all better? Performing your tasks, hah. Does your task include insulting the core you're sent to review? Don't think you're free of guilt here, mage boy. You entered my home without so much as a howdy-do. Where I come from, it's only proper for guests to introduce themselves and *request* entry, not demand it," Florence said.

Doug was aghast, trying to hide behind the pillar her gem was resting on.

"Intriguing. You are more self-aware than I had considered. I once again offer our apologies. I am Sar'narao, and this is my associate, Delvar. Thank you for hosting us while we perform our tasks," the elf replied, bowing.

"Apology accepted. I'm Florence Valentine. Pleased to meet you." Florence wished she still had facial expressions and could let Doug see how smug she was feeling at whipping these two into shape.

"Thank you. May I ask about your origin? Have you moved from another location?" Sar'narao asked.

"Yes, I did. I was originally placed somewhere else, but that there dog monster tried to crush my gem, and if it weren't for Bartleby's goop that we slathered on my gem, I'd have been a goner for sure." Florence kept quiet about her brief return to humanity and the licking skeleton's involvement. She didn't want folks to think she associated with the wrong sort. Given Berikoz's choice of folks to handle her relocation, she didn't expect he would be seen as a paragon of polite society.

"Sir, I think this Bartleby may be the merchant we've heard about, the one selling reward chests in the larger cities," Delvar added.

"That's the guy. Quite a huckster, but some of his wares are pretty good if you know how to strike a bargain, and everyone in Logan County knows that Florence Valentine can haggle with the best of them." She decided not to share the example of Marta Cantrell and the horrible deal she got on that ugly car she bought back in 2002.

"Thank you for that information. May we visit again if we have further inquiries?" the elf asked.

"Sure, and next time my kitchen should be all done up, and I'll set out a proper spread for you two," Florence replied.

"Thank you. It is obvious you're still in the process of sorting out your home. Until it is nearer to completion, I'll have to rank it A+ with a caveat that the defenders are level 4, so new adventurers should be wary. Your ranking will likely improve as you expand and add to your defenses. Until then, good day, and thank you for your assistance." The elf gave her a slight bow before the pair made their way out of her home. Once past the lawn, the elf cast that flashy teleport spell again, and when the light faded, the two were gone.

"Durn it, we were getting along so well. I should have brought up the door thing," Florence said.

"No, no you shouldn't. I somewhat expected that, despite the danger, you would continue with your constant insistence on agitating those with power," Doug lamented.

"Oh, don't you start with me. You're just embarrassed that you were hiding behind my pillar the whole time. Some brave tiger you turned out to be."

"It's not my fault you made me this tiny body. An upgrade would be nice, you know."

"We got too much to do and not enough money to do it with, so any advisor upgrades will just have to wait," Florence said. "Say, did you notice those two didn't give us all that much income while they were here? With their high levels and whatnot, I would have thought they could generate some solid income just by hanging around."

"Since our defenses were inactive, the ambient mana we can collect from them is negligible. Be thankful we received anything at all. These guild representatives can often use an ability to hamper our income absorption while they're inside."

"Did you notice I got an A+ again? This pair might have been rude initially, but they know quality and refinement when they see it," Florence said, pleased with her home's performance.

"Ugh, must we retread this ground?" Doug replied. "The ranking of A+ is not that high of an achievement. The rankings go from A to Z with a plus or minus when needed. Our current ranking places us squarely in the lower tiers and designates us as a minimal challenge. That's not entirely a bad thing. We're better off facing lower-level and less well-equipped adventurers, at least until we grow some more."

"You're just being a spoilsport. Say, why do you think they arrived so much quicker than they did last time? Have we spent more time than I thought getting things rolling?" Last time, adventurers had already been exploring Florence's home before the guild ever showed up. Maybe these guys were just getting lazy.

"I'm not sure what's considered typical as far as the first categorization exam of a dungeon goes, but typically they don't come out this soon. When a core goes active, they can scry its presence, but the process takes time."

"Well, we've got $12.55 to work with. I'm going to work on adding our hallway back in. Maybe you can rework your traps while I get started." Florence was itching to get back to work. Visitors were interesting and all, but she had a home to build.

Doug reworked the crossbow trap, making it so the trap didn't always appear. He and Florence spent $5 on it, so the trap could now fire at a more rapid pace, hopefully affording it at least two shots before it was taken out. Back in the fireplace, they spent another $5 to set up a flame burst trap. The new design was more powerful, and the burst of fire focused on a smaller cone, giving the device more damage but limiting it as an area-of-effect weapon.

"That should do it," Doug said. "I'll see about alternate placement for the crossbow trap. The flame trap can be left in place indefinitely. Parties will know it's there, but they'll be tempted to risk it if you place the reward chests in there occasionally." It was a good setup, and while Florence loathed giving anything away for free, sometimes it might do to reward a particular group. Having the rewards appear in the same place every time, a dangerous place, would make things more interesting.

The traps had taken most of her available funds, but the hall-way was a simple structure, and the construction would go quickly enough with just the tiny trickle of income that came in while the home was vacant. Now, if those adventurers would just show up and start exploring, she could really get things moving.

Chapter 7

"Matron of the Initiates, you are summoned to the scrying chamber," the young page said, handing her a scroll with the seal of the knight commander. With a sigh, Matron closed the tome she had been reading. The library inside the Brilliant Keep was her favorite place to find some solitude amid her busy day. Standing, Matron felt all the aches and pains that were the result of a lifetime of questing in service of the light. Those pains were becoming harder and harder to ignore. The specter of age stalked her, and age always took its prey.

While age might be slowly sapping the vitality from her body, her enthusiasm to serve overcame simple discomfort. If she had been summoned for a quest, it meant that despite her age, the light still had use for her. Sad would the day be when the summons no longer came and her usefulness in active duty came to an end. Continued service would still be there for her, but the duties she was assigned would no longer see her in the fray, trading blows with the foe. Even now, her position as Matron of the Initiates saw her teaching and instructing the new supplicants to the order; she got into the fight only if they needed her support.

A smile crossed her normally dour features as she thought of her latest charges. This group of aspiring adventurers might be her last, but they had more promise than any of the others she had worked with. Should this summons be for the reason she expected, they would have an opportunity to test their limits and grow in power. If this were to be her last quest, let it be one that made a difference.

Leaving the tome with one of the library attendants to keep for her return, Matron descended into the basement levels of the keep where Seer plied his trade. She asked years ago why Seer chose such a dark and foreboding location for his work. He simply replied that all those who inhabited this keep served the light, but to understand the light, you often had to face the darkness. She never learned Seer's name; he never offered it, and she never asked. Just as with her own name, it was gone, and her duty, her calling, was all that remained. She was Matron to her charges, so Matron she would be to all who followed the path.

"You summoned me?" Matron asked. Seer didn't even look up as she entered his room; all his focus was on a single candle atop the table at which he was seated. Darkness covered the chamber, pierced only by this one sliver of light.

"Ah, yes, my dear, but 'summoned' is perhaps the wrong term. 'Requested your presence' would be more accurate. How are your initiates developing?" Seer asked, reluctantly pulling his gaze from the flame to look at her.

"Well enough," Matron said. "The mages show some promise and could achieve great things if they would ever stop bickering. The rogue is skillful but foolish, lacking any form of caution. We still need to find them a healer, and I'm still puzzled why none of the clerics or aspiring paladins of the order have felt the call to join this team."

"The answer to your question is one that I might help with," Seer replied. "It's one I believe you know already. A healer for your initiates has already been chosen by the light, one that will bind their wounds with magic and become part of the whole. This one will not come from our ranks, but from outside, from somewhere we least expect."

"Vague as always. Does your skill always deal in ambiguity, or will I ever get an exact response," Matron replied, frustrated as she normally was with the signs and portends this old man dredged up.

"You dance around the main issue with your new charges and complain about my ambiguity. How fares the warrior of their group, the one member of the party you neglected to mention?" Seer asked.

"Powerful, deadly, but uncontrolled. I'm still not sure if she's an asset or a liability to the group. Only time will tell," Matron offered.

"Yes, time and your firm guidance. I have always respected that about you, Matron. You have a tough exterior but will do anything to see your initiates succeed. But bantering about your gaggle of fledgling adventurers isn't why I asked you here, at least not directly. My vision is drawn to the Crag Steppes and to a new dungeon appearing there. It is a strange one, a place that defies my attempts to look further," Seer said, his thoughts distracted as Matron watched him gaze into the candlelight once again.

"Is this new dungeon one that my initiates can handle?" Matron asked. Her group needed a place to delve and grow, and they were planning to eventually head to Brighton Harbor, where a lower-level dungeon had been found a few years ago. The dungeon had grown and developed since it was found, but it still contained suitable challenges on which a new party could cut their teeth. Brighton Harbor was a journey of several months, but while the Crag Steppes weren't easily accessible, it would only take them a few weeks of hard travel.

"Yes, the place is new, but not without dangers, I'm sure. The reason I want you there is because of something else. My vision saw more than just an unusual dungeon. It alerted me to a threat that is brewing. Watch your charges closely. Watch to see if this dungeon is tainted or if something else lurks nearby, clouding my vision. All I can say for sure is that the light wishes for you and your party to be there and that their success or failure will decide the fate of many." Seer handed Matron a map with a circle marking where he believed the dungeon would be found.

The circled area covered dozens of miles, but when she tried to ask for specifics, Seer ignored her, completely focused now on the flickering candlelight. She had seen him in this state before. It would be hours before he came to his senses, and even after that, it would take him days to recover. Something important was being revealed to him, something that didn't involve her or her party. Only once had she tried to gaze into the light while Seer was so distracted. Matron didn't remember what she saw, only that it would have driven her mad had she concentrated on it but a few seconds more.

Matron returned to her chambers. She sent a page to summon her party to the stables, giving them instruction to bring all their gear and rations for a month of travel. A myriad of tasks poured into her head, all the little things she needed to do before a long journey. The movements were almost automatic, and her travel duffel had already been half packed for weeks in anticipation of, well, she wasn't quite sure. Matron might not be a seer, but she could feel that there was something she would be called to do.

Her preparation stopped as she walked over to her armor stand. The suit of plate and chain was finely crafted, a reward for her years of service. It had protected her in battle countless times. The enchantments woven into the material would slowly repair any damage to the armor and the paladin who wore it. Faint marks on the surface were all that remained of the wounds that both the armor and she had taken in the fight against evil. Under her tunic, Matron's body had matching scars in many of the same places. The armor healed her as it repaired itself, but it didn't do so without blemish.

With only a thought, the armor disappeared from the stand and appeared on Matron, another expensive and worthwhile enchantment. Her hand sought out the war hammer propped up next to the armor. The weapon had a solid metal haft and a chisel-tipped head that could crush the skull of a dragon. Despite the runes carved into it, runes that reduced the weight of the weapon and improved its balance for her alone, it felt different. Her once-prodigious strength was fading, her body weakening a bit more each year. One day, even with the enchantments, her hammer would be beyond her strength to wield. But not today. Hoisting the two-handed weapon over her shoulder, Matron went to gather her flock.

Arguing voices greeted her as she entered the stables. As she suspected, the two brothers Frex and Chamm were at it again. The two were inseparable, but also unable to go for more than a few minutes without fighting. Things were much more problematic when the pair used their magic and not just their fists, but Matron had put a stop to that some time ago. She was a harsh teacher, but that harshness would help keep them alive.

"I take it that since you two have time to argue, all of your gear is squared away?" she asked the two brothers as she entered the stables.

"Aye, Matron, we're ready," Frex said, his quavering voice betraying the confidence he tried to show.

"Good, then let's do an inventory, shall we? We'll start with you, Frex." Matron had the party clear off one of the hostler's work tables, and the mage laid out what he had packed for their journey. It was a mess, missing several things he would need during their travels.

"I see you don't think you'll need more than one waterskin. What if our destination is in a desert environment and the water that we do find is unsafe to drink?" Matron asked.

"I can use my flames to purify it," Frex offered.

"Yes, use your flames and evaporate our precious water. Good call," she said, watching the young fire mage wilt under her glare. The rest of his gear was present, save for a backup ranged and melee weapon. Neglecting weapons was a common fault in young mages; confidence in their magical prowess often outweighed their mana pool. Other than that, he hadn't packed nearly enough food.

The others weren't much better. Only the berserker Jess was nearly squared away, but she had also misjudged the number of foodstuffs she needed to bring. Normally, they could hunt, forage, or purchase food from settlements along the way to supplement their supplies, but you couldn't always count on that. Valuable time was wasted as Matron sent them to correct their errors.

When they had returned and passed inspection, she finally told them the purpose of this little exercise. "Now that you are reasonably prepared and are done wasting my time, I'll tell you where our destination is. Seer has detected the emergence of a new dungeon in the Crag Steppes, and it is my intention to continue your training within this dungeon. Make no mistake, my presence is only to instruct you and to prevent disaster, not to do your work for you. Should one of you make a serious error, you will die, and even my prowess may not be able to save you. Remember your lessons and work together if you want to not only survive but also grow and prosper."

"Is this dungeon low ranked?" Jess asked.

"A good question, and one we don't have an answer to," Matron said. "Common sense would dictate that a new dungeon shouldn't be too challenging, but you can never tell with dungeons. Keep in mind that even if the defenders are weak, a dungeon is a cunning entity that would love nothing more than to slay a careless adventurer and feast upon the mana their death creates."

"Should we bring extra horses so we can carry all the loot I'll pilfer from inside our new dungeon?" the diminutive halfling rogue offered. Tipp was a work in progress, a youngster that was far too confident in his abilities. Matron had to admit the halfling showed promise as a rogue, not an uncommon finding among his people, but a promising young rogue could die just as easily as anyone else when he was not focused on his job.

"You know, we really should make some extra room for loot, Tipp," Matron replied. "Unfortunately, the order can only spare a few pack horses for our venture, so you'll just have to make do. Hmm, perhaps I have a solution. I want each of you to carry two additional duffel bags. That should give us a place to store all the treasures you find." The party groaned and cast death glares at Tipp. It might not sound like much, but they all knew from experience that any additional weight, even that of two empty duffel bags, would become pure torture during a long journey.

"Now, it's time for us to be off," Matron added. "We'll be moving at a fast pace and stopping only when absolutely necessary. One of the things I learned from my earliest dungeon delves is that being one of the first to the dungeon can give you a huge advantage. I want you to have that same advantage, so I expect no whining about how tired you all are. This is for your own good." Seer hadn't mentioned how long the dungeon had been active, and there was a good chance that others were already there, limiting the number of delves Matron and her party could complete.

They left the Brilliant Keep and the town of Klaxton that surrounded it, heading east toward the Crag Steppes. Her charges kept a good pace. It seemed the chance to finally put their skills to the test had given them a pep in their step. A trio of pack animals was led by the party, each heavily laden down with tents, supplies, and the things needed for an extended stay once they arrived at their destination.

Matron rode her trustworthy mount, Beauregard, a horse she had owned for several years now. Beauregard had been trained by the order's horse masters and was as deadly in battle as he was steady on the trail. Once in the countryside, Matron activated her armor's enchantment, sending the suit into the storage pack she had placed on Beauregard for this very purpose. Being able to summon her armor and weapons at will meant she could ride with a bit more comfort than the others, whom she required to remain fully equipped and ready for action whenever they weren't sleeping. The party cast a few jealous glances her way, but they knew she had earned the privilege of some level of comfort.

They made good speed on their trip, and Matron spent several hours each day quizzing them and having them practice their skills as a team, both in the light of the day and in the dark of the night, which better reflected the environment they would find themselves in while exploring a dungeon. As the journey progressed, the grassy plains and farmland gave way to bleaker terrain as they entered the outskirts of the Crag Steppes. The road also narrowed, and the constant traffic became a trickle that consisted of mostly stout-hearted merchants and those who wished for their journeys to go unnoticed by others.

"Ah, what have we here, lads? It looks like Grandmother is going somewhere," a voice called out from one of the rare copses of trees near the roadway. A scruffy man holding a loaded crossbow stepped out into the road. Another pair of ruffians holding spears stood by the man, all of them glowing a sickly purple in Matron's sight as their evil intent was revealed to her. Filthy and abused leather jerkins provided the highwaymen some protection, and the way they held their weapons revealed they were unskilled in their use. Still, an unskilled man could easily kill the unprepared.

She had expected some form of confrontation during their journey; they were moving farther from civilization with each step, and the wilds near the Crag Steppes teemed with dangers, not the least of which were the bandits that used the rough terrain to seek refuge from the authorities. The merchants that did face these roads usually did so with a strong escort. To these bandits, Matron must have looked like a lone elderly woman, one rich enough to afford several horses, but not wealthy enough to hire more than a few inexperienced guards.

"I will give you one chance, and only one, to let us pass," she said to the group.

"Oh, you hear that, lads? The old wench has some bite to her. Hop down off your horse, granny, and maybe we'll not skin you alive. Just look at the rest of these blighters, lads," the thug said to his comrades, gesturing rudely at her initiates. "Granny, did you actually hire this lot as your protection? You should pay us. We'll see you through safely. Won't we, lads?"

Matron gave a show of slowly dismounting Beauregard, not in any way to comply with the bandit's demands, but to keep her precious beast out of the line of fire of the man's crossbow.

A quick glance to either side revealed three more attackers standing up from where they had hidden on the other side of the road, foolishly giving away their presence in an effort to intimidate the group. Hand signals were passed among her charges, and each was assigned a target. The fledgling party could take care of the three newest attackers, none of whom held a ranged weapon, and she would handle the loudmouthed leader and his two companions.

"You are judged by the light and found wanting. No longer shall you trouble the innocent. Your lives are forfeit," Matron called as she summoned her armor and weapons. The bandits stood there stunned for a crucial, fatal moment as the helpless old lady in front of them became an armored paladin glowing with power. Recovering quicker than the other two, the leader fired off his crossbow. The bolt shattered against Matron's breastplate as she charged toward him. He fumbled to reload as she swung her hammer. The chiseled tip, designed to crush and penetrate armor, did horrible things to the man's skull.

Matron pulled from her mana, sending a bolt of energy into one of the spear-wielders beside the now-dead leader. Her target's scream of pain was cut short as the damaging power burned completely through him. The final spearman thrust his weapon. The rust-pitted point of the spear skittered off her armored vambrace. The man looked horrified as Matron's hammer swung once more to finish off her last foe.

With her three attackers dealt with, Matron turned her attention toward her initiates. Jess had a pair of steel axes in hand and was getting the better of her foe. Given the burnt and frost-covered bodies lying nearby, it appeared the mages had done away with all but the attacker whom Jess was busy with. Popping up, seemingly from nowhere, Tipp appeared behind the final highwayman, his dagger easily piercing the man's thin and patched leather armor. The wound wasn't mortal, but it did distract the man enough for Jess to land a pair of fatal blows with her weapons. It was over in less than ten seconds, and her initiates had done well. Six men had died, but that was due to their evil intent. Matron and her party were merely the instruments of righteous judgment; the only blame for the deaths lay with the highwaymen's actions, not those of her and her initiates.

"Well done. Next time, don't hold back, Jess. Tipp shouldn't have had time to reach your opponent," Matron said. Jess should have easily outmatched the clumsy highwayman. The young woman had so much potential, but she feared her class as much as the foe. It was with good reason; a berserker could easily lose themselves in the heat of battle, having trouble telling friend from foe.

"What do we do now?" Frex asked, looking a bit sick over the carnage in which he had just been forced to participate.

"They are gone, but we should not leave their belongings for others to abuse. Search them and look for their camp. Given the lazy nature of bandits such as these, it must be nearby. This was likely all of them, but likely doesn't mean certain, so use caution as you approach their lair," Matron ordered.

Taking the attackers' gear and valuables wasn't as clean as gathering loot in a dungeon, but it would be a good lesson for the initiates. The bandits were likely poor. She doubted they had more than a few coppers to their name, but nothing should be wasted. It would also serve as a reminder to her charges that a single mistake in battle could have fatal consequences. It could have just as easily been their party that was lying on the ground, dead, their pockets being rifled through by the victor. This was a hard world, one that had proven to be much more difficult than Matron would have ever expected when she started her journey as a new adventurer so long ago.

Chapter 8

"THERE, THE HALLWAY IS DONE," FLORENCE SAID AS THEY ADDED the final touches on her latest room. The wallpaper had to be just right, and she hated when the patterns were placed wrong. Tabitha Long's sitting room had that problem. Her grandson had put up the paper and didn't quite line things up correctly. Every time she visited, Florence found herself distracted by all the errors. She didn't know how long core gems lived, but it would surely be far too long to spend the time looking at crooked wallpaper.

"You're doing it again, aren't you?" Doug asked sarcastically.

"Just because you can hear my thoughts doesn't mean you need to eavesdrop on everything I think," Florence said.

"And just how am I going to avoid hearing your internal prater when you insist on thinking out loud? Do you really believe I want to listen in on your musings about some home improvement faux pas?"

"It's rude, and you should know better," Florence said. She was annoyed with her kitten helper but secretly kind of enjoyed bickering with him.

"Try to whisper your thoughts. If you do that, your internal musing will no longer be inflicted on those around you," Doug said.

"Wait, I can do that? Why didn't you tell me that when we first started?"

"I'm sure I did. Well, maybe. Nevertheless, please give it a whirl, if you don't mind."

Florence tried it out, and sure as shootin', the little guy couldn't hear her when she "whispered."

"Well, you learn something every day, don't you?" Florence said out loud.

"Hooray for you," Doug replied. He was still all mopey and annoyed because she had taken away his ball of yarn. She'd remake one for him, but not just yet. She didn't want him to think his antics had made her cave to his wishes.

"Oh, quit your yapping," she said. "Looks like we've got our first legitimate adventurers heading in."

Doug perked up and the pair watched as four elves left the dark confines of the tunnel and walked onto Florence's perfectly manicured lawn.

"That does remind me, Florence: we do need to replace your welcome sign when you get a chance," Doug said.

"I was waiting till we made it to the surface. I want my entrance to be open to the outside, not in the middle of some stupid cave. Now, be quiet. I want to watch our babies go to work," Florence said as Obi and Shadow began to stalk their way through the tall grass.

The adventuring party comprised a pair of elvish warriors armored in chainmail. Each carried a wooden shield in one hand and a curving scimitar in the other. Their skin was very pale, and Florence wondered if elves got sunburned easier than paler humans. Neither of the pair wore a helm, heads continuously scanning for threats. From their movements, she could tell they were nervous. They hadn't spotted the kitties yet, and Florence felt her babies had a pretty good chance to make their first attack a surprise attack.

Next to step onto the lawn was an obvious mage type. This guy was even wearing red robes. Couldn't these adventurers do something out of the ordinary once in a while? If the guy had been human, Florence would have bet good money on him having a long white beard and a pointy hat. Since them elves didn't seem to age like normal folks, they all looked like they were twenty-year-old whippersnappers.

"Hey, Doug, do them elves ever die of old age?" Florence asked.

"Yes, though their normal lifespan can reach six or seven hundred years," the kitten advisor replied.

"Do they ever look old, or do they just keel over one day still looking like a college kid?"

"Well, I suppose they would just keel over still looking young. Seven hundred years is a long time to survive in this world, and I believe that very few make it to that age before suffering some life-ending event," Doug said. She supposed it made sense. If she had lived that long back on Earth, at some point, she would be killed in a car wreck or something. Here on Aerkon, with all the monsters and dungeons and whatnot, there were more than enough ways to meet an untimely end.

The final member of the group was armored in soft leather, but it wasn't like the stuff the rogues usually wore. This looked more natural and bendy. She was either a rogue or some form of druid, Florence thought, given that she was dual-wielding clubs. These weren't iron-studded and reinforced like some warriors preferred. Nope, these were just a pair of plain but stout-looking sticks. Florence was looking forward to seeing how the stick lady fought.

"Teremai, this dungeon is unnatural. I sense the mind that controls it is not like any other," the stick lady said to the mage.

"Oh, if she only knew how unnatural your mind truly was," Doug chimed in. Florence let the comment slide since the kitties were just about to make their move.

"These here elves look like they know a little about what they're doing, and their gear is pretty good," she commented. While they weren't sporting high-end, enchanted gear, they also weren't wearing the hodgepodge of junk that new adventurers typically had to use at first.

"Yes, I'd estimate they are anywhere from level 3 to level 6," Doug replied.

"How come I can't see their levels? It's like sometimes they're revealed and other times it's locked," Florence said.

"Unlike the mindless monsters that wander in, attracted to your core, or even semi-intelligent beings like our old group of goblins, adventurers and their ilk are masked from us. It's something about universal balance and a way to prevent us from trying to target specific groups for destruction. Maybe someday the system will unlock more information for both of us, but for now, we're forced to work within its bounds," Doug replied. This was yet another thing she wasn't all that happy about, but her attention was drawn back to the front lawn, where the elves had stopped just outside of the range of Doug's mailbox trap.

"Hold. I hear something approaching from behind," the elf with the sticks said.

"Perhaps, Laranah, it's some creature native to the tunnels and not a product of this dungeon?" Teremai replied.

"Possible, though the native denizens of this place should have already been exterminated by the dungeon," said the stick lady, who was apparently called Laranah. "Nearby monsters and the like are typically thrown into a frenzy by the presence of a nearby dungeon core and killed off when they venture inside." She gestured toward the two elf warriors, calling them back from the lawn.

"Oh, man, just when we were finally going to get some income, they're running away," Florence said.

"I'm sure they're competent enough to deal with whatever's coming. Then they'll resume their delve. Have no worries, dear

Florence. These will be but the first of many to explore our lovely home," Doug reassured her.

The elves moved farther back into the tunnel, out of her line of sight, preventing her from getting a good look at how the party worked. Before long, she heard the sounds of combat and saw the flashes of light from spells being cast. She easily heard the war cries of the elves, but she only made out the occasional monstrous screech of their foes.

"Well, whatever came down that tunnel must be taxing the party. I didn't think they would take this long to finish off some of the simple creatures drawn to your core energy," Doug said, a hint of concern in his tone.

"Great, the adventurers are going to leave and whatever they are fighting will be killed out in the tunnel instead of inside our home. We're totally getting ripped off," Florence grumbled. The sounds of fighting built to a crescendo as a final spell lit the entire tunnel.

Florence and Doug waited for the victors to show themselves. The worst-case scenario was that the elves had won the fight but were too battered to continue with their delve. If the monsters somehow won, they would at least blindly continue into her home, where the kitties could tear them up. A figure moved in the tunnel toward their home. As it approached, they could see it was Laranah, the stick lady.

"She looks a bit worse for wear, doesn't she?" Doug commented. It was true; her armor was rent and torn in several spots, and partially healed wounds showed where whatever magical healing she had received didn't quite complete the task. One of her sticks was missing, and the other was covered in the goopy, spoiled-milk-colored blood of the spiders that had attacked Florence's home earlier.

"Must have been them spiders that attacked them, and the venom seems to be slowing the elf down," Florence noted. The elf stumbled forward in a daze, walking across the threshold of her home. Laranah dropped to her knees on the long grass, chanting as she cast a spell, a glow forming around her hand. The glow spread to her body, and while she was still torn up pretty good, the befuddled look on her face was gone, and she was moving a bit more normal.

"She must have druidic or nature magic of some type, which often includes a way to cure and prevent various poisons and venom," Doug said. At about that time, Florence heard skittering noises in the tunnel. It looked like the elves weren't the ones to survive this fight, and the critters that attacked them were coming to finish the job.

One of the elvish warriors stumbled into sight. His shield was gone, and his chainmail was ripped open in several places. Laranah gathered mana for another spell, and the familiar glow of healing magic infused the injured warrior. The two readied their weapons and waited for the attackers to arrive. They had a look of determination on their faces. These were a pair that weren't afraid to face death, bravely meeting it with steel and spell.

"I'm going to set the cats to passive for now. It doesn't seem sporting to hit those elves from behind when they're fighting monsters that were heading here to kill us," Florence said. Obi and Shadow had started to stalk the elves once they had wandered back onto the lawn, but now they held their places, hunkered down low in the tall grass.

"I agree with that, and we may be glad for every blow they strike against the foe," Doug said as the pair watched the attackers charge from the darkness. Four more of the creepy giant black widow spiders were back, but this time, they were joined by a scorpion that was just as large as the spiders.

"Where are all these crazy insects coming from?" Florence said with frustration.

"They're not insects. They're both arachnids," Doug corrected.

"Quit being a know-it-all showoff," Florence replied.

They watched the arachnids—she hated to admit Doug was right—launch themselves at the surviving elves. With a roar, the warrior charged the nearest spider, his scimitar slashing multiple times as he activated a combat ability. Hard-shelled or not, the spider felt those hits, each blow landing with devastating effect while the warrior dodged the creature's spear-like legs.

The elf druid swung her club at a spider charging toward her, but she found her attack interrupted as the scorpion snatched up her outstretched arm in one of its claws. A meaty *snip* was heard as the claw closed, causing the elf to shriek in pain as her arm was severed. The shriek was cut short when a spider landed on her and began to feast. The warrior was also down. He had hewn off the tip of one spider leg and damaged several others, but he couldn't hold out on his own. They had fought well, but these elves had been overwhelmed by the more numerous foe. Florence could only wonder how many more of the bugs were dead out in the tunnel. The elves might have inadvertently saved her home this day.

"Go get 'em, kitties," Florence said, kicking her defenders back into action. Obi and Shadow each picked a target. Their slow stalk toward the feasting arachnids went unnoticed. The overgrown bugs were so intent on getting a piece of each victim that they only noticed they were under attack when both kitties landed on their intended targets.

Obi landed on the abdomen of the spider with the damaged leg. His claws sank deep into the thing's armored shell, giving him a good grip as he started tearing away chunks of the monster with each ferocious bite. The spider let out an ear-piercing shriek of pain as it tried to roll over on the cat to dislodge it.

With a shriek to rival that of the spider, the scorpion tried to shake Shadow off its back. Shadow had landed just right, her teeth ripping into the joint where one of the scorpion's claws was attached. With the damage bonus from a sneak attack, only a pair of bites was needed to sever the limb, and then Shadow went to work on one of the scorpion's legs.

The remaining spiders closed in on the cats. One inadvertently wandered into the activation range for the crossbow trap inside the mailbox. A steel-tipped bolt flew into the spider's abdomen, cracking through the armor and piercing deep. The spider ignored the damage and skewered poor Shadow on one of its legs, allowing the scorpion time to land its deadly sting. Obi drove his claws deep into the abdomen of the spider he was attacking, and the monster shuddered a final time before collapsing.

"It's time to bring on more kitties," Florence said, activating her Summoner ability while targeting the front porch. Three flashes of light revealed a copy of Bhargath, Tater, and the recently departed Shadow. The cats hissed at the attackers, which were busy tearing apart poor Obi. The newly summoned trio jumped off the porch and into the fight.

The remaining claw on the scorpion sliced poor Obi in half as the invaders turned to face Florence's babies. A second crossbow bolt launched from the mailbox trap, the missile slamming into the side of the scorpion. Like before, the attackers ignored the mailbox, which began the process of reloading. This was one of the reasons Florence decided to summon reinforcements at the entrance; that trap was going to earn its keep today.

Bhargath slammed into the scorpion, which was off balance after killing Obi. The brawler kitty slashed his claws at the stinger-tipped tail, taking a chunk out of it and causing more bug goop to pour out. Tater was less lucky. He began grappling with a spider, giving better than he received, but another spider joined in, making it an unfair fight. Once it landed a couple of venomous bites, poor Tater started slowing down, unable to defend himself against the monster bugs.

The summoned Shadow tried to aid Tater, but she wasn't built for brawling face to face like Florence's other kitties. She clawed up one of the spiders real good, but with Tater out of the fight, several of the creeps were able to gang up on her. Bhargath was giving a shellacking to the scorpion; the monster had only one claw to defend itself with. The reinforced armor protecting the scorpion had been peeled away, letting every claw and bite from her kitty hit a vulnerable spot.

"Well, your trap did good today," Florence said to Doug as the crossbow mounted in the mailbox got off a third shot, slamming into the face of one of the spiders.

"Yes, with the defenders keeping the enemy's attention, it has proven a good value," Doug said. Florence could see him puff up a bit at the compliment. The little guy sure thought he was something.

With the scorpion down, the summoned Bhargath charged into the remaining spiders. He was fighting hard but was all alone out on the lawn. That was okay; the real Bhargath and his two buddies were waiting just inside the front door, ready to mop up any surviving creepy-crawlies.

Chapter 9

LIKE BEFORE, THE SPIDERS STABBED AT THE FRONT DOOR WITH their spiky legs. Shadow, Obi, and the summoned kitties had done well, whittling the number of attackers down to two, with a third spider alive but unable to move due to the damage to its legs. In the living room, Bhargath stood just inside the door, ready to engage the invading critters. Once the big guy had their attention, Tater and Midnight would leap down from the ledge over the door and smush them spiders good.

It didn't take long for the two attackers to tear the door down, and they wasted no time in charging toward their waiting prey. Florence watched Bhargath go to work. He slashed at the two spiders as the others waited for their opportunity to strike. Bhargath drew them farther into the room, and just when he was about to go down to a venomous bite, Midnight and Tater launched their attacks. Both cats landed on their targets, claws digging deep and their bites already crunching through the spider's armor so their teeth could get at the important bits inside. Within ten seconds, the final two spiders were down, and quiet descended over Florence's home once more.

"Well, that was unfortunate for the elves, but their loss seems to be our gain," Doug said. Florence took a quick peek at her information as she respawned their defenders.

Florence Valentine

Cat core, level 4

Experience: 649/1500
Funds: $276.88/$350
Defender expense: $110/$350

That was a lot of money for a pair of adventurers. Florence also had a slew of spiders and that scorpion critter keel over in her home, which would have added to the total. With the funds she now had, the rest of her home could be finished and the defenders re-summoned. Her home would be rebuilt like it was, but it wouldn't stay that way for long. Florence and Doug had plans for this here home—big plans. Another bonus of the last encounter was that her rocking chair and cane were finally back! Her gem now had a proper place to rest, and the cane would give a good shellacking to anyone that tried to cause problems in the core room.

"We need to get more adventurers in here as soon as we can," Florence said, already digging into the task of building rooms and repositioning the ones she had already made. She wanted to keep pushing toward the tunnel exit, not wanting her beautiful home to be stuck inside some scummy cave.

"Oh dear," Doug said with concern in his voice.

"Yeah, what's wrong now?" Florence replied.

"I just thought of something. We've only had one party enter the dungeon, and they met an untimely end. Though it wasn't our doing, their loss will be recorded in the logs that the adventurers guild tracks. The problem is that our home now has a one hundred percent lethality rate. Given that our home is new and there has only been one delve so far, we may be all right. Should the trend continue, we run the risk of being considered overly bloodthirsty, and when that happens, a kill team generally ensures our demise."

"It wasn't us. It was them creepy-crawlies that did those elves in. Don't try to put those deaths on me," Florence replied.

"I know that, and you know that, but no one else saw what transpired. We need to keep vigilant, and if these arachnid invasions continue, we may want to see about trying to more actively protect any adventurers that enter our demesne," Doug advised.

"Fine, I agree we should help a bit more if this happens again. I'm all for tearing up adventurers that have a fair shot, but I don't want outsiders slaughtering them inside our home, even if we get to rake in the cash for it."

"Good, we shall endeavor to mitigate the undeserved demise of any adventuring visitors," Doug said. "We shall also see to it that any intruders are dealt with in an expedited and violent manner. That, my dear Florence, I leave in your hands. We have a plan, so continue on that path, but I also require a bit more entertainment, if you please."

"Fine, if it'll keep you from bugging me and complaining, here you go." Florence created a variety of yarn balls for Doug to play with. The kitten advisor gathered the choicest of the lot and hauled them onto the rocking chair. Doug really liked to nap on that pillow, despite his complaints about her spending her initial money on a protective housing for her gem. After being resummoned, her defenders even joined in on the fun, the whole group playing nicely as Florence went to work.

Neither adventurers nor creepy bug things showed up while she worked, allowing Florence to re-create their old home the way it was meant to be. The expansion also had the added benefit of granting them a bit more income; the coins trickled in faster with each room she added. As each room was completed, Florence had the pleasure of resummoning her old babies in the home.

She couldn't track how long the whole process had taken, but it must have been several days, given that her Summoner ability had reset. Florence gave a mental sigh of relief once the last room was created. Basic furnishings were in, but fine-tuning the details would wait until the traps could be reset. Since Doug was upgrading his traps to the $5 versions instead of the $2 ones, several would have to be left out until she leveled up again and increased her defender expense.

"Well, what do you think, Doug?" Florence asked, waking the little guy from his nap. As her advisor, he didn't need to sleep, but somehow, the lazy guy managed to do it anyway.

"Oh, I see. Delightful to have our home whole once again and our defenders back at their labors," Doug said. He couldn't be bothered to walk through their home, but Florence could tell he was following along as she reviewed her home design and defenders.

The front lawn had extended farther down the tunnel, and while she could see light peeking out at the end, she couldn't quite reach the exterior just yet. Designing the right first impression would have to wait until she could finally grow their home all the way to the surface. Shadow and Obi stalked around the lawn, occasionally coming up to the porch to relax in the oversized rockers she had built for them. The shrubbery and flowers planted in front of the porch partially obscured the view, allowing her babies to slip into the tall grass unnoticed if visitors showed up.

The living room was now complete, and to reinforce her defenses, Florence resummoned the brawler kitty Baxter to join Tater, Midnight, and Bhargath. She also kept the fireplace trap as the location for random reward chest drops. The hallway was now populated with the lively trio of Buddy, Princess, and Mortimer. In the hall were two optional doorways, one leading to the sewing room, where Bob and Stubbs waited, and the other opened into the bathroom, where Charybdis and Scylla were patiently waiting for some victims. Florence had to nix the trap in the bathroom to save on her defender expense.

There was no link to the Home for Unwanted Goblins, and Florence kind of missed the little stinkers. She left some room in her home's layout to add the goblin home if she came across more goblins or other creatures that decided they wanted to join her.

Without the goblin home, the hall now led directly to the laundry room. Arya and Quirigua hid in the laundry baskets to get the drop on any explorers. Florence kept the clothesline trap in the room. Both defenders were mages, and they needed a bit of time to get their spells off. Doug's trap would hopefully gain them that time.

The laundry exited out to the optional garage, where Spud made his lair. Her stinky minor champion went where he pleased but did seem to enjoy spending most of his time in the dark and dingy garage. Florence felt a little sad for her delinquent kitty when he scratched at the wall where the door to the Home for Unwanted Goblins used to be. The poor little guy missed his friend Gabsug. With the goblin gone, maybe he would be a better friend to some of the other kitties. The minor champion wandered around, eventually coming into the core room. He looked up at Florence's gem as if to ask where his friend had gone.

"I'm sorry, baby. I don't make the goblins, and this is a new home," Florence said. "Why don't you try and be friends with the other kitties? Maybe someday other critters will join our home, but the goblins are gone."

Spud gave a pitiful mew that made her heart break. Doug perked up and looked down from his pillow perch on the rocking chair, eyeballing the sad Spud.

"No, unhand that right now!" Doug screeched as Spud grabbed ahold of two balls of yarn and then sauntered out of the core room.

"Calm down. He needs something to play with, too," Florence told the raging kitten.

"No, that is completely unacceptable. If it wasn't still on cooldown, I would demand you activate Deadly Doug so I can show that hooligan what for."

Florence ignored him and went back to inspecting her home. The laundry and the garage both exited into the library. Zeus, the lightning kitty, and his two brawler protectors, Fluffy and

Fluffy Junior, waited for any adventurers to make it into their abode. Florence also had Doug re-create his magic missile wand trap inside. Putting the kitten to work helped distract him from Spud's larceny.

Her game room came after the library, and it was one of the newer rooms in her home, only getting its first real workout when the followers of Kunrax invaded. Inside the large room, Astrid, Jurgen, Milk Tea, and Clementine waited for adventurers to try their luck at the games. Depending on how much the adventurers wagered, anywhere from one to all four of the cats could emerge from hiding and attack. If the bet was large enough, a trap built into the roulette table would activate. Depending on how the adventurers handled the scaling challenge, Florence would create appropriate reward chests for them.

If adventurers continued their delve past the game room, they would have a chance for some respite in the kitchen. Those that were respectful could even count on a delicious tea party waiting for them, the brew and snacks granting various beneficial effects. If the adventurers turned out to be the gem-smashing kind, well, she would just see to it that the tea and treats were doused with poison. It paid to stay on Florence's good side.

Those that chose to press on would face the dining room. Sasha, Kirabell, and Cookie would give them a good whooping before they took on her champions in the master bedroom. Chubbs and Zork were a formidable pair, and Florence was confident they would give any normal adventurers a run for their money. That left only Florence's core room, where her cane and Deadly Doug stood as their last line of defense against anyone wanting to cause mischief.

"Not bad, if I do say so myself. A true A+ home, if you ask me," Florence said, proud of her efforts. A lot of the décor was still needed, given how many of the rooms looked a little bare. Decorations would have to wait since her funds were now exhausted, and Florence would have to make do with whatever trickled in while she waited for more adventurers to show up.

"You've outdone yourself, Florence. I can't wait for the next stage of our home's development," Doug said, giving her the recognition she truly deserved.

"Yep, once we hit level 5, it's time for the second story, the new backyard, and the entrance we've been working on." Florence pictured what they had planned out during their time back on Earth. They had a rather unusual plan, one that might rub some of the guild folks the wrong way, but it was her home, and she'd run it any way she pleased.

"Do you miss it?" Doug asked.

"Miss what? Earth? Well, I'm not sure. I hope Tabitha and the kids at the game shop aren't too sad at my passing, but something about this life as a purdy core gem feels like the real me. Sure, it would be good to play a game or two of Dungeon Delve and go to another potluck at the seniors center, but can any of that compare to creating kitties anytime I want to?" Florence asked, not quite sure if she would want to go back to her old life at this point, even if it was offered to her.

"I guess it doesn't matter either way. This is our new life, and we should live it to the fullest," Doug said.

"Well, I'm stuck here. You can scurry off back to making core gems once you've served your time," Florence reminded her assistant.

"True, but I'm not sure I would want to return to that task. I had been content there, but it was all I had ever known. Now I think this mortal life of excitement might be more to my taste."

"Oh, you know you couldn't live without me. Making stupid gems would bore you to death now," Florence said, happy that her friend was at least considering staying the course with her. In truth, Florence wouldn't know what to do without Doug. Back in the past, her kitties would have been enough, but now she needed more; she needed someone to talk to and, if she was being honest, fuss at a bit.

"Oh, look, it appears your latest renovations are about to get a test." Doug drew Florence's attention to the tunnel, where a fresh party was making their way toward the front lawn. Her home was open for business, and her kitties were just waiting to take a crack at any visitors.

Chapter 10

"SO THIS LOT LOOKS A BIT LESS PREPARED THAN THE ELVES, DON'T you think?" Doug asked. He was right; the five adventurers approaching their home were definitely newbies. What little gear they had was mismatched, and they didn't have the confident but cautious stride of seasoned adventurers.

The group consisted of four human males who all bore a resemblance to one another, making Florence think they were related. Joining the brothers was a single young female. From what Florence could see, they had no semblance of a balanced party. All five appeared to be warrior classes of some sort, given their weapons and gear. While she had experienced some class-type surprises in the past, she didn't get the vibe that any of these were casters or healers.

"Is this it?" the man in the front asked, looking over the front porch with confusion.

"Yes, it has to be. How else would grass grow underground?" the girl snapped back, pushing the party forward.

"Oh dear, this isn't going to end well, is it?" Doug asked.

"Nope, these poor fools are going to be cut to ribbons by our kitties. What kind of rejects are the adventurers guild allowing to delve these days?" Florence asked.

"Perhaps there are no guild representatives on-site to manage the flow of adventurers yet. That would mean anybody nearby could venture down and take a shot at our new dungeon without knowing the true risk. I suppose it doesn't help that we've expanded significantly since those guild representatives arrived."

"No!" the girl shouted as the mailbox trap triggered, the steel-tipped bolt slamming into the lead adventurer. The man collapsed like a sack of potatoes, dead before he hit the ground.

Obi and Shadow used their distraction to cover their approach. The kitties each landed on a warrior, their claws and teeth tearing into their targets. The other adventurers stood there useless as the girl shouted for the last brother to do something. Florence never could understand folks like that, shouting for someone else to do something but doing nothing themselves. The remaining brother charged the cats, his efforts too late to save his kin.

Florence's cats finished off their first victims and then engaged the charging brother. While they weren't the greatest in face-to-face melee, the pair had little trouble against the single poorly equipped and trained adventurer that charged toward them. The girl shouted at them incoherently, slowly backing toward the exit. Her path took her too close to the mailbox trap. The weapon fired a bolt that pierced her left thigh. She dropped to the ground and slowly crawled toward the exit, managing to leave Florence's home just as the kitties finished off their latest victims and were charging toward the girl.

"I'll see you destroyed, dungeon. You didn't give us a chance," the girl wept as she stumbled to her feet and hobbled her way down the tunnel.

"How can I give them a chance when they're too stupid to prepare properly?" Florence lamented. Normally, deaths didn't affect her much, but this delve was just pure slaughter. Sure, she got a bunch of money for the four brothers keeling over in her home, but she didn't want to kill unless it was necessary.

"Sadly, until the guild structures and schedules entry into our home, it's open to all comers. There is something we can do, but not until we hit level 5," Doug said, reminding her of the jump in power her dungeon would receive once she hit that level. Levels 5 and 10 were big increases for a dungeon, improving their power and allowing them to choose a path.

Florence would have to choose whether to keep challenges in her home that matched her level of power or designate different power levels for each floor. If she kept her home at the same level of power as her core, all her defenders would match her core level and her home would sprawl out in every direction as she expanded. She didn't want some maze of a home and was leaning toward going with adding floors to her dungeon and scaling the challenge to appeal to a wider range of adventurers. Apparently, this choice was rare, with most cores wanting the highest-powered defenders they could summon. They made this choice despite the scaled-difficulty dungeons offering more defender expense to compensate for having some lower-leveled defenders.

"Hopefully, if we go with multiple floors with different difficulties, folks won't be so quick to get themselves killed," Florence said.

"True, but never underestimate the ability of an adventuring group to do something foolish," Doug replied. "Even with multiple floors of varying challenge ratings, we will still get those who push themselves too far or just happen to be unlucky. It's the way of things."

"Yeah, that may be, but the way of things can change, can't it?"

"That was our plan, though I should remind you that trying to shake up the order of things is not without some level of risk."

"Our home will be a challenge, but every single person attempting that challenge will know what the risks are," Florence said, more to herself than to Doug. That had been the plan they cooked up back on Earth: a home that was deadly when it needed to be but was a suitable challenge to those that played by the rules. Before she could build her dream, Florence had to expand and reach level 5. It looked like the entrance was clear for a bit, so it was a good time to review what the latest delve had gained them.

Florence Valentine
Cat core, level 4
Experience: 1085/1500
Funds: $126.22/$350
Defender expense: $350/$350

"Well, we didn't make a whole lot off of them, given they likely were newbs, but at least I have some funds to play around with. Too bad we're maxed out on our defender expense." Florence chuckled to herself. Without spending time back on Earth and learning about gaming, she would have never called anyone a newb or even had an inkling of what it meant.

"Nothing is stopping you from building the second floor. We can keep it sealed off from the rest of our home, at least until you can populate it with defenders," Doug advised.

It still irked Florence that she couldn't just do what she wanted when it came to opening or sealing off parts of her home, but at least the powers that be seemed to understand an empty floor didn't need adventurers poking around in it, getting all bored from nothing happening.

"I assume we're following the plan for our second story?" Doug asked.

"Sure, but which one?" Florence replied, trying to figure out which plan to go with. While on Earth, the pair had theory-crafted a number of expansions to her home, and the second floor had several variants.

"How about the great room version? I was always partial to the lovely windows you planned to create. You know, the windows with the wide ledges and the soft, cushioned sills? They would make the perfect place for a nap," Doug said.

"Alrighty, that's the one. I'll get to work. You keep an eye on things while I'm working my magic," Florence said.

"Very well. While you endeavor to expand our home, I will keep an eye on things as well as engage in a lively game of yarn ball chase with Bob and Stubbs." Doug ran off to the sewing room. Florence had to chuckle as she saw Spud perk up in his garage, the big kitty charging off to intercept Doug. That troublemaker loved to steal from the little kitten, and it was kind of fun to see Doug get all riled up over it.

Instead of listening in on Doug's cries of outrage, Florence went over her plans for the second floor. She would start off with a bang. The stairs to the second floor would lead into a large, open great room with plenty of places for her kitties to fight from. A pair of couches, a large fireplace, and several overstuffed recliners were placed in the room. Depending on how much of an increase her defender expense got at level 5, Doug had planned out several traps in this room. Defenders came first, but traps could help turn the tide, not to mention they were cheaper than kitties. Of course, they were nowhere near as cute, so traps would be placed only after the appropriate defenders were ready.

Florence was excited about creating and seeing some new kitties in the dungeon. While she had pages of perfect names memorized, Doug refused to tell her what he was going to choose for cat names, making her think the little guy would do something weird again. The hallway off the great room led to a bathroom that was, in turn, linked to a pair of bedrooms. She would decorate both bedrooms in contrasting themes. The hope was that the room design might trigger more variety in her defenders' skills.

One bedroom would have a nautical theme like in a kid's room. The second bedroom would be a western desert theme. Both bedrooms would lead to a large master bedroom that she wasn't quite sure what to do with. Maybe she would just roll the dice and see what kinds of kitties were summoned before determining its final theme. At the back of the master bedroom was a walk-in closet that contained a drop-down ladder leading to the attic, which would be where the champion of that floor would live.

The stairs leading to her new second-story addition would be placed in a small hallway that branched off from the champion room on the first floor. That was where she would start her new construction efforts. It was going to take some time and resources to build this all out, but Florence wanted things to be just right. It was their home, and it needed to be exactly how she envisioned it.

Florence was making good progress on the hallway and stairwell when her core reached a blockage of some kind. At first, she was worried the construction was going too close to the surface of the hill they were under, but her home was pretty deep underground and should be able to support several floors above her. No, this was something else entirely. Pushing harder, Florence started to make headway, only to feel something else push back.

"Uh, Doug, I think we have a problem here," Florence said.

"We have a huge problem. That deviant Spud is running roughshod over our home and is in extreme need of some punishment," Doug said.

"No, this isn't about your stupid yarn. It's about our home. Something's keeping me from expanding toward the second-floor rooms."

"Oh, well, perhaps your core is at the limits of its reach. It shouldn't happen this far into level 4, though."

"It's not the reach of my core. I get the feeling I can expand further, but something is pushing back when I try to go up," Florence said.

"I'm not sure what to say. This is very unusual. Try going up at a different spot. Perhaps we're hitting some mineral deposits that are resisting your core's influence. It would be a very good thing if we could get some valuable minerals to spawn inside our home. Those take time to assimilate, but once we do, they will provide resources for adventurers with crafting skills, resources that will take time to gather," Doug advised. The longer adventurers stayed in her home, the more money was pulled from their pockets.

"Do I have to pay to replace the minerals if they mine inside the home?" Florence asked. It wasn't a subject they'd spent a lot of time on, other than thinking about creating a garden with some exotic herbs. The problem was that she would need at least a sample of the herbs if she wanted to grow them. Getting things into their home from the outside wasn't an easy task.

"Not directly. They will regrow slowly by siphoning a tiny portion of our income. It won't be that much, and you will have a net gain in funds, given how long it takes to successfully mine a node."

Florence could almost taste the money. She would have to shift things around. She wasn't going to have some dirty mine inside her clean home. Nope, not going to happen. If there were minerals nearby, she would have to maybe build that basement level next or, better yet, create her backyard and garden.

"So what do I do? Just keep trying to place that area under my influence?" Florence asked.

"That should do it, but it will take some time," Doug said. "The longer it takes, the better, since higher-value minerals take longer to assimilate. I suspect we'll even get a windfall of experience once you're done with your task."

"I'm on it." Florence pushed her influence out once more. The resistance was still there, fighting against her. It was becoming a test of wills, but Florence Valentine was a strong-willed woman, and no fancy rocks were going to keep her out, no siree. Time passed as she focused on the task at hand. She didn't know how long she had been at it, but them mineral thingies were starting to weaken; she could feel herself gaining the upper hand in the fight.

"Hold on, Florence. Something isn't quite right about this. It's taking way too long," Doug warned.

"Hang on, Doug. I've almost got it. I can feel them weakening."

"Weakening is right. Look," Doug said, pulling her from her efforts.

"Now, I was almost there before you interrupted me, Doug. I'm going to take your yarn away for a month if I have to start all over again." Florence didn't like to waste time, but Doug seemed determined to get her attention.

"Look, I think you might have pushed too hard," Doug said with some concern in his little kitten voice. Florence had completed the small hallway off the master bedroom and had been halfway through creating the stairs leading to the second floor when she hit the interference.

Normally, the walls, floors, and ceilings of her home were nearly impenetrable since she essentially smushed all that material from her excavation into a super-strong layer to build them. There, at the top of the staircase, the ceiling was cracking. Dirt and bits of gravel were trickling down onto her clean floors. She began to absorb the material and compact the ceiling once more.

"Doug, these minerals might be more trouble than they're worth," Florence said.

"I'm sorry, my dear Florence. Perhaps I was a bit off in my initial assessment. Mineral deposits don't act like this, at least none that I've ever seen," Doug said.

The ceiling began to deteriorate faster than Florence could fix it. Cracks expanded, and they could now hear something on the other side. Something was digging its way into her home. Florence began to wall off the entire hallway but found that she couldn't. Whatever had been fighting her incursion into the area above her home was blocking her from making any changes. Almost like when an adventuring party entered, her hands were tied until whatever was doing this left.

With a loud crash, the entire ceiling caved in, and dust flooded the new hallway. Something about the dust blocked Florence's vision, which wasn't supposed to be possible. Inside her home, she was supposed to be able to see and hear everything that was taking place. A dull red glow was visible inside the dust cloud, a voice sounding out as the glow pulsed ominously.

"He took it from me. Now I'll take it from you," the voice said.

"Oh my," was all Doug could say as something climbed down from the level above, entering her home uninvited. Whatever was mouthing off in the dust cloud wasn't alone. Florence could hear lots of things skittering toward her. She could feel their need, their desire, to consume her gem. They were coming for her.

Chapter 11

"GET READY, KITTIES. WE GOT SOME UNWANTED GUESTS TO DEAL with," Florence called out.

"Be wary, Florence. These aren't your usual monsters," Doug warned as creatures emerged from the cloud of dust. It was more of the spiders, the ones that had already raided her home several times. The problem was, the spiders kept coming; there were too many for her to count. To make matters worse, the invaders were right on her doorstep, with only the master bedroom between them and her core. Thankfully, the master bedroom was protected by her most powerful defenders.

Zork and Chubbs prepared for the attack, with Zork already summoning the magical orbs he liked to hurl at the enemy. Chubbs hissed as the door to the room was knocked down, the big champion kitty doubling in size as he activated one of his abilities. Florence expected him to charge at the first spiders that were even now pouring into the room, but instead, he held back, a golden light encompassing him as Zork protected him with a magical barrier.

The dozen golden orbs circling Zork's head flew out in a blur, each one striking the spiders as they poured into the room. As the last orb connected, Chubbs finally launched his attack. He rolled into a fluffy ball of death that slammed into any spiders that survived the magical onslaught Zork had unleashed. With all the spiders in the room gone, Chubbs posted up near the door, swatting and biting at anything that tried to enter.

Functioning as a chokepoint, the doorway allowed Chubbs to avoid being swarmed. His claws were like long daggers, and his jaws could easily crush any part of a spider they bit down on. Florence's champions were holding back the tide, but it seemed like there was no end to the number of spiders pouring into her home. Her other kitties were also starting to respond to the intruders. The three cats in the dining room were already making their way to the master bedroom as the others ran to help.

"I need your core. I want to be whole again," the creepy voice called out.

Florence could see the outline of a new figure making its way from the hall, striding toward the master bedroom. The red glow she had seen earlier had come from this thing, and it looked like something out of one of them stupid movies Doug liked to watch back on Earth. The creature looked like a spider, just bigger than the others. Most disturbing was the thing's head; it had a human face that continuously babbled nonsense at her.

"Now that's just wrong. What's with this crazy world placing human heads on monster bodies?" Florence said to Doug. It was just like that three-headed dog avatar thingy that shattered her core the first time. The other one had a human head in the middle and was just as bonkers as this spider guy.

"Those crystal shards embedded in the monster look familiar," Doug replied.

"Hey, you're right. Those look like core shards. How did the spider man get those stuck all over his body?" Florence asked.

"I have no idea, and did you just refer to this creature as Spiderman?" Doug asked. Her kitten helper began humming the Spiderman theme song.

"You know what I meant. I knew it was a bad idea to let you watch all them superhero shows," Florence complained.

"All jokes aside, the crystals look like they have fused to the body. Perhaps this thing destroyed another core at some point, which may have caused this mutation," Doug said. Embedded in various points of the spider's hard carapace were small glowing chips of a core gem, and the human head of the spider monster had a large shard sticking out of its forehead.

"Maybe that one in his noggin is what's causing him to be all loopy," Florence suggested. The spider thing kept up an incoherent babble the whole time he closed in on the master bedroom. Unlike the creepy three-headed dog thing, this guy just seemed genuinely bonkers, and his words didn't possess any magical powers, at least not any that he had revealed yet.

"Loony or not, he is about to engage Chubbs," Doug said. The hallway attaching the stairwell to the second floor was placed as a small side passage off the master bedroom. If they made it past the champions, they would be right next to the door leading into her core room. At the opposite side of the master bedroom was the door leading to the dining room, and her first reinforcements were now arriving through it.

Sasha, Kirabell, and Cookie entered the master bedroom to help defend Florence. Kirabell faded from vision as she crept under the oversized bed, the perfect place for the commando kitty to launch an attack. Sasha, the big brawler tabby, charged in to join Chubbs at the door, ready to back him up if needed. Cookie was their little necromancer kitty, and she was already drawing on her mana to cast some kind of spell at the horde of creepy-crawlies.

If her babies could delay the attackers, the other cats would soon join in the defense. A powerful pair of slashes took down the last spiders between the spider guy and her cats. Not sure what to expect, Florence watched as the spider guy halted his advance.

The bulbous abdomen on his spider body shot forward like it did with spiders when they were going to sting someone. Instead of a stinger, goopy webs sprayed out, catching both Chubbs and Sasha.

Her kitties howled in pain as the webs tightened around them; an acidic venom of some sort coated the webbing. Chubbs was able to rip the webs off with his prodigious strength. Sasha was caught fast, and her health was dropping by the second. Chubbs was still in the fight, but ripping out of the webbing had delayed him long enough for a pair of spiders to skitter forward and attack. Chubbs crushed one in his jaws, but the second spider landed both a bite and a sting, the large dose of venom working quickly on her big fluffball.

Chubbs crushed his attacker with a kick of his back legs, but the damage was done. The doorway was cleared of defenders, and spiders poured into the bedroom, their attack met by the newly arriving defenders. Back in the hallway, the flood of spiders dropping into her home had slowed, but there were plenty remaining to keep the reinforcements at bay. Kirabell shot out from under the bed, her claws tearing off one of the spider guy's legs as her bite cracked open the thick shell over the monster's abdomen.

"No, keep away. I need the core. I need it!" the spider guy shouted as Kirabell attacked. Several of the nearby spiders jumped to his aid, burying Kirabell in a pile of fangs and stingers. It was at that point when Cookie unleashed her magic. A dark cloud hovered over the spiders attacking Kirabell, and wherever the cloud touched, flesh and chitin corroded away. Florence wasn't any fan of that undead necromancer magic, but old Cookie seemed to be doing much better at it than she remembered.

A pair of golden orbs slammed into the spider guy, causing him to squeal in pain as he charged for the door to the core room, sacrificing his other spiders to buy him time. In the master bedroom, her kitties had gotten the upper hand over the dwindling number of spiders, but that wouldn't help her none if that spider creep got to her core. Florence really didn't want to find out what he planned to do to her.

"You ready, Doug?" Florence asked as she used her Summoner ability.

"Yes, my dear, whenever you are ready." The little kitten hissed at the spider creep, arching his back and spiking out his fur like a tough guy.

Enough time had passed while building out her dungeon that both Summoner and Deadly Doug were off cooldown. Four kitties emerged from the summons, each one the same for some gall durned reason. Four Sashas appeared, and four squishy mage cats were exactly the opposite of what Florence needed right now. With no time to cast, each of the kitties attacked the spider guy. The mages weren't built for brawling and were only slightly larger than a house cat.

The spider guy tore into the summoned kitties, his spiky legs skewering two almost immediately. Florence activated Deadly Doug as another Sasha clone went down to a bite. Spider guy had transformed a bit, his mouth expanding as giant spider fangs appeared alongside his disturbingly human teeth. The final summoned kitty had enough time to cast a spell, and dark energy coalesced around her front paws, which she used to swipe at the nearest leg. The same necrotic corrosion occurred wherever she hit, but unfortunately, her paws were still pretty small.

Doug's paws weren't small anymore as he swelled to the size of a large tiger. Letting out a roar, her normally cute little helper leaped onto the spider creep, his claws tearing chunks the size of dinner plates from the monster. The creature squealed in pain, trying to scuttle closer to Florence as it bit down on Doug's shoulder. Doug roared in pain as potent venom was pumped into him. Her assistant wasn't a quitter, though, and kept a-slashing and a-biting for as long as he could, dealing horrible damage and distracting the monster just as it stepped into the range of Florence's cane.

She activated Shake the Cane and instantly unleashed five blows on the spider guy. Each hit caved in chitin and squished out some gross, milky-looking blood. Florence couldn't control where her blows went, and the first three cracked into the monster's legs, but the fourth hit was what she was waiting for. Her club connected with the human-like head of the monster. Whatever else that disgusting creature might have been made from, his noggin wasn't any tougher than that of a normal person. The blow caved in his skull, making the fifth hit on the thing's abdomen unnecessary.

"Consarn it, Doug, why'd you let that thing bite you?" Florence asked as Doug crawled out from under the monster's corpse.

"Sorry, I think you'll have to resummon me," Doug muttered as he succumbed to the venom flowing through his body.

"I got you, buddy. Don't you worry one bit," Florence said, choking up when she saw Doug transform back into his little kitten form after dying to the venom. She could bring him back, resummon him like a defender, but his tiny corpse was a pitiful sight that would have made her cry if she still had eyes.

It was only now that Florence realized that when the spider creep died, all the other spiders keeled over dead as well. That made things easier and also contributed to a large bump in income. She pulled up the menu to resummon Doug, spending the exorbitant sum of $50 to bring the little guy back. A timer counted down the fifteen minutes it would take for her kitten advisor to return. While she waited, Florence respawned her defenders and read the system prompts that had appeared as soon as she won the fight.

You have defeated the fragment of a vermin lord core. Bonus experience has been awarded for absorbing parts of a rival core.

Congratulations! You have reached level 5.

Congratulations! You have reached level 6. Please open your summary sheet to review any changes and make selections for your core's evolution.

A rush of energy filled Florence as she leveled up twice in a row, something she didn't know was even possible. Pulling up her interface, she reviewed the improvements as well as a few choices she could make for her core. True to the agreement they had made back on Earth, Florence would wait for Doug to be resummoned and get his input before finalizing everything, but for now, she could at least see what was unlocked.

Florence Valentine

Cat core, level 6

Experience: 117/6000

Funds: $555.27/$600

Defender expense: $350/$600

You have reached level 5 and must now choose a core path for your dungeon. Please choose from the following.

1. Level Scaling: Your dungeon challenges, including defenders, traps, and environmental hazards, will vary on each floor of your dungeon. This option will assign a set defender expense limit for each floor as well as a maximum level range. Overall, your defender expense limit will be greater than that of a core matched dungeon, but many of your defenders and challenges will be of a significantly lower level than your core.

2. Core Matched: The dungeon challenges created by you are matched to your core level. You have some variance, but typically, your defenders will need to be within 2–3 levels of your core gem's level.

A new core upgrade is available: Dungeon Affinity. An affinity is now available for your dungeon. While your

core type cannot change, an affinity will guide how the defenders inside will change over time. Note that your restrictive core type limits your choice of affinity.

A core affinity has been assigned. Due to the nature of your agreement with the being known as Berikoz, you have been assigned the undead affinity for your dungeon. The undead affinity will open several class options for your defenders. Given the nature of your dungeon, your defenders will continue to choose their preferred path but will be lured toward choices favoring necromancy when appropriate.

"Oh, no, I'm not going to agree to this. That licking skeleton has gone too far this time. I do not want any stinky undead things in my dungeon, and I won't have my kitties traipsing around with zombies and the like," Florence yelled.

The freshly respawned Cookie let out a sad meow and covered her face with her paws.

"No, I don't mean you, Cookie. You're a good girl and do that necromancer stuff the way it should be done," Florence cooed to her baby. She didn't like it one bit, but she also didn't want any of her kitties feeling bad about who they were. Florence took a few deep breaths to calm herself. She wanted to finish reviewing her options before Doug came back.

Core housing upgrade is now available for $250.

Protective avatar upgrade is now available for $250.

A new defender upgrade is available. Please choose from the following.

Empowerment: This upgrade will make all your defenders stronger, smarter, and more resilient. The changes will be geared toward their individual subtypes. Empowerment will be automatically upgraded at level 10 and every 5 levels thereafter.

Defender Classes: This is a further evolution of the defender subtype, allowing your defenders to unlock powerful classes. Since your core has chosen the Named Defender trait, there are many more options for your defenders to explore, including the chance for some of them to unlock powerful elite and prestige classes.

The following core abilities have improved.

Summoner: Your Summoner ability now has a chance to spawn a copy of one of your minor champions instead of several normal defenders.

Deadly Doug: The Deadly Doug ability now allows your advisor to choose from several classes when the ability is activated, fine-tuning and improving his ability to defend you. Due to the Named Defender trait, the advisor will be the one to decide on a particular class, and the core cannot influence his decision. The ability now lasts for up to 2 minutes and requires $50 to activate.

Florence had a lot more to work with now, given the expanded defender expense and the large income boost from defeating all of them spider critters. She knew what she wanted to choose, and first on the list would be the upgrades to her rocking chair and cane, but she held off, waiting for Doug's respawn timer to tick down to zero.

Chapter 12

"So what did I miss? I assume from the fact we're all still alive that our forces were victorious?" Doug asked as the little kitten popped back into existence next to her rocking chair. Waiting for him to return had nearly eaten up Florence. She really wanted to make her upgrade choices, but a promise was a promise.

"Of course we won the fight, and not only that, but I'm also up to level 6 and we've got a whole lot of decisions to make," she said. Doug, as her advisor, could look back on the system prompts as long as Florence gave him permission to do so, which she did in this case. Doug was silent as he read, the pause becoming almost as annoying as waiting for him to respawn.

"Choosing level scaling for our home is what we had planned. You should lock that in so we can see if there are any defender placement adjustments we need to make," Doug advised.

Florence made the selection, opting to review her interface after making the rest of her choices. "Well, hold up a minute. Before we get too far into this, what in the heck was that thing that attacked us? When we won, the prompt called it a fragment of a vermin lord core. You ever heard of that?"

"I never have. It looks like a new creature type that isn't in any of the data I possess. From what I can glean from our encounters with it and its minions, I believe it had the ability to create creatures, monstrous spiders in this case. We should be on guard for others, since if this was a 'fragment,' that implies there may be other fragments out there."

"What's going to happen when the next one shows up? Do we need to prepare for a creature that digs right into our core room?" Florence was curious about what had happened to the core this fragment came from. Was this her fate if her core was destroyed again? Turning into some mad creature roaming the depths?

"Our best defense would be in processing your upgrades and building up our home to better defend us. Focusing back on our objective, what was your preference for our defender upgrade?" Doug asked.

Florence took a deep breath in her mind, trying to focus on the task at hand and not worry about getting her core destroyed. "What's your preference on the defender upgrade?"

"I asked you first," Doug countered.

"Oh, this is silly. Let's just go with Defender Classes. That sounds like the most fun and will give my kitties lots of ways to grow," Florence said.

"Very good choice. I see merit with empowerment, but the gains from an ability like that are typically modest. Unlocking powerful classes could easily outpace any kind of blanket improvement of our defenders."

"Then why didn't you say so?"

"I didn't say so because you can sometimes be quite a contrary person. By the mere mentioning of my preference, you might have chosen the opposite just to spite me," Doug replied with a smug and self-righteous look on his face. It never ceased to amaze her how a kitten could have such a variety of facial expressions.

"Everyone knows that Florence Valentine is not a contrary person. I consider all sides of an argument. There was one time at the seniors center—this is before your time on Earth—when I got into it with Hilda Wellington over what show to watch. I was completely open to her argument and I even listened for several minutes before I turned the channel to the show I wanted. She who controls the remote controls the . . . Hey, Doug, where are you going?" Florence said as Doug wandered out of the core room, ignoring her and her captivating tale.

"I don't wish to hear it, and until you're ready to discuss our home, I'll occupy my time somewhere else. You should be building and creating new defenders, not wasting time on stories or reminiscing about television shows. Just make sure not to waste money on the core housing and protective avatar upgrades."

She didn't need any kitten with an attitude telling her what to do. Florence would show him. She spent five hundred of her savings on upgrading both her core housing and the protective avatar. She could feel the magical shell over her core strengthen. Its power would resist anyone who wished to do her harm. In addition, it would give a magical shock to anyone or anything hostile that touched it.

Her cane also improved with the protective avatar upgrade, giving Florence the ability to imbue her weapon with her choice of elemental enhancements. To top things off, the cane would also hit harder, and her Shake the Cane ability could now launch six strikes instead of five. It was a nice upgrade, but she also kind of wished she had waited and left more money to create kitties.

"Thank you for proving my point," Doug said as he walked away. He must have seen their funds drop when she purchased the upgrades.

Florence wanted to ask Doug about being stuck with the undead core affinity, but there was no way she was going to try and ask him questions just yet. When she was good and finished with being mad at him, they could have a conversation about it, but for now, she'd just move on to building the second floor and populating it with whatever kitties she could afford. When she pulled up her interface, it looked like she had more decisions to make and some kitties to shuffle around.

Florence Valentine

Cat core, level 6

Experience: 117/6000

Funds: $55.88/$600

Defender expense: scaling

First Floor: level range 1–3 ($350/$350). This floor can be assigned 1 minor champion and 1 champion.

Second Floor: level range 3–5 ($0/$250). This floor can be assigned 1 champion.

Third Floor: level range 5–6 ($0/$150). This floor will house the dungeon champion.

Dungeon affinities: undead

"Doug, you need to stop moping around and get over here to help. We've got a lot to do, and I need your advice." Florence really did need him to help, and she would be the bigger person and ignore their little spat from earlier.

"Fine, let me take a look." Doug got all glassy-eyed as he read the interface.

"How come I got stuck with that stupid undead affinity? I didn't choose or want that. The licking skeleton shouldn't have been able to make that decision for me. It's my core," Florence complained.

"Yes, about that, I'm sure it's only a result of the method of preserving your memories, not anything more. Now, let's put that aside and take a look at what we have to work with. Well, the level scaling seems to have given us a nice boost to our home's total defender limit. With a third floor to house our dungeon champion, we should see about building out both floors now that we have a chance. Our home hit a milestone level when we reached level 5, so we should be able to close things off for some time while we make changes."

"Fine, but I'm going to want to change out our dungeon affinity as soon as I find a way to do it," Florence said. "It looks like all my kitties were assigned to the first floor, but I get the feeling we can move them around a bit if we want to."

"Yes, you can do that. The critical aspect is that before we re-open, you'll need to have champions assigned and at least some defenders on each floor. Now, would you rather promote one of your cats to be the second-floor and dungeon champion, or should we create new ones?" Doug asked.

"That's kind of a tough decision. I'm kind of fond of having everyone stay where they are on the first floor. They like it here and even have their pictures on the living room wall. As for a second-floor champion, I think Spud should get a crack at that if he wants to. Besides, the extra distance might keep the two of you from bickering so much. I'm not sure about a dungeon champion, though. I'm going to rename that position to home champion. You'd think the interface could get it right that this is our home and not some creepy dungeon. It's like it tries to do the right thing sometimes, but other times, it just insults me with calling this glorious place a dungeon."

"I agree with the decision on Spud," Doug said. "The further away, the better, but I don't want him to be our home champion. That would give him too much power. The dungeon champion—excuse me, I mean the home champion—will be an order of magnitude more powerful than a floor champion. They are meant to be an epic encounter that many will refuse to attempt even if they are at the appropriate level. Correspondingly, the home champion will drop the best loot our home can produce, with a chance at legendary items that are influenced by our home's theme."

"Okay, Spud will get moved from the garage to the attic, and we'll create some new kitties to replace him. What about our minor champion here on the first floor? Somebody gets a promotion, or should we create something new?" Florence asked.

"Let's wait and see. We can't promote Spud until the floor is built, and once we do that, there is a chance the system will pick a minor champion for us, just like it did with Spud."

"Fine, we'll hold off on trying anything more until I'm done building. For our third floor, we'll make that backyard we had planned. With a limited defender expense, it will likely just be a single warmup encounter and then the big champion fight," Florence said. They had the expense limit but not the funds to make enough kitties to populate her expanded home just yet.

The natural trickle of funds that came into her home had improved by a noticeable amount after she gained two levels. Given the time it took to build rooms, her balance would grow even while she spent some on construction efforts if she didn't worry too much about décor just yet. It wasn't a lot, but it would help. To start with, she repaired and finished up the stairwell leading to the second floor. The creeps had gotten in through a natural side tunnel that skirted where she intended to build, causing her to make sure she reinforced the walls anywhere near the tunnel's path.

Once the stairwell was complete, Florence got to work on the second floor. It wasn't as large as the first floor, having only seven rooms in total, though the great room was pretty huge on its own. For now, the rooms were just roughed in, with Florence only creating interior items if it was absolutely necessary. She had an idea for the two bedrooms leading off the bath. She would make them an either/or proposition. The system seemed to agree with her efforts, allowing only one of the doors to the rooms to open at a time. She would change the bedrooms occasionally, mixing up the challenge and throwing a twist to the parties that went the same way each time.

The second-floor master bedroom was done in a modern style she'd seen on one of her shows. It wasn't a style she would want to live in, but for her home here on this world, it would be rather unique. Instead of the comfortable carpet like in her other bed-room, this one would have bamboo floors with tasteful rugs placed in key areas. Those places would also open up into hidey-holes for her kitties, allowing them to leap out from under rugs to launch their attacks. For now, she just dug out a dozen hiding places and created a tunnel system linking them together. The adventurers exploring this room would need to have eyes in the backs of their heads to watch every possible point of attack.

With a smaller space, the walk-in closet presented some de-sign challenges. She was even contemplating making it a trap-only room since the adventurers would face the floor champion in the next room. Spud seemed to like his garage, and Florence figured the attic space would capture the dark and musty environment he seemed to prefer. She was kind of curious how his powers would change once he accepted his new position as floor champion.

Her final touch was to create a small window on the side of the attic. One of them emergency fire escape ladders would be kept underneath it, giving the adventurers a place to climb down to the third level of her home: the backyard. There wasn't much to do for the backyard. It would be a large lawn with some planters to break up the line of sight and a gardening shed that her home champion could use as a place to hide. The ladder from the attic would leave the party at the small side lawn, where she would place any addi-tional kitties she wanted for this level. She would decorate things after summoning her kitties, and by the time she finished roughing out the backyard area, she had $98.11. The basics were done. Now it was finally kitty-making time.

Chapter 13

"Okay, it's bare and ugly, but the home design is done. I just have to push out the front lawn and build what we planned for the new entrance," Florence said.

Doug perked up from where he had been fake napping on the rocking chair pillow. "Very good. Let's get to work with our defenders, shall we?"

"Yep, and first off is Spud's promotion. Come here, my stinky little boy," Florence cooed to Spud, who listened for once and trotted his way into the core room, rubbing up against her rocking chair and taking a halfhearted swipe at Doug.

"Stay away from me, you uncultured yob," Doug hissed as Spud continued to annoy him.

"Leave Dougie alone, Spud. Does my little baby Spud want to become a champion for our new floor? You would have to stay in your assigned room, though. No more wandering around when adventurers are inside our home," Florence asked, laying down the ground rules.

The kitty mewed excitedly, nodding his little head, and then ran upstairs to the still undecorated floor. He circled the attic, finding a good spot to nap and leaving his mark on other areas, much to Doug's disgust. A system prompt interrupted the enjoyment of watching Spud.

You have begun populating your dungeon's second

floor. All defenders placed on this floor will have their levels adjusted to match that floor's difficulty rating.

You have created your second champion in a scaling difficulty dungeon. A bonus has been added to your cash balance for reaching this milestone.

Continue to populate your dungeon. It will be forcefully reopened in 72 hours if you have not willingly opened it by that time. If a forced reopening is required, you will experience reduced passive mana absorption for a period of 30 days.

"Woah, they don't mess around, do they? Come to think of it, who's sending these prompts and whatnot? How can they do stuff to my home or give me more money?" Florence asked, still confused over the rules governing her new existence.

"I'm not entirely sure," Doug admitted. "I worked in a different department and didn't get to interact with, well, anyone other than the souls I was transforming into cores. I just know the system works, and no matter how hard we try, some things can't be avoided. On the positive side, it looks like they've given us additional funds equal to the cost of creating the new floor champion as well as the dungeon champion. You might want to know that the dungeon champion requires $100 to create while the floor champions will cost you the normal $50 that we were charged previously."

Instead of paying to promote Spud, she found her balance had gone from $98.11 all the way up to $198.16. She watched as Spud grew, going from the size of a large dog to that of a pony. He looked impressive, and Florence could see the greenish cloud of crud that followed her baby around. His class had also been tweaked, and he was now a level 5 plague charger, whatever that was. The wacky system that controlled this world was somewhat stingy with information. No worries, though—she would see how he had improved when the adventurers started showing up.

Another wave of change went over all the kitties on the first floor. They shrunk down and looked, well, weaker than they had before. The defenders on the lawn, in the living room, and in the hallway were now level 1, with the others somewhat stronger at level 2. They all went to level 3 after the kitchen, which seemed fair, given that her kitchen was kind of the last refuge before a party would challenge the more dangerous bits of her home.

A level 1 defender just looked like a freakishly large house cat: huge, but not something that would make people call 911 back on Earth. Around level 3, the larger brawlers started approaching the size of a golden retriever. She'd have to create more kitties to find out how the rest of the level 5 and 6 kitties looked. Spud's newly enhanced size might be partially a result of him becoming a champion. With her stinky champion squared away, it was time to create her home champion, but then something crazy happened.

The creation of your dungeon champion has been overridden. Your dungeon affinity has selected a champion from among your other defenders. The new dungeon champion will be Mortimer Skullshaper.

"What! You mean I don't get to even choose my own home champion?" Florence growled as the funds drained from her account and flowed toward poor Mortimer, who looked confused about the whole ordeal. Under some compulsion, the kitty ran through the house, heading to the second floor, and then jumped all the way down to the backyard, which was also changing before her eyes—changing into something she didn't approve of one bit.

"Oh my, that is a rather unexpected development," Doug said. "Normally, a dungeon affinity is only a mild influence. It appears you possess a much closer bond to that affinity than you would like. I should point out that it might also make our home champion stronger than that of a normal dungeon champion."

Florence ignored him, distraught over what was happening to

her lovely home. The backyard was just an empty section of the cavern, with the back wall of the house blocking it off on one side and the cavern wall on the other. She had intended to make it a bright and cheery place, with artificial sunlight and lots of landscaping, even a nice painted fence to cover up the cavern wall. In addition, she wanted to have a garden with herbs and the like for the adventurers to harvest if they survived the encounter with the champion. Now her backyard had transformed into a dark and partially dying lawn that sat under the glow of a full moon.

Tombstones pushed up from the ground, with the mounded earth of a gravesite attached to each one. Some of the mounds burst open to reveal crumbling ancient coffins full of dried bones. A few shrubs that were mostly brambles and thorns were strewn about, and the small gardening shed that she wanted to build became a caretaker's shed with shovels and things for digging graves, not planting herb gardens. And to top things off, poor Mortimer was turning into some new type of kitty, one that Florence wasn't sure she approved of.

Mortimer grew to a size just a bit smaller than Spud, but with a sickly physique. His black fur became scruffy and brittle-looking while the white markings on his face became more pronounced and really made him look like he had a skull drawn on his head. When the transformation was complete, her newest champion gave a cute little mew as he started to explore his new space. For all the trauma of the transformation, not to mention being forced away from his friends, Mortimer seemed perfectly content. It would have broken Florence's heart if one of her kitties were sad. New information on her baby populated her vision, giving only a hint at what he was now capable of.

Mortimer Skullshaper, Level 6 Dungeon Champion, Necrocatster

"What in tarnation is a necrocatster?" Florence asked.

"I'm unsure, but I expect our little Mortimer will be considerably more powerful than a normal dungeon champion, given he has what appears to be a completely new class," Doug offered.

"Well, at least he seems happy enough. We should probably see about getting him someone to play with up here, but we've got a lot of cats to make right now." She had just about $100, enough to make ten cats, less if she wanted to replace the minor champion on the first floor. "Let's make the minor champion next. Hopefully it won't be something forced on us. Should I go for a fresh one, or do you think one of our kitties might need a promotion?"

"Hmm, there are several viable candidates, but most seem happy just hanging out where they are now. Let's do a new summons, and I get to name it," Doug said.

"All right, here we go," Florence said. She was about to get annoyed at Doug for trying to claim the first naming, but then again, back on Earth, she had lost that game of Dungeon Delve they had played to decide who picked first. Her balance dropped by $25 as a new kitty formed in the core room. Doug and Florence looked on in anticipation as the first new kitty that wasn't part of the old home arrived.

It was a beautiful Maine Coon with long, luxurious fur that was almost too fluffy and cute for her to stand. He was orange and black with a white belly and paws. Florence thought that he had a very regal look about him. Her newest champion gave a rub on her chair, then touched noses with Doug in greeting, along with the obligatory sniffing cats always did when meeting someone new.

"I believe you will be Loki," Doug proclaimed.

"Not too bad. I was worried you'd saddle our minor champion with something weird. Okay, Loki, go find your place," Florence said. Spud had claimed the garage as his when he was on this floor, but Loki didn't seem like the chap that would be found living in a garage. His class populated her vision, giving her an idea of what to expect from the newest addition.

Loki, Level 3 Minor Champion, Raider

"Oh, I know this one," Doug said. "The cat's new class resembles one that adventurers can train to be. A raider specializes in hit-and-run tactics, almost like our commando kitties, but they are willing and equipped to stay in the fight longer. They usually have an ability that allows them to disengage when they need to, often pulling out of the fight completely to recover. This one will be interesting to watch when he gets into his first fight."

Now that Florence thought about it, Loki did look a bit like someone who would be a raider. Her new kitty didn't seem to be bound to a particular room. Instead of staying put, he started patrolling for intruders and making friends with all his new brothers and sisters. Once he had made the initial round of introductions, he kept his patrols confined to the areas that held the level 2 and 3 kitties. He was a good sport and didn't want to beat up on adventurers who were just cutting their teeth on the initial challenges of her home.

There was enough defender expense remaining on the first floor to summon one more kitty, but she wanted to save that for a special project when she pushed the entrance out toward the surface. It was probably a good time to get started on that, considering she was on the clock. Seeing outside would be nice, even if she did feel much more comfortable underground the longer she spent as a core gem.

Florence pushed her influence from the front lawn toward the surface, moving past more and more of the tunnel, keeping her home sealed up during this whole process; she didn't want some wandering creeps to jump in when she wasn't looking. They weren't all that far from the surface when she hit a block. It was in some ways similar to the problem she had run into before the spider guy had attacked, but this time, she didn't feel that anyone was directly trying to get into the dungeon. It was just some force that was blocking her from assimilating more territory.

There was a small tendril of space in the cavern wall that she could move her will through, a narrow passage that led toward the actual mouth of the tunnel. Her influence was limited since the surface area she was able to control was small, but eventually, she found herself looking outside and viewing the surrounding territory. It was the same rock-covered hill that the adventuring party of jerks had dragged her through to fulfill their deal with the lich.

Alongside the barren landscape that she remembered from her trip, Florence could see the beginnings of a new town being built. A pair of larger structures were a hub of activity as workers built further additions and outbuildings while adventurers camped nearby. Already a dozen firepits lined the area. She was going to have a busy home once things were ready to go. Well, the force blocking her from assimilating the whole entrance area didn't prevent her from working on the actual tunnel opening, so she could build a proper entrance. It would be slow going, given the limited control she had over the area, so she didn't have time to waste on a proper entrance just yet; she had more kitties to make.

Funds were now at $74.22, so she wouldn't be able to summon everyone she wanted, but it was enough to at least make the second floor not look like it was abandoned. Starting with the second-floor great room, Florence summoned three kitties, one of each type. This room would eventually have five or maybe even six defenders, but it would only be three for now. Starting with the mage, Florence summoned her cats. Money flowed out from her gem, and the first cat sprang into existence. Her newest mage kitty was a white-furred cutie with blue eyes that looked around the room before she tried out her magical power. The cat launched several blasts of ice and snow and even froze a table leg to the floor, which would be a good crowd-control ability.

"This one is Winter," Florence pronounced. Without hearing any negative comments from Doug, she went ahead with the second cat. A sleek and sassy-looking Siamese appeared. Her build was perfect for the commando class.

"Your turn, Doug," Florence said, worried about the name he would choose.

"Hmm, I think I'll call this one Willow," Doug said.

"Not bad. I knew that letting you watch all those old fantasy movies would pay off," Florence said as she started work on the next cat. Her brawler kitty was another Maine Coon, which was pretty popular today for some reason. The cat wasted no time in running up to introduce himself to the others.

"What will this one be named?" Doug asked.

"This one is Winston. He's going to be a good boy," Florence proclaimed. She could summon four more before her funds ran too low to continue, but where to place them? For now, she'd leave the third floor as it was; Mortimer would be fine on his own for a bit longer.

Some rooms would have to stay empty for the time being, and she didn't want to only place one cat in a room. This was the second floor and was supposed to be a bigger challenge than the first. Two in each bedroom would have to do until she had enough money to populate the rest. She formed a kitty for the first bedroom, the ball of cash coalescing into a pretty tabby with coloring that looked like gravel.

"Doug, you're up," Florence said.

"Oh, that one's coloring is nice, like a bunch of pebbles in a stream," Doug said.

Florence saw her opportunity and jumped in for the kill. "Okay, Pebbles is a good one, Doug. The next one is mine to name."

"Wait, no, that wasn't what I was going to name her," Doug protested.

"Well, it's too late now. Next time, be more careful," Florence chided, loving that the name Pebbles had stuck. She hadn't selected a class for Pebbles, too intent on scamming Doug, but the system seemed to have assigned her as a commando kitty. There was little cover inside the undecorated bedroom, but Pebbles was able to make her fur shift color to match the bare stone walls. She was going to be great at her job if she could hide in an empty room.

"Don't worry, baby. I'll get you a friend and decorate your room nicely as soon as I can," Florence said. The next cat was a long-haired black cat that looked a little chubby. It was no surprise the big boy was a brawler; he sure looked the part.

"I suppose it's your turn, or do you want to actually be fair and let me have one more?" Doug asked.

"This burly guy is Cooper. I think that fits him," Florence said. Cooper and Pebbles left their assigned bedroom to travel through the home and meet all the other kitties. While she loved to stop and watch the kitties get to know each other, she had another room to populate. A new cat was summoned in the second bedroom. This one was a mage kitty, a petite white little critter.

"My turn," Doug said. "Let's see . . . A mage needs a proper name. I think we'll go with Archimedes." The cat seemed to approve, giving a little bow before joining the others. It wasn't too bad of a name, but it wasn't one Florence would have picked. She conjured up the last kitty, at least the last one until she could get more money. This was another gall durned Maine Coon. What was going on with them today? It was a cutie pie, though. He was a super-deep orange color that Florence thought suited the brawler very well.

"All right, you're going to be Sherbet," Florence proclaimed.

"Your imagination continues to astound me." Doug's sarcasm

was getting a little out of hand, but Florence was far too busy to deal with him just now. Time was running out, and she would spend what little she had remaining before the dungeon opened to finish decorating her new rooms. Her home needed to look its best for the guests that would be arriving soon.

Chapter 14

"Matron, I believe the dungeon must be near. Look," Jess said, stating the obvious. They had been traveling through low hills and rocky scrub for the last few days, and from the abundance of fresh tracks all around, Matron assumed they were heading in the right direction. People didn't venture out into the Crag Steppes unless they had a purpose.

Once they made it around the bend of yet another large hill, they saw signs of civilization. Or at least the beginnings of one. A dozen campfires burned in the small valley at the base of a nearby hill. Two large buildings were under construction, workers just now finishing up their day as the afternoon turned into evening. Clusters of tents were placed around each of the campfires. Likely, these were different adventuring parties queuing up for their chance at a delve. Matron had hoped to beat the rush, but at least there were only a dozen at most, not the hundreds of adventuring parties that flooded the more established locations.

"Jess, you know what to look for. Find a place for our camp. I'm going to go and find out if there's an adventurers guild representative on-site and get us into the queue. Tipp, you're with me, and I assume I don't have to warn you about keeping your hands off any merchandise that might be lying about," Matron ordered. The rogue, Tipp, wasn't criminally minded, but he sometimes forgot the rules of ownership when a particular item caught his eye. The young halfling would have to temper his spontaneous nature if he wanted to survive and thrive as an adventurer.

They skirted around the encampments, and Matron noted that most of the other groups had that poorly equipped look that identified them as new adventurers. One of the pair of buildings being constructed was an inn, but Matron's initiates didn't have the funds to live in such comfortable accommodations. Her charges would have to prove themselves and gather treasure from the dungeon if they wanted to sleep on a soft bed each night. Matron turned toward the other building, A roughly hewn wooden sign proclaimed the place to be Junior's Adventuring Outfitters. The symbol of the adventuring guild was etched above the door, letting her know this was where she needed to go.

"Welcome to Junior's. How can I help you today?" a middle-aged man asked. A genuine smile was plastered on his bearded face. He looked the part of the shopkeeper, but there was also something familiar about his features.

"I'm here to register a group for the dungeon. I assume you're the guild representative?" Matron asked.

"Yes, ma'am," Junior replied. "My family have been accredited delve administrators for two generations. Step right up and sign. If you'd like, I can see about outfitting you with some better gear. Normally, I'd have a dungeon guide for you to purchase, but this place is a bit odd."

"Odd how?" Matron asked. Once she signed her party up on the roster, the magical document tracked the delves and organized them into an appropriate flow that wouldn't overtax the dungeon.

The dungeon challenge rating listed at the top was encouraging. An A+ dungeon with a beast subtype would be just what her charges needed to gain experience without too much risk. Of course, there was always risk in a dungeon, but she would be accompanying them, at least for the first run, in order to conduct her personal evaluation of the place. Matron's presence would reduce the experience her charges would gain, given her much higher level, but it would only be for one or two delves if things went as planned.

"Odd in the . . . Well, take a look at the delve tab in the back," Junior said, sounding like he was reluctant for her to see it.

A dungeon log was a magical construct entrusted to those that had been approved by the guild. The queue was its main feature, but more data was listed in the back, showing the number of delves and the mortality rate of those entering the dungeon. So far, only two delves had been made, and neither of those parties had returned and were assumed dead. The kill-to-delve ratio stood at one hundred percent, an unheard-of number and one that would see this dungeon core destroyed if the trend continued.

"Were these new adventurers that were lost, and is that why all the others are sitting in their camp and not delving?" Matron asked. There were plenty of people in the queue, but nobody was shown to have actually entered the dungeon for some time.

"One party were fools, underequipped and with a poor party composition. The others were better equipped and should have had no trouble with a dungeon of this ranking. Shortly after the last group entered, the place sealed itself up and that was that."

A dungeon typically could only seal itself off when expanding or when adventurers were inside. Having been sealed for this long indicated the dungeon was expanding rapidly; killing off two full parties would do that for a new dungeon. With her power supporting them, Matron's party shouldn't meet the same fate as the others, but she would need to be cautious. She finished signing up her group, noting that a dozen groups were scheduled ahead of hers.

"My charges are looking for a healer. Have you had any solo adventurers inquire about joining a party?" Matron asked. The light would guide the correct person to her fledgling party, but sometimes the light would use the obvious to achieve its purpose. Many people were constantly looking for deep meaning in the light's purpose, ignoring the solution that might be staring them in the face.

"No, sorry. There were a few pairs that inquired, but those have all found a group. If I hear of anyone, I'll be sure to send them your way," Junior said.

"Thank you. We'll be camping nearby and I'll check in on occasion," Matron said.

"Will you be accompanying your charges on their delve? I don't mean to pry, but there could be an opportunity for your group if that is the case," Junior asked. Matron was obviously a seasoned adventurer, despite her age, and Junior would have been pretty poor at his job if he didn't recognize that.

"Until they find a healer of their own, I intend to accompany them, at least on the first delve," Matron replied.

"Very good. I can see you're experienced, and, well, the others gathered here aren't. If you were guiding the party, I might be able to get you promoted to the top of the list. You see, with this dungeon's kill ratio, I'm afraid it won't be tolerated by the guild for long. With an experienced adventurer among the party, you'll no doubt survive and be able to assuage the nerves of the other groups. My whole future is tied up in this place. If the dungeon were to prove a bust, I would be bankrupt."

"Get us the first slot, and I'll be glad to give you a rundown of the dungeon and its threats. Of course, if you intend to sell that information, I will expect a fair percentage of the profit," Matron advised. It wasn't uncommon for the merchant overseeing the dungeon log to sell information about the dungeon, its threats, and its rewards. Typically, it was offered for a nominal charge, but her party needed funds if they were to improve their gear.

"You have a deal, though I may have to insist on store credit initially for any income we receive from the guide. I'm a little light of coin, and without adventurers bringing it out of the dungeon, I'm afraid everything of value I possess is locked up in inventory," Junior said.

"Fair enough. When things start improving here, I expect a shift to hard currency. I also insist you trade with my party at a fair price. No gouging just because they are using store credit," Matron demanded.

"Fair, and I agree. Junior Bingman's word is his bond."

"Bingman, eh? I thought you looked familiar. I've shopped at your father's establishment a time or two," Matron replied. The Bingman family was well known for offering adventuring supplies as well as for their other, less common ventures. They had a good reputation, and she could take this man at his word. Besides, lying to a paladin of the light was a difficult thing to do.

"Excellent. I'll send someone to find your camp once the dungeon reopens," Junior advised.

Matron gave Tipp a hard stare, making sure he hadn't gotten sticky fingers while she was talking with Junior. They left the shop and searched the other encampments for Jess and the rest of the party. Their camp was set back a bit from the other line of tents. Her students had chosen a proper location near a stream that fed fresh water to the place, but it was far enough away that any minor flooding would miss their tents.

Being away from the other adventurers also had the added bonus of a quieter environment. New adventurers were loud and boisterous, especially if they had just completed a profitable delve. The subdued nature of the other adventurers showed their apprehension about entering the potentially deadly dungeon. Matron didn't have much fear. The guild would have never missed a challenge estimate by much, and it would take a dungeon several orders of magnitude more challenging than an A+ one to have a chance to harm her.

"Where are the others?" Matron asked as she walked the campsite.

"Frex and Chamm are out gathering firewood," Jess replied.

"Good. If you're leaving camp for any reason, always travel in at least a pair. Monsters and dangerous animals can sometimes be drawn to a dungeon's power," Matron advised.

She didn't really have to mention it; the theory was part of their education. A dungeon attracted some animals and nearly every dangerous monster in range of its influence. Normally, these creatures were killed off by either the dungeon or the adventurers gathering to delve into the place. After a few months, most of the nearby threats would be eliminated and a dungeon town became, strangely enough, one of the safest places you could live.

The twin mages returned not too much later, and the party soon had a cheerful fire going. Matron explained the potential danger of this new dungeon, but it did little to dampen the group's spirits. Young people were so convinced of their invincibility. A foolish notion that Matron had been forced to abandon long ago, much earlier than she would have liked.

"Matron, did you meet anyone that might become a good healer for our party?" Jess asked.

"No, the light will reveal its choice when it is time," Matron replied. Their attention turned to a pair of laborers that approached their campfire.

"Uh, ma'am, Junior wanted me to tell you that the dungeon entrance has been a-rumbling something fierce and should be ready for y'all to delve in the morning," the man advised.

"Thank you. We shall go at dawn. Let me know if you hear anything else that might be of interest." Matron tossed a copper coin to each of the men. Information was valuable, and a few coppers given here and there to the simple folk just might ensure she found out something important before anyone else.

"So we're going in at first light? What information do we have on the dungeon?" Jess asked. The girl was very analytical for a berserker; her logical and deliberate way of thinking was strange, given her chosen class.

"Only that it's an A+ beast dungeon," Matron answered.

"Sorry, ma'am, you forgot the part where it's gone all murdery and killed everyone that's entered," Tipp added.

"Don't pay that too much heed. These dungeons test new adventurers to their limits, and only two parties have attempted it so far," Matron replied. She wanted her charges to be wary, not terrified, when they went on their first delve tomorrow.

"Exactly. It was only, what, eight or ten people that have delved it, none of whom lived to tell the tale," Tipp continued.

"Do you wish to recant your membership in the organization? The light has chosen you, but you are not forced to live this life if you deem it to be too dangerous for your liking," Matron said, staring hard at Tipp.

"Oh, no, not at all. I just wanted everyone to be ready. You know, on their toes and all that," Tipp said. She knew the halfling was just running his mouth, but it was good for him to realize that words could have dire consequences at times.

"Good, and since you're just trying to be helpful, you can prepare the evening meal and do the dishes," Matron ordered.

The others began to finish setting up the camp. Tipp started on the meal while the tents were being set up. Matron merely pulled a small canvas swatch from a pouch at her belt and placed it on the ground, where it unfolded into a small but well-equipped tent. Inside, she had a comfortable cot, a small writing table, and a secure chest in which to store things. The magical tent had been another expensive purchase years ago, but the magic was just as strong today as it had been on the day she bought it.

Her charges looked on in envy as they continued to do things the old-fashioned way. Age and experience had their privileges, and Matron was getting too old to rough it if she didn't have to. It was also good for them to see the potential rewards of their chosen profession. They needed something to aspire to, and the dungeon delve tomorrow would be their first true steps on that path. The time for training and theory was over. Now the danger—and the rewards—were real.

Chapter 15

"I GUESS IT'S THAT TIME, AIN'T IT?" FLORENCE SAID, EXCITED TO reopen her home and nervous that everything wasn't exactly how she wanted it just yet. Hopefully the early groups of adventurers wouldn't make it past the first floor and she would get the funds and time needed to build out and populate the rest of the place before it was seen.

"And here we go. It shouldn't be long until the first ones arrive, given the burgeoning settlement outside," Doug commented. She focused her view on the tunnel entrance. The sun was just starting to rise, and she could see some activity in the settlement. Fires had been started as people began their day. She had to give it to the folks here; they sure weren't ones to sleep in and be lazy like a lot of folks back home.

"Oh, look, Doug. The first ones are on their way," Florence said excitedly as five figures made their way from the town to the tunnel entrance. She pulled her view back, looking over the first floor to make sure everything was as it should be. Once adventurers were inside, it became impossible to change most things; she could only spawn reward chests. This was her first impression, and she wanted to make it a good one.

It took a while for the party to make their way to her home. There were still some side passages leading off the main tunnel, but until her control over the area improved, she was unable to seal them off. At least she had killed off that spider guy, which seemed to have stopped the critters from scampering around the place. Her vision over the tunnel area was limited, but she caught enough glimpses to see they were going in the right direction.

"Well, let's see what we have to work with here," Doug said as they looked over the approaching party.

"Not bad on their gear. Basic but well-made stuff. But what gives with the hero lady?" Florence asked.

The group was fairly standard. The two human men wearing normal clothing and carrying staves screamed mage to her, and the little halfling guy in the leathers was a rogue of some type. A young lady in leather reinforced with bits of chainmail at critical points might have been their tank, even if she was dual-wielding axes instead of going with a shield. The odd one out was the final member of the group. A woman wearing shiny plate armor with a full-face shield and wielding a two-handed war hammer strode behind the others. Her gear was top-of-the-line and glowed with power in Florence's enhanced sight.

"Hmm," Doug mused. "Perhaps they are from some adventuring organization and have brought a minder to make sure they aren't wiped out on their first try. Sadly, if that plate-armored woman is as high level as I suspect, it will reduce the income for us and greatly reduce the experience the party receives."

"We'll have to hope she's just serving as training wheels for their first run. I don't want to kill people if I don't have to, but I also don't approve of boosting runs by high-level adventurers." Florence didn't ever get into MMO games, playing Dungeon Delve pretty much exclusively, but she did learn a bit about how things operated in them from the kids she gamed with.

"Hold, what is this?" the armored lady said. She sounded like someone from the seniors center, not a young adventurer.

"Are they bringing their grandma to help them?" Doug mocked.

"Shush, let me hear what they're saying," Florence replied, watching as the younger one with the two axes addressed the armored lady.

"Matron, what do you mean? Is there some special threat with this dungeon we should be wary of?"

"No, this is just . . . Well, it's unusual and resembles something I've seen before. Proceed, but be wary," this Matron lady replied. It must have been a title or something, giving weight to Doug's theory that the party belonged to some organization that sent along a babysitter.

"Since when do dungeons make themselves look like houses? This is weird," the halfling said as the party stepped onto the lawn, officially entering Florence's home. The party readied their weapons and strode forward into the long grass. Florence both loved and hated that lawn. The long grass was necessary for her babies to stay hidden, but she also didn't want anyone to think she didn't take care of her lawn. After all, that Ruby Mays let her lawn go and the city forced her to have it mowed, and if she didn't, they would fine her. That memory brought up a troubling thought.

"Hey, Doug, there isn't some kind of dungeon homeowners association, is there?" Florence asked.

"No, of course not. Now, focus on the task at hand, Florence. Our defenders are about to strike," Doug said.

Obi and Shadow leaped from the grass and onto the girl with two axes. They timed their attack to coincide with the mailbox trap going off, but that durned little rogue popped into view behind it, having disarmed it without anyone seeing it happen. Her kitties were just about to get some good licks in when the girl with the axes was covered in a golden shield their claws and teeth couldn't penetrate. Their efforts made horrible sounds, like nails on a chalkboard, as they tried to attack their foe. Just when the kitties decided to run after easier prey, the old lady in the armor crashed into them, her glowing hammer smashing them down with no trouble.

"You, dungeon, I know you can hear me. This mockery of a dungeon design is an affront to her memory. I will see you destroyed for this," Matron spouted as she charged at impossible speed toward the front door. The rest of the party looked on, just as confused as Doug and Florence over what was happening. With a crash, she broke through the door, hammer striking poor Tater, who was trying to stop her charge. The little guy was turned into kitty pulp with one blow.

Matron wasn't even surprised by Bhargath and Baxter leaping down from the ledge over the door, and another swipe of her hammer took the pair out. Only poor Midnight was left. The kitty bravely charged around the sofa to engage the crazy lady that was invading their home. Hammer raised to strike down Midnight, the Matron lady held her blow when the cat gave a long, pitiful meow. The kitty showed no signs of aggression as she looked at Matron.

"Consarn it, get in there and fight, Midnight. That Matron lady's a-going to destroy our home," Florence pleaded. Instead of attacking as ordered, Midnight crept forward slowly, claws sheathed and meowing cutely at the enemy.

"No, it cannot be. She was killed. Are you really here, Midnight?" Matron asked.

"Woah, hold on here. How does she know the cat's name already, and what in tarnation is Midnight doing?" Florence growled. Midnight walked over to Matron, who lowered her hammer and removed her helmet, kneeling to give the kitty a scratch behind her ears, then a belly rub when Midnight rolled over for more attention.

"It is you, isn't it, Midnight? You're still a good kitty, aren't you?" Matron cooed.

"Perhaps it is some kind of charm ability," Doug said, "though with her gear, I would have said this Matron person was a paladin or warrior, not a class that should have access to such magic."

"You stay back. Leave the dungeon until I deal with this," Matron ordered to her party members, who were cautiously approaching the front door. They obeyed, moving out of Florence's home and standing just outside where the lawn began.

"Dungeon, if you are who you pretend to be, speak. I know you can do so if you wish. Speak through your defender and tell me why I shouldn't kill you for trying to mimic that dungeon from long ago," Matron ordered.

"How dare she make demands in my house. I'm about to give her a piece of my mind," Florence said, both confused and angry with the lady saying not-so-nice things about her home.

"I would recommend against speaking to adventurers, but when have my well-reasoned arguments ever swayed you toward the appropriate path?" Doug replied with a kitten sigh of resignation.

"You wait for just one minute, missy," Florence barked. "You don't go barging into someone's home and start ordering them around. Where I come from, guests are a bit more polite, but apparently, you were raised wrong. Now, release my kitty from the charm spell and get on with your adventuring."

"No, it can't be. Is it really you, Florence Valentine?" Matron asked.

"What? Well, yeah, it's me, but how do you know my name?" Florence asked, more confused than ever.

"It's been many years since I was that young adventurer. But I was among one of the first parties to delve into your home. You might not remember or recognize me. Time changes our appearance so much, but Midnight here remembers me, don't you, girl?" Matron said. The name struck Florence then: the one person her kitty had taken a liking to.

"Shara, is that you?" Florence asked.

"Yes, Miss Valentine. It is," Shara replied.

"Well, I'll be, Shara. It's good to see you. I guess I was gone longer than I thought," Florence said.

"What happened? I thought your core had been destroyed by the followers of Kunrax. We tried to stop them, but there were too many, and the price we paid was high that day. Vanderman gave his life to protect us, and I'll never forget his sacrifice," Shara said.

"I was destroyed, but, well, let's just say it wasn't a total destruction type of situation and I was able to come back from my injuries. I'm back now, and I'm getting my home sorted out so folks can enjoy it again," Florence said.

"The ones waiting out on the lawn are my new initiates. They're here to test their mettle against your home, if that's all right with you," Shara said. Florence still couldn't believe that one of the few people she knew in this world was here.

"Sure, tell them to go right ahead. You know I can't do anything to help them, and if something happens . . . Well, sometimes these delves go wrong. My home should be a bit more friendly for newbs—I mean new adventurers. I've decided to go with level scaling. The further they go, the more dangerous things will become. Now, I do have to insist that you don't tell them anything about what's waiting for them inside. That would be cheating." Florence was glad to see an old friend, but she wouldn't approve of any unfair advantages.

"Of course. I'll give them no knowledge of what your lovely home has to offer, other than explaining to them the normal things they'll need to prepare for when delving into any home or dungeon," Shara agreed.

"Fair enough. Would you like to come over for tea sometime? Doug and I do like to have guests over," Florence asked.

"Yes, that would be lovely. Whenever you have time, I'll be

available. For now, we'll leave my charges in the dark as to your rather unusual nature," Shara said.

"Great. When we visit, you can tell me what happened to your friends and I can tell you about my old world, if you're interested."

"I'll see you soon, but for now, I'll leave so these new adventurers can get their full experience out of their first delve." Shara gave Midnight a pat before leaving to speak with the youngsters.

"That's a nice surprise. We didn't spawn in our old location, so I wasn't expecting to see any of the adventurers that had delved our home before," Doug said as he and Florence watched Shara explain to the group that they were on their own for the delve. True to her word, Shara didn't spill the beans about Florence and their conversations, merely telling them that the home was functioning properly and that her earlier fears were unfounded.

"I suppose time doesn't exactly match up between Earth and this place, does it?" Florence asked, still a bit shocked to see an elderly Shara.

"No, the transition back to a core was less time-consuming than the first time, but it seems that it did take several years of this world's time before you were back in your gem," Doug replied.

"Here they go," Florence said, watching the four new adventurers resume their delve. The lawn was cleared, but they didn't take that for granted, showing caution as they neared the now-demolished front door. Midnight was all alone, so she decided to give herself every advantage she could, leaping up to the perch above the door.

"Matron may have said this dungeon was normal, but I've never heard of one that resembled a house before," the halfling said.

"It doesn't matter what it looks like, Tipp. You need to pay attention to your task," the girl with the axes advised. The halfling rolled his eyes but did get back on the job, entering the living room cautiously.

"Ahh, get it off me!" the halfling shouted as Midnight leaped down onto his back. Her claws ripped into the thin leather armor that protected his back while she latched onto the back of his neck with her powerful jaws. The kitty was only level 1, which sapped a lot of the little brawler's oomph, but she was still dishing out some damage. Two magical balls of light shot into the room. The pair of mages outside were lending aid to their struggling comrade.

The magic attack burned one side of Midnight and froze the other, the two mages revealing their schools of magic in that one attack. To his credit, the halfling guy they called Tipp stayed in the fight, lashing out with a pair of daggers as he struggled to his feet, blood still weeping from the wounds the kitty had inflicted on him. Midnight was too slow in her follow-up attack, and the rogue's blades sunk deep into her back, taking down the brave kitty.

"Frex, bandage up Tipp. Chamm, help me search the room," the girl with the axes ordered.

"I'm no healer, Jess. My magic brings the fires of destruction down on our foes," Frex replied.

"Quit complaining. We have bandages for a reason." Jess's eyes scanned the room for threats while the other mage, the one named Chamm, looted Midnight.

"Only a handful of coppers and one of whatever this is," Chamm said, holding up a doily featuring Obi. Florence had been rather proud of her dungeon doily loot and was glad to see the items make a return in her new home's loot tables.

"Stow it for now. We'll divide everything up later. Tipp, are you doing okay or do you want to stop for the day?" Jess asked.

"Let's at least check another room. The bandages are helping," Tipp said. Florence could see none of them were healers, but they did seem to each have a large supply of bandages. A faint, almost imperceptible glow of magic was emanating from the rolled-up gauze they used to patch up Tipp.

"Magic bandages?" Florence asked Doug.

"Yes, they can help in a pinch but only numb the pain a bit, staunch bleeding effects, and allow for somewhat better health regeneration. Not something you'd want to use as your primary source of healing during a delve, but better than nothing," Doug replied. Florence could see this here party needed a healer badly if they wanted to make it past more than one or two rooms each time they delved.

"Ha, they missed the fireplace trap," Florence noted. She hadn't spawned a treasure box there; this crew hadn't done nearly enough to warrant that kind of reward just yet. They did spend some time reviewing the pictures on the wall, visibly confused.

"What's with the pictures? Are all these cats and things in the dungeon? Is that a dragon?" Tipp said, looking over the photos.

"The dragon may have been a bit much," Florence admitted to Doug. To keep the adventurers guessing, she rotated the pictures, including images of random creatures to keep them on their toes.

"Oh, they're about to face the hallway. Without a healer, things could get a bit interesting," Doug said as the party prepared to continue. Only two cats remained in the hall after Mortimer's promotion to home champion, but they were sneaky and had lots of ways to cause some serious damage. Florence couldn't wait to see how her babies did.

Chapter 16

THE PARTY STARTED OUT WITH JESS IN THE LEAD, TWIN AXES IN HER hands. Behind the warrior, Florence watched Tipp scrutinizing the hallway as he scanned for traps. This left the pair of mages at the rear, a perfect target for Florence's kitties. Just as she suspected, the two hatches near the mages opened, and out charged Buddy and Princess. The cats landed devastating slashes on the back of each mage's leg, causing both to howl out in pain and blindly unleash their magic, but their blasts of frost and fire hit nothing but the floor.

"Watch yourselves. They have more than one exit," Tipp said, finding and opening one of the hatches that Florence's cats had used. The halfling shrieked like a little girl and fell back on his bottom as Princess chose that moment to shoot out of the hatch he was messing with. Florence had to hand it to the rogue; he was quick, getting both daggers up just in time for her precious baby to impale herself on the blades. Being level 1 with the less robust commando body meant the attack was fatal for poor Princess.

Buddy shot out from the opposite side to avenge his sister. The tabby furball led with a sharp claw swipe that managed to get under the rogue's shoulder armor, digging a deep and painful-looking furrow into his flesh. That one kid with the axes, Jess, wasted no time, swiping the pair down as Buddy flew past. The first axe missed, but the second one was timed perfectly to chop Florence's little baby down.

"Back to the other room," Jess ordered. The bleeding party stumbled its way back to the living room, where they broke out the magic bandages again. A few minutes later, everyone was patched up, and with the mages holding spells and ready to cover her, Jess rushed out to gather the loot from the two fallen kitties. She found a silver coin and another handful of coppers, not a haul the party was pleased with.

"This stinks. The loot is horrible and we're already out of action. I don't want to go further. The wounds are making it hard to concentrate like I need to," Tipp said.

The party agreed and moped their way out of her home, returning to where Shara waited for them just outside the entrance. A glow covered the older woman, and healing energy poured into the group. Tipp started to head back in, but Shara stopped him and warned that if she had to heal them, it was the end of their run. Florence overheard Shara tell the party that she wasn't going to have her charges running out of the dungeon so she could patch them up each time they got hurt. That would teach them nothing and might even result in decreased experience gain.

"What is it with these rogues always complaining about the loot?" Florence said.

"I think they were just unhappy they couldn't proceed further," Doug replied.

"Well, it's not my fault they were too dumb to bring along a healer, and what do they expect for taking on only three normal defenders that were level 1? They got some coin for their trouble and even got an Obi doily drop," Florence murmured angrily. She didn't like ungrateful people but would reserve judgment on the group until after they made some more runs.

"If you're done with your complaints, see how much cash we received from that little jaunt," Doug said.

"Oh, don't boss me around," Florence replied, still a bit angry, but she did indeed pull up her interface to check on the results of the limited delve.

Florence Valentine

Cat core, level 6

Experience: 204/6000

Funds: $28.77

Defender Expense:

First Floor: level range 1–3 ($340/$350)

Second Floor: level range 3–5 ($120/$250)

Third Floor: level range 5–6 ($100/$150)

She had enough to build a couple more defenders, and since building defenders meant making kitties, she jumped right into the process. The question was, where would she place them? The second floor was still lightly populated, and the final floor only contained Mortimer, but since Mortimer was like the final boss fight of her home, it was fine if he was on his own for now. Selecting the unoccupied second-floor bathroom, Florence made another brawler kitty. The cash flowed from her gem and turned into a rather sorry-looking fellow. Her new kitty was brown and mangy. Not only that, but he was as scrawny as could be and had a meow that made him sound like a three-pack-a-day smoker.

"Ah, I think I broke something," Florence said.

"What do you mean? Oh dear, that poor fellow. Hmm, no, it looks like he's working as intended, and you've discovered a new defender type," Doug said.

Florence zoomed in on the new kitty, the system filling her in on the details.

A new defender class has been discovered: undying. The undying beasts have the rather unique ability to come back to life after being dispatched by adventurers. Undying defenders have a lower-than-average health pool and damage rating and possess no special attacks,

but their ability can create quite a danger to distracted adventuring parties when the dead defenders rise once more to attack.

"Now that's not what I had in mind, but the little fella still needs a name. You're up, Doug." Florence really wanted to complain about her unwanted dungeon affinity kicking in again but didn't want her newest kitty to feel bad about himself.

"Now, a new class deserves a special name. Let's go with Acheron, named after the river of woe in the underworld of your Greek myths," Doug said.

"Well, that's not *too* weird, so on to the next kitty. Let's give Acheron a buddy." Florence conjured up the last kitty her limited funds would allow. The ball of money pouring from her core turned into a bright light, revealing another sickly-looking kitty, just like poor Acheron.

"Oh, allow me, please. I have the perfect name for this one," Doug said. Florence kind of felt sorry for the new kitty; it had white fur, but it was all matted and dirty-looking, even though she knew it was clean. Florence would not abide by a dirty cat in her home, and Spud didn't count because that was his ability and he deserved to be the type of cat he wanted to be.

"Fine, you can have this one, but I get the next three," Florence said.

Doug looked excited over this, agreeing to her demands. "This cat will be Styx, named after yet another river in Hades," he said, very proud of himself.

"Sure, whatever, okay. Styx and Acheron, go meet everyone. Then be ready for duty," Florence said.

"What now? Our funds are rather depleted," Doug asked.

"I was fixing to start decorating the second floor," Florence said.

"Before that, we should consider moving the core room," Doug offered. He was right, she hated to admit. They had planned to do this, continually moving her core gem to the best-protected place in the home as they grew. For now, the most protected place was under the shed in Mortimer's graveyard. Inside the shed, she would create a stairwell leading to the core room.

Any attackers that meant them harm would have to fight their way through all three floors to get at her. Later on, she'd have to think of something else. Once the home became more than five levels in size, it was sort of mandatory to have a way for adventurers to choose which floor to start on. Higher-level folks didn't want to waste their time fighting level 1 defenders that didn't give them any experience and afforded very little loot. She needed to grow a lot in power before that could happen, though, but with the town and the slew of adventurers milling around outside, Florence felt she would grow quickly.

It would have been slow going to physically move her core room, so instead, Florence dug out a new one underneath the gravedigger's shack. Her old room would remain where it was; eventually, she planned to craft some kind of dummy core and lots of traps to catch anyone trying to sneak in and give her the business. She spent a bit of coin on the new core room, making several nice places for Doug and the other kitties to hang out if they wanted: lots of scratching posts and soft pillows to nap on. She also crafted hidden compartments to allow her defenders to ambush folks trying to kill her.

Once the new core room was complete, she had to make the move, a difficult task when you're a gem and all of your defenders are cats without opposable thumbs. She first tried to have her kitties drag the rocking chair through the home, but the stairs put a stop to that. Frustrated, she finally looked at her interface, searching for a solution to her problem. It turned out Doug knew the answer the whole time and was having too much fun watching her flounder about to tell her the solution. She was so getting back at her little kitten advisor.

Core Gem Translocation: Once per week, your core gem can teleport to any location in your dungeon. This ability cannot be used when the dungeon is occupied by outsiders.

She could send herself anywhere she wanted once per week, but only if there weren't any adventurers poking around. That was too bad, as blinking away at the right moment could save her life. Doug was finally forthcoming enough to let Florence know that her core housing and protective avatar would automatically be brought with her. With a thought, Florence activated the translocation thingy and found herself in the newly created core room. This location did feel a bit cozier than the last, even if it was positioned under a graveyard.

"Well, that's squared away, despite your lack of help," Florence said once the process was complete. She was going to hold a grudge about this for a good long time.

"Excellent, I assume you're going to continue the home decoration plan?" Doug asked. She most certainly was, tuning out her annoying assistant while she dug into the details of making her home just right.

The great room on the second floor was first. It ended up being a lot like the living room at the entrance, only bigger and without a fireplace. Two sofas and a pair of recliner chairs took up much of the space, their gleaming plastic slipcovers ready and waiting for guests to enjoy. Lots of hiding places for her kitties were built into the surrounding furniture, including false interiors on the end tables near each sofa. A round coffee table was placed between the two sofas, and she would let Doug have a crack at some traps in here, but that would only happen after she was finally able to fully populate the place with kitties. Avocado-colored shag carpeting finished off the design. She could never figure out how such a nice flooring option had fallen out of favor.

The bathroom with Acheron and Styx was left dark and foreboding, a perfect place for her two strange new underworld-inspired kitties to operate. A commode and a pair of sinks were placed in the room, with a glass-enclosed shower taking up the rest of the space. It would be tight quarters, giving her defenders their best chance at scoring some damaging blows. She hoped the reanimating ability would have some delay and the adventurers would have already moved on to tackle one of the bedrooms when her reanimating cats surprised them by jumping into the fight.

Two doors led off from the bathroom, each one randomly connecting to one of the two regular bedrooms. She did up her first bedroom in a nautical theme, giving it a dark blue carpet with fish wallpaper. A waterbed was placed in the room; Doug insisted he had the perfect trap ready for it once they had enough funds. Pebbles and Cooper seemed to enjoy the new setup. Both of them took the time to pounce on the waterbed and curl up on the thick bedding for a nap. She was a bit worried they would pop the bed and let water ruin everything, but her kitties were careful with their new furniture.

Her second bedroom was going to have a desert theme, with sand-colored carpet and a small bed crafted from desert rocks. The rocks weren't going to be all that comfortable for her babies, so Florence added a thick pillow-top mattress and bedding that matched the rest of the room. A large dresser stood opposite the bed and would scream "trap" to most adventurers. It wasn't trapped, but the clothes-filled interior would be the perfect spot for a kitty to fight from. Sherbet and Archimedes settled in, with the mage kitty choosing to climb into the clothes stacked in the dresser. Florence added some decorative trim that hid the openings in the dresser door, allowing Archimedes a firing port for his magic. A lock on the inside of the dresser would let the kitty secure himself inside, delaying adventurers and, hopefully, letting him cast more spells.

The second-floor master bedroom was next. It had a fancy open and spacious design with some bamboo flooring and modern-looking artwork everywhere. You could even see under the bed. No lovely, frilled dust ruffle would hide kitties from the adventurers. Nope, all her kitties were hiding *in* the floor. Rugs were strewn about, covering several possible angles of approach. Hopefully the adventurers would get plumb dizzy by the time they cleared the place.

After the master bedroom, a large walk-in closet would be the access point for adventurers that wanted to try out the champion for this floor, Spud. A pull-down ladder was here, and the closet was stuffed with the kind of clothes and junk that people accumulated and never seemed to find the time to throw out. There wasn't any plan for kitties in here, just a bunch of traps, including one of Florence's own design. Lack of funds delayed trap construction for the time being, so there was nothing to delay adventurers from climbing on up into the attic.

Her attic was dimly lit and had a simple plywood floor. Boxes lined the place, and there were several dark nooks and crannies for Spud to hide in. The newest champion seemed to want to do some personal redecoration, pushing the boxes into long rows, leaving a single wide path that led to the window holding the ladder to the backyard. Spud was free to arrange things how he wanted, and there must have been a reason for his actions.

The second floor was decorated just how she wanted—and just in time. Another party was making its way toward her front lawn.

Chapter 17

"WHO DO WE HAVE THIS TIME?" DOUG SAID, WATCHING A FAIRLY ordinary party make their way onto the front lawn.

"I don't know, but with their gear, the first floor should be just about their speed," Florence said.

The party had five members. The two in the lead sported leather armor reinforced with chainmail in critical areas. She figured that armor design must be the most popular starter gear for the warrior and tank types. One of the pair had a longsword and shield, while the other held a two-handed axe. An older man in robes walked behind the pair, waving a metal ball on a chain. This wasn't some weapon, at least not at first glance; it was some kind of incense burner.

"What's the deal with the older guy, Doug?" Florence asked.

"I'm not sure, but if I had to guess, he's some form of healer, and that incense censer may be giving them a buff of some form," Doug offered. It was logical enough, and she'd find out for sure once Obi and Shadow got to work. A woman in leather armor with a short bow at the ready was behind the incense guy, looking for targets. The final member of their party had disappeared right about the time they crossed over the lawn. They must have been another rogue.

"They're well balanced as long as that guy is a healer, but they seem to lack a mage or any arcane support," Florence said.

"Yes, but save for the older gentlemen, the others appear young enough to modify their classes as they gain experience. Maybe the archer could turn into an arcane archer, or the rogue might acquire some hybrid mage skills," Doug replied.

Obi and Shadow stalked their prey, each cat approaching one of the lead warriors. It wasn't the most efficient attack—Florence would have preferred they focus on the squishier and less well-armored adventurers—but her level 1 kitties couldn't be expected to form complex plans; cuteness didn't equate to cunning. The cats waited, timing their attacks for when the mailbox trap triggered. It wasn't going to happen this time; the party's rogue appeared behind the mailbox after having successfully disarmed it.

"Doug, you're going to have to change things up out there. Everyone keeps disarming that thing," Florence complained.

"I already have a plan for that," Doug replied, too engrossed in the fight between the warriors and the kitties to elaborate.

Obi and Shadow managed to get their claws past the warriors' armor, but once revealed, they fell quickly to the counterstrikes and arrows. The guy with the incense swung it faster, chanting as the wounds on the two warriors started to close before their eyes. When she concentrated, Florence could see waves of mana coming from the man, the censer acting as the focus for his magic. It was an area-of-effect healing energy that was a great way to handle multiple injured party members, but without a focused and more powerful direct healing spell, the party could be in trouble when pitted against a champion.

"So they cleared the lawn. How far do you think they'll make it?" Florence asked.

"I'll say they make it to the library at most," Doug replied.

"Yeah, I think I agree with you. Unless he has some power or ability we haven't seen yet, that healer's going to be out of mana long before they make it to the champion."

They had it almost right. The party fought their way through the living room, taking injuries from the fight, but the healing magic put them all back together again. Their rogue was able to locate and disarm the fireplace trap. Her skills proved their worth again in the hallway when she figured out where cats would emerge based on the sound of the claws scratching on the wood as they made their way to their attack points.

Their thoroughness led to them clearing the bathroom and sewing room, taking more damage in the process. Florence's home confused the group; it wasn't what most people would expect from a dungeon. It wasn't her fault that the other cores were boring and didn't have good taste in home design. She was a true A+ home and things were only going to get better as she expanded and improved.

The party ended their delve in the laundry room. The warrior with the big axe charged in, reaching the pair of caster kitties inside, only to nearly decapitate himself on the clothesline trap. With a few well-placed arrows, the archer took care of Arya and Q, but the damage was done. The group poured what looked like a healing potion over the warrior's throat. Florence didn't think that potions worked that way, but it seemed to do the trick, buying their healer enough time to get ahead of the damage. He was able to stop the worst of the bleeding, but after he was done, his throat still had a gross-looking open wound as the healer announced that he had reached his mana limit for the day.

"Not a bad run. They did well enough and stayed long enough for us to collect some cash," Florence said, her funds now up to $33.15 as the party left.

"With both this and Shara's party making it out without casualties, our kill ratio should start moving in the right direction," Doug said. "We're becoming more powerful by the day, but I still wouldn't fancy our chances against an adventurers guild kill team."

"I thought you said we had some time to make things right since we're new?" Florence liked the fact the guild kept things organized and there weren't ten groups trying to enter her home at the same time, but she wasn't sure she liked the power they had over her home.

"That's a worry for another day, and I believe you have some new defenders to summon, don't you?"

"Yep, let's see." Florence looked over her home to see where the new additions would be placed. The second-floor master bedroom needed kitties, so Florence got to work summoning the three she could afford. Her ultimate goal for the room was to have five defenders, three of which would be commando kitties that could utilize the trapdoors and tunnels she had built into the place. She'd make the commandos now and then later add a brawler and mage to finish the place.

Florence held her breath as $10 flowed from her core and the first kitty appeared. She had specified commando kitties for these three, but that didn't guarantee she'd get what she wanted. What she really didn't want was more of them undying kitties. Sure, she'd love her undying babies as much as the others, but she wanted cute fluff balls, not haggard-looking ones. The first kitty resolved into a sleek white and gray tabby commando.

"This'n will be Marshmallow," Florence said with confidence as she started on her next creation. Another $10 poorer, she had a dark brown shorthair cat that jumped around like she was on a sugar high.

"My turn?" Doug asked.

"No, you get the next one. This here cat is going to be Brownie," Florence told her advisor. Doug gave a huff of disgust at her choice of name, but Florence ignored him since his annoyance was only jealousy over her naming skills. A brown and black tabby appeared for her final commando kitty.

"Oh, how about KitKat? Those always looked delicious, and I really wish I could have eaten chocolate back on Earth," Doug lamented. She couldn't tell if the little guy was pulling her leg or not, but the name stuck, and it was pretty good considering the room had other food-named kitties inside, so she was happy enough with it.

"Go on. Go meet your family and get to your places," Florence told the newest trio of babies.

They played in the trap doors and room tunnels for a bit. They seemed to enjoy popping out from under the rugs to pounce on their friends. While everything was fun and games now, one look at the level 6 commando kitty claws told Florence that her babies were ready for trouble. Their play did reveal a problem in the room design, however; the rugs got all rumpled after the kitties jumped out of the tunnels they were hiding in, making each exit a one-use proposition for the battle.

"Doug, what should we do about those rugs?" Florence asked.

"Oh dear, I think we should pay attention to the tunnel rather than the rugs at this moment." Doug drew her attention to the main tunnel. The party that had just left her dungeon had stopped out there to bandage their remaining wounds and allow the healer to use the last trickles of his mana to repair the worst of the remaining damage.

Out of one of the nearby side tunnels, more of the scorpion creatures emerged, claws and stingers tearing into the rogue; she had wandered around a bit, exploring while waiting for the others to finish. The girl only gave a short squeal of pain before one of the creatures dragged her body back into the dark side tunnel. Reacting quickly, the warriors readied their weapons. The one with the two-handed axe was having trouble moving his head; the wound hadn't been completely healed, and Florence could only imagine how much a slashed throat would hurt when trying to fight.

Five of the scorpion monsters exited the side tunnel, but who knew how many more of them bugs were hidden away in the dark? Florence's vision was blocked just past the side tunnel entrance, and she suspected that was due to another of them vermin lord core fragment thingies. None of these bugs had glowing gem shards stuck in them, so their boss must still be hiding away.

Blocking a stinger with his shield, a warrior hacked off a claw that was trying to clamp onto the axe-wielder. His attempt to help his buddy turned out pretty bad for him as another of the scorpions worked its way behind the warrior and lashed out with its stinger. The axe guy hacked the new attacker. His powerful blow caved in the head of the big creepy-crawly, killing it in one blow. It was too late for the other guy, though; the venom was already going to work, and while the axe guy had been fighting, another scorpion scuttled out of the tunnel and dragged the now partially paralyzed warrior away.

The archer didn't have time to use her bow and was instead trying to fend off a single attacker with her shortsword. Sadly, the healer didn't last for more than a second, being both unarmored and armed with only a small dagger he pulled from his belt. With the healer being dragged down the tunnel, the axe man and archer were the only ones left. They faced off against one scorpion each, but more were even now running from the side tunnel to join in. Their fight backed them closer and closer to Florence's home. She wished they would cross over; then her kitties could help.

"If they make it back here, I'll designate them as neutral so the cats will focus on the bugs," Florence told Doug.

"Good call. It looks like they just might make it." Doug's words seemed to jinx the pair, as the archer fell just after he said them. The remaining warrior didn't have long before the dog-sized scorpions flanked him, so he turned and charged back onto the front lawn. A pair of stingers stabbed through his armor, paralyzing the man as he stumbled the last few steps into Florence's home.

A pair of scorpions shot onto the lawn, lancing their stingers into the paralyzed man to finish him off, unaware they were, in turn, being stalked by her defenders. Florence's kitties were only level 1, but coming from stealth, their attack power was multiplied. Kitty claws and teeth crunched through arthropod exoskeletons, the dying bugs leaking gross stuff all over her pretty lawn. The remaining scorpions didn't seem like they wanted to tangle with her defenders and instead ran back to their side tunnel, dragging any corpses or pieces of the fallen they could get ahold of.

"This isn't good. It might have been better if the poor chap had died outside our home. Now we'll be credited with his death and perhaps even the deaths of the entire party," Doug lamented.

"Nah, them bugs got to 'em, and nobody can blame us for that," Florence said.

"Well, I hope you are correct, Florence, but we need to do something about these pests outside our home."

"Not much we can do. I can't exert my influence into that side tunnel they're hiding in, and it's not like we can send our kitties out there on their own," Florence said, frustrated over the lack of options she had for dealing with the constant incursions.

"If they keep attacking adventuring parties, eventually one of those groups will get the better of the arthropods. They may even seek to clear out the nest in hopes of some treasure," Doug offered.

"I don't think so. Them bugs seem too strong for the ones exploring our home to handle."

"True, but the scorpion creatures weren't all that powerful. The party they just killed might not have fallen if they were prepared, but the monsters waited until they had left our home, their mana was depleted, and one of the fighters was sporting serious injuries."

"Well, Shara's supposed to come back and visit. When she does, maybe we can make her an offer," Florence suggested. There were a lot of things to be happy about in her new life, such as building a home and creating kitties and whatnot, but not being able to leave was kind of a downer. Sure, back when she first arrived in this world, that wasn't a problem, but Florence had changed since then and had found that she enjoyed the company of other people from time to time.

"At least we did recover some income from the whole affair. Like it or not, we were recompensed for the adventurer dying inside our home, not to mention the two scorpion kills," Doug advised. Her balance was up to $77.18, and maybe making more cats would take her mind off of things.

"Okay, Doug, let's finish up populating the second floor. We can worry about the guild and killing off the scorpion shard later. Nothing we can do about it now."

The plan was for six more cats on the second floor. The rest of that floor's defender expense would be taken up by the traps Doug had in mind for the place. Two more kitties were placed in the great room, bringing the total to five. Both of these were brawlers. One was a long-haired white kitty with one blue and one green eye. Florence named her Puddin. The other brawler was a tabby with short brown and white fur. This one was named Buttercup. She needed some extra support in each of the bedrooms, so she made one cat for each. These she had to let Doug name, unfortunately.

"Doug, you're up. We've got a new kitty in the nautical bedroom, and she's a doozy," Florence said. The kitty was unusual in that her short fur had a blue tinge to it, a perfect fit for the room she was placed in. Maybe this system thing got things right once in a while.

"Oh, lovely. A water mage. This seems strangely appropriate

for the room. Let's see . . . How about Lusca, the Blue Death?" Doug pronounced.

"Poor baby. We'll just call you Lusca, if that's okay," Florence said as her newest addition made the rounds.

"It's a perfectly good name. I derived it from sea monster tales from your world," Doug argued after the cat had left the core room.

Florence had held her voice until now, not wanting to make her newest little one feel bad. "Well, just because it's from my old world doesn't mean I like it. You hated that one cat food I got for you, remember? The one on sale that you said tasted like dirt? I didn't force you to eat it. No, I bought you the good stuff afterward, just to make you happy. You repay that favor with some obscure name for one of my precious babies?" she argued, none too happy the whole name for poor Lusca had stuck.

The next kitty was going into the desert-themed bedroom, and it was a tan shorthaired kitty with gray eyes. Very cute. Her newest addition was a commando, and her fur helped hide her in the sand-colored environment. Florence even spent a bit of time tweaking the room's décor, adding a litter box in one corner for the new kitty to hide in if she wanted. It was time to name her new cuddle bear, and if she gave Doug this one, she'd be able to name the final pair in the second-floor master bedroom, and she wanted to keep the snack theme she had going for that room.

"Try this one, Doug. Keep it normal," Florence ordered.

"Oh, fine. Let's try this one your way, shall we? Where to begin? A cat with fur colored like the theme in the room. A new litter box in place. This is easy. Your new cat is Sandy," Doug said in a mocking tone.

"Good, you did fine on that one." Florence made a point to ignore his tone. She had other things to do—namely, two more snack-themed kitties to conjure up.

Her first cat was a light orange tabby that was a bit on the big and chubby side. He was a brawler, so she supposed it sort of fit. The big boy made his way through the home to his assigned room while she conjured up the final cat for the second floor. This one was a sleek black mage kitty, showing a specialization in illusion magic. With three commandos in the room and lots of hiding places, an illusionist might be a perfect choice.

"Doug, meet Cheddar and Licorice," Florence said proudly.

"Hello, you two. I suppose I should be happy that the room is complete. I wasn't looking forward to seeing you create cats named Granola Bar and Corn Flake," Doug mocked.

"Don't you worry about it. Just get to work on them there traps. You've got $20 of defender expense to use once the funds roll in. I want to finish out the floor before we summon the other cats for the backyard," Florence told him.

Doug perked up at the chance to implement his plans but was distracted by movement in the tunnel. "Here we go. Another group coming to try out our home, and these look very well prepared for the task."

Florence watched the newest group of adventurers approach but couldn't shake the feeling that the scorpion creeps were watching everything from the shadows, waiting for the right time to strike.

Chapter 18

"So that's it, nothing too deadly, just some strange cats as the defenders in the place. No other monsters or beasts, just cats?" Junior asked.

"Yes, sir. Other than a pair of traps, the only defenders we encountered were overgrown cats," Jess replied. Handling information for the dungeon guide was good training for Jess, given that she seemed to be the natural leader of the group. Matron took a moment to look for Tipp, whom they had also brought along to the shop. He was just browsing and hadn't pocketed any of the store's goods, at least not yet.

"Well, that is an odd one," Junior said. "You've explored only a small way into the place, so there's no way to know what type of champions it has or if there are any other creature types, but this early information will give us something to publish. The deal stands. Store credit for five percent of the profit the guide makes."

"The deal does stand, but the percentage should be fifty percent. After all, we're the ones risking our lives in there," Jess countered.

"Ha, Matron, I like this one. She's sharp. She's wrong, but she's sharp. Since I'm fronting the cost of everything, I'll do a bit better for you. How does ten percent sound?" Junior asked, a grin plastered on his face the whole time. Matron never really learned to enjoy haggling over things, but she supposed it would be a critical skill if you were a merchant.

"Ten sounds better, but let's just cut to the chase and go with twenty-five. That's my final offer," Jess said.

"Normally, I like to go back and forth a bit more, but I can tell you've had a rough day in the dungeon. Fifteen is my final offer," Junior said.

"Fine, that will do." Jess glanced over to Matron as if seeking her approval. Matron didn't indicate one way or the other; her thoughts were on the dungeon and the strange being that ran it.

This odd dungeon core named Florence Valentine had returned, something that Matron hadn't thought was possible. Seeing her also brought back the bad memories. The day the dungeon was destroyed was the day she lost her friend Vanderman, someone she still thought about from time to time. She had lived the life he had always wanted to live, that of an adventurer.

Vanderman's death had changed her. She was no longer Shara, the friendly healer. She was now Matron, a harsh taskmaster, consumed by her duty to the light. Shara was something long past, a name and a person she had tossed aside to protect herself from the hurt and loss that inevitably followed from caring too much. At least she had thought that person was gone. Now, it seemed, Florence Valentine had reminded her of what had been, of what could have been.

"Hey, you! You're the one I was supposed to find. Kunrax has commanded that I seek you and your party out," a loud voice called out from the doorway to the store. Matron's hammer and armor were summoned, ready to fight a follower of that evil deity.

"No, none of that in my shop. If you want to scuffle, you'll do it outside, Matron," Junior commanded. She held the magic energy she was about to unleash, a blast of pure light that would have obliterated this follower of evil and her stinking hound from this world.

"Woah, crazy old bag. I'm not here to fight. I was commanded by Kunrax to join you," the woman in the doorway said, holding her hands up to show she wasn't a threat. The oversized hound at her side had its hackles up, and it gave a low growl, recognizing the threat Matron represented.

"Outside. We'll honor the proprietor's wishes." Matron motioned for the woman in the doorway to move back onto the dirt path in front of the store. The woman . . . No, she wasn't a woman, just a kid of no more than twenty summers, if Matron had guessed correctly.

As they made their way outside, Matron thought about what this person had said. She wished to join them. It took someone who wasn't right in the head to follow Kunrax, the Hound in the Night, but surely this girl couldn't be so daft as to think a paladin of the light would deign to allow her to join the party. A thought struck Matron then, one that she couldn't shake. What if this person was the one meant to join her charges, the one meant to heal their wounds? The light wouldn't choose one such as this to add to the party, would it?

"State your business. The followers of your dark god are not welcome in this place," Matron demanded as they left the store. The girl backed away, realizing that her life was in danger and that Matron was a threat, despite her age. Power and a bright glow enshrouded Matron as she called upon the light.

"I'm not following a dark god. Kunrax is misunderstood. He seeks to bring those in his care down into their final judgment. Isn't that the same thing your light claims to do? Do you not claim to bring judgment to those deemed worthy of their fate?" the girl argued. She had a point, but it wasn't one Matron wanted to consider.

"Misunderstood? Tell that to Vanderman and the others that were killed for no reason by your fellow cultists," Matron hissed.

"Hey, I know there were some who did horrible things in the name of Kunrax—some even still do it to this day—but they weren't true followers. Kunrax is casting ones such as those aside, denying them his power. They are winnowed from the flock when found. I'm merely a neophyte, seeking to spread the truth about his will. I seek to make amends for the sins of the past, to show the true nature of my master."

"For what it's worth, Matron, I've heard rumblings of this. There's a schism in their faith, and some, like this one, are claiming that Kunrax isn't an evil deity," Junior called from the doorway. Merchants kept tabs on these types of things, knowing the troubles of a pantheon could mean an opportunity for profit. At the very least, it would allow him to know whom to bar his doors to and who to let in.

"I'll stay my hammer, for now. Speak your piece and then be on your way." Matron's gut reaction was to fight, but something about this situation was odd, tickling the back of her mind.

"Thank you. I truly have been guided to you and your party. The dreams showed me all of you as clear as day. My deity wishes me to use my powers to heal the wounds of those in your care. I am to protect them with my life, to value their lives as I would that of my bonded." The girl motioned toward the large hound at her side. Some of the followers bonded with hounds, their god granting them both powers from the joining. There were also detriments, as the death of one meant the death of both.

"You may have had some dream, but the twisted dreams of your god have no sway over the light. If the light wished you to join us, it would have been made known to me," Matron argued.

"But hasn't it? I assume that you came from one of your keeps. Tell me, do the followers of the light lack for healers among your kind? Was there no one capable in that entire place that could join you? Were there none worthy of the task? Why, tell me, didn't the light provide a healer for your group while your party journeyed here? Why didn't the light have one of your kind waiting here for you? Why didn't one of the other so-called good-aligned powers step forward to have one of their followers join? I'll tell you: it's because the light knows that this position is for me, not for any of the others. I, a follower of what you think is evil, have been chosen by the light to prove my worth. By proving my worth, I'll prove that my god is what he says he is, not what the misguided want to make him out to be."

Was this it? Was this brash young lady truly sent here for a purpose other than the furtherance of evil? Matron couldn't bring herself to believe it, but that voice in the back of her mind seemed to confirm it. There might not be a pillar of light descending from the heavens to announce this was the one, but perhaps the person in front of her, the unlikely choice, was the correct one.

"The light provides, Matron. I think that, despite my dislike of her on sight, this one was meant to join us. I can feel it," Jess said, a shocked look on her face.

"Sure, why not? I always liked doggies." Tipp appeared from behind the follower of Kunrax, sheathing the twin daggers he had held poised to strike should things have gone another way. The hound gave a yelp of surprise and snapped at the rogue, who quickly drew out of bite range.

"I'll leave the decision up to you, Jess. If you are to lead this party after my instruction is done, you will have to learn to make the hard decisions and live with the consequences of them," Matron said. As much as she wanted to slam her hammer into a follower of Kunrax, she had to let her student follow her own path. It was time for Jess to do so, to take up the mantle of leadership and make her own decisions.

"What is your name?" Jess asked.

"I'm Isa and this is Gnaw," the girl replied. The hound gave a small yip when he heard his name, standing protectively between Isa and Tipp, who backed away farther.

"If you wish, I will allow you to join us on a trial basis. We'll see how you do in our next delve and then we can make a determination as to whether you will be a good fit with our party," Jess said with confidence.

Matron stood down, dismissing her armor and weapon back into storage. Jess had made her choice, and Matron would abide by it, but that didn't mean she would trust this Isa just yet.

"Tipp, take Isa inside and sign us up for another run," Jess said. There were mutterings around them, and a crowd had gathered. Matron had been so focused on the fact that a follower of Kunrax was here that she hadn't even noticed. A foolish oversight on her part.

"Sure, come on in, Isa and Gnaw. So just what type of healing do you do? I'm not going to have to bark or something just to get healed, am I?" Tipp asked as they walked back into Junior's shop. Isa gave a small chuckle, and the tension of an impending fight faded away.

"Did I make the right decision?" Jess asked. Matron was about to reply, giving more advice and admonishing her for a rash decision, but she held her tongue. Those days were done; they ended the moment Jess stepped up and took control of the situation.

"It's no longer my place to say. You have your party, and the time for my guidance is nearing an end. Lead with the same confidence I saw you exhibit just now, and you'll do fine. As for whether you made the right decision or not, time will tell," Matron said, leaving Jess to her thoughts and fears.

Matron made her way back into the shop, wanting to see how long it would be when her group could make their next delve while at the same time trying to figure out when she could sneak away to visit with Florence. The shop mostly was stocked with adventuring gear, but perhaps there was something on hand that might make a good gift for her odd dungeon friend.

"Who is that behind the counter?" a loud voice boomed from the doorway. Something about this shop attracted loud and strange people, but this person was someone Matron remembered.

"Who do you think it is? Don't you recognize your own kin?" Junior replied.

"Ha, if it isn't my third favorite nephew. Come over here and shake Uncle Bartleby's hand, Junior," the man said.

"Welcome, Uncle. I was wondering if you would show up." Junior gave his uncle a big hug.

"Tell me, Junior, is this dungeon worth my time? I've not heard good things from the guild. They fear this place may be one of the bad ones, if you get my meaning," Bartleby said.

"Excuse me, Bartleby. Sorry to interrupt, but my charges recently delved into the dungeon, and while it's unusual, it hasn't gone murderous and mad," Matron said.

"Thank you, Shara, and yes, I recognize you. Old Bartleby never forgets a face or a deal. Don't take offense, but aren't you a little long in the tooth to be clearing dungeons these days?" Bartleby asked.

"Long in the tooth? You're older than I am, even though you look the same as the first day I met you. How does that happen?" Matron asked. It was true. When she first met Bartleby, he was the same middle-aged human she saw before her now.

"I've quite a few more miles under my feet, but my line of work does have some advantages. Junior, I'll get with you in a bit. I'm going to catch up with Shara here." Bartleby led Matron across the street to the inn, offering to buy her a meal and an ale in exchange for her story. Matron was a bit nervous about leaving her charges, but Jess needed some freedom to work on her own.

"So are you going to tell me the secret of your youth?" Matron asked as they began their meal.

"A very rare and valuable item was requested by a very old and established dungeon," Bartleby said. "In return for finding said item . . . And before you ask, no, I will not tell what the item was. Now, for finding the item, I was rewarded with a legendary reward chest. Normally I'd sell such a thing for a tidy profit, but something told me to keep this one for myself. I don't know if the dungeon had a hand in that. I suspect he did, but right then and there, before I even left the dungeon, I opened the box. Inside was something I only heard rumor of: a potion of longevity."

It was an astonishing find, a truly legendary prize. "How much longer will you live?" Matron asked.

"I don't know for sure. The dungeon said something like another hundred years or so. Not bad for a human, I tell you. Now, your turn. Tell me about this new dungeon."

"Well, I don't want to spoil the surprise. Let's just say you'll enjoy meeting this dungeon. I'm sure it's perfectly fine for you to visit," Matron replied.

"Ah, mysterious. I like mysterious. I think I'll go bug my nephew to put me in the queue. Hopefully being part of the family will move me up the list," Bartleby said.

"He better not. My party is scheduled to go in before you, and if you jump place in line, I'm not going to be happy about it," Matron joked.

"We'll see. You can't blame me for trying."

Matron enjoyed spending time and enjoying a meal with an old acquaintance. It was good to put aside her duties and just enjoy the moment.

Chapter 19

"There goes poor Zork. I thought that going to this world would mean all the cheaters were gone, but here we go with four pally again," Florence complained as the party finished off the last threat in the master bedroom. Just like the most popular build in Dungeon Delve, here were four paladins, clearing her home out with their cheating ways.

"Well, at least we'll have our first adventurers that make it to the second floor. Don't compare these adventurers to the game we played back on Earth. They've had a solid run so far, but I'd bet my ball of yarn they're running low on mana. Once out of mana, a paladin is just a normal warrior," Doug replied. He was right, not that she was going to give him the satisfaction of telling him that. The four dwarves didn't say much during their delve, but whatever deity they followed must have specialized in earth magic of some sort.

The party had somewhat better gear than most, leading Florence to believe they were likely level 3 or 4 and not completely new adventurers. Paladins, shamans, and sword mages with healing affinity could all do about the same thing. This group had used magic to bolster their leather and chain armor with a rocky shell and enhanced their weapons with a magical glow that gave them heavier impact. The early encounters didn't even make the four of them break a sweat, but hitting more of the level 2 defenders and tangling with Loki forced them to start burning through their resources.

Florence hadn't seen too many dwarves in this crazy new world, so she was kind of pleased to have a chance to watch them work. Given they were in a hilly area and there were large mountains in the distance, the area was probably perfect for a dwarf clan to live in. The fact that they were all the same class didn't seem to detract from their ability to fight, though the few traps in her home did get some good licks in. The flame trap in the living room had crisped up a couple of them, which forced their first use of healing magic.

"Without a rogue in their party, your traps are doing well. We'll have to turn you loose to build what you had planned. When these four leave our home, there should be more than enough cash to work with," Florence said.

Doug perked up when she mentioned that he would get to play with trap designs soon. "Indeed, I look forward to mixing things up a bit and have some good ideas for the second floor."

They stopped talking so they could watch her babies do their thing in the great room. The dwarves took the stairs cautiously; they must have known a new level meant greater challenges. But with greater challenges came greater rewards, so that egged them on. Buttercup, Puddin, and Winston had been napping on the chairs and sofas in the room, but they scrambled into action as the adventurers approached. All her babies in the great room were level 3, and being brawler kitties, they were as large as a medium-sized dog and heavy with muscle. Hissing, arching their backs, and bristling out their fur, the kitties made ready to fight.

The paladins didn't waste any time, the party of four cautiously approaching the brawler kitties. Two of the adventurers wielded axe and shield, while the other pair sported oversized two-handed axes, forgoing the extra protection offered by a shield. Having cleared the first floor, they tried to keep an eye out for any surprises, and given the number of commando kitties in Florence's home, their wariness was justified. Willow had been hiding under one of the end tables. She launched her attack, but one of the dwarves was ready, and his huge axe swooped in to cleave her little baby in two.

Just before the shield bearers closed with her brawlers, Winter popped up in the far corner of the room. The glow of ice magic was already surrounding Florence's white-furred mage kitty as she unleashed her first spell. Shards of sharpened ice flew from her paw, peppering the paladins and slowing their advance. One of the dwarves disengaged from the brawlers, his two-handed axe raised to chop into poor Winter. Stubby dwarven legs charged across the great room, but Winter was a smart one; she had anticipated this type of attack. Dropping her ice spray, the mage kitty instead focused her magic on the floor in front of her, coating it with a thin layer of ice.

The dwarven paladin hit the icy floor, and Florence was surprised to see just how slippery frost-covered carpet could be. With a shout of surprise, the dwarf went down, sliding past Winter and slamming into the back wall of the house. Her mage kitty wasted little time as she began forming more ice spikes and hurling them at the downed dwarf. It looked like Winter would score a kill, but even the higher-level second-floor kitties only had so much mana. Her babies seemed to run out at the worst time, and Winter had run out just as the dwarf regained his feet. With no other option, Winter charged the dwarf, her puny mage claws doing little against his protective armor.

With a single swipe of his axe, the dwarf was able to finish off Winter. Florence's other kitties were just about done in as well. Buttercup and Winston were down, and Puddin was on her last legs. With a final hiss, the bloodied Puddin latched onto a dwarf's leg, tearing a deep wound even as she succumbed to the axe blows raining down upon her. It took the dwarves a few moments to pry Puddin's jaws apart and free their comrade and even more time to cast healing magic; all four of the party members sported wounds of some type.

"Brothers, I'm nearly out of mana. Should we continue?" one of the dwarves grumbled as the others looted her babies.

"Aye, at least a bit further. We'll need the extra coin for repairs," another replied. It was true; they had swatted down her kitty defenders, but even if their wounds were healed, the dwarves had taken a beating. Chainmail links were snapped, and leather was torn to shreds in places. The shields that two of them bore had deep claw marks all over the surface. Florence wasn't sure how long a shield was good for, but if it was all clawed up, that meant it might break soon, didn't it?

"Fine, move slow but cautious. These beasts are getting stronger," another mentioned.

"Aye, brother. Stronger but not all that different. I've never seen a dungeon populated by pets. It's disturbing and a bit sickening," a dwarf grumbled.

"Sickening! How dare he, Doug. Who does that net-decking little hooligan think he is? Why, I've a mind to drop my summons on top of them at the next champion room. That will show them. Insulting an old woman's home like that. The nerve of some people," Florence ranted.

"Hold on. They likely don't know any better and don't realize you're different than most other cores. Remember, we need to keep the kill ratio down if we don't want to attract unwanted, and likely fatal, attention from the guild," Doug argued, somewhat panicked that Florence was going to do something rash.

"Don't get your fur tangled up, Doug. I'm just mad, not stupid," Florence replied. She had been planning to drop her summons on them in Spud's room if they made it that far, but she didn't want to give Doug the satisfaction of knowing he was right about her doing something that he thought was "rash."

"Very well, you had me worried. Oh my, they didn't do all that well, did they?" Doug said, drawing her attention to the bathroom, where her two undying kitties had been hacked down in seconds. They were kind of scrawny and only about as strong as a mage kitty, but without any magic, they were easy targets for a well-armed and armored party.

"At least we'll get to see how their ability works. Hopefully it isn't too gross. I don't want no zombie cats dripping gunk all over my floors," Florence said.

They settled in to watch as the dwarves selected a door to proceed through. Both bedrooms were waiting, but once they selected one, the other would be locked. Florence wasn't sure if she liked the way that worked yet; she wanted the bypassed kitties to have a chance to defend their home, and it did seem like kind of a waste to have one set of them locked up if they were under a big threat. Maybe Doug would know something. She hated to admit that he had some good advice every once in a while.

"Hey, Doug, is there any way we can set the kitties loose in the bypassed room?" she asked.

"Hmm, not normally with the type of setup you've devised, but you can override it and set them to release after a certain time frame has passed," Doug replied. The kitten advisor was quiet as the party selected the door that led them to the desert-themed bedroom.

Inside, Archimedes fired off a flare of light as soon as the party entered, blinding them temporarily. Her babies must have been practicing because the other two were already on the move, looking away at just the right time to avoid being blinded. Sherbet bowled into the lead paladin, knocking the dwarf over and going to town on him with oversized claws and teeth. Sandy materialized to launch a devastating stealth attack against another dwarf.

Her claws continued to dish out extra damage as the flash-blinded dwarf blinked rapidly to regain his sight.

The paladin in the back hadn't been affected, and he conjured a magical hammer of light in front of him. The glowing weapon was hurled into Sandy, who gave a pitiful yelp before keeling over, dead. Archimedes responded with a pair of magic spheres that slammed into the dwarf that had killed his friend, penetrating the armor and disrupting the heal spell he had been working on.

Sherbet continued to maul the dwarf he had knocked over, clamping his jaws onto one of the paladin's wrists as the adventurer tried to take a swing at him. Shaking his head from side to side, almost like a dog would do, Sherbet pulled back as the bones in the dwarf's wrist gave a disturbing crunch before the entire hand was pulled away. Howling in pain, the dwarf with the dismembered hand was finally rescued by his fellows; a pair of axes slammed into poor Sherbet and knocked him off their comrade. Her baby clawed and scratched, unwilling to open his mouth to add his bite attack, as that would mean giving up the dwarf's hand.

"Look at that, a dismemberment. That's something new," Doug mused. The little guy was really getting into the fight.

"Serves them right for insulting me and my home. Good job, Sherbet." Florence didn't know if her babies could hear her in combat, but she thought she caught a gleam in his eye; the kitty knew she was proud of him. Sadly, the battered Sherbet wasn't a match on his own, and Archimedes was fighting a losing battle against one of the dwarves. The mage kitty proved no match for the paladin's skill with a two-handed axe.

"Hold still, brother. I need to see the wound to restore it," one of the dwarves said as he poured healing magic into the stump that was still splattering blood all over the sand-colored carpeting. Florence had thought the dwarf was a goner, but while the others were finishing off Archimedes and Sherbet, he had managed to pull a potion from his belt with his one good hand and slugged it down. It didn't stop the bleeding completely, but the magic in the potion must have kept him from croaking due to blood loss. More magic was expended, and after prying the severed hand from Sherbet's jaws, the dwarves were able to reattach it.

"I know these guys are probably higher level than the others that have tried out our home, but even these jokers have to be just about out of mana now," Florence said hopefully.

"I believe you're right. I've estimated based on their spells and abilities that these four are around level 5. Maybe one or two could be level 6. Given standard stat distribution and mana regen caps for their class, the well is about to run dry, so to speak," Doug confirmed. He tried to explain to her all that nonsense about levels and stat distributions and whatnot, but she really didn't care to get into that much detail.

It was then, with all of them focused on healing up the guy with the bum hand, that her undying kitties showed up again. Now, them little critters weren't stealthy and all that, but since the dwarves were distracted, both of her babies were able to finally do some damage. Much to her disgust, the poor kitties did look like a pair of zombies from them spooky shows that Doug would watch late at night sometimes. Florence didn't cotton to that type of entertainment and would have put a stop to it if Doug hadn't insisted that they were educational. She let him have his fun as long as he only watched them types of movies when she was already in bed.

"Not the best of fighters, but these undying variants of our defenders can be useful, I must say," Doug added as they watched the dwarf cradling their wounded comrade shout in pain as two zombie cats attacked. Like before, these undying kitties weren't powerful and fell quickly to the party's axes, but they had landed more shots and the wounds would have to be healed. Florence couldn't imagine anyone wanting to go trooping through a dungeon after getting scratched by zombie claws.

"That is it, brothers. We should return," the dwarf that had just been scratched said as one of the others healed his wounds.

"Agreed, we've done well enough for our first run and at least know what to expect now," another said. They gathered themselves and made their way cautiously toward the stairwell, eyeing each kitty corpse for signs of reanimation.

"They did well, though I must admit to a bit of disappointment over not seeing our home champion in action," Doug said.

"Yeah, and Spud too. He got a new class, and we don't even know what the guy can do yet," Florence added.

"Spud is not someone that I wish to associate with or watch unless it is absolutely necessary," Doug said, pouring on the attitude.

"Ware the shadows, brothers!" a dwarf shouted as one of their number was attacked.

Florence was confused. She didn't have any commando kitties left; at least she didn't think she did. But it turned out it wasn't a kitty at all. A lanky goblin in leather armor appeared after dealing his deadly strike. The dwarf slid off the goblin's twin knife blades, convulsing as whatever poison coated those weapons went to work. Fighting broke out among the other adventurers as more goblins appeared from the shadows, launching their own attacks.

"I's come back like I promised, pretty little gem. Now, Blivix will take his prize," a very unwelcome voice said.

"Oh dear, I know that guy and I think we may be in trouble, Doug," Florence said.

Chapter 20

"You know that rapscallion?" Doug said incredulously.

"It's that little green turd that carried me here," Florence said.

"They appear to be a batch of assassins, and they must have followed this party in, waiting for your defenses to be depleted and the adventurers to be weakened before striking," Doug said. Florence could see it now; that Blivix guy had snuck through the whole delve, waiting for his chance. With the adventurers heading back, the goblin couldn't let them leave and give Florence the chance to reset her defenders, so they had chosen the most opportune time to attack.

Things weren't going well for the dwarves. The one Blivix had stabbed was dead, and the others were fighting a losing battle against a swarm of the creeps. At least the other goblins didn't seem anywhere near as skilled as Blivix, but they had all launched their first attacks successfully from stealth. They must have had some gunk on their blades as well, since the paladins weren't moving and fighting as well as they had against her babies. As she watched, one paladin glowed bright as he cast a spell on himself. The magic must have cleansed whatever was running through his system. The lethargy was gone, and the dwarf was chopping down one goblin while fending off another with his shield.

"Consarn it, where did that Blivix goober go?" Florence asked, losing sight of the assassin. The goblin reappeared behind a paladin, his twin daggers taking down the target as the surviving pair of adventurers fought their way back to the corner of the room.

"He is likely high enough level to possess abilities that allow him to disappear while in plain sight. It's common for assassins to do such things. The dwarves are being smart, though, protecting their backs with the wall," Doug replied.

"Should I pop my summons and add kitties to help the dwarves?" Florence asked.

"No, I think it would be better to reserve your ability for a more opportune time, like when this crew is engaged with a champion."

It galled her to do nothing to help the dwarves, but adding a few cats to the mix wouldn't really help much. The pair were slowing down, and the goblins were landing more and more hits, despite losing two more of their number. When the two-handed axe of a dwarf got caught in a goblin's ribcage, he took too long to dislodge the weapon, allowing a pair of daggers to slash his throat. On his own, the last dwarf took another goblin with him, screaming curses and war cries as he succumbed to the poisoned blades.

"How many of the little green creeps are there? I can't get a good count?" Florence asked. The other goblins couldn't disappear in plain sight like Blivix, but as soon as her attention was drawn elsewhere, the jerks were able to turn invisible.

"It's hard to tell. They are a slippery lot. There could have been anywhere from fifteen to two scores of them, but that's just a guess," Doug answered.

"Well, at least them poor dwarves thinned the herd for us." Florence counted a total of seven fallen goblins. These ones had dark leather armor and long daggers, just like Blivix, but their gear didn't look enchanted or anywhere near as well made as the gear of the leader of this band of cutthroats.

Every few seconds, a goblin would pop into view, looting something from the corpse of friend and foe alike. By the time they were done pillaging the fallen, Florence was able to lock her view onto one of the critters, refusing to be distracted so the goblin couldn't elude her. Figuring that they were all going the same way, she could track their progress by watching where the one goblin went. It looked like they were heading deeper into her home as the goblin walked past the bathroom and opened the door to the bedroom. Sadly, since the home hadn't been reset since the paladins had gone through, the other bedroom couldn't be accessed. Florence would have loved to let her other kitties take a crack at these guys.

"They're going into the master bedroom," Doug said, his comment distracting her and making her lose her lock on the one goblin.

"Dang it, Doug, I lost my focus on that guy. Oh no, it looks like my babies don't know what's heading their way," Florence lamented. The door to the master bedroom creaked open. She'd have to fix that; it wouldn't do to have a creaky door in her home. There was that one bedroom door in her house that always creaked when the humidity got too high. She had been meaning to have Tabitha's grandson come in and fix it, but the whole dying thing happened first. Florence wondered who would buy her house now that she was gone. Would they fix the creaky door?

"Florence, pay attention," Doug chided, bringing her focus back to what was about to go down. The kitties knew something was up. The doors in her home didn't open on their own, but they weren't quite sure what to do. Marshmallow, Brownie, and KitKat must have figured it was an attack of some kind, because all three disappeared into the tunnels underneath the master bedroom. Cheddar stood at the foot of the bed, trying to protect Licorice, who had been napping on the pillows but was now casting some spell.

"At least Licorice has illusion magic. It should work nicely in this situation," Doug predicted. Florence didn't care about the type of magic. All that mattered was that her kitties were ready to fight.

Licorice finished her spell just before Blivix appeared behind her, knives stabbing out to eliminate the magic support before the fight really got started.

Another pair of Cheddars appeared, illusory copies of her kitty snapping into place as the spell completed. The real Cheddar, which Florence had no trouble telling apart from the illusions, charged Blivix. One of the illusion kitties popped out of existence as several of the other goblins appeared around it, stabbing what they thought was the proper target. The second illusion popped as others attacked it, and poor Cheddar gave a squeal of pain as a single goblin launched a surprise attack on the real brawler kitty.

Cheddar turned away from Blivix to rake his claws across the goblin that had hurt him, his enhanced natural weapons easily shredding the diminutive green killer. Blivix wasn't able to make his escape just yet; Marshmallow already had him in her sights as she launched at him from under one of the rugs at the side of the bed and initiated her own sneak attack. Blivix reacted quicker than Florence thought possible, twisting away from the slashing claws of her commando kitty even as he brought up his blades to counterattack.

Marshmallow was able to adjust her attack slightly, causing her right paw to rip into Blivix's shoulder. Green blood flowed from the wound, but it wasn't a crippling injury. The goblin's counterattack was, though; his blades pierced deep into Marshmallow as she flew past, ripping her up from front to back. When she landed on the floor, Florence's poor kitty gave a little meow before collapsing.

The other commandos launched their attacks at the goblins that had suddenly become visible in their midst. If they hadn't been inside the tunnels, they, too, would have fallen in the initial attack, but instead, they were tearing into the visible goblins. Their fight was a desperate one, and more and more goblins dropped stealth as they joined the attack. With kitty commandos and goblin assassins everywhere, the fight sure didn't last long. Florence's babies had lost the battle, but eight more goblin corpses decorated the room, her babies exacting a huge toll on the invaders. Unfortunately, Blivix's corpse wasn't among the fallen. The little creep disappeared again soon after finishing off Marshmallow.

"Fourteen, I believe," Doug said.

"Fourteen what? Fourteen minutes until you drive me batty?" Florence asked. She hated when Doug tried to be all cryptic and stuff.

"No, fourteen goblins are still alive. That doesn't count this Blivix individual, though."

"You got some counting skills I don't know about?" Florence asked, irritated that Doug could count the invaders and was acting so confident about it.

"No, I could be off by one or two, but I was able to discern some distinguishing characteristics about the little hooligans and had some success in keeping them sorted during the last kerfuffle."

"Good job, I suppose. At least we know what we're dealing with. We only got Spud and Mortimer left between them and us," Florence said, starting to get a bit concerned.

"While I have no confidence at all in our floor champion, given his lack of discipline and overall slovenly behavior, I am certain that Mortimer will give a good account of himself," Doug assured her.

"Don't discount old Spud just because he bullies you. The big stinker will do a good job. He's a champion now," Florence said, starting to get a little concerned.

"He's about to get his chance," Doug said as the hatchway to the attic opened.

"Look, Spud's an old alley cat scrapper. He knows something's up, but them goblins is all stealthed and whatnot." Florence was worried that Spud would just get stabbed down with poisoned daggers and sneak attacks before he could really get going. The champion kitty sniffed and gave that low growl that kitties gave when they were really irritated but not quite irritated enough to go into full hissing mode.

"Gads, was that what I think it was?" Doug asked as burbling noises came from the kitty's rear end. A green cloud started to spread from her big plague charger.

"Ha, way to find them goblins, Spud. Stink 'em out of hiding." Florence laughed. While she didn't approve of public flatulence, she couldn't argue with Spud's effectiveness. As the cloud spread out, several goblins appeared, gagging from the stench. They had been approaching the kitty in a mob, but Blivix wasn't there. Either the leader was able to keep from gagging or he was hiding somewhere the stink couldn't reach.

"Can you imagine the stench in there? How bad must it be to make goblins gag? They're some of the most vile and odiferous creatures on the planet," Doug said. Florence took his statement as a compliment on Spud's abilities as a champion.

Hissing and spitting, Spud began to run toward the mob of goblin rogues, a glow settling over his back as he activated one of his new abilities. A saddle appeared, and seated in the saddle was none other than Gabsug, the diminutive goblin that Spud had befriended all those years ago. This version of Gabsug wasn't the real one, and instead of the filthy rags the goblin had worn, this one sported filthy armor instead. A long lance was couched and ready to strike, shield held in the goblin's off hand to protect both mount and rider.

With a crash, Spud hurled through the goblins, claws lashing out to take down a pair of invaders as a third was skewered on the end of Gabsug's lance. As he passed, the stink cloud around her baby made several of the other goblins fall to the ground, where they retched and barfed all over the attic floor. At least the attic floor was simple plywood and not her lovely shag carpeting.

Spud had one flaw in his new charge attack: it took him time to slow down and get turned back in the right direction. It was then that Blivix decided to make his appearance, twin daggers glowing with poison and some ability he had activated. When the daggers hit Spud's flank, they released the stored energy, exploding against her baby's hide. Spud hissed and lashed out, the agile goblin assassin dodging his paw. Blivix might have dodged Spud, but the summoned Gabsug was also attacking, the lance stabbing into Blivix's belly.

Blivix backpedaled. The lance was pulled from his belly, but not before taking a chunk of goblin with it. The assassin threw down a small marble-sized object that exploded in a cloud of smoke, enabling him to disappear once more. Spud must have been out of gas, because he didn't toot again to try and flush out Blivix. Instead of trying to track down the wounded assassin, Spud turned his attention back to the other goblins, who were starting to recover from the stench around them.

A second charge left three more goblins down, and then the summoned Gabsug lookalike disappeared as two goblins appeared behind him and attacked. Spud slashed down the two attackers, only to have more appear. Shrugging off the blows, Spud fought through the wounds he was sustaining. A champion was much tougher than a normal defender, but Spud was taking an awful beating. Each time he turned to defend himself, another attacker would appear. Not only were the attacks that landed on him enhanced by rogue abilities, but many also added various poisons into his system.

Damage over time was bleeding off Spud's health, and his counterattacks came slower and slower. Eventually, even her big champion kitty succumbed to the relentless attacks of the invaders. Blivix reappeared, landing the final blows on Spud as he shredded apart a goblin that had been too slow to avoid his paw. The champion slumped to the ground, and Blivix shuffled over to loot the corpse. Florence didn't see and didn't care what loot had been found, but she was glad to see the assassin was forced to down a health potion to heal the damage that the summoned Gabsug had done to him.

"Not bad. Blivix has already used a potion and he's down to four minions," Doug said.

"Yeah, I hope that Mortimer is up to the task. I mean, he's never even tried out his new class and he was just a regular old commando kitty before," Florence said. Would her little necro-catster be able to hold his own against an assassin? Florence sure hoped so.

Chapter 21

"Oh, look at that. Mortimer can see them," Doug said excitedly. It was true; since her cat could see the invaders, Florence could see them as well.

"How is he able to and none of the other kitties could?" Florence asked.

"Likely due to his new class. I know you're not sold on the whole undead affinity thing, but one ability that many powerful undead possess is the ability to sense life. That's what Mortimer is doing now, sensing the lifeforce of the attackers. Can't you tell how everything about them looks different?" Doug was right; she was seeing the goblins, but it was in strange colors, the shades growing brighter on the more powerful Blivix.

Mortimer wasn't fooled one bit, but he was sure putting on a good show, pretending to just walk around the graveyard all normal-like. Since the enemy was revealed, it was time to unleash her summoned kitties. Florence concentrated near Blivix, wanting her summoned babies to attack the biggest threat. The summoning felt different, and instead of three or four normal defenders, the minor champion, Loki, was summoned. Instead of being level 3, the summoned minor champion matched her level of six. That was something she was worried about; the normal defenders were random copies of cats in her home, and it would be horrible if they summoned all level 1 kitties when she needed

them most. It looked like that was one thing she didn't need to
worry about.

Mortimer's vision seemed to extend to not only Florence and
Doug but also to Loki, who activated one of his raider abilities. The
cat charged in to swipe and bite at the nearest goblin, a normal
rogue, unfortunately. The minor champion's attack tore the goblin rogue in half. Loki's class enabled him to jump back instantly,
avoiding Blivix and the other goblin's retaliatory attacks.

Blivix tried something new, throwing his daggers at Loki, who
noticed the attack too late. Both daggers dug deep into the raider
kitty and then did more damage as the enchanted blades returned
to Blivix's hands. Loki limped from the wound but still charged
into battle; the summoned kitty was fearless in his attempts to
stop these invaders. Loki was tough. He was a minor champion,
and his Raider class, despite using hit-and-run tactics, wasn't as
fragile as the commando kitties.

"What's up with Mortimer?" Florence asked.

"I have no idea. He's using mana, but I don't know for what
purpose," Doug replied.

Power gathered around the home champion, dark energy in-
fusing him, but instead of blasting the bad guys and whatnot,
Mortimer sent thin tendrils of dark mana out toward everyone.
The tendrils ignored the summoned copy of Loki but were absorbed by all the goblins. Florence could see the tendrils—it was
her dungeon, after all—but the goblins were none the wiser.
With that spell complete, Mortimer pulled up more energy, coating his paws in a sickly-looking combination of green, black, and
mustard-yellow energy.

While Mortimer readied his next spell, Loki struck down the
last of the goblin rogues, leaving only Blivix. The assassin had
the upper hand, though, and his blades were slamming into poor
Loki one after the other. Stacks of poison damage were draining

Loki's health at a rapid pace, and just as his health reached zero, the summoned kitty disappeared. It was Mortimer on his own against Blivix. The assassin was wounded, but none of his injuries seemed to slow him down much. Standing perfectly still for a second, Blivix then began to creep toward what looked like an unsuspecting Mortimer.

"That dummy thinks he's invisible, doesn't he?" Florence taunted.

"Yes, not the sharpest tool in the shed, that one. Cunning and dangerous, yes, but smart? Not so much," Doug replied.

With a hiss, Mortimer leaped at the assassin, who deftly avoided the necrocatster. A pair of quick stabs left poor Mortimer on death's door, but they also hurt Blivix. When he struck, the necromantic energy covering Mortimer's paws flowed up the weapons and into the goblin. Where the energy hit, flesh rotted and muscles atrophied. Not giving up just yet, Blivix leaped back and threw his daggers at Florence's last defender. Both daggers struck true, the range too great for Mortimer to retaliate with his powers. Blivix wasn't moving as fast as normal, but he was plenty fast enough to outrun the wounded Mortimer, kiting the poor kitty around while throwing his daggers whenever the skill was off cooldown.

"That's not fair. Mortimer needs a ranged attack or something." Florence was disappointed in her home champion's performance in the fight but wasn't going to say anything since she didn't want the little guy to feel bad. She was sure he was doing his best, but after the third toss of the daggers, Mortimer fell.

"Now, pretty gem, it's just you and Blivix. I think you're all outs of catses, I do. No more defenders. How sads for youse. I promise to make your death painless. Blivix is nice like that sometimes," the assassin said as he limped his way toward the gravedigger's shed that served as their core room.

"You ready to fight, Doug? Draw him in good and close so I can whack him with my cane. It's just you and me, little guy," Florence said, steeling herself for the fight to come.

"Well, I don't think we're quite alone. Look," Doug said. Mortimer stood back up, only it wasn't the scrawny little kitty from before; it was a gooey zombie version. In addition, the four goblin rogues did the same thing, turning all zombified and moving in front of Mortimer to protect him as they advanced.

"Tricksy core, I'm tired of fightings. Go away, dead things," Blivix said as he raised his daggers in the air.

"Oh my, it seems the goblin has some powerful ability he's trying out," Doug said, concern creeping into his voice as hundreds of daggers rained from above, peppering the zombified home champion and his zombie helpers.

"No more trickses. Now I kill you slow and painfuls for wasting my dagger storm thingy," Blivix said, the goblin visibly drained from using what must have been a daily, or perhaps even weekly, ability.

"Impressive. Look at Mortimer go. You can't keep a necrocatster down, it appears," Doug said. Mortimer and the four goblins rose once more, but this time, all the flesh sloughed off their bodies as they stood. The skeletons moved a bit faster than the zombies, and the goblins were on Blivix in a flash. The rogue tried to swipe with his daggers, the magically enhanced blades doing damage and snapping bones, but Florence knew that even with the magic, a piercing and slashing weapon like a dagger did reduced damage to skeletal creatures.

"He sure can stay in the fight, can't he?" she said, proud of her Mortimer.

Blivix tried to stealth again and again, but unless he could mask his lifeforce somehow, Mortimer knew where he was. Skeletal goblins dug their claws into Blivix, who kept fighting, blasting bones from his attackers with each strike. His struggles ended when

Mortimer pounced and landed atop him. Dying seemed to make Mortimer stronger, and his claws dug deep into the invader. At the same time, her home champion seemed to draw the life right out of Blivix. A few whimpers of pain were heard as the goblin assassin finally fell still.

"Who's a good boy? Mortimer is, that's who," Florence cooed to her brave baby. Mortimer stood up straight, Florence lavishing praise on him as she reset their home. Unfortunately, she still had to shell out money to respawn Mortimer. It looked like if he died even once in the battle, he needed to be resummoned. What a rip-off.

"Florence, look at your interface," Doug said. It was all there in black and white. She had hit level 7.

"How'd we go up a level after only a couple of delves?" Florence said. Not that she was going to complain. She just didn't understand it.

"It's not too hard to figure out. Those four paladins had a long run before dying inside our home. The death of four adventurers that were somewhat higher level than the average is a windfall. When you add to that all the goblins that died and that Blivix scoundrel, we've had quite the haul. That assassin was the highest-level adventurer we've had inside, and he died, giving us a huge boost," Doug advised.

"Uh-oh, what about our kill ratio? Are these guys going to be added to our score?" Florence said.

"Unfortunately, yes. I can only hope we have more successful delves before the guild gets around to looking more closely at our numbers," Doug said. Florence was worried, but there was too much to do now that she had leveled up. She pulled up the interface to dig into the changes.

Florence Valentine

Cat core, level 7

Experience: 119/8500

Funds: $700/$700

Defender expense:

First Floor: level range 1–3 ($340/$400)

Second Floor: level range 3–5 ($230/$300). You may now summon or promote a minor champion for this floor.

Third Floor: level range 6–7 ($100/$150)

Summoner: Your summoner ability has been upgraded, and the chance to summon a minor champion instead of several normal defenders is increased.

Deadly Doug: The Deadly Doug ability now allows your advisor to choose from several classes when the ability is activated, fine-tuning and improving his ability to defend you. Due to the individuality upgrade, the advisor will be the one to decide on a particular class, and the core cannot influence his decision. The ability now lasts for up to 2 minutes and 30 seconds. Deadly Doug can only be activated once every 24 hours.

"So, no new abilities, just upgrades for what we have, more defender expense, and whatnot," Florence said. "We're also going to get another minor champion for the second floor. The level range for the third floor also increased, but the others look like they stayed the same."

"Yes, eventually we'll have to expand more to keep the level ranges from being too wide for each floor, but it will be a while before we have to worry about that," Doug advised. "As far as new abilities go, you'll see those less often as we level, but the ones we do get will generally prove to be more impactful. As we go forward, look for big changes at level 10 and then at every five levels after that."

"That's fine. The extra defender expense will help with you

creating those traps you wanted, and I can finally create the last of our defenders."

"We need to spend something soon. Our balance is maxed out, and every moment it remains that way, we're losing the normal trickle of income our home provides."

"Then go ahead and build your traps, and I'll see about finishing up that new area I wanted in front of the lawn. I'm going to call it the welcome center," Florence said. Being a frugal woman, she liked having a full bank account, but she knew there was a time to spend money, and that time was now.

She started by pushing out her home past the front lawn. She wanted to create a safe area before a party started in her dungeon. The goal was to give everyone that visited a fair warning of what they could expect and even give new adventurers a chance to test themselves on an easy encounter. The front lawn was now set apart from her new area by a fresh, waist-high white picket fence with a gate. Her new area was covered with short-cut grass. It was a comfy lawn, the kind you just wanted to lie down and take a nap on. People wouldn't even have to worry about bugs and mosquitos biting them out here.

Florence had planned to have the front entrance to the tunnel system as her home's main entrance, but with her power still being blocked by something out there, she would just make do with this new area. A portion of the new area near the cavern wall was surrounded by another picket fence, and inside that area, she created a new kitty for the first floor. Cash flowed out, and sitting there as proud as you please inside his little pen was an adorable long-haired black and white brawler kitty with markings that made it look like he was wearing a tuxedo.

"Why, aren't you the sweetest little thing? Okay, little kitty, you're going to have a dangerous but very important job. The odds will be stacked against you, but I think you're a tough little guy, aren't you?" Florence asked. The kitty meowed and sat proudly to display his bravery for all to see.

"Oh, I believe it's my turn for a name," Doug said.

"Nope, this one reminds me of a kitty I used to have. This is going to be Morris—or Mo, as I liked to call him," Florence pronounced. Mo prowled around his pen, then leaped over the waist-high fence to go meet everyone else in the home. Florence set this one area as neutral. Mo wouldn't mess with anyone that didn't mess with him. He would also stay inside the assigned fenced-in area; at least she thought he would. A gazebo was placed on the other side of the cavern, with lots of seating for adventurers to relax on while they healed up or discussed their plans.

When adventurers showed up, they would see the gazebo to their left and Mo hanging out in his pen to the right. A flower-lined path led through the area and stopped at the front gate to the main lawn. A glowing sunlike light source was placed on the cavern ceiling to give the place the feel of an early spring afternoon. She needed to make a couple of signs to let adventurers know what was going on. She started with one where the welcome center met the rough stone of the tunnel floor.

Welcome to the Valentine residence. This is a neutral area where you can rest and plan your delve. Please use caution and wipe your feet before entering the home.

Beware of Doug.

There, that would do it. A way to announce this was where her home started. But the next sign, which was placed in front of Mo's pen, would take a bit more finagling to get right. It was something Doug had helped her with earlier.

Remember, adventurer, this is a dangerous place that you shouldn't enter unless you're in a balanced party with appropriate equipment. The farther into my home you progress, the greater the dangers you will face. Mo here will be a good test of your skill before you enter. Try your strength against him before deciding to delve through the main home.

To finish things off, Florence placed a picnic basket inside the gazebo. It held some sandwiches, regular ones, not the fancy ones you had with tea. Bags of chips, some pickles, apples, and a big jug of sweet tea would be found in the basket. These refreshments were delicious, but Florence could also enhance them with buffs for parties that needed a little extra help. Of course, she could always make the food do something bad to anyone that ate it, but that particular version of a picnic was reserved for those that meant her harm.

She felt better about her home now. The place was just as dangerous as before, but now she had done her best to warn away those that shouldn't be here. If they ignored her warnings, well, she was still a core gem and would gladly accept the rewards that came when someone croaked inside her home.

Chapter 22

"Doug, what did you come up with for traps?" Florence asked. He was still moping around a bit since she named the last kitty, but talking about traps seemed to perk the little guy right up.

"Oh, I didn't realize you were done creating new defenders. Did you run out of names?" Doug whined.

"No, just show me what you done and stop being passive aggro or whatever it's called," Florence said.

"The phrase is passive-aggressive, and I've only had time to work on something for the mailbox trap." Doug showed her the upgrades he'd made. The old mailbox trap was the same $5 version he had upgraded to before, but now the mailbox was situated inside the middle of a ten-foot-deep pit trap. Wooden spikes waited at the bottom for anyone unfortunate enough to fall in.

"That should help counter the constant annoyance of rogues disarming the mailbox," Doug said, proud of his work.

"Hmm, I like the new trap, but won't rogues just disarm the durned thing like they do the mailbox?"

"Yes, they can, but it will take them time to find the trap and then disarm it. That whole time, the mailbox will be chugging out crossbow bolts at the adventurers."

"Nice work. What are you going to work on next?" Florence asked. The pit trap was a nice addition, but she could see parties sending their rogues over to disarm it and the mailbox before they ever stepped into range. That was fine; the front lawn was the first test a party took on, and it wouldn't be fair to overload it with traps and defenders.

"If you're not going to add additional defenders in the hallway, I was going to add a couple of traps in there next, as well as update the fireplace trap," Doug advised.

"Sounds good. I'll call you over when I make some new kitties. You'll get to name the next one, I promise. I'm going to finally finish populating the third floor next. Mortimer could use some kitties to raise from the dead if the adventurers aren't nice enough to bring him any corpses to work with." It was a bit gruesome to think of it that way, but her home champion really did need bodies to use, and having a few kitties there in the side yard should work perfectly.

Florence focused on the side yard, creating another kitty. This one turned out to be a big old orange tabby, a true brawler kitty if she ever saw one. She wanted to name the newest addition but had agreed to let Doug do it, and he was still tied up with working on a trap in the first-floor hallway. Fine, she'd let him finish up before naming this guy.

"Sorry, big orange guy, you'll have to wait on Doug to give you a name, but don't worry. I won't let him give you something weird," Florence promised her newest baby. The kitty looked up at her and gave a small mew. She could tell he was disappointed, so she'd better give him a friend as soon as possible.

Her next kitty was a bit odd but in a cute, not creepy way. Sitting there next to the unnamed orange cat was a strange long-haired black and brown calico kitty. The kitty's eyes would occasionally flash with white light, and its body would sort of fade out of existence. She had never seen anything like it, and Florence Valentine was a woman who had seen a lot of things in her time.

"Oh, that's a lovely new cat type you've discovered, Florence.

Since it's my turn to name a cat, I shall call this one—" Doug started to say.

"Nope, I'm naming this one. It's Spooky—" Florence started before Doug interrupted.

"—White Eyes of the Hunter," Doug shouted, having the nerve to try and shout out a name for the cat, both of their voices blending together as they tried to speak over each other.

"Now, listen here, Doug. You're not going to try and talk over me, especially not when I'm trying to name our kitties," Florence said, chastising the white kitten advisor.

"Well, though the method may be deemed rude, I felt I had to expend the effort if I didn't want to be the victim of your negligent behavior. How dare you skip over my naming turn multiple times. It was my turn, and just look what your unfair shenanigans have done to our latest defender."

Florence was constantly surprised over the range of emotions a kitten could have. Right now, Doug had both fury and disdain plastered on his fluffy white face. Looking at her latest baby, Florence had to admit their argument had spun the naming process for a loop.

Spooky White Eyes the Hunter, Ethereal Assassin

"Fine, that didn't go well, and if I cut in line, I apologize. Now, to make things up, you can name this jolly kitty here." Florence pointed toward the orange kitty still waiting for a name. Doug was obviously in the wrong here, but she was going to be the bigger person, like she always was, and let Doug have a go at naming.

"Very well. Since you admit your culpability in the matter, I'll come up with an appropriate name for this fellow." Doug placed a paw up to his chin in contemplation.

"Don't take all day. I know you have a whole list of dopey names floating around in your head. We talked about this back on Earth," Florence said, irritated at the little guy for wasting their time.

"Fine, this brave defender shall be named Sun Wukong!" Doug pronounced loudly. The orange brawler kitty seemed to like the name, even if it was ridiculous.

"What kind of name is that? Calling a cat Sun King Kong isn't right," Florence replied.

"It's Sun Wukong. The name is from Chinese mythology. It's the Monkey King."

"The fact that you have to explain it means it's not a very good name. Imagine naming a poor kitty Some Kind of Donkey Kong and having the nerve to also call him a monkey."

"Nowhere did I mention anything close to Some Kind of Donkey Kong. It's Sun Wukong," Doug argued.

"Okay, you're done here. For now, go back to your traps. I'll handle the naming for a while," Florence ordered, ignoring Doug's further protestations. She turned her attention back to the third floor. She had two more cats to create here.

The next cat looked almost like a twin of Spud. It was, thankfully, less stinky-looking, but he was a bit scuffed up, like he was a guy that got into a lot of fights. She named him Scamp, which seemed to fit him perfectly. For her final kitty on the floor, Florence watched as yet another fluffy Maine Coon cat appeared, already meowing and greeting Scamp.

"What gives? We've been getting far more Maine Coon cats than I thought we would. It's a good thing they're fluffy and cute, or I'd be mad about the whole situation," Florence said to herself. She loved that breed of cat, but her home needed some variety, of course, as long as that variety didn't include any dead zombie cats. "You're going to be Lizzy. You look like a Lizzy. Say hi to your friends, and let's see what classes you and Scamp here have become."

It turned out Lizzy was a mage with a conjuration magic affinity. Scamp was something different. She thought he was going to be a brawler, but his class was showing him as a bully instead. She wanted to ask about it but was still irritated with Doug.

With the four new defenders on the third floor, Florence was using up $140 out of her $150 defender expense limit. The remaining $10 would be used for some traps to bolster Mortimer. Whether she was annoyed with him or not, Doug was good at figuring out the perfect trap for the situation. The third floor was done, but with the expanded defender expense she received for reaching level 7, she took a look at the second floor. They didn't have any traps yet, so most of her funds would be required for that.

The rest of the floor had good coverage. Maybe she could add some defenders into the walk-in closet. She had planned to do traps in there, but perhaps she should add one kitty to distract adventurers from the possibility of traps. She summoned one more defender, but this time, she got something different. Instead of a normal-sized level 6 kitty, she had what looked like a kitten. She was as adorable as you could make a cat, but why a kitten? She couldn't force a kitten to fight, could she?

Vala, Level 6, Puppet Master

What in the heck was a puppet master? Was her kitty going to put on some kind of kids show or something? Things were getting weird, but as long as the little cutie contributed to her home's defense, Florence was glad to have her. The second floor now needed a minor champion. She thought about promoting one of her babies, but it might be nice to create something new.

Twenty-five dollars were pulled from Florence's core, and when the process was done, she had her second-floor minor champion. It was another short-haired tabby, but she was rather, well, chubby. To top things off, the poor cat had an unnaturally small head. What in tarnation was going on with this cat?

"Doug, what's with this new minor champion? She's got a weird small head, and I haven't heard of this class before," Florence said, pulling up the cat's information.

Tachi, Level 5, Chronomancer

"Chronomancer is a rare and powerful mage sub-class," Doug said. "Our newest defender will be able to control time itself, though at her power level, I suspect she will do something simple like slowing enemies and speeding up allies. When combined with our other defenders, Tachi here could really help push our forces to victory. As far as the diminutive cranium is concerned, that is an unfortunate side effect of this class."

Florence watched as Tachi made the rounds. Never settling into a room of her own, Tachi was content to wander the second floor. By the time the day was out, her newest minor champion should figure out the best places for naps across the whole floor.

"Are you still working on the first-floor traps? We need to finish things up on the second and third floor," Florence said.

"Yes, the work here is complete. I was just doing some additional testing," Doug said. Florence could see her defender expense for the first floor was now maxed at $400, so Doug must have been pretty busy.

"Run me through the changes," Florence asked. She could detect where new traps were placed but wanted to hear Doug's reasoning behind what he did.

"Very well. The first change is in the hallway. With Mortimer gone from the room, the place needed a bit more danger. Some of the adventurers have discovered that they can hear the defenders moving around in the walls as they prepare for their next attack. I've placed two random spear traps, along with some noisemakers, to simulate a cat attack. When adventurers move to cover an opening, it might be a cat or it might be a spear to the face," Doug said, obviously proud of his work.

"That's good, but I noticed you've not placed any traps in the sewing room and the bath," Florence said.

"True. Those rooms are optional, and as we discussed before, I don't want to waste defender expense on them. In the laundry room, however, I've added a second clothesline trap. Now the adventurers can't just duck under the first line, or they'll run into the second one that is placed a bit lower. While they're trying to disarm things, our summoners will be busy throwing creatures at them."

"What about the garage? It's optional but you have four traps in there, if I'm seeing things correctly."

"Yes, it is an optional chamber, but I propose we place a reward chest inside for the first few runs," Doug told her. "That way, adventurers will be drawn inside and have to run the gauntlet I've created. Just inside the room, I have a pair of large litter box traps. They'll have to find some way to cross over them safely, and when they finally do cross over, the second pair of traps will activate. For those, I've added several drills that will shoot up from the sand."

"Nice work, Doug. What's left down here?" Florence asked.

"I added the second magic missile trap in the library, and inside the dining room, we now have a silverware catapult. This is a command-activated trap, and the kitties inside can trigger it when they like, or you and I can trigger it remotely if we so desire." The trapped tray was filled with sharp knives and forks, all ready to be flung into an adventurer's face. With the manual trigger near the dish Cookie liked to sleep in, the cats defending the room should have a pretty good chance at firing off the trap before the adventurers got to them.

"I like it, and I've left you $35 of defender expense for the second floor and $10 for the third," Florence told him. Before Doug could get back to work, a strange figure arrived at the front of the lawn.

"Hello there! It's me, Bartleby! I've got my bountiful bag of baubles for your dungeon. May I come in?" the man asked.

"Florence, it's that man that sold us the cat mech. We should see if he has any more of those," Doug said. Florence could remember how much Doug loved that thing, but she also remembered that this guy never mentioned anything about her losing her memory if that soulbond liquid activated.

"Why, of course, come right in, Bartleby," Florence said.

The man looked confused as he approached. "Florence Valentine, is that you?" he asked as he walked through the front door.

"Yes, it is, and you've got some explaining to do, mister!" she growled. Bartleby started to look a bit concerned as the cats in the living room bristled their fur at him.

"Oh boy," Bartleby mumbled as the front door closed behind him.

Chapter 23

"WELL, THIS IS A PLEASANT SURPRISE. IT'S GOOD TO SEE A SATISFIED customer once again. I wondered where you had run off to. I had heard they said you were destroyed, but I knew you were a lucky purchaser of my soulbond elixir," Bartleby said. The somewhat slimy salesman was not quite able to cover his discomfort over the situation.

"You forgot to tell me a certain little tidbit about that particular product, didn't you?" Florence asked.

"No, did you experience some side effects? There was a rune placed on the vial warning that some side effects could occur. Something that powerful has some risk. Anyone knows this," Bartleby argued.

"Well, you're going to make that up to me, aren't you?" Florence said. The unspoken threat was there, but of course, this guy had walked out of more dangerous dungeons than hers. Still, she wasn't going to let some two-bit huckster pull anything over on her.

"Oh, most assuredly. Bartleby is known for fair dealing. Dungeons and, um, homes all over the world are my customers," Bartleby said.

Florence gave him credit for remembering her home was a home and not some creepy dungeon. "We'll see if that reputation is deserved or not, but before we start talking turkey, I must apologize for not offering you refreshments." She summoned snacks and tea for her guest. It was one of the few things she could do while her dungeon was occupied, and Florence Valentine would not have a guest think that she had shirked in her duties as a hostess, even if it was a guest she was still a little annoyed with.

"Thank you, that is quite thoughtful," Bartleby said.

"You're welcome. Now, do you mean to tell me that you were unaware that the product you sold, the soulbond goop, would erase my memory when it activated?" Florence asked.

"Well, I'll be honest: yes, I knew that. Think about it, though, my dear Florence. If your choices are death or life with some memory loss, most cores are just happy to be back. They don't remember much, but they do buy the product again when I remind them that the elixir is what kept them alive."

"I do suppose you're right, to some extent. Unfortunately for you, I didn't lose my memory."

"Okay, I get it, and I apologize for my somewhat less than forthcoming description of my wonderful product. But how did you survive and come back as, well, you?" Bartleby asked.

"Well, that's enough rehashing of the past. I assume you've got something in that bag that I might be interested in," Florence said, ignoring his question.

"Absolutely, I have everything a dungeon or home could need. From the sands of the Yawning Pit to the depths of the Sea of Teeth, I've collected the very best inventory." Bartleby dug through his bag. Doug perked up, having already crept into the living room to see what was on offer. The little guy just loved shopping, and Florence had taken him everywhere she could back on Earth. He was still a bit put out that he couldn't go into the grocery store, but they didn't allow pets, even if they were core gem assistants.

"How about more of that soulbond goop? Do you have any that

doesn't require me to lose my memory if I get crushed again?" Florence asked.

"Sadly, no. You see, normally, I'd have no qualms about selling a regular old bloodthirsty dungeon a second dose, but I like you, Florence. I'm going to shoot straight with you: the soulbond compound only works once."

"But hey, you just said you sold this to other cores after they had used it once."

"Yes, but only for the cores I didn't care for. There are some rather disreputable dungeons out there, not at all like yourself and your lovely home. If they get destroyed a second time, it's not like they can complain about it, can they?" Bartleby said with a conspiratorial smile plastered on his face. She would have to be on top of her game with this one. All this hullabaloo about liking her was just sales lingo, and he was just as likely to give her a bad deal as he was them other cores.

"At least you're honest about your dishonesty, if that's a thing. What do you have that won't backfire, kill me, or leave a stain on my carpets?"

Bartleby started removing things from his bag, placing them on the coffee table. He even dumped a couple of large crates and a barrel on the floor. The cats sniffed at the items, curious as they usually were. To her horror, Doug jumped onto the table and started batting things onto the floor.

"Doug! Mind your manners," Florence chided.

"Oh, my apologies. I sometimes do that without even realizing it. I forget that most folks don't understand that things always need to be knocked off high places," Doug said.

"No problem at all. We all have our quirks." Bartleby returned the fallen items and pushed them protectively toward the center of the table. "Before we begin, I have a question. Do you still have those lovely doilies in your loot tables? They were quite the hit with my customers." This guy had quite the scheme worked out, buying dungeon reward chests and selling them to normal folks in the cities.

"Yep, that hasn't changed much. We're still just kind of getting started up here, so I can't tell you if there's anything new," Florence said.

"Excellent, just what I was hoping for. Now, for my first offering, I present to you a decorative item. A little something to liven up your home." Bartleby removed the lid on a small box to reveal a gem-encrusted stone. Florence examined the item to see what it did.

Illusory Home Décor Stone: These items are popular among the up-and-coming nobles who haven't quite acquired the means to decorate their estates in the manner they wish. When activated, the stone will project one of several filters over the room, changing the visual appearance of the items inside to fit the particular theme selected. This is illusion magic and subject to dispelling as well as disbelief the longer a person stays inside the affected room. This stone holds the following 3 illusions.

1. Torture Chamber: Transform your room into a horrifying place of pain and suffering.

2. Disorganized Mess: Transform your well-organized chamber into a complete mess with illusory debris piled everywhere.

3. Haunted Chamber: Your room will look the same as always, but something will be a bit off. Haunting noises and faint images of ghostly horrors will randomly appear.

This exciting item is offered today for the low, low price of $25.

"Who'd want that?" Florence said, unimpressed with the first item.

"Usually nobody, but someone in your particular career path may have some use for it. This particular stone was created as a cursed item, the purchaser thinking she was going to transform some simple rooms into something lovely for those she wanted to impress. Instead of impressing them, a rival used this item to embarrass her to no end," Bartleby said, explaining the origin of the stone.

"Shoot, those nobles are as petty as some of them ladies at the seniors center." Florence thought about a pair of ladies in particular who irritated her to no end.

"I believe we could use the third setting on that stone to improve the ambiance of Mortimer's backyard. I should also mention that I disagree with your earlier statement. Matilda and Lulu at the seniors center were lovely people and not petty in the least," Doug said, knowing exactly who she was thinking about.

"Bah, you just like them because they slipped you treats. Okay, Bartleby, I might be interested in this as a novelty item, not something I'll pay good money for," Florence told him.

"Understandable. It isn't a particularly valuable item, so why don't I give this to you, free of charge, as a way of apologizing for my earlier indiscretions?" Bartleby offered.

"That's a fine gesture. Thank you, Bartleby. What else do you have to offer?" Florence asked.

"Ah, this might tickle your fancy more than the illusion stone did," Bartleby said as he pushed another box forward, lifting the lid to reveal a set of small figurines. They reminded Florence of the minis that she had used to play Dungeon Delve. The information on the figures was revealed in her interface.

Minor Figurine of Summoning: These figurines are concentrated one-use summoning spells. Triggered by either a command word or gesture, these figures will activate, and the depicted creature will be summoned to

fight at your side for 30 seconds. The summoned creatures will be somewhat weaker than their normally summoned counterparts, as the process of creating the figurine saps some of their power. This collection includes the following.

1. Orc warrior

2. Orc shaman

3. One-legged ogre

4. One-armed troll

5. Displacer beast

6. Fitzfizzle Zizzlefitz Jones, the gnomish inventor

Start your deadly collection today for only $50 per figure!

"These could be useful. The only problem is that they seem to be, well, shall we say, distressed merchandise," Doug argued. It was true; two of them were even missing parts.

"Who wants to summon some ogre that will just flop around on the floor with a missing leg? I'm not sure I want to buy the rejects, but the orcs seem okay. What's with the weird gnome guy?" Florence asked.

"I understand your concern. The ogre and troll are somewhat impaired but still deadly in the right location. Keep in mind that they are also cheaper, and a true troll or ogre summoning figurine would be quite costly to match their power. As for the gnome, well, I'm not sure. It's a bit unique and was part of a larger batch of these I bought from a school of mages in the Karmark Duchy," Bartleby explained.

Doug looked over and gave her a small nod of approval. She figured he was going to use these items in some trap or whatnot.

"Okay, place them in the 'we might want to buy if the price is right' pile," Florence said, eager to see the next item.

Bartleby walked over to the two large crates and pulled a

crowbar from his inventory to pry off the sides. With a thump that caused the defenders to jump in surprise, the sides of the crates dropped down. Bartleby apologized for the noise and pulled some pet treats from his bag, treats her kitties seemed to like. They normally didn't eat, being sustained entirely by her core energy.

"Hey, what did you feed my babies? They're on a strict diet, you know," Florence said, a bit annoyed. She hated when people tried to slip Doug treats back on Earth. They had no concern for his well-being. Everyone knew that an advisor kitty, just like her defenders, needed to be on a strict diet to stay in top form. Now that she thought about it, Matilda and Lulu probably only fed him because they knew it would get her goat.

"These are completely harmless and in fact can be beneficial for defenders. I keep a good supply on hand to placate the less well-behaved defenders I interact with. Of course, your kitties are perfect ladies and gentlemen." Bartleby handed over a small brown bag of treats for Florence to look at. Tater, Midnight, Bhargath, and Baxter all looked happy with not only the treats but also the compliments.

Binkerlin's Pacification Pieces: These treats can be offered to dungeon defenders to calm them and make them less likely to attack. Please be advised that these treats do not function on defenders you are currently engaged in combat with.

"Fine, don't feed them too many, though. I don't want my babies getting sick all over the carpets," Florence said as she took a good look at the strange contraptions the crates held.

Andy and Skyler, Parakeet Battle Mechs, Level 5: Gnomish inventors combine technology and magic to create these incredible automatons to defend their homes. This duo is a matched pair, and their abilities are enhanced when they fight together. Gnomish battle

mechs are a perfect way to bolster your dungeon's defenses without taking up any of your precious defender expense. This pair of parakeets is on sale today for the deeply discounted, buy-it-now price of $250. If you purchase the pair today, a valuable accessory item will be added, free of charge!

"Oh, these are the same mech type as Kyo. I don't much care for them being giant birds, but they could be useful," Doug offered.

"Yeah, bird people are weirdos, but we might have a use for this pair. Why do they already have names? Who names robot birds Skyler and Andy?" Florence asked.

"You have defenders named Cookie, Bob, Tater, and Spud. I don't think you have grounds to complain regarding gnomish mech nomenclature," Doug chided.

"Oh, and you're so great at picking names," Florence snapped back.

"Sounds like these will go into the purchase category," Bartleby said, tactfully interrupting Florence and Doug's argument.

"Not in the purchase category. We don't have one of those. We only have the 'we'll see what kind of deal we can work out' and the 'no way in hades' categories. What else you got?" Florence asked.

"Just one more item for today. I found your home on my way back from a long trip, so my inventory is a bit more depleted than normal. I should be able to return in a few weeks, though, with a collection crafted specifically for your home." Bartleby gestured toward the large barrel placed to the other side of the sofa.

Barrel of Gnomes: This barrel can be used as a powerful trap or a last-resort defense option. Suspended inside are several gnomes who may or may not attack when they appear. The actual count of gnomes varies, but our new and improved barrel technology guarantees at least 13 gnomes per container. Buy yours today for only $100.

"A bunch of gnomes that may or may not do anything isn't all that exciting. The last one you sold us was at least full of guys with rabies. They stunk at fighting, but they sure did go after them cultists," Florence told him. In her previous home, the barrel of rabid gnomes had done some work, fighting the avatar of Kunrax, but they just weren't very good.

"I agree. This is the last thing I have in stock that matches your home," Bartleby said, realizing that trying to defend this particular product was a lost cause.

"Well, what do you have that doesn't match my home?" Florence wondered if Bartleby was holding back the good stuff.

"Each dungeon, or home, is a unique entity. Some of the things I have in stock would be diametrically opposed to you and seek to destroy you, not help. I generally like to avoid killing my customers," Bartleby told her.

"Sounds good to me. Now, if that's all you got, let's get down to brass tacks." Florence got her game face on. Well, she would have put her game face on if she still had a face.

"Very good. As you know, I'm interested in the minor reward chests. Those offer the best value to my other clients, who do love your doilies. I do have to ask . . . It has nothing to do with our business here today, but it was bugging me. Why are your doilies knit and not crochet? My grandmother used to enjoy crochet so much."

"Why? Because I like to knit, and that lady, Pearl Lamar, who did the crochet class at the seniors center was an old bitty." Florence was still sore over that lady trying to tell her that her stitchwork was horrible.

"Understandable. Back to the business at hand. Here we have an amazing collection of items that are perfect for your home. Individually, these products would be priced at 130 minor reward chests, a great bargain as it stands. Today, for my old friend Florence, I'll give you the entire lot for only 128 chests. A fine deal."

"A fine deal for you, a total rip-off for me. You've got some decent stuff, like the birds, but the figures are mostly damaged, and the barrel is kind of dumb." Florence paused to take stock of her finances. They had been maxed out, but she had been creating cats and decorating, and Doug was still working on traps. The balance was at $598.11, which equated to a maximum of 119 chests, given that they cost her five bucks each. She still had more to do in her home and couldn't spend it all. "I'll give you forty chests for the lot, and that's only because you promised to bring me the good stuff next time."

"Florence, Florence, Florence, I know you were upset over the soulbond misunderstanding, but that's no reason to be insulting with your offer. Given that misunderstanding and in the spirit of friendship, I'll give you an additional discount. I'll sell you the lot for the low price of 120 chests," Bartleby offered. She could tell he was enjoying the back and forth as much as she was, but while her initial offer was low, his was still way too high.

"I appreciate the effort, but why don't we adjust the deal a bit? I don't want the broken figures or the barrel of gnomes. Take those off the table and sell them to some other sucker. If you do that, I can bump my offer up to forty-five chests," Florence countered.

"I can't break up this lot of goods, and to give you the discounts I'm about to propose, I need to get rid of everything. This is a once-in-a-lifetime deal. This entire spectacular array of goods will be offered for the insane price of 110 chests. Even you can admit this is a fine deal."

Florence could see they were going to do a deal; Bartleby had lowered his price to the point that it was almost reasonable. She figured he had a little more give in his price, so she'd try for one final discount.

"You know, Bartleby, I think I'll bump up my offer to ninety chests. That's all I can afford, and if you can't do it, then no hard feelings," Florence said.

"I do believe that we're close to an agreement, Florence. I'll make one more offer. This is it, though. No further negotiation or I have to take my leave. I'll give you the whole lot for one hundred chests, no less."

"Deal. I'll get to making the chests. While I do that, why don't you let Doug here take you on a tour of our home? Maybe that will help you figure out what goodies to try and gouge me on the next time you're in town," Florence agreed, closing the deal.

"A great idea. Lead on, Doug." Bartleby followed the little kitten around and seemed genuinely interested in her home, dutifully offering treats to the cats, but only one each, which was fair. Spud tried to swipe the entire bag, but Bartleby was too quick. Contenting himself with batting Doug around a bit, Spud took his one treat and settled down for a nap in the corner of the attic. Bartleby collected his reward chests, using the strange glove to place them into his Bag of Holding.

"Oh, before I forget, here is your free gift for the purchase of the parakeets." Bartleby pulled another large crate from his magic bag.

"Thank you," Doug said as Bartleby walked away, the man waving as he stepped off the lawn and into the tunnel. Florence hoped he would return soon with something really good. For now, she'd try to figure out what to do with her new purchases.

Chapter 24

Florence felt that she had at least a little time after Bartleby left to finish up what she wanted on her home. Her balance was down to $98.22, which should be enough to summon the last few cats and for Doug to round out things with his traps. The second-floor bath needed another defender. The surprise attack from reanimated undying kitties was good, but it would have less of an impact when the adventurers got a few runs in and knew what to look for. She summoned a new kitty, and as she suspected, this one was just as haggard-looking as Acheron and Styx.

"Doug, do you want to name our newest addition? I thought you had some weird river thing going with their names or something," Florence offered. The new kitty was a skinny gray short-haired one, and even though it looked like it was half starved, the kitty seemed to be enjoying himself while he played with the others.

"Oh, thank you. This one shall be Lethe," Doug proclaimed.

"I suppose that's another one of them rivers?"

"Yes, the river of forgetfulness in the underworld, to be exact," Doug said before going back to work on his traps. It turned out he had done a good job with trapping the walk-in closet. Vala was hiding in there behind the junk stashed on the top shelf. If anyone tried to climb up there, several boxes filled with caltrops would drop down, making any movement on the floor a difficult proposition. In addition, he had placed two traps on the pull-down door leading to the attic.

If someone tried to pull down the ladder, it would descend with overwhelming force, slamming into the unsuspecting adventurers. When it triggered, or if someone tried to climb the ladder, a crossbow trap hidden in a storage box would activate. The room would be confusing and deadly, especially the first time a party tried to clear it.

For the last two traps on this floor, Doug decided to do something in the great room. There was a strong force of five defenders protecting the room, but it was currently just a normal type of battle for the adventurers. He went with a new design, combining two traps into one. Using the venerable crossbow trap, Doug inserted two of the devices into the coffee table situated in the center of the room. From that spot, the entire room would be in range. It would make this one of the more dangerous rooms, but Florence was fine with that. If adventurers wanted to go from the first level to the second level of her home, they were going to be challenged.

Both the first and second floors were now at their defender expense limits, with the third and final floor having $10 left. Florence was going to just make another kitty and call it a day, but Doug was really excited about trying something new there. She let him have his fun, and the little kitten placed traps in two of the coffins lying about the graveyard. If anyone got too close to them, they would lurch forward and snap shut, doing damage and holding their victims in place for a bit. It would probably scare them half to death as well; nobody wanted to get eaten by a coffin while trying to fight a necrocatster.

"Doug, what do you think we should do with the stuff we bought? I was thinking of using the haunted rock thing to make Mortimer's backyard even creepier," Florence said.

"That's a good use for that item. As for the others, I'll rig up the barrel of gnomes as I did before, using one of the kitchen cabinets. In fact, I'll place the figurines there as well. If we're seriously threatened, we can drop them all on the unsuspecting attackers and have quite the swarm of defenders," Doug advised.

"That will work." Florence watched as Doug put the finishing touches on everything. For now, the barrel of gnomes would stay in the core room. Without the goblins and their opposable thumbs, nobody in her home could lift it up. The figurines were small enough that they could be carried up to the counter, but that barrel was a biggen.

"My dear Florence, I think that the home is now complete. We've reached the defender cap on all three floors, and we're as ready as we can be for anything the adventurers can dish out," Doug said with pride.

"I agree. You did some great work on them there traps, Doug. I can't wait to see them in action," Florence said.

"I think we're about to get that chance. Shara and her charges are back."

They watched as the party stepped onto the new starter area for her home. Seeing her welcome center for the first time, the group stood there for a bit, gawking at the gazebo and the fenced-in area with Mo waiting inside. It was then that Florence heard a noise that she most definitely didn't like. It was barking.

"I knew I should have put out a no-dogs-allowed sign." Florence eyeballed the newcomer with Shara's group. It was a young lady dressed in shabby leather armor. She had a dagger belted around her waist and wore bracers with strange sticks shoved into them. The dog itself was a monster, a big old boy with a mean look to him. It hit her then; this newcomer was one of them there Kunrax hound people!

"Is that what I think it is?" Doug asked, his kitten fur

bristling when he realized what type of dog was being brought into their home.

"Hey, you get on out of here. I don't want no followers of that stupid Kunrax dirtying up my home!" Florence shouted out. The party, save for Shara, was stunned that a voice was coming out of big Mo, whom Florence had used as her mouthpiece.

"Woah, a talking cat," Tipp said as they approached the fenced-in kitty.

"All of you, head back out into the tunnel for a moment. Let me explore this on my own," Shara ordered.

"But how are we to learn if you keep what you're doing hidden from us?" asked the girl, Jess.

"I am still your Matron, and you will do as I command!" Shara ordered.

The girl looked like she was going to offer further argument but held her tongue and led the others into the tunnel.

"I should have warned you, this young lady, Isa, is joining the party on a trial basis," Shara said to Florence. "She claims that her god is just misunderstood, but I have my doubts. She is as green as my other charges, so I don't believe she could be a threat to you, even if she wished. I hate to admit it, but I think there is a purpose to her joining up. Can you put aside your justifiable anger and let these young ones attempt to delve into your home?"

Florence was furious at seeing a follower of Kunrax, but she trusted Shara and would agree to her request. "Very well. They can delve, but one wrong move from this Isa and her mutt, and I'm bringing everything I can down on her."

"Thank you. I'm not in the party with them today, so do you think we could visit together while they work on their delve?" Shara asked.

"The fact they're not in a party with you will help them some with the experience drain, but your mere presence inside our home will still hamper their growth a bit," Doug said. He trotted out of the house and into the gazebo, motioning for Shara to join him. She went back and told the party to go ahead, saying she would wait at the gazebo for them to return.

"I have some sandwiches and other snacks for you inside the basket," Florence said.

Shara helped herself to a ham and cheese as the party assaulted the front lawn. Doug had her tell them not to hurt Mo; he was just there for testing the newest of adventurers.

"What happened to the rest of your party?" Florence asked, curious what had become of them.

"On the day you were attacked, the town tried to fight off the invaders and Vanderman gave his life, affording us a chance to escape," Shara said.

Florence could see the time that had passed did little to diminish the woman's pain over losing her friend.

"As for the rest of us," Shara added, "we continued as a party for a while, occasionally adding an additional member when needed. We were quite successful, but one day, Roland just up and left. He said he was done with the adventuring life and wanted something more peaceful. He never kept in touch, so I'm not sure what became of him."

"Well, he was kind of irritating, like most rogues are," Florence interjected.

"Rogues and similar classes can be . . . challenging. As for Ox and Nala, they retired soon after Roland left. His father had passed away, and Ox took over the business. They're married and have had a wonderful life with five children. The two mages in the group, Frex and Chamm, are their grandsons," Shara said, a smile on her face as she remembered her good friends. "I kept on with adventuring, eventually taking over the training of new initiates in my order. But enough about me. Where did you spend all these years?"

"Me and Doug went back to my world until the gem was ready again. Time works weird when you're involved in all these core gem shenanigans. For us, only three years passed before I returned to Aerkon. It took Doug a bit longer to find me, but we're doing just fine now." Florence didn't feel comfortable going into too much detail about Earth. Perhaps it was something to do with being a core, the influence pushing her away from revealing too much.

Florence shared with Shara how the party was doing on their delve. They had made it past the hall and were clearing the bath before trying the sewing room. So far, that dog lady wasn't causing much trouble, other than her filthy pet seemed to have quite the hankering for biting her kitties. She used them sticks on her bracers quite a bit, throwing them down to summon totems that healed or fired off bolts of energy at her babies. Florence hated to admit it, but her class seemed effective.

They hit a snag in the library. Between Zeus and the magic missile traps, they were banged up pretty good, calling it a day just in time; Loki's patrol pattern through the dungeon meant that he would have reached them soon if they'd stayed. As for the loot, they didn't do too bad, with lots of coins and several doilies. They didn't get the rare drop, Tater, but they did get four of the others. A couple of normal weapons also dropped. Shara said they could trade them in at the shop for gear that was appropriate to their classes.

"Thank you, Florence, for a wonderful afternoon. Your home is lovelier than ever. I hope you'll have me over again when these kids run their next delve," Shara said.

"Of course. We're always glad to have you visit. Come by anytime," Florence said.

"I still don't trust that Isa, but other than her presence, they were a nice group," Doug said as the party made their way into the tunnels.

"Yep, I don't trust her, either, but until she does something, we'll let her join them in their delves," Florence said.

A commotion near the tunnel caught their attention. Shara had summoned her armor and weapons, calling upon her power as the party formed up behind her. Florence could feel mana being used as Shara unleashed spells to smite down whatever was attacking them. She had the party back toward the home entrance, which caused Florence to hurry and resummon her missing defenders. Once the party crossed into the welcome center, Florence would be blocked from rebuilding her defenses.

"Disgusting. I despise these arachnid invaders. Shara seems to be doing a number on them, though," Doug said. Florence looked up from her work and could see swarms of them jumbo-sized scorpions flooding out of the tunnel. Shara was giving them what for, her hammer crushing an ugly bug with each swing. The others fought as well, their weapons slamming into any of the scorpions that tried to circle behind Shara.

Unfortunately, the farther she backed away from the tunnel, the wider the area she had to defend. That dumb dog lady threw down another of her totems. This one glowed red and shot off small fire bolts at any bug that got within its range. Another totem went down. This one caused roots and whatnot to grow from the cavern floor and entangle the monsters. Florence had seen something similar when the cultists invaded, but Isa's magic wasn't nearly as powerful. Her dog was happy enough to chomp down on a bug or two, but Isa called him back when a sting left the dog's movements lethargic from the venom.

"This is my last totem," Isa called as she dropped a stick that glowed green and began to heal the party by a small amount every few seconds.

"They're backing off. Do not pursue," Shara called as the bugs fled back into the tunnel.

"What do we do now, Matron? They may be waiting for us in the tunnel and the dungeon is at our backs," said the rogue that Florence thought was named Tipp.

"Head into the dungeon for now. I need to work on something in the gazebo. As long as you don't go past the first area, you should be fine," Shara said, stumbling her way toward the gazebo.

"Shara, are you ill? Did them critters poison you?" Florence asked, concerned for her friend.

"No, it's not poison, just my years catching up to me," Shara answered.

"I've heard of this phenomenon," Doug said. "As an adventurer ages, they still retain the powers of their class but will rapidly lose energy during a fight. Long, drawn-out battles could leave an elderly adventurer on the ground, gasping for breath despite their impressive abilities." It was sad, but Florence kind of figured there had to be some way in this world for folks to get old. Eventually, old folks just got too run-down and it was time to pass on. That was what had happened to her.

"Your companion is correct. In my younger days, I could fight for hours, if necessary. Now my energy runs out quickly. The time I can fight is becoming shorter and shorter each year," Shara admitted, looking a bit sad about the whole thing.

"I know that feeling, dear. It happens to us all," Florence said, trying to comfort her friend.

"These were to be the last of my trainees. I can only hope the light grants me strength enough to see them complete their instruction." Shara finally caught her breath while enjoying a cup of sweet tea that Florence had placed in the basket for her.

"I'm sorry about them critters. The place is lousy with them. Some core got destroyed and it turned a couple of the critters into crazed monsters. I had to kill the spider guy already, but the scorpion one, who I hope is the last of them, has been hiding in the tunnels like a coward."

"Clearing out this scorpion abomination would be a good test of my party if they weren't exhausted from their earlier delve," Shara said.

"I'd pay good money to have them critters exterminated—" Florence started to say, only to have a system prompt pop into her vision. From the shocked expression on Shara's face, it looked like she was seeing something similar.

You have offered a quest to a party of adventurers in your dungeon. They have been tasked with eliminating the source of the scorpion shard creatures that keep assaulting your dungeon. Select a reward level and turn-in location for this quest. Note that your dungeon will be hostile to adventurers even if they are just there to turn in a quest. The cost of the reward will be deducted immediately and returned to your balance if the quest is not completed in the allotted time.

A time limit for this quest will be automatically generated.

Quest Reward Options:

1. Minimum Reward: This reward level generates $25 worth of reward chests. The reward cost is $25.

2. Moderate Reward: This reward level generates $40 worth of reward chests and an item unique to your dungeon. The reward cost is $50.

3. Maximum Reward: This reward level generates $50 worth of reward chests and an item unique to your dungeon for each party member, up to a maximum of 6. The reward cost is $100.

It was a tough choice; her current funds were low after she and

Doug finished up the home and placed the last of the traps. The maximum reward was out, and after selecting the moderate reward, she was left with $18.33. Being a frugal woman, Florence would have rather gone with a minimum reward, but if Shara and her crew could take out the scorpion bug guy, she would have one less thing to worry about. Florence then selected the gazebo as the turn-in location, not wanting to force them to battle through her home just to turn in a quest that was helping her. She confirmed her choices and watched as Shara and the others agreed to the quest.

"This is quite a surprise, Florence. I didn't realize you could do such a thing," Shara said as she accepted the quest.

"I didn't, either, but I guess it's kind of a crazy situation since the bug guys were part of a core gem at one point," Florence replied.

"We'll take our leave and then try to resolve your scorpion problem in the morning," Shara said.

"Thank you, dear. I'll be waiting to hear from you."

Chapter 25

THE PARTY, ALONG WITH SHARA, LEFT, AND GIVEN THE LACK OF noise, Florence figured they had made it back to the tunnel exit without any further problems. She spent some time sprucing things up, putting little decorative details throughout the home. Doug worked on his traps; he wanted to move things around a bit between delves to keep the adventurers on their toes. Florence normally liked these quiet times—it did her good to just sit back and watch her babies—but she couldn't quite enjoy it this time. She didn't feel well. Her gem itched all over and she could feel a pressure that bordered on pain starting to form in her mind.

"My goodness, are you all right, Florence?" Doug asked.

"I don't know, Doug. Can core gems get sick? I . . ." Florence couldn't complete the sentence as the pain intensified. It almost felt as if her gem was cracking, but that wasn't possible, was it? She heard a voice, the sound coming straight from the source of the pain.

"Florence, do not resist me! I command you to let me through," the voice said.

"Shut up, whoever you are. Get out of my head!" Florence shouted in her mind. An image appeared. It was that creepy licking skeleton guy, and she could tell he was trying to use her gem for something. Whatever he was doing to her gem wasn't going to end well for her if she let him. Florence redoubled her efforts, pushing back against the lich with all the stubbornness she could muster. She could feel the lich's anger at her resistance. Every time before, the guy had been creepy but polite enough. This time, there was a desperation in his actions.

"Very well, little core. I'll seek rebirth elsewhere, as my need is urgent this day, but your time will come soon enough. Your gem is my plaything, a part of me, and I will not be denied," that skeleton guy said. He released his hold, and Florence could feel the pain recede, but it didn't completely dissipate.

"Florence, are you well?" Doug asked. The little guy was concerned about her.

"I don't know, Doug. That lich guy just tried to take over my gem. I gave him what for and he left, but he said something about coming back again. What do I do?"

"You fought him off this time. You'll do so again," Doug reassured her. He looked down as if he was embarrassed over what he was about to say. "I'm afraid that I have a bit of a confession to make. This all might be partly my fault."

"What do you mean? How did you have anything to do with that lich guy trying to steal my gem?" Florence asked.

"To save your memories after your gem was shattered, I had to work fast. The collar on my neck that the lich gave me—Berikoz is his name—led me right to him after it activated. He wasn't interested in helping, but he did want to strike a deal. I had no other option, so I agreed on your behalf, and he saved your mind."

"What did you agree to?" Florence would normally be pretty darned mad at Doug, but she was still feeling poorly.

"I agreed to have your gem transformed into a phylactery for the lich. When his body is destroyed, he can re-form it using his phylactery. He told me that there were hundreds of these things stashed around the world and odds were minuscule that he would ever need to use yours. That might be what he was trying to do.

Some adventurers or some creature must have managed to destroy the lich, no mean feat, and he was going to use your gem to restore himself. Your resistance must have pushed him to use a phylactery that was easier to access," Doug said. It was a lot to take in, especially when she was feeling bad.

"You did what you thought was best for me, Doug. I appreciate that. In the future, let's try to not make bargains with liches and the like. I gave old Berikoz a whooping, even if it hurt me as well. He ain't going to come around for my gem anytime soon."

"That may not be entirely accurate. A being like a lich can be hard to predict, but I know one thing about them: they are very proud. You thwarted his efforts, which will likely elicit a response from the creature in order to put you in your place. I'll try to think of something, but I'm not sure what. Perhaps we can ask Bartleby the next time he shows up. A man with his connections might be able to do something for your condition," Doug offered. It wasn't much, but it was a plan. For now, she had to see to her home and the next batch of adventurers that were arriving to try out her challenges.

Florence's beautiful gem was cracked. It wasn't a big crack, just one of them hairline ones that was faint and hard to see. She could see it, though, and not only could she see it, but she could also feel it. It was a throbbing pain that was hard to ignore, but over time, it changed into more of an itchy feel. She didn't like it one bit, but the itching seemed to coincide with the crack getting smaller. Doug told her that a core gem could repair itself over time, so she had that going for her.

Thoughts about the lich were always in the back of her mind as she watched the new party attempt the challenge her home presented. Eventually, the lich would need to be dealt with, but that was a trouble for another time. This new party had six members, and they seemed to be reasonably well equipped. With her body itching something awful while it healed, she couldn't focus on the delve as much as she would have normally liked to. Her babies had done a good job, though, even if she wasn't watching all that attentively.

"The adventurers didn't do too poorly, did they?" Doug said.

"No, they did just fine. Do you think we'll see some more powerful adventurers before long? So far, nobody's been able to even make it to the third floor, and them goblins don't count since they cheated," Florence replied.

"Yes, the ones going through our home will grow in power just like we do. I suspect Shara's trainees will make it to the first-floor champion in a few runs, then to the second floor a few runs after that."

"I hope they can just stay alive. Hey, what's that going on out in the tunnel? No, not again!" Florence said as the party leaving their home fled back toward the lawn. Pursuing them were more of the insect creatures, this time a whole slew of them scorpions along with one that was double the size of the others.

"It appears the neighborhood core shard madman is at it again," Doug said. "Unfortunately, it looks like he's been raising quite the army." The party stopped near the tunnel mouth, their numbers down to only four by this point. Florence wanted to help, but should she try and communicate with the group? Talking to Shara was one thing; talking with even more adventurers was inviting trouble. If they entered her home, Florence would try to do something, but out in the tunnel, her influence was very limited.

The final stand was short but brutal, the group killing a dozen of the scorpion monsters and wounding the biggen before the last adventurer fell to claws and venom. While they had fought, Florence had time to reset her home. Best she could guess, there were around twenty or so of the monsters, not including the bigger one. That one had an odd look in his disgusting bug eyes. It was smart, not just a stupid old bug; that one was plotting and planning. It must have figured that her home was going to be too much for the remaining creeps to handle, ordering the others away.

The scorpions dragged off all the corpses, once again leaving the tunnel floor clear. From the limited view that Florence had outside, darkness was setting in, which meant the delves would stop for the evening. Doug had assured her she could run 24/7 once they leveled up a bit more, but for now, the number of delves each day was somewhat limited. Florence figured that was a good thing; everyone loved a party, but at some point, they wanted the guests to go home.

She would have liked to watch the town more closely, but pushing her view outside the tunnel complex was draining, and with creepy bug things lurking around, she didn't want to keep her focus off her home for too long. Maybe when she finally finished off the scorpion shard, she would have better control over the things around her.

"Florence, look at this. One of the parakeet mechs has an onboard piloting feature!" Doug had been messing with their purchases and seemed especially fascinated with the mechs.

"Hey, what's in the crate that we got for our free bonus gift?" Florence asked, almost forgetting about the mystery gift.

"Oh, that isn't something too helpful, I'm afraid. It's a portable tool kit for gnomes, and we lack both the opposable digits and the gnomish passwords needed to open it. Thankfully the mechs came preassembled and the instructions are pretty good. They are highly configurable, and I just might be able to pilot one once I figure everything out."

"Just don't break them. We can't repair them until Bartleby returns." Florence was a bit worried since Doug had pried open one of them mechs somehow; she thought it was the one called Andy. She could tell Doug wanted to be the one to pilot the mech around like them robot cartoons he liked so much. She could never get into them. Too much yelling, too many bad hairdos, and too much nonsense as far as she was concerned.

"Spud, no! Drop that right this instant!" Doug shouted as the plague charger wandered into the core room, snatched up a pair of the summoning figurines, and ran for the hills, Doug in hot pursuit.

"He just wants to play, Doug. You know that yelling at him only makes him want to hassle you more," Florence said, laughing at her assistant.

"You don't understand. If he bites down on the figures too hard or drops them too far, they will activate. These types of things are not in our control and would likely be hostile to our home. They're for a trap and need to be preserved for an emergency," Doug argued, his little kitten legs not able to keep up with the huge champion.

Spud led Doug on a long chase through the house. Florence had thought the big guy would camp out in his attic, but he was enjoying Doug's whining too much to give up the chase. It was all fun and games until Spud made it to the ladder leading down to the first floor. The big guy let out a hiss and squeal, jumping back when the figures glowed with light and began to grow as they tumbled down the stairs.

A pair of screams were heard as the figures summoned their live counterparts. A roar of anger and pain competed against a high-pitched shriek of terror. Spud had apparently grabbed the one-legged ogre and Fitzfizzle Zizzlefitz Jones, the gnomish inventor. The gnome continued his terrified screech as he rolled down the last stair, his rotund body continuing to roll until he stopped inside the master bedroom, face to face with an equally surprised Chubbs.

Back in the stairwell, the ogre was a-hollering up a storm. It turned out the one-legged figurine wasn't sporting some old healed-up battle wound. Nope, this guy had a freshly severed, ragged stump that was spurting blood all over the place. He was all riled up with pain and anger, hurling the club that had materialized in his hand. The weapon flew over and smacked poor Spud right on the noggin.

Now Spud was a big boy, but this here ogre was a good nine feet tall, and his head would have brushed the roof of her home if he hadn't fallen over because of the whole one leg thing. Wasting no time, Spud summoned his Gabsug rider and charged down the stairs toward his attacker. If the ogre had been fully capable, Spud's charge wouldn't have stood a chance, but all that blood loss must have made the ogre a bit loopy. The slow swipe he made at the charging plague mount missed, allowing Spud to tear into the ogre while the rider buried his lance deep in the ogre's chest.

It turned out that ogres were kind of stubborn, and that biggen refused to die, his lumbering hands grabbing ahold of Spud as his charge crashed home. Her big boy gave a screech and hiss, but the ogre ignored the champion's oversized claws and squeezed harder. Florence couldn't watch, turning her attention away as her baby's hiss ended with a meaty crunch. The ogre didn't last much longer. He finally bled out all over the bottom of the stairwell, the gore running into the master bedroom and staining her carpets.

"No, stay back. Where am I?" the gnome stammered out, letting loose with another high-pitched girly shriek while he backed away from the pair of first-floor champions. He was dressed in strange clothes and was unarmed as far as Florence could tell. It struck her then; these weren't normal summoned creatures. The ogre didn't just disappear when he died, and her home had reprocessed the body, not to mention she had gotten a good chunk of money from his death.

"Hold up there, Zork and Chubbs. This'n might not be a threat. Hey you, gnome guy, what were you doing inside that figurine?" Florence asked. The champions backed away, keeping an eye on the gnome as Florence waited to see what the gnome would say.

"Who's there? I don't want to fight. Don't let these lions eat me!" the gnome shouted in terror. The cats seemed to puff up with pride; being mistaken for a lion must have been pretty flattering to them.

"They aren't going to eat you unless I tell them to. Now, answer my question. How in tarnation did you get inside that figurine?" Florence asked.

"Well, as long as you keep them from eating me, I'll try to answer your questions. Where are you? Who are you?" the gnome asked, looking around. He could hear Florence but couldn't see her.

"You first, buster. Who are you and why were you in that figurine?"

"If I might add," Doug interjected. He had sauntered over to the stairwell, and the appearance of a talking cat seemed to confuse the gnome guy even more. "It appears you are not some summoned creature and were, in fact, trapped. Perhaps we should start with the last thing you remember." The little guy was actually being helpful.

"Oh yeah, sure, umm . . ." the gnome started to say. He took a deep breath, gathered his thoughts, and continued, speaking rapidly. "I was working, or trying to, when some of the guards nabbed me. They took me to a cell, and then the last thing I remember was an elf with glowing hands chanting words of power that made me feel sleepy. Next thing I know, I drop onto the floor with a bloody ogre howling and these rather overgrown cats looking like they want to have Mrs. Jones's youngest son as a snack."

"Hmm, you neglected to mention why the guards were there to interrupt your work. What exactly is your trade?" Doug asked. He was a-doing just fine, so Florence let her advisor continue the interrogation. Who would have thought all those police shows the kitten watched would come in handy?

"It wasn't something criminal or anything like that. I was captured against my will and was just trying to find a way back home," the gnome said.

"Who captured you, where did they capture you from, and why?" Doug asked.

"Well, I never met which one of the wizards captured me personally, but as from where, I was on my ship when they took me. As for why? I think I just got caught up in some nonsense magical experiment. I overheard they were disappointed they found me instead of what they were looking for, and, well, you see the results." The gnome was becoming more comfortable now that it appeared he wouldn't be eaten just yet.

"So you broke free and were messing around in a wizard's workshop to find a way home?" Doug asked.

"Yep, pretty much. I'm a tinkerer and figured if I had enough time in that workshop, even if it was a wizard's workshop and not a proper gnomish one, I'd figure some way out of wherever it was they had me," the gnome replied.

"Enough with the questions, Doug. This guy isn't going to cause us any trouble, are you?" Florence asked.

"Uh, no, ma'am. I just want to . . . Well, I'm not sure what I want to do, but I know I don't want to be a prisoner and I'm absolutely sure I don't want to be eaten by giant cats."

"Well, this is my home, and unless you do something to deserve it, my defenders will leave you alone," Florence said. "You're free to go. There's a town starting up nearby, but you might want to wait for the next party of adventurers to escort you since the tunnel outside my home is lousy with giant scorpions."

"That's an unexpected relief. Thank you. Who exactly are you, ma'am, if you don't mind my asking?" the gnome asked.

"My name is Florence Valentine, and this is my home. Now, before you ask, yes, this home is a bit different than most since I am a core gem. You're welcome to stay as long as you need, so long as you don't get into any trouble. Doug, show him around and let him eat his fill from the picnic basket in the gazebo. But first, have him run outside the home for a minute so I can bring Spud back."

"Excellent, pleased to meet you, Florence Valentine. I'm Fitzfizzle Zizzlefitz Jones, at your service. So your home is like a dungeon, then? I've never been inside one before. The whole idea of adventuring kind of struck me as a completely foolish and deadly way to try and make a living. Nope, give me a well-stocked workshop and I'm completely content to sell a few gadgets and gizmos to pay my way in this world," Fitzfizzle Zizzlefitz Jones said.

"First off, buster, this is a home, not a dungeon. Second, do you have something like a nickname or whatnot? I'm sorry, but your name is kind of a mouthful." Florence didn't get mad at the slight of him calling her home a dungeon; the gnome didn't know any better, and he seemed like a good enough sort now that he wasn't shrieking like a little girl.

"My apologies. I won't make that mistake again. My friends used to call me Fizz, so that will work. I'm not saying you have to be my friend, but I'd like our interactions to remain on a cordial and not on a cat-eating-me basis. So now that we got that out of the way, there was mention of something to eat? Being trapped by an evil wizard in a magic figurine has a way of making you kind of hungry."

"Fizz is fine, and yes, we'll work on a friendly basis here. So long as you don't cause any trouble, you won't get eaten up by my babies. Doug, take Fizz here on a tour and let him eat his fill," Florence said.

"Well, Mr. Fizz, you say you're a tinkerer," Doug said. "Tell me, how much do you know about gnomish parakeet battle mechs?"

The two were chatting up a storm as Doug led the gnome around on the tour. It did her heart good to see Doug make a friend. It also meant he would be out of her hair for a while, something she wholeheartedly approved of.

Chapter 26

"Jess, did your run go well? Greetings, Matron," Junior asked as Shara led the party into the shop, his eyes locked onto the berserker and only noticing Shara at the last moment.

"Yes, Ben, we did pretty well overall. I think we all gained a level this time, and the loot wasn't horrible," Jess replied, using the man's real name rather than his nickname.

"You two work out our purchases. I'm going to enjoy a hot meal and an ale." Shara made her way over to the tavern portion of the business. It was time to loosen the reins on her charges. Not to mention, even she could see that Junior had a crush on Jess, and she seemed to be pretty taken by the shopkeeper as well.

Shara didn't need any gear, but the others in the party would. This scorpion shard seemed like a tough challenge. At least it was one that she felt perfectly fine in joining. Delving a low-level dungeon would greatly dilute their experience, and possibly their loot, but creatures outside a dungeon didn't operate by the same rules the system imposed on dungeons. If they contributed to the battle, everyone would receive a decent experience reward. The ratio of individual experience would be skewed a bit to give the higher-level party members a greater share, but the system was much less punishing outside a dungeon.

They had all leveled up on the last run, a good thing to see. It would give them some confidence and reassure them that their hard work would generate results. Training in the keep had its limits, and once the party had reached level 2, training could no longer be used as a means to gain experience. The training still served a purpose, however; experience points and levels weren't the only important thing for an adventurer. Learning to fight smart, knowing your enemy, and working as a team could be the difference between life and death.

For their first two levels, Shara had guided them on abilities and the choices they should make based on their class options. Now they were on their own. The importance of choosing a solid foundation had been taught to them, but if they chose foolishly at this point, it was on their head. As a group, they had worked well together, but Shara was still not happy with the healer, Isa. It was clear that the light had some hand in guiding her to the group, but was that for a purpose other than helping the party? It wasn't something she could figure out at this moment, so she chose instead to focus on the hearty bowl of stew that had just been delivered to her table.

"Matron, would you like me to place us into the queue again?" Jess asked.

"What do you think?" Shara replied. There wasn't any heat or criticism in her tone; she just wanted Jess to think things through without relying on her mentor for everything.

"No, we should wait until we return from our quest. The dungeon quest is unusual and should take priority," Jess answered.

"Exactly, not to mention it would be poor form to return to the dungeon without having at least attempted its quest," Shara added. Jess nodded and ran off to finish her shopping.

Knowing the party had limited funds, despite a successful run, Shara called over the server. She gave her a pouch of coin and instructions to head into the store and purchase whatever antivenom or poison antidote potions Junior had for sale. Scorpion venom was no joke, and she had doubts about whether the party would think of spending their limited funds on expensive potions to counter the venom. A few minutes later, her purse was sufficiently lightened, and another small pouch with six antivenom potions was now safely waiting in her pack.

She would like to go immediately to wipe out the scorpion nest, refusing the creatures a chance to replenish their numbers. Sadly, her body was all done in for the day, and without a good night's rest, she would be useless, and she had a bad feeling they would need her power before the quest was completed. The party returned to join her in a hearty meal, showing off their new purchases. It wasn't much, but each new piece of equipment was a small victory for an adventurer. Shara found herself caught up in the excitement, remembering her first runs into Florence's home and the rewards her friends had found inside. Shara thought a lot about her old friends as the party returned to their tents and tried to rest before starting their quest to destroy the scorpion creatures.

**

"Does everyone have their gear ready?" Jess asked the group. Shara would have liked her to be more assertive, but she was doing what she should do to verify the group was ready.

"Yes, let's get moving," Tipp whined. Jess shot him a harsh glance and then verified everyone had what they needed. It turned out the party didn't have enough coin to purchase any of the pricey antivenom potions, so all they had were the ones Shara had bought, but they did purchase some bandages that were enhanced with magic to help them shrug off the effects. Bandages like these were a poor substitute for a potion; they worked slowly and didn't completely remove the venom from your system.

"Each of you, take one of these. Keep it handy. These scorpions have potent venom." Shara passed out a potion to each party member. She didn't keep one for herself; she was immune to such things, a trait her class had granted her at higher levels.

They made their way toward the tunnel, waving off a tense moment when another group thought they were trying to cut in line. After Shara explained about the scorpions and the threat they represented, the other group gladly waved them on. She equipped her armor and hammer. The weapon gave off enough light for them to see by, but Frex also conjured a globe of light that would follow the party, providing a backup source and not requiring anyone to hold a torch instead of a weapon or shield in one hand.

While the main tunnel passage led toward Florence's home, there were several side passages and large openings, any one of which could harbor a hostile creature. Most ended in a dead end or tightened up enough that the dog-sized scorpions couldn't fit through. One passage, though, was larger than the others, and when they followed it, they found more than enough evidence to locate the nest they were seeking. Bits of clothing, armor, discarded weapons, and ominous bloodstains were found here and there.

"Look out!" Tipp shouted. One of the daggers in the halfling's hand flashed as he threw it at a scorpion they had all missed. The monster bug was hanging from the tunnel ceiling, hidden among the shadows created by the passage's rough-hewn surface. The dagger flew true and sunk into the scorpion's armored carapace even as Jess, the monster's intended target, leaped to the side. With a clattering sound, the scorpion missed its target, righting itself before trying to continue its attack. Chamm was ready, conjuring shards of sharp ice that pelted the monster, slowing and damaging it. Jess finished off her attacker with a slash of one of her axes.

"Eyes out. These things can attack from any direction," Shara advised. She was ready to fight, but given her limited endurance, her power would best be unleashed on a target the party couldn't handle. Random individual scorpions should pose them little risk.

The tunnel opened up into a larger cavern complex. Unexpectedly, the cavern then opened up into a huge chamber, the center of which was dominated by rubble and the remains of collapsed buildings.

"Matron, you said that the shard of a dungeon core may be responsible for these creatures?" Frex asked. She had told them as much as she could about the threat they faced without giving away Florence's secrets.

"Yes, that was the information I received," Shara replied.

"Perhaps this is where it once laired. These collapsed walls and piles of rubble are not ancient. This happened not that long ago," Frex offered. The young mage was right; this could have been some old dungeon that collapsed in upon itself when the core that held it together was destroyed.

Movement among the rubble caught Shara's attention. "I believe you're right, Frex. Not just because of the ruins, but also because of what is lurking in them," she replied, drawing the party's attention to the swarm of scorpions that were charging out of their hiding places.

"They're all around us. Frex and Chamm, thin them out. Tipp, stay with the group," Jess ordered, taking control of her party.

Blasts of fire and ice hit the approaching horde as the twin mages went to work. Their area-of-effect spells weren't powerful enough to destroy the creatures, but the damage slowed them and made it easier for follow-up attacks to prove fatal. Shara placed herself near the thickest concentration of scorpions, hammer ready even as she activated an armor-enhancing ability, strengthening the protections on the party around her.

Tipp threw a pair of daggers, dropping two of the attackers, while Isa tossed down one of her totems. Shara could feel the power inside the magical device activate as it pierced the ground. A swath of ground around the totem erupted in a cluster of grasping vines, tying up several of the attacking scorpions, at least for as long as the magic held out.

Jess laid into the horde, her axes a blur as she activated her class ability and lost herself in the red haze of a berserker. It made her more powerful than a simple warrior, but the longer she stayed in that state, the more she would have trouble telling friend from foe. Shara was proud of the team she had trained; they were working well together, and other than a few swings of her hammer, they needed little additional support.

In less than a minute, a dozen of the creatures were shattered and bleeding out on the ground. A similar number had retreated into the rubble, chased by blasts of magic from the fire and ice mages. There was no quarter against creatures such as these, no honorable warrior code to follow, and killing them while they fled was better than fighting them again later.

"I think around ten escaped. Do you think we killed enough of them to satisfy the quest?" Tipp helped the others check the corpses littering the ground, making sure they were truly dead and recovering the knives he had thrown. Shara would have liked to see him develop a better ranged attack skill, but the halfling was fond of his daggers.

"There is something here that is creating these monsters. We need to destroy the source if you want to earn your quest rewards," Shara advised.

They pushed on, deeper into the ruins, finishing off two more scorpions that hadn't picked the best of hiding places. Jess led them toward the center of the rubble, where the cause of this trouble likely resided. The scorpions made several attacks as they progressed, but the monsters were coming two or three at a time. Her charges didn't escape unscathed; Tipp and Isa's dog both took bad wounds from the monsters' powerful claws, and one of the scorpions was able to sting Chamm. The mage wasn't doing all that hot but waved off Shara's attempt to give him one of their limited antivenom potions. An enhanced bandage was keeping the venom from overpowering him, and given enough time, the adventurer would shake off any ill effects.

"Oh, this doesn't look ominous or anything," Tipp said as they discovered a stairwell leading down into the dark. Carvings of monstrous insects covered the areas around the doorway where the passage of countless scorpions had brushed back the dirt.

The diminutive rogue disappeared as he used a class ability to hide. Hiding in the shadows might not be all that effective against monstrous creatures like the scorpions, but the darkness was comforting to adventurers with Tipp's particular skill set. Shara's hammer and the light globe hovering over Frex illuminated the passage. They entered what must have once been the champion room of the dungeon. As the party entered the large chamber, scuttling noises came from the stairwell behind them.

"Isa and Chamm, cover the stairwell," Jess ordered. The rest of them approached the only other way out of this room: a partially collapsed stone door that led into a dark chamber where the core room would normally be located. A huge claw appeared from the dark, closing around the door and ripping the remains out of the way. Then, finally, the creature responsible for all of this appeared.

"So the food comes to me, for once. Thank you. I'll need a good meal if I'm going to create enough pets to take care of the other core," an otherworldly voice said as the new monstrosity showed itself. Shara heard combat behind her but didn't turn to watch. Chamm and Isa should have no trouble holding back the remaining scorpions trying to assault them from the rear. The staircase made a natural chokepoint that was easily defended. Shara would be needed here, against this new abomination.

Standing nearly seven feet tall was an amalgamation of half man, half scorpion. A human torso was melded to a scorpion's body. One scrawny human arm hung lifeless from the torso, and the other arm was replaced with an oversized claw. The human head's normal features made it even more disturbing than if the creature had held the visage of a monster. A scorpion tail swayed over the monster, waiting for the right time to strike.

"This foe is mine. The rest of you, handle the smaller scorpions," Shara ordered. She couldn't sense the power of the dungeon-core-turned-monster, but she could tell it was beyond the ability of the rest of the party.

"Old woman, you will be tough and stringy, but that will not matter. My venom will tenderize your flesh," the monster said as it scuttled toward her. It was then that Shara noticed it was drooling, the spittle cutting a trail through the gore of previous victims that stained its mouth and chin.

"Begone, abomination! I have slain more powerful creatures than you." Shara answered its charge with one of her own. A new aura surrounded her as she activated one of her paladin abilities. The claw tried to grasp her even as the stinger-tipped tail shot forward. Claw and stinger skidded off her protective barrier, unable to penetrate or find any purchase. In response, Shara charged her hammer with power and slammed it down on the overextended claw, shattering the carapace and pulping the sickly flesh beneath.

"No, make the pain stop. No, we know the pain only stops when we eat. Eat the old woman first, then the more succulent young ones," the mad creature muttered to itself. The glow covering Shara faded. Her age made itself felt even in the short time she had been fighting; the energy required to keep the powerful barrier up was draining her mana more quickly than she could sustain it. She needed to end this now, before her elderly body betrayed her.

The stinger was fast, but her plate armor was not only thick but also enhanced with numerous enchantments to defend against just such a strike. Greenish-yellow venom sizzled on the surface of the armor, but the sting did not penetrate. A second swing of the hammer slammed into the tail even as it jabbed over and over again in an attempt to find some weak point in her defense. A horrible squeal burst from the monster as the destroyed tail dropped to the ground with a wet slap.

"I end your suffering. May you find the light in the next world." Shara brought her hammer down for the third and final time. The weapon crushed the monster's head, ending its foul existence. The sounds of combat faded behind her. Shara turned to see the stairwell full of dead and dying scorpions. When the master controlling them died, so did they. Shara had seriously underestimated their total number. She figured her party had faced off against six or seven, but there must be nearly fifty of those things wedged in the stairwell.

"This is just gross, but I'm glad all of them didn't try to ambush us outside," Tipp said.

"Yes, it must have taken time for them to gather, or for some reason, that poor creature didn't want them to interfere in his kill," Shara offered. She couldn't shake the feeling that at some level, the monster secretly wanted her to end its existence.

"I'm going to have nightmares of that thing for a while, I think." Isa fed her antivenom potion to the dog, Gnaw. From where he was slumped over, the beast must have held back the bulk of the attacking scorpions.

"If you choose the life of an adventurer, the odds are that you will see even worse things than that abomination," Shara advised.

"Too bad it doesn't have pockets. Let me check out its lair," Tipp said, skirting past the monster as he went on his way to the now-vacant core room. Shara followed him in, curious to see what was there. Engravings of various bug-like monsters adorned the walls, and tiny bits of red gemstone littered the floor. The room was cold and quiet; the last vestiges of the will that had once run this dungeon were now gone.

"Nothing, not a single copper for all this effort," Tipp said with frustration.

"Uh, Tipp, you might have some treasure out here, if you want to grab it," Jess said.

Shara followed the rogue out of the core room, only to find Jess poking at the ruined head of the monster. There, inside the pile of gore, was a faintly glowing stone. Tipp poked it with his dagger, unwilling to touch it.

"Gather that up. It will prove we have completed our quest," Shara ordered. Pulling an old rag from his pack, Tipp used it to pull the gem from the carnage. With a sickening pop, the gem came free. The rogue wrapped it in the cloth so he didn't have to touch it with his bare hand.

"Now, let's go get our reward," Tipp said with a dopey grin plastered on his face.

Chapter 27

"DOUG, QUIT YER TINKERING AND GET OUT TO THE GAZEBO. IT LOOKS like Shara and them kids are back," Florence called out as she spotted the party nearing her home. Doug and that gnome had been getting along like a house on fire, messing with them stupid bird robots. The gnome, Fizz, had been ecstatic when Doug showed him the parakeet contraptions. The two talked about the things after finishing a quick tour and the contents of two picnic baskets worth of food. For such a little feller, that gnome could sure put away the vittles.

"Okay, dungeon thing, here's what you wanted us to do," the dopey halfling rogue said, dropping a slime-covered rag onto the table of her pristine gazebo.

"Show respect, Tipp. This is more than a dungeon, as you can see. It's a home," Shara chided. "Unwrap your prize and see if we have done what the core has asked of us."

The rogue didn't look too pleased about touching the goop-covered rag, but he followed her instructions and a sliver of a core gem clinked down onto the table. A system prompt appeared in Florence's view as four minor reward chests appeared on the table, as well as a velvet-covered object. They looked like they were going to gather their loot and leave, but Florence really wanted to see what she had unknowingly created for them.

Quest complete. The previously designated rewards have been generated.

"Hold, adventurers. You may reveal your rewards here without threat. Please enjoy the spoils of your efforts." Doug leaped up onto the gazebo bench from where he had been hiding.

"It's a talking kitten this time. It's adorable," Isa said as her hound growled at Doug.

"I am no mere kitten. Nae, I am the Great and Mighty Doug, caretaker and advisor to this home. You may now receive your gifts." Doug laid it on thick, enjoying the attention.

"Thank you, Doug, for your generous rewards. Tipp, go for it. I know you're itching to do the honors," Shara said.

"I'll save the best for last." Tipp carefully moved the wrapped item as he started on the reward chests. They held pretty much what Florence expected: a few coins, a doily. One even had a minor healing potion in it. The party didn't seem that disappointed and were eagerly waiting for Tipp to reveal the wrapped item. He finally got around to it, pulling away the rather luxurious velvet to reveal a stout-looking dagger with an elaborately engraved handle. The blade's length was nearly that of a shortsword, and Florence could see the faint glow of enchantment. Pulling it up in her interface, she reviewed what her home had created to reward these kids.

The Claw of Doug: This dagger was infused with the power of a dungeon, giving it enhanced damage and accuracy. Once per day, the wielder can activate an ability that creates a magical cat's claw. This claw can be targeted with a range of up to 20 feet and deals the same damage as a normal strike.

"Very nice. Thank you, Doug!" Tipp said, laying claim to the weapon, much to the displeasure of the other party members.

"Hold on. We'll discuss the distribution of our gains at a later time. For now, we need to rest, and you need to get back into the queue to explore this excellent home again," Shara said, ushering her charges out of Florence's home. Tipp reached out to pat Doug on the head, which he tolerated, probably only because he was still pretty full of himself.

"They were rather pleased with our rewards, weren't they?" Doug said.

"Oh, you're just all puffed up because the little knife was named after you," Florence said.

"Jealousy is not becoming of you, my dear Florence. Now, what do you intend to do with that shard? It's larger than the one that was inside the spider-shard madman we defeated earlier. I daresay this one might offer you some insight into its destruction, much like the shard you purchased from Bartleby during your first stint as a core gem."

"Let me take a gander at this thingy," Florence said, ignoring Doug's comment about her being jealous; everyone knew Florence Valentine was a woman not given to jealousy. As her influence touched the core gem shard, it was absorbed by her home, and Florence was drawn in, just like the last time she had tried this.

"Observe my final moments, and avoid my mistakes," the shard said to her as her point of view changed to that of the now-deceased core. Florence could see a modest-sized dungeon with two floors. It was a vermin-themed core with various creepy bug things: rats, cockroaches, and whatnot. Who would want that to be their home?

"A foolish deal. My greed for more power was my undoing," the voice said.

"Hey, hold up there, bug guy. Who are you? It's rude to start talking to a lady without introducing yourself," Florence chided. The voice didn't respond. Some of these other cores were so rude.

Florence watched as a half orc entered the dungeon, obliterating any defenders with a simple wave of his hand. Eventually, the orc made his way to the core room, and when he spoke, the voice that came out of him was familiar.

"Dungeon core, I could easily destroy you, but instead, I offer you power if you will agree to my terms," the orc said.

"Hey, that's that licking skeleton guy, Berikoz!" Florence shouted. The core shard didn't respond, and she was beginning to get the feeling that this one was much more degraded than the other she had consumed.

"What do you offer?" the core asked. Florence couldn't see the details of their deal, but she got the feeling the core was very pleased with what it had gotten. Time sped forward, and the dungeon grew another floor almost immediately. Whatever the lich's gift had been, it enabled the core to grow quickly.

"And now, view my destruction," the core said. Florence watched what she understood to be something that happened not that long ago. The gem pulsed and hairline cracks appeared all over it. With a flash of red light, the gem shattered, and standing right there in the core room was Berikoz. The lich left without a word, and before their connection was lost, Florence could feel pain and madness overtake the destroyed core as it desperately tried to cling to some semblance of life.

"Woah, Nellie. That's what that durned lich was trying to do to me, wasn't it?" Florence asked. Doug could observe some of what she experienced, and she really needed his advice now.

"Yes, it does appear so, and this makes finding a way to avoid this fate even more important. It is unusual, though. A lich is powerful and difficult to defeat in battle, but this Berikoz has been dispatched several times recently. Something more is at work here," Doug advised.

"Thanks, Doug. We'll have to hope that old Bartleby can give us a hand with this. Of course, I won't go down without a fight, and if that lich thinks he can just shatter Florence Valentine's core, he'd better think again," she said with a confidence she didn't necessarily feel. The last encounter with the lich had very nearly done her in, and she didn't think it would get any easier the second time he tried to use her core.

"Um, hey, yeah, sorry to bother you, great and mighty core, but may I ask you a boon?" Fizz schlepped his way into the core room, still looking a bit spooked.

"What? Yeah, what do you want? Oh, I'm sorry. Totally forgot about you there. I know I promised to send you out with an adventuring party, but the deadly critters out there are gone, and you shouldn't have any trouble leaving under your own power," Florence replied.

"Oh, no, I wasn't wanting to leave. I was wanting to stay. That's what I wanted to talk to you about. Me and my clan were always getting pushed around by the big folk. Here, I can experiment without any trouble, and I'd have a whole dungeon—er, I mean home—full of kitties to defend my labors."

"What's that? Don't you want to return to your people? I know my home is a beautiful place to be, but what kind of gnome wants to skulk about here by himself?" Florence asked.

"That's the other part of my question. You see, when you purchased me, you also purchased most of my clan. I can tell they're here, somewhere. Do you have more figurines stashed away somewhere? If you can free them, we'll make stuff to improve your defenses," Fizz offered.

"Well, I don't have any other gnome figures, just a one-armed troll, a couple of orcs, and a displacer beast," Florence said.

"They're here, in your home, somewhere. Gnomes can tell when their gnomies are near. Our connection to the clan is strong."

"Gnomies? Really?" Doug said with annoyance. "You know, there may be one place we haven't looked. Follow me." The kitten assistant led the gnome to the corner of the core room, and there, hidden behind the sofa, was the barrel of gnomes he had meant to rig up as a trap at some point.

"This is it! My gnomies are inside. Let them out, please!" Fizz pleaded.

"Fine, whatever, just stop your squawking. Me and Doug don't have opposable thumbs, so you're going to have to do the honors yourself." Florence didn't really care about the barrel of gnomes; the one she had used before had been something of a disappointment, and they had rabies. These ones were plumb normal types that probably weren't too good in a fight.

"Thank you. Let me see . . . The right tool for the job. Ah, here we go." Fizz ran over to the gnomish toolbox, which was left near the partially disassembled battle parakeets still cluttering up her core room. Fizz had chosen a huge hammer and started whacking at the side of the barrel. After about three hits, the seal broke, and the barrel started a-hissing real good. With a pop, the top flew off and a horde of little gnomes spilled out onto her floor. Florence was mortified when a couple of them lost their lunch after tumbling out.

"At least we didn't try using that as a trap against an actual foe, though they might have died laughing at the ridiculousness of our feeble attempts at creating a trap," Doug said as the raucous bunch all started shouting questions at once. Fizz took some time to get them in order. He even had to slap a couple that were wandering too close to her core for comfort. She didn't know any of these little guys running around, but she didn't feel they meant to be a threat. If one had gotten burned up by her protective shield, it would have been bad.

"Everyone, be quiet!" Fizz shouted, finally getting the attention of the baker's dozen of gnomes that had emerged from the barrel. "We were all nabbed from our ship, and this here nice lady Florence Valentine has been kind enough to free us. Before you ask, yes, this is a dungeon, and no, the defenders are not going to eat you unless you attack them first. I should also warn you that you must call this place a home, not a dungeon. Miss Florence has gone through a lot of trouble to make the place look nice, so mind your manners."

"Who died and gave you the red hat of command?" asked one of the gnomes, a rather surly-looking fellow.

"What's a red hat of command?" Florence asked, and the gnomes gasped in surprise at her ignorance.

"I believe it is their symbol of leadership," Doug replied.

"What does the hat look like?" Florence asked.

"Do you remember the label on those baked goods you overindulged in? The mascot was mislabeled an elf, but in reality, they were more akin to the gnomes of this world. The conical hats they wore are similar to a hat of command," Doug advised.

"Thanks. I always did think those little critters on the package looked nothing like an elf. For the record, I did not overindulge in cookies. I merely ate one or two after dinner as a treat." Florence pushed out a few coins to create her own version of a red hat of command, complete with a rearing cat on the front. The hat materialized next to her rocking chair, to the surprise of the assembled gnomes.

"Sure, just a few cookies," Doug said sarcastically.

"Hush, Doug. I'm working," Florence said.

"You were working back then as well—working on finishing off a whole pack of cookies every few days," Doug mumbled under his breath. Florence chose to ignore him. She had better things to do than deal with her petty advisor.

"There you go, Fizz. You were the first one here, so I'm giving you the hat." Florence offered him the hat she had created. The hat was a lovely creation, trimmed in white, with the image of a cat sewn into the design.

"Hey, it doesn't work that way. We need to decide, and there are protocols we need to follow," the surly gnome interjected.

"Listen here, mister. Do not try to tell me what to do in my own home. While you're in here, you'll mind your manners and speak politely to me. I make the rules here, and don't you forget it," Florence said sternly, summoning Mortimer down to intimidate the lot.

That surly fellow uncrossed his arms and backed away as her champion gave him a dirty look and summoned dark necromantic energy. "No disrespect meant, ma'am. I'm just a traditionalist, but it's your home, your rules."

"Go on, Fizz, put on your durned hat and either get on your way or agree to become part of the home. I'll have no freeloaders running around the place."

"Can you give me a minute?" Fizz asked.

"Sure, but move this gaggle over to the kitchen. It's too crowded in my core room for this. When you're ready to talk, just speak up. I can hear you anywhere in my home."

While they meandered through her home, Florence set out a spread on the kitchen table. She was polite enough not to listen in as the group started babbling but given the *oohs* and *ahhs* from them as they made their way through the various rooms to get to the kitchen, they were impressed. Of course, they should be impressed; her home was rated A+ by the adventurers guild, after all.

"Doug, do you think we should let this many hang out in our home?" Florence asked.

"Absolutely, they can be an enormous help as our allies. We still have the Home for Unwanted Goblins that remains vacant. If you clean it up, I'm sure they can set up living quarters and a workshop inside," Doug said.

"That might work. I'll get the place up to code while they blabber on. At least these ones seem smart enough not to make a mess of things in there like the goblins did."

"I believe we would like to stay, Miss Florence, so long as we can work out something that we'll both be happy with," Fizz said.

A small clan of gnomes has offered to join your dungeon. Do you wish to enter into negotiations with the Fizz Clan: Y/N?

"Hey, look at that, Doug. They got a system name and everything now," Florence said, hitting the *yes* prompt.

"It seems these are far enough from their original clan to warrant being a separate entity," Doug replied.

You have entered into negotiations. Here is the Fizz Clan's first offer.

1. The clan gains the protection of the dungeon.

2. The clan will make items and inventions to benefit the dungeon. Raw materials for these items and their personal experiments will be provided by the dungeon.

3. Accommodations made to the clan's specifications will be provided by the dungeon free of charge or obligation, with the option to expand if necessary.

"Doug, do your thing," Florence said. He had handled their negotiations with the goblins back in the day, and while she loved to haggle now and again, she had to admit that Doug was a bit better at doing it on this world. Now, if they were at a car dealer, she'd take charge and give that salesman a good thrashing, but for gnomes, she'd let Doug take the lead.

"Ah, my good gnomes, I'm sure your initial offer was just an accidental miscalculation. We won't hold it against you for such an insulting offer. I'm sure it was made in good faith," Doug said as he crafted his counteroffer. Mortimer gave a low growl to emphasize Doug's point.

Your counteroffer has been sent.

1. The Fizz Clan joins the core as an ally and is required

to defend it in times of need. A time of need is determined by the core or her advisor, not the clan.

2. The core is not obligated to provide material support save for the most basic of materials. The quantity, quality, and timing of material support are to be determined by the core or her assistant. Foodstuffs will be provided, and the type and quantity will be determined by the clan.

3. The core will protect the clan to the best of her ability. The extent and nature of this protection are determined by the core and her advisor, not the clan.

4. At the request of the core, the clan is required to venture from the dungeon to perform simple acts on behalf of the core. The core cannot make more than 1 such request per week, and a request can only be made if the clan has a reasonable chance of success in the requested endeavor. Additional requests per week may be made by the core, but the clan may accept or reject those requests without consequence.

Florence watched as the gnomes huddled together and discussed the counteroffer. She noted that unlike their deal with the goblins, Doug hadn't placed a time limit on their deliberations. If it turned out that gnomes spent hours discussing stuff, she wasn't going to be so happy with Doug. The last thing she wanted to do was wait around for the little guys to come to a decision.

The Fizz Clan has accepted your offer. Gnomes are not compatible with any of your current affinity types, and their link to your core will be limited.

"Welcome aboard, Fizz. Doug will show you where you'll be staying. Tell him how you want the place set up and I'll take care of it," Florence said.

Just like with the goblins, the link to her core was minimal with the gnomes. She suspected the link would keep them fed but was willing to give them other food if needed. Of course, she couldn't respawn them, either, so they would have to be careful, and she couldn't count on them rebuilding their numbers in the same disgusting manner the goblins had. Another problem she had was with keeping them equipped and having enough materials for use in their workshop.

Florence's defender limit was maxed out, and she would need to free some up to supply the gnomes. The only place not being used that much was the garage. It held four traps and a treasure chest. Eliminating them would free up $20 of her defender expense. Florence would need to seal off the room since it would be vacant, but with $20 of defender expense, she could create upgraded weapons and armor racks, as well as work something out to provide resources for the gnomes.

Doug had worked with her back on Earth to fine-tune some of the ancillary things that could be constructed in her home. A resource generator was a way for a core to create something to attract adventurers, like an herb or mining node. Sure, those could be found at times when she expanded, but they could also be created at the price of eating up some of her precious defender expense, something she normally wouldn't think of doing.

1. Improved Weapons Rack: This rack will hold an array of weapons appropriate to your inhabitants' preference. A single rack can provide weapons for up to 50 inhabitants. The gear will be appropriate to their level and scales up to a maximum of level 10.

2. Improved Armor Rack: This rack holds an array of armor types appropriate to your inhabitants' preference. A single rack can provide weapons for up to 50 inhabitants. The gear will be appropriate to their level and scales up to a maximum of level 10.

3. Resource Node, Variable: This resource node can produce up to 1 cubic foot of material each day for your inhabitants to use in their endeavors. The more valuable or rare the material requested, the less of it the node will produce.

The resource node was the toughest to make and the most expensive at $10 of defender expense. Upgrades to the node could be made, but the expense started to skyrocket at anything better than the one she had built. Even though it said one cubic foot of material, fancy stuff like gems or gold might eat up that whole limit to only produce a tiny fragment per day. Simple stuff like iron or leather could be produced easier.

She had gone with the improved version of the weapons and armor racks for her gnome residents. They took up $5 of defender expense each and only provided gear for fifty people, but the gnomes would likely need better gear than the goblins, and there weren't all that many of them, so she felt better having them well equipped. The initial cost to construct all three of the upgrades wasn't cheap and would eat up most of her remaining cash reserve. As an added benefit, Doug seemed to like hanging out with the gnomes, which meant he would annoy her less than he usually did.

Chapter 28

"Wow, they just got right to it, didn't they?" Florence told Doug. The kitten advisor had finally tired of his amateur tinkering and was back for a nap on the rocking chair cushion.

"Yes, gnomes are quite industrious, and I have to admit I enjoy it myself. They are intrigued with Skyler and Andy. Fizz said he was implementing some improvements, but he wanted to keep the final results a surprise."

Florence had spent some time tweaking their new home, even expanding it a bit to give each gnome their own personal space. Despite the workshop smack dab in the middle of their home, the gnomes were fastidious about keeping the place clean, much to Florence's delight.

"I'd be happy if all they do is repair the robot birds," Florence said. "I hate buying them only to use them once. That Surly even seems to have made friends with Spud." She hadn't bothered to learn the other gnomes' names, with all their fizz and fazz nonsense, so she just gave them all nicknames.

"I try not to bother myself with Spud. I pity the gnome that befriends that yob," Doug said with disdain.

"If you had been nicer to him, maybe he would have been nicer to you. As long as those two are playing together, I'm happy." It did Florence's heart good to see old Spud make a new friend; he had been down in the dumps ever since she brought him back.

He missed his old goblin friend Gabsug, but Surly seemed to not even mind the smell around the big plague charger kitty. He even jumped up for a ride now and again. Whereas the other gnomes liked to work together, Surly had created a makeshift workshop for himself in Spud's attic.

The gnomes would take some time to wander the home and even play with the kitties. Florence did have to warn a few not to put their feet up on the sofa, but other than that, they were perfect houseguests so far. Her home was coming along nicely, and other than maybe doing a few decorative changes, she really didn't have much more to do until she leveled up again. The activity had improved her experience a good bit from the last time she had checked, but she had a long way to go before hitting level 8.

Florence Valentine
Cat core, level 7
Experience: 4485/8500
Funds: $22.18/$700
Defender Expense:
First Floor: level range 1–3 ($400/$400)
Second Floor: level range 3–5 ($300/$300)
Third Floor: level range 6–7 ($150/$150)

With them core shard bug people gone, Florence was able to finally push her influence toward the outside without restriction. She worked on reshaping the entrance to the tunnel into something that had more curb appeal than a dumb crack in the side of the mountain. It wasn't her home proper out there, but she did want to welcome folks. She carved out the opening so the adventurers wouldn't be so crowded. A wooden frame painted white like her home surrounded the plain stone tunnel entry, giving it a homey feel.

Florence also placed a couple of flower beds just outside the entrance, giving the dull browns of this area a pop of happy color. She also wanted to advise people that this was the right path but that this here tunnel entrance wasn't the start of her home. The answer was to create a street sign, one arrow pointing toward the growing town and one toward the tunnel. Florence didn't know if the town had a name, so she just labeled it *Town*. The other arrow into the tunnel entrance was larger and painted with what she hoped was a fair warning. If some other monsters crawled out from the depths of the tunnels and ate up some adventurers, she didn't want her home being blamed for their deaths.

This way to the Valentine residence. The owners of the residence aren't responsible for encounters you may have on the way to their home, so use caution when traveling inside the tunnels.

Beware of Doug.

She had to throw that last little bit in there; Doug loved it. Florence also put a couple of other signs inside the tunnel, pointing the adventurers toward her home and away from dark side passages where who knew what lurked inside. The signs were more taxing than creating things inside her home since she only had influence and the area wasn't a direct part of her home yet.

A loud explosion distracted Florence from her work. The entire first floor shook, causing the cats to all run around crazy. It didn't take a genius to realize the source of the explosion; it was the gnomes. Their room was filled with smoke, and it took her home a few moments to clear it out. Expecting to find bits and pieces of gnomes scattered about, Florence instead found the lot of them crouching behind a large steel barrier and looking at a black spot on the far wall.

"What in tarnation are you doing to my home?" Florence shouted, annoyed that her previously well-behaved guests were becoming a nuisance.

"Oh, sorry for the noise. It's just an experiment. We wanted to see how some of our new blast powder did against a core-reinforced wall," Fizz said. The other gnomes looked down at the ground like a bunch of kids caught doing something they shouldn't have been.

"Why would you want to do a fool thing like that?" Florence asked.

"For science!" Fizz proclaimed.

"Whatever, you keep it down in there. Just look how upset all my kitties are," Florence ordered, looking at her babies.

"My apologies. Come on, lads. We'll need to cancel the second blast. Team One can work on weapons and armor. Team Two can work on the mechs, and Team Three can get started on internal defense," Fizz ordered to the other gnomes.

Having nipped that explosive nonsense in the bud, Florence looked over her kitties, letting them know everything was okay and they weren't about to be blasted to smithereens. Or at least she hoped not.

Movement at the entrance to the tunnel drew her attention. A pair of humans were riding horses toward her home; mounts were something the low-level adventurers she was used to seeing couldn't afford. The morning sun glinted off the armor that one of them wore, and as they drew closer, Florence could see they had a determined and confident look about them. Another adventuring group was just preparing to enter when the newcomers waved them off. Florence expected an argument to break out, but the party just nodded in agreement and walked back toward town.

"Doug, what do you make of this pair? They just cut in front of the other group and the adventurers didn't seem to have a problem with it."

"Oh no, I fear these are more guild representatives," Doug said.

"Durn it, we just got rid of them bugs that were killing everyone. Why couldn't they show up in a few weeks when our kill death ratio had a chance to improve?"

"I don't know. They are likely powerful adventurers, but at least it doesn't appear to be a kill team," Doug advised.

"So do we just stand down? Or do I have to defend myself?" Florence asked.

"Stand down, at least for now. If they declare your termination at the entrance, then all bets are off."

The two humans chatted among themselves, confused by her new sign. Unfortunately, her view outside the tunnel was just that: a view. She had no way to listen in on what they were discussing. One man was dressed in robes, and the other wore full armor. The quality of their gear was high, but it wasn't quite up to the level of that other pair of guild folks that had first visited. While the other pair had arrived to give Florence the much-deserved A+ rating, these two didn't seem to be here for the same purpose. The pair made their way into the tunnel, making note of the signs along the way, and eventually showed up on her front lawn.

"Dungeon, we are representatives of the adventurers guild," the guy in the robes called out. "An unacceptable kill ratio has been reported at this location and we will investigate its cause. Stand down your defenses and do not interfere in our investigation. Any attempts to disrupt our work will be met with deadly force."

Now that they were close, Florence could take a better gander at them. Like she had noted outside, the pair were well equipped and likely way over the level of the average adventurers that delved in her home, but she didn't think they were as all-powerful as Doug had feared. If push came to shove, her kitties would have a good chance at swarming the pair, especially if Florence dropped her summons on top of them at the same time.

"Florence, do as they say and mind your tongue," Doug advised. "They appear to be investigators, but I have no doubt a kill team is on speed dial if something were to happen to them or if they deem us a true threat." Florence did as he said, setting her home to neutral as they watched the investigators work.

"This dungeon is as odd as the initial report indicated. Look at this sign and the caged defender," the man in armor said.

"Aye, and the warnings are something I haven't seen before. It's not what I would expect an out-of-control dungeon to create, but they can at times be cunning enough to try and lure adventurers into a false sense of safety," the guy in the robes replied.

Like the initial assessment team had done, these two wrote down notes about the defenders, defenses, and any unusual features of her home. They made several comments on the décor, which had them confused. Of course, they were probably just stunned to see such a wonderful design; she doubted any of them other dungeons were anywhere near as nice as her home. They passed the hallway, and then Florence realized they would be able to see the Fizz Clan's room, even though it wasn't active. These guys could see through anything a dungeon tried to use to hide a room.

"Hey, Fizz, we got some visitors that will likely barge in. They're a pair of adventurers guild representatives, so don't give them any trouble," Florence said.

"Okay, not a problem as long as they aren't here to steal our designs," Fizz said. Florence assured them the investigators weren't there for any corporate espionage, calming the gnomes down before the guild folks arrived.

"These are not defenders, but I can see a faint bond with the gnomes. Inhabitants, I would surmise," the man in robes speculated.

"Yep, Fitzfizzle Zizzlefitz Jones, at your service, gentlemen. My clan recently relocated here to safely work on our projects without any outside interference," Fizz said.

"Yes, I can see your connection is recent, so any control the dungeon has over you would be minimal. Might I ask you a few questions?" Robes asked. Since these two weren't offering up their names, Florence decided to call them Robes and Armor.

"Go right ahead, though I should warn you that Florence doesn't like her home being called a dungeon. I mean, just look at the place," Fizz replied.

"The dungeon's preferences are not our concern for this visit. The high mortality rate of adventurers that venture inside is. Have you observed any of the delves that have proceeded through the dungeon?" Robes asked. Florence didn't like the tone of his voice one bit. He was way too snooty and condescending for someone that was a guest.

"I can't speak to that," Fizz said. "We've only been here a short time, and most of that time was spent working on projects. What I can tell you is we were trapped by a mage, and Florence not only set us free but offered us a place to stay."

"What do you mean?" Robes inquired.

"We were there, you see, sailing across the sea to a gig making automatic lighting fixtures for the Zebulaw Collective when our ship hit a magic field. There was lots of shouting, explosions, and magic spells going off, and somehow during the ruckus, a spell hit me and my fellows here. I was turned into a figurine of summoning, and they were all shoved in a magic barrel."

"Yeah, and even though it was a magic stasis field holding us in, we could still smell, and having thirteen of us in that small space made for some unpleasant odors, I'll have you know. If you folks want to go around investigating, why don't you investigate who did this to us?" Surly argued.

"Your abduction is not guild business. A dungeon that is far more deadly than it should be is. Back to the question at hand. Have any of you noticed any aberrant behavior on the part of this dungeon core? Have you noticed anything that would lead you to believe it is acting irrationally?" Robes asked.

"Other than the fact the place is lousy with cats? No. Florence has been good to us," Surly answered, the rest of the clan shaking their heads in agreement.

"Fine, your cooperation has been noted. If the destruction of the dungeon becomes necessary, your clan will be offered safe passage, provided you do not participate in any resistance," Robes advised.

"Just leave Florence alone," Fizz said. "She's a kind person. Any other dungeon would have either killed us for the mana or imprisoned us to work for them, but she offered to let us go and was even willing to let the next adventuring party guard us when we left to keep the beasts in the tunnel away."

"Beasts in the tunnels? We saw nothing threatening out there. What do you mean?" Robes asked.

"I don't know the details. You'll have to ask Florence and Doug about it," Fizz offered.

"Very well. I think we'll have a conversation about that shortly," Robes said. The pair left the Fizz Clan's home. The investigation that would determine if Florence lived or died continued without interruption.

The pair finished their examination of the first floor, noting every tiny detail for their report. The second floor went faster; there were fewer rooms, after all. A brief spot of trouble happened when they entered the attic. Spud was behaving, but it wasn't like he could entirely turn off the stink that surrounded him. Now, Florence couldn't smell anything in her core gem body, but she could see the greenish haze that filled the attic.

The two almost attacked but realized that the debuff from the stench aura was a passive ability, noting that the simple floor champion could not toggle the aura off. In the backyard, they stopped to examine Mortimer for a while, noting the undead affinity her home had picked up. Florence was kind of embarrassed about it, but it seemed the affinity was a good thing, making her home appear a bit more normal to the guild reps. Finishing up with Mortimer, the pair descended to her core room; it was time for her and Doug to face the music.

Chapter 29

"CORE GEM, I KNOW YOU CAN HEAR AND SPEAK WITH US. I REQUIRE that you do so now. Tell me, without any subterfuge, how it is possible so many adventurers have met their demise inside your dungeon," Robes demanded.

"Okay, mister, two things. First, my name is Florence Valentine. I'm a lady and expect to be addressed as such. Second, this is a home, not some creepy dungeon," Florence said forcefully. Doug moved behind her rocking chair, covering his head with his paws. The scaredy-cat didn't want her to speak out, but Florence Valentine was not going to abide folks barging into her home uninvited and trying to order her around without so much as a "how do you do?"

"You are not the ones to make demands. The guild is here to investigate and render judgment. Now, answer the question as to why so many adventurers died inside your dungeon," Robes said, reiterating his demands.

"Your poor mother, she must be mortified to have a son that treats an elderly woman so poorly. Fine, I'll answer your question if it'll get you to leave. Some folks died inside my home, but did I go on some murder spree? No sirree. My home is dangerous, but the folks that died inside it knew the risks they were taking. I know you saw the signs on your way in. I gave every loving one of them the chance to back out before they got in over their heads, but the ones that pushed too far, or just ran into a spot of bad luck, well, that's the life of an adventurer, isn't it?"

"You are correct that dangers can be expected, and that reflects in the expected mortality rate. Your *home* has a rate of nearly one hundred percent. How can you explain that?" Robes demanded.

"That weren't my fault at all. Nope, your adventurers guild is to blame for that," Florence argued.

"What? How are we responsible for you killing everyone that comes into your dungeon?" Armor spouted out.

"I'll tell you how. It's because you weren't doing your job. Do you know what killed those folks? It weren't me. It was a completely bonkers core gem that did it. Some other core was residing here, or somewhere nearby, and it shattered, causing core shard creatures to start roaming around the tunnels, killing everything and trying to eat up my core as well," Florence told them.

"Another core in this area? Dinlam, check the records," Robes said. "A core shard creature, you say. I doubt it, but we'll know shortly. Even if that was the case, the deaths happened in your area of influence."

"Sir, there were reports of a core in this area years ago, but the dungeon went inactive. Here are the details," said the armored guy, Dinlam.

Robes grabbed the magical scroll with the information on it, reading before starting his interrogation again. "If this core shard did as you say, you would know what type of dungeon it was. What types of creatures attacked you?"

"Critters. You know, spiders and scorpions. I wanted to call them bugs, but Doug reminded me that those are arthropods," Florence replied.

"Hmm, that could be accurate. It was a B– vermin core dungeon. That doesn't put you in the clear. The deaths occurred inside your area of influence, and I find it hard to believe these core shards would remain inactive for so long," Robes argued.

"Not to mention this core is trying to place the blame on our esteemed organization," Dinlam interjected.

"Fine, that bit about you being at fault may not be entirely true. It's more the lich's fault than yours, but you shouldn't let him go around victimizing core gems. You'd think that an organization as *esteemed* as yours would want to protect your livelihood," Florence said.

"Now you're blaming a lich for your actions?" Dinlam said incredulously.

"Yeah, Berikoz. That jerk even tried to take over my gem, but I ran him off. He's using us for phylacteries," Florence advised.

"I know that name, Randman—I mean sir. Many of our guild-affiliated high-level adventuring parties have been offered an outrageous sum by the Kingdom of Fintok to destroy that monster. The information should be in the register. It was noted since many of the high-level dungeons have had few visitors, as most parties are tracking down that fiend," Dinlam said with a shocked look on his face as he pointed out the entry in their magic scroll to Randman, the guy she had been calling Robes. Florence wished she could get a peek at the durned thing, but it was protected from her view by magic of some sort.

"Interesting, this undead fiend has found a way to thwart even high-level parties," Randman said to himself. "Normally, there are several magical means to keep the monster from its phylactery, but if that phylactery was masked by the magic inherent in a core gem, he just might be able to avoid destruction."

"That is only conjecture, and it still doesn't answer why nobody has seen or been attacked by these core shard creatures since it was destroyed," Dinlam said.

"Something tells me this wasn't exactly a highly populated

vacation spot, so it's no wonder folks wouldn't have been around for the creatures to attack," Florence interjected. "I should also mention that, purely without my input or consent, I just might have accidentally entered into a pact with this Berikoz character. Maybe that connection woke the critters up. They sure seemed keen on eating my core, I'll have you know."

"That could be it, but it is very unlikely," Randman argued.

"Unlikely, sir, but these core shard creatures aren't entirely unheard of, and if they did populate the tunnels, like this core suggests, their latent energy may have masked where the adventurers had fallen," Dinlam offered. "We see they fell in a dungeon, but we never considered there could be something else giving off dungeon mana. Our assumption that this dungeon was responsible may be inaccurate."

"Well, some of them adventurers did die in here," Florence told the investigators. "A few were just durned fools and got themselves killed through their stupidity, but them core shard critters liked to wait for the parties to leave, when they were out of resources and vulnerable. A few groups were chased back inside my home before they were killed by the shard monsters. I tried to help, but there was only so much I could do."

"I think we'll take some time to investigate further," Randman said. "For now, we'll allow your core to function as it has been. If this whole unlikely chain of events did occur, the mortality rate inside this place should drop precipitously. In the meantime, I'll investigate this lich Berikoz further. If he is truly involved in using core gems to further his own ends, that could be a threat to our entire organization."

"That's mighty kind of you. I'm sorry if I said some unhospitable words earlier. I didn't realize you were going to give me a fair shake," Florence said.

"Make no mistake, core. I will get to the truth, and if what you have told us is false, I will personally sign the kill team order. We have a group standing by, just for that purpose. Good day to you," Randman said, then turned and led his flunky Dinlam out of the core room.

"Doug, I think that went about as good as we could have hoped for," Florence said.

"Don't get too comfortable. They may still decide to end you just to make sure they've covered all their bases. I should have never entered into an agreement with Berikoz. I'm sorry, Florence," Doug said.

"I told you there was no need to apologize for that. You did what you had to do, and I appreciate you saving me. Now, that doesn't mean I'm going to put up with your nonsense, but I will always be grateful."

"Thank you for that. I believe I will help the gnomes work on the battle parakeets. They've just finished up rebuilding Skyler so that I can pilot it. Imagine that: a fierce warrior kitty using a bird mech to wreak havoc on our foes."

"Ha, a kitten in a chicken. Not exactly fear-inspiring, but I guess it does keep you out of trouble, so have at it," Florence told Doug. She suspected that he and Fizz would become fast friends, just like Spud and Surly had become. In fact, Surly was back in the attic, trying to attach some mechanical contraption to the back of Spud, who seemed to barely tolerate the gnome's efforts.

Florence had hope as she watched the adventurers guild investigators walking across the front lawn of her home. Her position was precarious, but the guild might just be the key to getting rid of Berikoz and his hold over her core. With the power and resources at their disposal, a way to prevent the core gems from being used as phylacteries shouldn't be too much trouble.

"I sense something. Beware!" Randman shouted. Glowing magic started to gather around his person as Dinlam stopped to draw his sword, looking around for the danger that Randman was warning him of.

"You fools! I told you not to get too close. Kill them both. They spotted us," a voice called out from the gazebo. As Florence watched, three humans materialized on the lawn, halberds thrusting toward Randman. A magic shield around the investigator flashed as the weapons struck, deflecting the attack with the screech of nails on a chalkboard.

Two arrows thudded into Dinlam. One shaft hit his unarmored neck while the other shattered against his breastplate. Small bursts of flame peppered the pair as a man in shabby robes appeared behind them, magical flames pouring from his hands. Randman cast the spell he had prepared, and a wave of energy flowed across the lawn and the welcome center. No fewer than thirty opponents materialized, a scruffy lot that wasted no time in pressing their attacks.

"Doug, get out of that bird suit and look at the front lawn!" Florence shouted, trying to figure out if she should do something to help but not wanting to unleash her kitties only to have the investigators think she was part of the attack.

The wave of energy revealed two rogues that had been hidden just behind Dinlam. Quick despite his armor, the investigator thrust his blade deep into the chest of one rogue; his target's leather armor did little to stop the enchanted blade. The second rogue rolled past the investigator, dodging his second attack and slashing a curved dagger across the back of Dinlam's knee, causing him to stumble.

Randman fired off a burst of magic missiles, the bolts of magic slamming into the trio of halberdiers assailing him. The attack dropped all three, but not before the second thrust of their halberds shattered Randman's magical shield. Archers around the gazebo poured arrow fire into the guild mage while the rest of the attackers closed in.

While not as powerful as the other pair of guild representatives that had first visited them, the pair battling for their lives on the front lawn were skilled. Unfortunately for them, skill didn't look like it would overcome the sheer number of attackers that were currently engaging them. That was when she recognized one of the attackers, the mage. He was dressed not in the typical robes with a staff or wand. No, this joker was wearing common peasant garb and had only a simple dagger belted to his waist.

Scanning the others, Florence picked out the two she expected to see. Durg, the orc in heavy plate, was charging across the lawn toward Randman, his spike-covered shield ready to impale the guild investigator. The man with the gravelly voice, Kam, was over by the gazebo, barking out orders even as he drew the two scimitars on his belt and jogged over to join the fight.

A ball of flame left Randman's hand, aimed at the charging orc. The blast hit, flames exploding outward, but the orc just shrugged it off. Activating an ability, the orc instantly leaped to his target, spiked shield leading the way. Spikes skittered off some new layer of protective magic, but a heave from the powerful orc broke through Randman's defenses, and sharp spikes dug deep into the guild mage's body.

Randman raised a glowing hand, ready to smite the orc, but before he could release the power he had gathered, the orc's axe swept down. With its blade glowing red, the axe clove through Randman's hand, drawing a shriek of pain from the mage. The sound was cut off when a second axe blow slammed deep into his chest, permanently silencing him. Only Dinlam remained, and it didn't look too good for him.

A half dozen attackers had gathered around the beleaguered guild warrior, his blade lashing out to intercept the incoming weapons. Dinlam was continuously peppered by arrows. A blast of green goo hit him in the face, and the acid spell partially blinded him. Kam reached the fight, his twin swords a blur of motion as he laid into Dinlam. The guild warrior deflected the first two strikes, but being partially blinded by the acid spell, he missed the next pair of attacks. One scimitar slashed into the warrior's leg, nearly severing the limb, while the second blade raked across his throat. The guild investigator, choking on his own blood, dropped to the ground under a rain of blows from the swarm of attackers around him.

"Doug, we might have some more problems here," Florence warned. "It's the rest of them creeps that brought me here, and it looks like they've brought a whole passel of friends with them."

Chapter 30

"WHAT DID YOU DO TO IRRITATE THESE HOOLIGANS ENOUGH TO MAKE them come back after you?" Doug asked.

"I don't know. They were creeps, but I couldn't even talk to them when I was being carried here. That lich guy had some geas on them that prevented them from hurting me during the trip, but that obviously wore off," Florence replied.

"That might be the reason. The geas wore off and now they are under no restriction. Killing even a low-level core would net them quite the experience reward. There is also a lucrative market for shard fragments since alchemists use them for several high-level elixirs. Of course, killing a core would result in a price on their heads from the adventurers guild, which probably led to them killing the investigators. These aren't the type to leave witnesses to report their actions."

"They probably thought I was some newbie level 1 or 2 core gem. Well, they're about to find out that our home and its defenders are quite a bit better than that," Florence said.

"True, they were counting on the invisibility magic to bring them right to your core room without a problem. The good news is that an invisibility spell powerful enough to cover the mob out there likely drained a good chunk of mana from their wizard. I assume he's the poorly dressed fellow that was hurling spells," Doug said.

"Yep, his name's Harmon. The guy with the two swords is Kam, and the ugly orc in the heavy armor is Durg. They're dangerous, but so am I. Okay, our home is now hostile. Let's get our kitties into the fight," Florence said, trying to get an accurate count of their opponents while the defenders went to work.

Obi and Shadow were already stalking their prey. Both had remained hidden in the tall grass during the investigation and hadn't been spotted by the invisible invaders lurking around the lawn. They knew Mo was there, but he was inside his pen. They must have thought he was stuck in there, since a pair of poorly equipped hooligans approached with little concern, taking their time in loading their crossbows.

Mo leaped over the top of the short fence, his pounce landing on one of the approaching invaders. The man screamed in terror and dropped his crossbow as the defender tore into him with core-enhanced claws and teeth. Seeing their target wasn't as helpless as they thought, the other guy with the crossbow went into overdrive. He tried to arm the weapon as quickly as he could, fumbling to load a bolt as Mo finished off his first victim and turned toward his second course.

"Florence, it looks like there are thirty-three of the common hooligans in addition to the three nefarious adventurers you're already acquainted with," Doug said.

She was focused on Mo's fight, but upon closer inspection, it did appear that most of the other invaders were wearing little to no armor. They did, however, have decent weapons. It was like the trio of adventurers had hired as many goons as they could on the cheap. That was fine with Florence—better these creeps than a well-equipped army. The three adventurers would be a problem, but her home should be able to strip away the chaff fairly easily.

"Make that thirty-two. Mo got his first kill and is starting in on the other one," Florence said. Other invaders were rushing to the aid of the pair that had been sent to kill Mo, but it looked like her baby was getting some good licks in on the second fellow with a crossbow. He had loaded his weapon in time, shooting the poor kitty, but Mo shrugged it off and ignored the pain as he tried to defeat at least one more invader before bleeding out.

Arrows sprouted from Mo's hide as four archers armed with short bows fired from near the gazebo. Her kitty was only level 1, and the attack was just too much for him. He did good, though, killing one enemy and wounding another. Obi and Shadow used Mo's distraction to launch their attacks, each surprising an invader and easily dispatching them with their commando stealth attacks. Once out of stealth, her poor kitties fell prey to the same archers that had done in Mo. The front lawn and welcome center were a wide-open area, with only some tall grass for her defenders to hide in; it was perfect for archers. Once inside the home proper, the archers would be much less effective.

That guy Kam seemed to be in charge, and after making sure the defenders were all cleared out, he organized the invaders to breach the front door. One of them wandered too close to the mailbox, activating the trap inside. A crossbow bolt wounded but didn't kill him. Another, this one dressed and armed more like a rogue, ran toward the mailbox, presumably to disarm it, but instead triggered Doug's new pit trap. The man landed on several spikes, screaming in pain and unable to lever himself off the wooden stakes piercing his back and legs.

"Fools! Watch where you're stepping," Kam said. "This should have been an easy in and out, but somebody decided to get too close to that pair of adventurers leaving the dungeon. Now we got to fight our way through this whole place, and anyone doing dumb things from here on out can forget about their cut." The man had activated some ability that instantly teleported him to the mailbox, which was just about to finish reloading. A few swipes of his scimitars disabled the trap, and another slash ended the cries of the man trapped in the pit.

"Well, I suppose killing your employees is one way to avoid paying them," Doug said.

"Yeah, these other fellers should do the smart thing and run on out of here while they can," Florence said.

"I doubt that anyone has ever accused this bunch of being smart. Dangerous, yes, but not smart," Doug added.

They watched as the survivors re-formed into a semblance of a formation. The other wounded defenders weren't killed and instead worked to place bandages on their wounds. Though enhanced with magic, the bandages were a poor substitute for healing magic. Any of these creeps that she was able to injure would be much less effective. This Kam guy must have tried to do this on the cheap, hiring poorly equipped thugs and not wanting the expense and trouble of finding a healer to join them.

As the invaders readied themselves to enter the home proper, Florence finally got a good chance to see what faced her. In addition to the three adventurers, there were a dozen of the thugs armed with shortswords and bucklers. Looking like rogues, six of the attackers wielded only long daggers, and all four archers were still around. Near the front door, five more attackers held halberds. Florence knew that halberds could be very effective at holding a narrow entryway, but they were cumbersome in close combat. The wounded attackers waited near the rear of the formation, in pain and trying their best to hold onto their weapons. Kam would no doubt end them as soon as they ceased to be useful.

"Here they come," Doug said as the pikemen burst through the door and charged into the two cats waiting for them. Baxter and Tater stood their ground but couldn't get past the reach of the pikes, the weapons tearing and chopping into them. As the pikes pushed into the room, the archers followed, firing arrow after arrow into Florence's poor kitties. This was their first time inside Florence's home, and the fact that they didn't check the ledge above the door told her that these clowns hadn't shelled out the few coppers needed to buy a guide from the merchant.

Bhargath lived up to his name, rending the foes as he leaped down upon the archers from the perch above the door. Midnight joined in as well, jumping farther and hitting the back of one of the pikemen. It was too late for poor Tater and Buddy, but the other two were on a roll. Both had dispatched their first opponent and were going to town on the next target. Unfortunately, Durg was following behind the initial attack. The huge orc hewed down Bhargath with his axe and then slammed the spiked shield into Midnight. Her babies had done their job, though, reducing the enemy's number by four.

The foe decided to assign their wounded to the task of gathering loot. It was a smart choice; they were the least able to try and make a run for it, and if they didn't give up the loot after the battle, they would be easily overpowered. What they didn't count on was Doug's fireplace trap. Florence had placed a small reward chest inside, knowing the lure of loot would be too much for these clowns to resist. The guy wounded by the crossbow bolt reached in to grab the chest, only to eat a face full of fire. His body blocked the blast from doing more damage, but it was another kill, and the enemy had a long way to go before they could reach her core room.

The hallway was next, and this time a half dozen swordsmen led the way, with Durg behind them and the rest of the gaggle waiting in the living room for their turn to move forward. Buddy wasted no time, dashing out from a side panel to slash the back leg of one of the lead swordsmen. When the man turned to face the threat, Princess flew out of a higher-placed panel. Her claws opened up a horrible wound on the back of the man's neck. The swordsman dropped to the ground, moaning in pain, as the other looked for the threat in every direction.

"Back out, you fools. I'll take care of this," Harmon ordered. The mage leaned into the hallway, casting a quick pair of spells. Green energy formed on the ground, and the glow resolved into a pair of large snakes. The beasts wasted no time, slithering into the nearest panels as they hunted Florence's babies.

"Hey, that's not fair," Florence complained.

"Fair or not, it does seem effective," Doug said. Her kitties seemed shocked to see the snakes slithering in behind them. The pair of level 1 kitties were soon overpowered by the snakes, whose levels would match that of their summoner. Wrapping several coils around the kitties, the snakes dragged them out of the panels and into the hallway even as they crushed her poor babies to death.

"Loot the kills and get in the back of the formation," Kam ordered to the fallen swordsman, who was fumbling to place bandages over his wounds. The man knew he was dead meat if he didn't comply and pushed through the pain, reaching out to grab the reward both her babies had left behind. A faint rattling was heard in the panels as he moved forward. The two snakes assumed it was more victims and slithered into the noisy panels to chase after their prey. This time, it wasn't prey, but instead, it was Doug's trap. Two spears shot out. They pierced through the snakes' thin bodies and drove deep into the wounded man behind them, killing him and despawning the summoned snakes.

"Yes, just as I planned. It's a powerful and devious set of traps, but sadly, it only can fire once before it needs to be reset," Doug said.

"I think you did just fine there, Doug. You killed two snakes and finished off that wounded goober to boot," Florence said, praising her assistant's good work. A sound distracted them as a pair of gnomes struggled to drag the battle parakeet mech, Skyler, inside.

"Here you go, Doug. It's ready for battle," a gnome said. The pair waved and ran off toward the Fizz Clan's home. The enemy would be there soon, and the clan would need every gnome on deck to defend the place.

"Doug, it don't feel right to risk them gnomes like we did with the goblins. Those little green creeps could replace their losses easy enough, but the gnomes are more like, well, people," Florence said.

"Do what you feel is right, Florence. The room can be sealed off, but it's no guarantee that their wizard won't find it. Just remember, we may need these gnomes in the end. So far, we've been bleeding the enemy dry, but eventually, we'll have to face the trio of adventurers and then we'll be happy to have every blade at our disposal."

"That may be the key, Doug. Good idea." Florence pushed her voice into the Fizz Clan's home. "Hey, Fizz, there's a whole slew of bad guys heading your way. I've sealed off your room, but that may not fool them. You need to head back to my core room before it's too late."

"Huh, that's what all the racket was? Okay, we'll just grab the important stuff and head over to you," Fizz said.

"Wait, they're almost to your home. Use the escape tunnels," Doug advised.

Florence had almost forgotten there were small crawl spaces that led from the former goblin home into the garage, which would buy them some time. The invaders had stopped to argue for a bit; Harmon wanted to push straight to her core, while Kam wanted to clear out everything to make sure nothing would attack them from behind. Kam won the argument, and they were now clearing both the bath and the sewing room at the same time.

The gnomes were a blur of activity. Instead of running, they were gathering bundles of gear and tools, pushing them through the escape tunnel. Inside the garage, a pair of gnomes loaded themselves down with so much gear that Florence thought they were going to be crushed. They were surprisingly able to stagger their way forward. It would take them time, but they should make it to the core room ahead of the enemy. That was two down and twelve more gnomes to go.

"Hey, get a move on, Fizz. They're heading your way, and it's only the laundry room standing between them and the garage," Florence said, worried they would get caught in the middle of lugging their junk.

"Okay, but we can't leave all this behind," Fizz argued.

"It doesn't matter. You can make more stuff after the fight is over," Florence argued.

"Fine, move it, boys. Just what you've got in hand," Fizz relented. Each gnome in the group gathered a pair of bags and started crawling toward the garage.

"Here, there is a hidden door. Open it," Harmon said, doing exactly what Florence had feared: finding the hidden door that would normally protect the Fizz Clan from discovery. For the mage to find it, his level must be higher than Florence's core level of seven. That meant these adventurers might be more powerful than she had thought.

The bathroom and the sewing room defenders had helped thin the enemy's number, at least. A rogue and three swordsmen were down, and another rogue was sporting a bloody bandage on his arm. The three surviving halberdiers and the archers formed up in front of the Fizz Clan's home. The door became visible as Harmon cast something that dispelled Florence's attempts at concealment.

"Get moving, boys. I'll hold them off. It's battle bird time, and my parakeet has upgrades!" Fizz said, walking toward the battle parakeet named Andy. The gnome pulled a lever, and the bird mech opened to reveal a rather comfortable-looking cockpit. Fizz jumped in, and the contraption started to walk around, a horrible, very fake-sounding bird-like screech ringing out every few seconds.

"Egad, that isn't the sound a parakeet makes. It sounds like the fake hawk noise they use in all those cheesy movies. I hope my mech doesn't do that," Doug complained.

They watched as the door was opened and the trio of halberdiers charged without hesitation at the man-sized bird contraption in front of them. Fizz wasted no time getting into the fight, charging forward even as a red metallic hat of command extended from a panel on the back and was secured on the bird mech's head. The hat glowed and the volume of that horrible bird noise increased to what must have been painful levels. The halberdiers faltered in their advance, dropping their polearms to hold their hands over their ears.

Harmon seemed unaffected by the horrible noise. He calmly cast a spell that created a large blob of acid that flew directly into the hat, melting it off the bird's head. Fizz wasn't no one-trick pony, though, and he brought the wings forward. Sharp edges cleaved into the lead halberdiers even as more acid landed on his mech, eating away at the armored suit. Sparks started to erupt from the damaged areas of the parakeet battle mech, and Fizz was having a hard time keeping it on course. He laid into the second set of halberdiers, who had recovered enough to grab their weapons and stab deep into the parakeet. With an eruption of sparks, the mech crashed to the ground. Flames licked at it from several points while the metallic feathers flew out to shred the remaining halberdiers.

"Oh my, I hope that Fizz is still alive in there," Doug said.

"I can sense life in there, but it doesn't look good," Florence replied. Thankfully, the rest of the invaders seemed to think the mech was a trap of some sort and steered clear of the sparking and burning contraption.

"There's nothing here but some useless tools. Keep moving," Kam ordered. "We don't have all day. Eventually, another group of adventurers is going to show up, and I don't want them running out to spread the alarm."

Chapter 31

DURG TOOK THE LEAD, PUSHING ASIDE THE SWORDMEN THAT WERE forming up in front of the laundry room door. He kicked the door and charged inside. Arya and Q were already starting to summon creatures to defend themselves, but the armored orc wasn't going to let that happen. His charge took him directly into the clothes-line traps, but his armor and shield snapped the razor-like cables easily. A single goblin was summoned, but Durg's axe was already going to work, easily dispatching Florence's poor babies. The little summoned goblin jabbed the armored warrior with his wooden spear, doing nothing before being turned into a pincushion by the archers who were waiting in the doorway.

"At least the rest of the goblins are going to make it," Florence said to Doug, watching as the overburdened little guys made their way from the library into the game room, waddling ever closer to the core room.

The library was a bloodbath. Durg led the way once more, but this time, he was met by a bolt of lightning magic from Zeus as well as hits from the magic missile traps hidden in the room. Fluffy and Fluffy Junior were level 2 brawlers, but they stood no chance against the armored killing machine. That didn't stop her babies from try-ing, though, and they were further reinforced when Loki wandered in to help. Loki used the charge ability from his raider class, landing the first hits other than magic damage that seemed to bother the orc.

A spiked shield met the raider's next attack, and poor Loki impaled himself. The minor champion was tougher than a regular kitty, but even his prodigious health pool couldn't withstand the rain of axe blows that Durg hammered into him. Zeus was dropped by the archers as a pair of rogues took out the magic missile traps. One of them ate a blast before he could disarm it, adding another wounded invader to the others shuffling along at the back of the formation.

"The armored fellow seems to be hurt a bit." Doug watched as Durg waved the swordsmen and archers forward to take the lead, downing what must have been a healing potion.

"Good. How many of those things can they drink down before they don't work?" Florence asked. Potions were supposed to be expensive in this world, so the orc wouldn't have used one unless he needed to. Lightning from Zeus was the perfect attack to use on the metal-armored opponent, not to mention the magic missiles and Loki's battering hits.

"There is a limit to what potions can heal," Doug advised. "The maximum is usually around their total health pool, but the number is affected by their constitution rating, which means that our armored friend there can probably heal quite a bit. After the limit is reached, healing potions begin to become toxic, dealing damage instead of healing." That was good news; they couldn't just sit there and drink potions to survive forever in her home.

Inside the game room, the attackers were having some trouble dealing with all the threats. Florence wasn't playing around and didn't activate the game mode. Instead, she let all four kitties go to town, not to mention the rather effective roulette trap. Milk Tea kept up the buffs on the other kitties, letting them hit harder and move a bit faster. Astrid, Jurgen, and Clementine were fighting well, each having taken down a swordsman.

The battle turned against her kitties as Kam entered the fight.

His twin scimitars were a blur of sharp death, and he easily fended off incoming blows and killed her babies before they could lay a claw on him. An archer was killed by the roulette trap, which, along with the three swordsmen casualties, left a good dent in the number of remaining invaders.

"Let's finish this," Kam said, waving forward Durg and Harmon. The adventurer was getting frustrated with the delays and his hirelings' lack of results.

"I've been waiting for this," Doug said with an evil grin on his kitten face. The adventurers had entered the kitchen, looking confused that there were no foes inside.

"We must have eliminated most of the defenders. I think we'll only have a final champion to deal with before we reach the core," Kam speculated.

"Oh, he is so wrong. Wait for the party to make it to the dining room, Doug," Florence said. Doug watched as the three adventurers tore into the defenders protecting the dining room. The remaining hirelings were waiting inside the kitchen and staying out of the way. Several cabinet doors in the kitchen creaked open, and a handful of figurines dropped to the floor, landing with a flash of light.

Screams and roars of anger thundered in the kitchen as the trapped creatures found themselves in an unfamiliar location and under attack. An orc warrior, an orc shaman, a one-armed troll, and a displacer beast were added to the room full of hirelings. The orc warrior hacked into the nearest rogue while the shaman started to cast a spell.

Magic energy fizzled as the orc shaman was grabbed by the one-armed troll. Green blood pouring from the stump of his severed arm, the seven-foot-tall troll chomped down on the shaman, tearing into the flesh, using the food to hasten his powerful regeneration ability. Already, the blood spurting from the stump had slowed to a trickle. Two dagger-wielding thugs stabbed at the troll, but you needed fire to put a troll down for good.

The displacer beast was even more impressive, no doubt because it resembled a big kitty with tentacle thingies. It was completely obliterating the mass of thugs in the room with its teeth, claws, and spikey tentacles. The troll reacted to the rogues that were stabbing it, hurling the dead shaman at one and grasping another to feast upon. With his comrade dead, the orc warrior wasted no time in attacking the troll, and the mighty blows of his axe cleaved the remaining arm from the monster.

"It appears our troll has been disarmed," Doug offered with a smug look on his face.

"That's pretty bad, Doug, and don't think I missed the fact your trap is spending as much time fighting itself as it is fighting the invaders," Florence replied with a groan.

"In hindsight, I perhaps should have distributed them a bit differently," Doug admitted.

The hirelings were all down, and having easily taken down Florence's dining room defenders, the party was just now realizing there was a threat behind them. Harmon held the party back, a ball of fire growing in his hand. With a gesture, the fireball shot into the kitchen. Another spell grew in his hand even as the first detonated. Flames whooshed from the doorway, and Florence could feel the impressive heat the spell had caused. This mage was going to be trouble, but at least the trap had eaten up a couple of higher-level spells. The second fireball finished off the charred troll and the displacer beast, which was barely able to stand after the first blast.

"We're on our own now," Harman noted.

"Not a problem. That just means we don't have to pay them," Kam added.

"Go," was all Durg said, indicating the door to the master bedroom, where Zork and Chubbs waited.

Following his own suggestion, Durg burst into the bedroom, only to eat a swarm of magic missiles cast by Zork. The spinning ball of cuddly fur that was Chubbs rocketed out from under the bed and slammed into Kam, who was just entering the room. A bolt of lightning flew from Harman, striking Zork. Florence figured the mage was sharp enough to realize he should take out the caster first. Durg roared in anger, charging the mage champion while Kam got into the fight, fending off Chubbs's blows and keeping the pudgy champion from rescuing his buddy Zork.

Zork was a champion, and even if he was only the champion of the first floor, he wasn't a pushover. Florence's little mage kitty blinked out of view just as the orc's charge reached the bed. Her baby reappeared on the dresser, orbs of magic already swirling around his head. Harmon spotted the move. A glob of acid hurled toward Zork as three more magic missiles slammed into Durg, the magic seemingly able to ignore the orc's heavy armor.

Chubbs was holding his own, activating an ability that made his fluffy fur turn sharp and spikey. Every time Kam landed a blow, bristles of fur dug into his hand and arm. The defensive ability was distracting enough to allow a swipe or two from Chubbs's claws through Kam's defense. Things might have gone better for her chunky champion if he wasn't forced to face all three adventurers at once. Zork hadn't survived the combined damage from a blast of lightning, an acid blob, and a few hits from the orc's axe.

"Considering the probable level advantages of their opponents, our first-floor champions didn't fare too poorly, did they?" Doug said.

"Yep, and look, they're having to gulp down more of their potions. Do those mana potions do the same thing as the healing ones do?" Florence asked.

"Yes, they do. It doesn't matter which type you consume. The toxicity is combined so you can't down mana potions to your limit and then consume the healing variety without ill effects. I should also mention that the mana potions do nothing to increase your daily mana limit. That still exists, and the potions only help them regenerate faster," Doug assured her. That was good. She hoped the mage would get hurt and be forced to drink some healing potions; giving him more mana was dangerous with the powerful spells at his disposal.

"So much for this dungeon core being the equivalent of a toddler." Kam gestured toward the stairwell leading to the second floor.

"It doesn't matter. The second level will have more dangerous defenders, but it will be smaller than the first. We'll be done shortly," Harmon assured the others.

The trio of evil adventurers crept up the stairs, stopping at the landing and peering inside. While it appeared vacant, there were not only five hidden kitties but also a pair of crossbow traps waiting to trigger as soon as someone entered the room. Durg raised his shield and Harmon crouched behind him, casting. Kam followed up last, ready to engage any defenders that appeared. Harmon finished his spell just as the kitties went into action. Three brawlers charged forward while Winter began to summon her ice magic. Willow slunk around in stealth mode, trying to creep behind the attackers. Durg and Kam met the brawlers, their skills and weapons holding back Winston, Puddin, and Buttercup without much trouble.

Harmon's spell turned out to be another summoning. This time it was a large armored beetled with sharp, oversized pincers for a mouth. The summoned creature materialized right next to Winter, and pincers closed around the ice mage kitty. Winter pelted the bug with ice shards, slowing it and cracking its shell, but she could do nothing about the pincers that clamped down hard.

"There goes Winter. I'm really sick of bugs," Florence commented.

"I have the same sentiment, my dear Florence," Doug agreed.

The beetle ate it when the twin crossbow traps triggered; the bolts easily penetrated the already damaged shell. Kam and Durg were dominating the three brawlers, burning down their health, while the mage hung back, conserving his mana. What Harmon didn't count on was Willow striking from behind with a surprise attack. Her commando kitty didn't hold back, continuing to land blows and distracting the mage from casting a spell. Florence was on the edge of her seat, waiting for the mage to bite the bucket when he teleported across the room, using a spell similar to the one Zork had used earlier.

"Durn it, I thought we had him there," Florence said.

"No matter. He's seriously injured and was forced to use up more mana," Doug replied. She was fine with that. The mage was already slugging back a healing potion, bringing him that much closer to the limit.

Willow tried to help her fellow defenders, but by the time she reached the fight, the last brawler kitty, Buttercup, went down. The two powerful warriors didn't have much trouble with Willow; a commando wasn't too good once it was spotted. The mage was forced to drink a second healing potion, much to Florence's delight, and the others were only lightly injured, choosing to wrap bandages around the few minor cuts and bites they had sustained in the fight.

The bathroom and bedrooms went by quickly. They were straightforward fights, and other than an exciting moment when Pebbles surprised Harmon as he stepped on her hidden form, they had little trouble clearing things out. Little trouble didn't mean no trouble, though, and Kam was forced to down a potion and mentioned to Durg that he only had one left. The second-floor master bedroom was next, and her newest minor champion, Tachi, had decided to make her stand there, along with the other five defenders.

Harmon began casting even before he entered, tossing a fire-ball into the center of the room. The five cats that called the room home were partially protected from the blast; each was camped out in one of the many hidden attack spots in the room. Tachi was standing right in the center of the room, where the fireball was headed, and it looked like curtains for her, at least until she used that chronomancer magic of hers.

Everything but the minor champion seemed to move in slow motion. Tachi ran forward, landing several powerful blows against the gaps in Durg's armor before running back out of the way of the fireball blast. Time snapped back to normal inside the room, the invaders confused by what had just happened to them. Durg touched his bleeding neck, not quite sure what had inflicted the wound. Cats began to erupt from all over the room, way more than Florence remembered placing inside.

"What in tarnation? Where'd them cats come from?" Florence asked.

"Oh, that would be Licorice. She's using her illusion magic to summon false targets," Doug advised. Florence had almost forgotten about that. It was getting hard to keep track of all her babies and the special talents they were developing.

"Illusion. I will dispel it," Harmon told the other adventurers, who were finding half their blows were flowing right through their targets. Hits were getting through as the real kitties got to work. Marshmallow, Brownie, and KitKat were all commandos and put their skills to good use, while big old Cheddar just waddled up to the nearest invader, Durg, and started swatting at him.

Tachi spotted her opening, racing forward to engage the mage. Her magic sped up her movements, but it was nothing like her ear-lier spell. A claw got through and shredded Harmon's arm, but he kept his concentration and summoned a bundle of grasping black tentacles under the chronomancer kitty. The shadowy appendages dug into the minor champion, causing her to mew with pain and thrash around as she attempted to get free.

With the immediate threat gone, Harmon sent out a blast of mana that dispelled the illusions and revealed the actual kitties. In addition to Tachi and the five cats that lived in the room, three more kitties shambled in from behind the adventurers. Acheron, Styx, and Lethe had come back. The undying kitties weren't very powerful, but they did distract the mage, who wasted more mana summoning acid blobs to take them out. Brownie and KitKat also went down when Kam activated an ability and became a swirl of sharp steel that chopped anything he touched to bits.

Durg used Kam's distraction to deliver powerful blows on the trapped and hurting Tachi. Giving as good as she got, the minor champion managed to get a paw free and swatted back at the orc each time he attacked. Cheddar fell just as Kam's ability finished up. The warrior was running after Licorice, the last of the room's assigned defenders that was still on her feet. Having only illusion magic, Licorice made for a poor melee attacker, and it only took a single blow from Kam's scimitar to dispatch her.

Tachi was free; the spell had expired, freeing her up to paw and bite at Durg. Occasional blows seemed to blur with speed, dealing more damage as a passive time buff ability was triggered every few attacks. Harmon had little trouble with the undying kitties. In their zombie form, they were too slow to catch him, and each acid blob was able to kill one. Durg was looking a bit ragged by the time the three adventurers finally took down Tachi. Florence's minor champion with the absurdly small head did a good job, focusing on the orc and really giving him what for.

More potions were consumed, and Durg announced that he had reached his potion limit. Kam had come through with only minor injuries, and Harmon said he was close to the limit and could only consume one final minor potion. His mana was also reaching his daily limit. They had gone too far to quit now, and the trio moved into the walk-in closet. Junk lined the shelves, and Durg shouted in alarm as an old doll stood up and launched itself at him, needle-like claws and teeth out for some orc blood.

"What are these things?" Kam asked as more and more toys came to life and attacked.

"Now that's just creepy, Doug," Florence said of her baby's power.

"And you were worried that Vala was just here to entertain children," Doug said.

"We better not let any kids see that. They'll get nightmares for sure."

The dolls proved to be somewhat disappointing despite their disturbing appearance. Vala had to poke her paw out from hiding to work her magic, and Kam eventually spotted her, his blade ending the creepy puppet show. Kam had been lucky on the floor so far, but when he reached up to pull down the ladder, his luck ran out. The ladder slammed down into his face with unexpected force as caltrops showered down on the party. Florence thought she heard bones crack as the man dropped to the carpeted floor, stunned.

A box opened to reveal a crossbow trap, but Durg was on the ball and got his shield up to block the attack. The trap didn't get a chance to reload, and after pouring a healing potion down Kam's throat, they started up the ladder. It was up to her floor champion, Spud, to stop them. Her third floor held the home champion, but there were now very few kitties standing between her core gem and the invaders.

Chapter 32

"Sit still, you big stink bag," Surly chided as he tried to fasten a harness around Spud's big belly. Florence couldn't believe it; the big plague charger was allowing the gnome to strap what looked like a mechanical saddle to his back. The gnome finished up the task, securing a pair of shields to the saddle with clamps built for that purpose. The gnome then added a long tube to each shield. The tubes reminded her of the barrels of a cannon.

"Hey, Doug, did that gnome just mount cannons onto Spud?" Florence asked.

"No, I suspect they're not quite up to the standard of modern weaponry, but they will do something horrible to whatever they're pointed at," Doug advised.

"That's too bad. I could use more cannon kitties in my home," Florence said, giving up the idea of fielding a cat-based armored division.

The gnome finished up right in the nick of time, the party climbing up after Kam had recovered his senses. Dark and dingy, the attic wasn't all that easy to see inside. Florence kept the light down. Only the moonlight coming in from the window illuminated the place. Old Spud could see just fine, but the adventurers took a moment while Harmon summoned a simple light spell for the party.

"Charge!" Surly held onto the saddle for dear life as Spud leaped forward. The gnome had secured what resembled a gas mask to his face, and he looked completely ridiculous atop the plague charger champion.

Surly might have looked ridiculous, but he knew how to use those strange weapons he had strapped to the shields. As the champion neared the foe, Durg moved to place himself in front of the angry kitty. From the barrel of the weapon, a large spear shot forth. The orc caught the spear on his tower shield, but the momentum from the charging cat, as well as the deceptively powerful weapon, drove the spear through the metal shield, splinters stabbing into Durg's arm.

Spud batted the orc aside. A second swipe opened deep wounds on Kam before Spud pulled back for another charge. Before he left the vicinity of the party, a familiar burbling noise came from behind the kitty, and a green cloud of stink began to fill the space. The party struggled as the foul odor caused them to gag and vomit, watering eyes having trouble seeing anything in the dark attic.

Spud reached the far wall, where he turned for a second charge. The attic floor shook as the champion sprinted toward the party once more. Harmon finished casting a spell, despite the overpowering stench. Fresh air blew across the attic, removing some, but not all, of the champion-generated fumes. It was enough for the party to regain their feet, right when Surly fired the second weapon. This time, the spear didn't meet a heavily armored shield—it met the magically reinforced garb of Harmon. The magical reinforcements to his clothing were meant to turn a knife blade or render a fatal wound less serious, but they were never designed to hold back a spear fired from the back of a charging plague mount.

"Harmon!" Kam shouted as the spear pierced his comrade's body, digging into the attic floor and holding the now-deceased mage upright.

The fatal attack canceled the clear air spell that Harmon had cast and allowed the stench to return to its full effect. Both Kam and

Durg gagged once more, distracting them from the deadly claws of Spud. Charging into the fight was Spud's thing, but Florence knew her baby was just as deadly close up. The enhanced champion's claws tore through Kam's chainmail, opening deep wounds in his chest and stomach.

"Take that, you son of a goblin!" Surly shouted. The gnome had pulled a crossbow from somewhere inside his bulging pack and fired it into the wounded Kam. This was no normal weapon. Nope, this was one of them there gnome tinkerer deals, and it fired two bolts at once. The twin projectiles slammed into Kam's upturned face; fighting from atop a mount gave the diminutive gnome a commanding view of his target.

Kam staggered back, scimitars swinging feebly at Spud as the cat leaned forward and took the man's head in his jaws. With a gross snap, headless Kam dropped to the attic floor, Spud swallowing loudly and looking like the cat who had caught the canary. Durg was having none of it. The orc took in his fallen comrades and made a beeline for the attic stairwell. Florence wasn't going to let any of these creeps escape and used her summons to drop a kitty right in his path. The summons turned out to be a good one this time, and Chubbs appeared, her first-floor champion blocking the path of the retreating orc.

"Nope, you're not making it out of here alive," Florence said.

"Agreed, to let one of these escape would only invite a retaliatory assault from a vengeance-seeking survivor," Doug said.

Durg was heavily armored and skilled with his weapons, but that didn't matter when he was trapped between two champion kitties, not to mention that gnome Surly wasn't done yet, either; he was trying with some difficulty to reload his crossbow while atop the bucking Spud. First, the orc's shield was ripped away by Chubbs. Then Spud was able to land several blows, including another powerful bite that failed to decapitate his target but did leave large holes in his armored torso. A second volley of bolts struck true, and then Chubbs dealt the final blow, ripping a deep wound that the adventurer's armor and health couldn't withstand.

"Ha, take that. Well done, my babies, and thanks to you as well, Surly," Florence said.

"Surly? Nope, core lady, my name is Bizzlenap Ipipip Smith," Surly replied.

"Uh, I'll just stick with Surly, if you don't mind," Florence replied.

Surly just shrugged and went with it, dismounting to examine the armor and weapons the adventurers had dropped.

"You can salvage what you can from the invaders. Just leave anything you don't want on the ground. Oh, make sure you get someone down to check on Fizz. I think he's alive, but he's trapped in that parakeet robot thingy," Florence said.

"Hold up. I don't think this is quite over yet, Florence," Doug said, drawing her attention to a group entering her home through the front door.

There were five of them. The lead pair were heavily armored with gear that practically glowed with enchantments. Behind the lead pair was another armored figure, and if she had to guess, this one was a healer of some type. A mage followed, protective spells twisting around his form. The final figure was almost ethereal, a shadowy rogue class that was so powerful it was hard to see even when she wasn't trying to hide.

"What in tarnation are they doing here, and who are they?" Florence asked.

"I doubt they're affiliated with the party of hooligans we just dispatched, but they are surely not here for a delve. A single piece of their gear is likely more valuable than every drop in our home," Doug said.

"They seem a bit confused, which is understandable, given the dead bodies and whatnot all over our home." Florence desperately wanted to respawn her defenders but was unable to do so with this new party already inside.

"Spud, you're a good boy. Go on back to your normal spot and let the attic air out a bit. These folks don't look like the type we want to start a ruckus with," Florence said. Her often strong-willed champion obeyed this time, trotting back to the corner but standing ready to defend his home if needed.

"Hey, Surly, jump on down and join your fellows. If this goes sideways, I don't want you caught in the crossfire," Florence said.

"I'll stay up here with my friend, if you don't mind," Surly said.

"Sure, but don't blame me if you get turned into a toad or something," Florence warned.

The party wasted no time heading through the first floor and onto the second. Once they had their bearings, they made their way to the attic, the rogue disappearing and no doubt already in the attic somewhere. One of the armored warriors reached the top of the attic stairs, looking over the room before speaking.

"First live defender has been spotted, a floor champion. Dispatch it, but leave the gnome. It's not tagging as a defender, and we may need it for questioning later," the armored warrior ordered. After he finished, Spud dropped to the ground, dead. A brief whisp was all that was seen of the rogue; her poisoned daggers killed Florence's baby without trouble.

"Woah, what's going on here?" Surly barked as he rolled from his now-deceased mount.

"Keep silent. We're here on guild business," the mage said as he climbed the stairs. "You're not a dungeon-created defender, so your life will be spared as long as you don't interfere in our work. I should warn you that pestering us with questions constitutes interference."

"Uh-oh, this doesn't look good. I think I'm going to be sick," Florence said as the team climbed down the ladder to the backyard.

"I don't know what to do," Doug said. It wasn't like him to be without a plan, even a stupid one. The sick feeling got worse, and Florence worried it wasn't just due to the adventurers guild kill team closing in on her.

With no effort, the rogue took care of Spooky, Sun Wukong, Lizzy, and Scamp. Mortimer moved toward the party only to be dropped by a spell from the wizard. It was their turn to be surprised when Mortimer and all four kitties rose again, this time as zombies, all of which attacked. It was only a brief respite, and the zombie versions of her kitty defenders were taken out without landing a single hit. Things were definitely out of control, and Florence doubted they would survive the next few minutes.

Chapter 33

"Matron, something's going on over at Ben's place," Tipp said.

"What's going on, and why do you think it's any of my business?" Shara replied. She was getting ready for a rest when the initiate had stuck his head into her tent.

"I don't know, but there are lots of wagons outside and they're being loaded up," Tipp said.

"Very well. My rest can wait a bit longer. Let's see what's gotten you so excited."

It wasn't normal. The shop and tavern usually received lots of goods and didn't need to ship things out. A few grumbling adventurers were walking from the shop, but she didn't stop to ask them what was happening; she preferred to hear it directly from Ben. The shop was a bustle of activity as the staff worked on packing up all the goods into large shipping crates. She had Tipp, who had been tagging along, wait outside. This much activity and so many unwatched valuables might be too big a temptation for her fledgling rogue.

"Matron, come to say your farewells? Or do you need some last-minute item before we're gone?" Ben asked.

"What is this all about? You have a thriving business. Why quit what should be a perfect location?" Shara asked.

"It is a perfect location, but it won't be shortly, I'm sorry to say," Ben answered, shaking his head.

"Why is that? Quit being evasive and tell me the whole story," Shara demanded.

"You hadn't heard? Sorry, I thought everyone knew. I forget you set your camp away from most of the other adventurers, and I don't suppose you're the sort for idle gossip. Where to start? Our friendly local dungeon has proven to not be so friendly and the guild is closing it down."

"Why? I know there were a lot of deaths inside, but it turned out most of those were due to those creatures we cleared out," Shara said.

"I know that, and I was going to explain that to the investigators when they left the dungeon," Ben replied.

"Are they still inside? I'll go tell them myself. A paladin of the light's word should still hold respect among the guild investigators."

"They would undoubtedly lend your arguments a lot of weight, but sadly, the investigators are dead, murdered by the dungeon."

"No, the dungeon wouldn't do that. It must be those creatures. Perhaps there were more in the cavern that we missed." Shara worried something bad was about to happen to her friend. An even more disturbing thought entered her head. What if Florence truly was mad? Perhaps the dungeon felt some bond with her but was a bloodthirsty monster with other parties. No, she didn't want to believe that, and Florence had never given her any cause to believe she was anything other than what she claimed to be.

"It's too late," Ben said. "A powerful adventurers guild kill team left just a few minutes ago to destroy the core. I'm sorry. I know you had high hopes of using this dungeon to train your charges. You'll have to come up with another plan now."

"Maybe not. Let me see what I can do." Shara summoned her horse as soon as she left the building.

"Matron, what's going on?" Tipp asked.

"I've got to go inside the dungeon to try and save it. The guild thinks the place is mad and wants to destroy it. A kill team is heading inside, and I've got to speak with them before they make a huge mistake," Shara explained.

"I'll get the party together and we'll join you," Tipp offered.

"No, gather them and stand ready near the tents, but don't go near the dungeon entrance. Wait for me to return." Tipp looked confused, and Shara didn't blame him one bit.

"Yes, Matron. Please don't hesitate to call on us if you need assistance," he said, surprising her with his discipline. A few short weeks ago, the halfling rogue would have argued until she demanded that he stop.

Her horse, Beauregard, galloped toward the dungeon entrance. It wasn't far, but time was critical. Leaving her horse tied to the entryway, Shara moved as fast as she could inside the tunnel. Florence had done some work out here. The entrance was nicely decorated, and there were even signs guiding potential adventurers toward their destination. Surely this wasn't the work of a mad killer, was it?

The tunnel led toward the lovely lawn and gazebo that Florence had created. Instead of the tranquil surroundings and starter defender to challenge new adventurers, Shara found a scene of carnage. Bodies were strewn about the lawn, and there was no sign of the defenders that would normally be stationed here. The mailbox trap was disabled as well.

This was odd. Even if a kill team had entered here, they were typically few in number, usually four or five of the most powerful adventurers the guild had a contract with. Where did all the bodies come from? To make things even more confusing, there was no glow of loot. If the kill team had swept through, they would have no trouble dispatching Florence's defenders, but they wouldn't delay their task to loot a few coppers and trinkets. Their time was much more valuable than that.

Things didn't look any better inside the house, where more carnage greeted Shara. She even checked the side rooms; they, too, were in the same state as the rest of the house. The kitchen was an even stranger sight. The room was charred like a fireball or two had gone off inside, and if she wasn't mistaken, the corpses of a troll and a displacer beast were lying there among the burnt human and orc corpses.

The second floor was new, and since she hadn't been here before, Shara called forth her armor and weapons. Similar sights as the floor below met her gaze, and when she used mana to enhance her hearing, she thought she could hear fighting.

"Don't worry, Florence. I'm on my way." Shara ran as fast as she could through the dungeon, hoping she wouldn't be too late to save her friend.

Chapter 34

"Stop, do not harm this core. It isn't to blame!" Shara climbed down the ladder from the attic to confront the kill team.

Just how many folks were going to visit Florence's home today? The kill team had held her entire attention, and neither she nor Doug even noticed Shara's arrival.

"And just who do you think you are?" the wizard asked.

"I'm the Matron of initiates for the Brilliant Keep and I speak with the authority of the light," Shara said.

"You tell them, Shara!" Florence said.

"Dungeon, you will be silent!" the mage ordered before turning his attention back to Shara. "While I respect all followers of the light, we are tasked with the destruction of this aberrant core and will abide no interruptions."

"At least stay your hand until I explain what has happened here," Shara said.

"Go on. Out of respect for your position, I will hear you out, but know that my patience is limited," the mage said.

"Thank you. I brought a new team of initiates here to train, the light guiding me to this newly created dungeon. While here, we learned the dungeon was beset by creatures who roamed the tunnels and killed adventurers as they left the dungeon. I hunted down the monsters, and they should trouble this place no longer. The dungeon is of only modest difficulty, and it would be a waste to destroy it for a simple misunderstanding."

"I have no doubt you believe that, but the fact remains, an investigation team was sent here to find out the truth of this dungeon's character, and they were slain inside here less than an hour ago. As you know, Matron, such a thing cannot be tolerated, and my team was teleported here at great expense," the mage argued.

"While I can't claim to know about this investigation team's loss, I believe you should hear the core out before rendering a final judgment," Shara countered.

"If I do, will you relent and leave us to our task unimpeded?" the mage asked.

"Yes, she is unusual, but I think you'll find that this core is not excessively murderous."

"Very well. Dungeon core, we're entering your core room, and any threats of violence will be met with your instant destruction," the mage advised.

"Well, in that case, come on in. Would you like any refreshments?" Florence asked.

"I need nothing from you other than answers to my questions," the mage told her as the whole gaggle of them climbed down into the core room. Florence was happy that she had made the new core room larger than her other one. She had planned on making it a place for her kitties to hang out, but now there was a gnomish clan, a kill team, a cat advisor, a parakeet battle mech, and her friend, Shara.

"I have one question for you, dungeon core: how did our investigation team die? I know it was inside your dungeon," the mage asked.

Florence gathered her thoughts, something that was becoming more difficult by the minute as a familiar pain began building inside her gem. "First off, my name is not dungeon core. My name is Florence Valentine, and I'm a . . . Uggh!" She grunted in pain as the lich once again made a play for her gem—at the worst possible time, of course.

"That is it," the mage said. "The poor thing is mad, and we are likely doing it a service by putting it out of its misery. Stand aside, Matron."

"No, she is in pain, likely injured in the attack she just fought off. I'll try to heal her. I won't lose another friend like I lost Vanderman." Tears ran down Shara's face as she cast a spell in Florence's direction.

The attempt to use magic elicited a deadly response from the rogue that was hovering right behind her. Florence looked on in pain and horror as her friend, perhaps the only one in this world other than Doug, was attacked. Thankfully, a paladin was not that easy to kill, and a contingency spell activated. Instead of her friend being impaled on the rogue's magical daggers, she blinked out of view, teleporting to what Florence prayed was a safe location. The pain encompassing her increased, and Florence tried with all her might to hold back the lich once more.

Divine Restoration has been cast upon your core stone by a neutral party. Do you wish to allow this beneficial spell to take effect: Y/N?

"Hit *yes*, Florence. It's your only chance!" Doug shouted before he was cut down by one of the warriors. The gnomes looked on in horror. Some held up their hands to show they weren't a threat while others went about constructing a makeshift bunker out of all the parts stored in the duffel bags they had lugged into her core room.

Florence was losing it, her mind unable to comprehend both the loss and the pain. She hit *yes*, accepting Shara's magical help even as the pain overrode the last of her focus. Her very being was shattered as her gem broke into a handful of shards. The pain receded, but as it faded, Florence could tell her hold on this life was also fading. Perhaps it was Shara's spell, but somehow, she was still able to hear and watch from her core shard as Berikoz appeared, standing right next to her rocking chair.

"Unwanted guests everywhere. That must have disturbed you to no end, Florence. I'll deal with them as a final reward for your sacrifice," Berikoz said.

"A lich. This core has summoned a lich. Destroy it quickly!" the mage commanded as he drew in mana.

The lich wasted no time, pointing at the pair of warriors. The men shriveled up like a pair of prunes as all the moisture was drawn from their bodies. A wave of Berikoz's other hand created a rain of fire in the room, and now the gnomes started screaming as well, retreating into the partially completed bunker. Florence wanted to shout at everyone so they would leave the gnomes be, but her voice was gone, vision slowly fading as Berikoz ignored the deadly spells being cast in his direction.

Appearing behind the lich, the rogue thrust her blades, only to have the weapons deflect off a magical barrier. The lich spoke a horrible word, and the dead in the room rose once more, attacking the living members of the kill team. A flash of light from the healer obliterated the newly summoned undead, but the healer then caught another of the wilting spells from Berikoz.

"The guild will end you for what you have done today, lich!" the mage shouted.

"I hope they try. Tell your betters that their minions were slain by the mighty Berikoz. I look forward to killing more of you. It has proven very amusing," Berikoz said as the mage teleported away. "Hmm, it seems one more is lurking about. Oh, there you are." Berikoz fired a black ray of energy into the middle of the room. The rogue appeared from where she had been hiding, and a second blast of magic disintegrated her.

"Goodbye, Florence. It's been fun, but I have things to do and can't stay for your final moments. My apologies. I'll see myself out," Berikoz taunted as Florence's vision faded for a final time.

Chapter 35

WELL, BEING DEAD THIS TIME WAS KIND OF BORING. SHE COULDN'T see, hear, speak, or do anything other than think. Florence knew she was, well, somewhere, but had no idea how much time was passing. How long would it take for her to go bonkers in here? Now, of course, Florence Valentine wasn't the type of woman to lose her marbles, but that would happen in a place like this eventually, wouldn't it?

She tried to keep her mind occupied, but all thoughts drifted back to the horrible and chaotic last moments of what she guessed was her fourth life. Shara had tried to save her, and she could only hope her friend was safe. Poor Doug. He couldn't survive without her core around.

One thing she did know: if it were at all possible, she was going to put paid to that lich, Berikoz. That guy was going to get his comeuppance if she had any say in the matter. Too bad she couldn't say anything or even listen in on what was going on around her. It wasn't too bad, she supposed. There weren't none of them lakes of fire and whatnot. She couldn't see anything, but it wasn't dark and creepy; it was more like a comforting gray haze all around her. The haze parted briefly as a system prompt appeared.

The final adjudication of the life-form/core known as Florence Valentine will commence.

"There is some confusion over this one. I will solicit input from the life-form directly," a voice said. What was this adjudication nonsense? Was she on trial for something? Were they going to put her in some kind of dead person jail?

"Hey, you, the voice guy. Can you hear me?" Florence asked, surprised as her ability to speak returned.

"Yes, of course. Now, I'm trying to complete your file, but I seem to be having some difficulty in confirming your death. There's an interference involved. Can you describe to me your last moments?" the voice asked.

"I most certainly can, but who in the heck are you, and why are you asking me all these weird questions?" Florence asked, confused over this whole ordeal.

"One moment. Oh, there it is. I see in your file that you've been labeled as a rather, shall we say, challenging individual to deal with. I note several heated interactions with core gem creators, one of which ended in the creator's demotion to the position of core assistant. You seem to have difficulty working with another entity unless there is a certain personalization to the interaction. To that end, you may call me the master adjudicator for entity disbursement."

"Nope, how about I just call you Mike? Yep, that will work. So, Mike, where am I, and what's going to happen to me?"

"You're at the end-of-term processing department, and as for what is going to happen to you, that is what we are trying to figure out," Mike said. "On a side note, I'm not sure if I like the moniker you are using. Did you not wish to call me by my title?"

"That title nonsense is only for hoity-toity folks that think they're more important than everyone else. You seem like a nice enough guy, at least compared to the others I've dealt with. I can call you Mike, or, you know, I could even go with Michael if you prefer a longer name," Florence offered.

"Michael will be sufficient. Oh, that's what the core gem

creators meant when they said you would draw them into the strangest conversations. That might be the first moniker conversation I've had in my existence. It is quite a treat to have a new experience. Thank you. Back to the task at hand, can you tell me what happened to you just before and during your death?"

"Sure, Michael. Wait, which death do you mean? I've had three of them so far. Four, if I really did just die."

"Uh, the most recent one, if you please."

"Okay, well, I was there in my home, minding my own business, when these hooligans entered and tried to destroy my core. They were tough and all, but my kitties were giving them the business." Florence paused to gather her thoughts.

"So, destruction by adventurers, then?" Michael asked.

"No, hold your horses. I'm just getting started. Let's see . . . Yeah, Spud killed them adventurers. Then the guild sent a kill team after me." The memories of her last few moments on Aerkon were a bit fuzzy, so she took a bit to sort things out.

"Ah, so it was the organization known as the adventurers guild on your world that dispatched your core," Michael said.

"Wait, no, that weren't it, either. It was that lich guy that done me in. The guild folks were the ones that tried to kill my friend, Shara. They also killed poor Doug, my assistant." Sad thoughts overcame her excitement at being able to talk to someone again.

"That's what I needed. Thank you. Now that I have more information to sort through the final moments of your core's existence, I can zero in on what is causing the problem with your adjudication. Oh my, there is something rather unusual there. A fragment of that world's mana is attempting to prevent your passage."

"I don't know what you're looking at, but if it was mana, it might have been when Shara cast that Divine Restoration spell on me. I didn't know she could do that. Usually only the harmful stuff worked on a core gem," Florence said.

"Interesting. An inhabitant of that world has used a form of divine magic to bind your soul to your body," Michael said. "Our normal process would be to terminate that link and move you along without delay, but this requires some more investigation. I'm sure it's a one-off occurrence, but I will need to develop new guidelines and procedures to work through a potential recurrence of these events in the future."

"Well, I'm sorry if my death has caused you some extra work," Florence said, a bit annoyed. Sure, this guy was polite enough—he even knew how to say thank you—but her death wasn't some homework assignment.

"No, it's not a bad thing. This is wonderful. I love a new challenge, and it's been a while since I've done anything of the like," Michael replied.

Long moments passed, with Michael not saying anything. Now, Florence Valentine was as patient a woman as anyone you could name, but sitting in the nothing, back in that durned silence, wasn't something she was going to put up with.

"Hey, you still there, Michael? What's going on?" Florence asked.

"What is it? I'm working on the new guidelines," Michael said.

"I'm just kind of sitting here in the nothing. Isn't there somewhere I can go? Or maybe, you know, I could head on back to Aerkon?"

"That would be impossible. Wait, hold on." Michael's voice started to get excited again.

Florence sat in the nothing. And sat and sat and sat.

"I've created an option for you, should you wish to exercise it. The mana causing this entire holdup can also be used to link you back to that world, bringing you back to life, in a manner of speaking," Michael said.

"Woah, hold up there, buster. What do you mean back to life in a manner of speaking?" Florence asked, worried this Michael might be some flimflam artist or trying to turn her into some undead creep like the lich.

"Well, you have a link back to this Aerkon world due to the spell cast upon your core. Of course, that link is tenuous, and it would require some effort to recraft a physical form that fits within the guidelines. You've been rather pleasant to deal with, not nearly as difficult as the gem-formation specialists would have me believe, so I'd be willing to whip something up for you," Michael offered.

"Sounds good to me. Zap me on back whenever you're ready," Florence said, excited to return. If she was back, she could resummon Doug and save him from whatever was happening to him.

"There will be some restrictions, and your time there would be limited to the length of time it takes me to craft new guidelines and procedures to deal with this sort of event," Michael advised.

"How limited are we talking? I can't imagine it would take all that long to craft new procedures and whatnot." Florence wasn't sure she wanted to go back for a couple of hours only to leave again.

"In local time, exactly 199 days. Was there some goal you wished to accomplish? Will this be enough time for you to do so?" Michael asked.

"It'll be tight, but I think I could make that work. That lich that did me in, he's a-planning to do the same thing to other cores, and I'd like to stop him. Now, them other cores aren't likely to have a paladin casting spells to keep them alive, but I suppose there is the possibility the lich will cause you some problems if folks like me keep popping up all the time."

"Hmm, it would be rather inconvenient to have a continuous influx of entities in your particular situation. Of course, my new guidelines would help, but I had planned on crafting them as a one-off, not something that would be used as a regular process. I think I can see to it that you're given a chance to accomplish your goal. Please understand that I can only give you a chance and I cannot, and will not, influence events in your favor," Michael told her.

"That works for me. Send me on back. Oh, and as a personal favor, can you see to it that my assistant, Doug, is returned?" Florence asked.

"I think that can be arranged for your assistant. I should also advise you that should you be destroyed again on Aerkon, your death will be permanent," Michael warned.

"So I'd end up back here to hang out with you?" Florence asked.

"No, if you perish during the 199-day window, your afterlife will be . . . most unpleasant. I need you to understand that your return is not some simple excursion. It is one that has substantial risk."

"So I get just under two hundred days to deal with the lich, and when my time's up, then what?" Florence asked.

"Well, I can't say just yet what will happen after the 199 days. That is something I am most definitely not permitted to disclose. So do you wish for me to send you back now that I have informed you of all the potential risks?" Michael asked.

"Hmm, so you're saying you haven't decided what to do with me after the 199 days and something bad will happen if I die again before that? Hmm, yeah, whatever. Send me on back," Florence said.

"Here you go. Enjoy your return, Florence Valentine. It has been a pleasure," Michael said.

Florence tried to thank him, but her vision faded out again.

Chapter 36

YOU ARE UNDER THE EFFECTS OF DIVINE RESTORATION. As a core, this intervention has resulted in the transformation of your being. Your class has been adjusted to accommodate your previous experience across multiple lifetimes. Please review your status.

That was weird. Florence was still kind of out of it, unable to see anything other than the system prompt. Her core felt weird, too, not like it normally did and most definitely not in a bad way like when Berikoz was zapping her gem. It was almost like she could feel things around her, not just sense them with her core. Florence took a moment to review her status screen, hopeful it might shed some light on the newest version of her existence.

Florence Valentine, Hybrid Entity

Core Gem / Catomancer (Domestic Housecat Subtype), Level 1 (0/2000)

You have been returned to life, but your dual nature as both a human and a core gem has created a new hybrid entity. As a hybrid entity, you will acquire experience at a reduced pace.

Health: 100%

Mana: 100/100

Stats: N/A. As a core shard, you do not have individual

attributes. As you level, your health, mana pool, and melee attack power will increase accordingly.

Core Shard Restrictions: You are a hybrid, but your dual nature is not always in perfect harmony. Once every 7 days, you will need to find a suitable area and transform into your dungeon. After 24 hours in your dungeon form, you may once again return to your hybrid body.

Core Shard Traits: Note that new traits will be unlocked or improve as you level.

1. **Indomitable Will:** You have survived multiple lives with your mind and sanity intact. It will be very difficult for anyone to influence your mind through magical means or with natural abilities.

Catomancer Restrictions: Your previous experience has unlocked a unique class, the catomancer. A catomancer summons and empowers creatures to do their bidding. In addition to your summoning abilities, limited direct-damage and enhancement spells can be unlocked at higher levels.

When you are transformed into a dungeon, the majority of your catomancer-based spells and abilities are unavailable.

Catomancer Traits:

1. **Companion:** You can summon to your side 1 feline companion beast to assist you. Your companion beast has already been assigned and is the entity known to you as Doug. Doug's level will match your own, and he will be responsible for selecting new abilities and powers for himself as you level. Should Doug perish in combat, you may resummon him after 24 hours have passed.

Hybrid Class Abilities:

1. **Instant Dungeon:** This ability can be used once per

day and is only available in your hybrid form. Instant Dungeon will anchor you in place, re-creating a random room from your dungeon around you. This room will be populated with the defenders and traps that were present when your core controlled a dungeon, but the other items inside will be illusions. Your current level will affect which room is randomly selected. As you level, this ability will improve.

Magic: You have access to the following spells.

1. Summon Defender (Catomancer): This spell requires 25 mana and will summon a single random cat defender to protect you for 1 minute per level. The summoned creatures will reflect your class subtype (domestic housecat) and will have powers and abilities equal to your level.

2. Empower Beast (Catomancer): This spell requires 25 mana and will infuse power into either your companion or one of your summoned cats. If cast upon a summoned cat, it will extend the length of the summoning as well as improve its abilities.

Combat Traits and Abilities (Hybrid Form Only):

1. Soulbound Weapon: Your cane has been selected as your soulbound weapon. This item cannot be stolen from you or permanently destroyed. Should the weapon be destroyed, it will re-form within 1 hour. You have been granted proficiency with this weapon, and as you level, the weapon, and your skill in wielding it, will improve.

2. Soulbound Armor: Your armor has been selected for you, providing the same level of protection as padded armor. This armor cannot be permanently destroyed, re-forming after an hour when necessary. The armor

provides very limited protection from physical attacks and environmental factors.

After reviewing her new, and rather odd, status screen, Florence found her vision and control returning. She was still a bit wobbly, but it wasn't scary like something was wrong with her. Instead, it was more like when you first woke up. Standing up to look around, Florence could see that she was inside the ruins of her core room. Scorch marks and the signs of the earlier battle were still there, but thankfully, none of the bodies remained.

"Oh dear. I really loved that chair," Florence said, a bit saddened to see her rocking chair shattered on the cavern floor.

Class ability unlocked.

Core Vision: You can see in every direction and in any light. All companion creatures and summoned defenders will be granted this ability.

"I say, Florence, what exactly has happened to us?" Doug asked. Her kitten advisor was here, only he wasn't a kitten anymore. Standing right there in front of her was what could be described as a white tiger. Her Dougie had grown!

"Doug, what got into you? You're huge!" Florence exclaimed.

Doug seemed to shake off the same lethargy she had experienced, his tiger eyes going wide as he looked back at Florence. "What's got into you? You're human again!"

"I am? Well, look at that. I didn't even notice until you pointed it out," Florence said. There she was, standing on her own two feet and dressed in her favorite outfit, looking exactly like she had back home. Despite the fact that she looked like an old woman, she felt like a twenty-year-old. None of the aches, pains, or weaknesses of her old human body were there. It was wonderful.

"Don't we make a pair, Doug? I've got a whole story to tell you, but first, let's get out of this place. It's not our home any longer," Florence said. It was true; the home was no longer connected to her and was just a rather tastefully decorated portion of a dark old cavern. Doug followed her out, climbing into the attic and then down the ladder into the second-floor closet.

"So what do we do now?" Doug asked as they made their way to the first floor. As she thought about it, a system prompt populated her vision.

Quest issued: Stop Berikoz. The lich, Berikoz, is corrupting and destroying dungeon core gems, using them as his phylacteries. Find the remaining cores that are under his influence and liberate them. This is a timed quest, and you have 199 days to complete it.

Rewards: unknown

"Well, Doug, it looks like we're going to delve some dungeons and kill a lich," Florence said.

"That sounds delightful, and not at all suicidal for a level 1 adventurer," Doug replied sarcastically.

"Good to have you back, Doug, though I'm sorry to see that becoming a big kitty didn't improve your disposition none."

"It's good to have you back as well, Florence. Shall we?" Doug pointed forward with his oversized paw.

"Yep. No time to waste, Doug," Florence said, leading them out of their old home and into a new life.

Epilogue

"Hey, where am I?" Aaron Lavelle called out. He couldn't see anything, and his mind was fuzzy. This didn't feel like a dream, but it also didn't quite feel real, either.

"Welcome, human! You have been selected from among the billions of your kind to be granted a great honor," a voice called out.

"Hello? Who said that?" Aaron asked, more confused than ever. It was then that he realized the voice wasn't actually speaking; he was hearing it in his mind. He tried to remember what was going on before this, how he wound up here, but it was like parts of his memory had been stripped away.

"Do not worry," the voice said. "While you have passed on from your previous existence, a new one awaits you. This new existence will be one you have trained for all your life."

"Wait, passed on from my previous existence? What does that mean? Did I, like, die or something?" Aaron asked.

"Yes, the mortal life of a human is a short one, but now you will have a potentially unlimited lifespan," the voice replied.

"This must be a dream or a hallucination. Wait, you said something about training all my life for something. I don't remember doing any training. Dude, I don't remember much of anything, to be honest."

"You have been a top one hundred player on the competitive ladder for several games, and because of that, you will now be granted a second life as a core gem. As a core, you can create and grow a dungeon in the new world you are assigned to. Very few meet the requirements for this honor, and you should be proud that your experience has made this possible for you."

"You mean a dungeon, like a game dungeon or the other kind?" Aaron asked.

"The game type, of course. Extradimensional incarceration is handled by a completely different department. As a dungeon core, you will use the skills you have gained on Earth to create something amazing. The only limits to what you create are your imagination and skill," the voice assured him. That was weird. Aaron could remember almost everything about gaming, but the rest of his life was sort of a blur, the memories refusing to form in his brain.

"I don't remember much. I was walking out of the store after picking up some energy drinks and beef jerky when something happened." Aaron thought this whole thing was some game-induced nightmare. It was summer and he had decided not to take any university classes so he could focus on gaming for a couple of months. Maybe he had been overdoing it with the twenty-hour runs? He remembered that much, but when he tried to remember what he had studied or even where he lived, his mind just couldn't seem to conjure it up.

"Sadly, your human life was terminated when you walked in front of a large conveyance while distracted by your handheld entertainment and communication device. It has all turned out for the best. Now you can become something much more than a human," the voice said. Aaron couldn't remember much, but becoming something new was fine, especially if this new life resembled the games he liked to play. Something in the back of his mind told him to be concerned, but he was flooded with happy feelings about this, feelings that overpowered any qualms he might have had.

"Fine, that sounds cool. What happens now?" Aaron asked.

"Now, I have completed your transformation into a core gem, and I must say, you retained much more of yourself than the average human does. Sometimes, that becomes problematic, but I believe you will slide right into your new life with very little in the way of acclimatization difficulty. You will be assigned to the world of Aerkon. Normally, you're sent to a random location, but there have been quite a few openings for new cores of late, so you may choose between the three open locations that I currently have available."

"What do you mean 'starting locations'? How are the rules for the game set up? I'll need to know about each place if I want to min-max my build properly. How do skills, abilities, and expansion work if this is really like a dungeon game? What sort of magic system is there? Is there even a magic system or is it a tech world with magic-like nanobots?" Aaron asked, all the gaming possibilities swirling together in his mind.

"You'll have to figure those things out for yourself once you have decided on your location. Rest assured, a proper assistant will be assigned to guide you through the process," the voice said.

"Hold on, you don't mean some stupid fairy. That's how these games work, right? You send me some hot-looking fairy who flirts a whole bunch and only gives the bare minimum of information. No way, I want someone, or something, that will actually help, not some window dressing."

"Rest assured there will be no salacious manipulation of your emotions. In fact, those types of feelings are no longer a part of your being, so a 'hot' fairy is of no use other than as an information conduit. Knowing your preference, I will endeavor to have an appropriate being assigned to assist you. Now, my time is limited and work is backing up here, so make your choice," the voice told him.

Choose your core gem installation site.

1. Varnham Wastes: Some cataclysmic event in times

long past caused this once vast, open sea to drain. The area was subsequently transformed into a wasteland haunted by dangerous beasts. Rumors tell of unnatural creatures deep below the surface, ones that seek to refill the sea and use it for their nefarious purposes. This location holds affinity bonuses for aberrations, undead, and reptilian cores.

2. Fire Pits of the Steel Mountains: A volcanic region that is unstable and dangerous to all who try to traverse it. Creatures of flame and rock battle with stalwart explorers who look to exploit the resources of this dangerous land. This location holds affinity bonuses for igneous, draconic, and deep dweller cores.

3. Frost Peaks of Ulmore: These frozen mountains are desolate and dangerous. Hardy tribes of barbarians roam about, attacking all outsiders, while hideous creatures, cloaked in frost and shadow, wait for fresh victims. This location holds affinity bonuses for frost, humanoid, and giant cores.

"Dude, how can I choose a location based on some flavor text? How do affinities work and what types of mobs can I create from each of these affinities?" Aaron asked. How could he be expected to min-max properly if he wasn't being given the whole picture?

"You will be fully instructed by your assistant, but I must insist you make a choice now. I have been lenient so far, as I feel you have potential, but my patience is at an end. Choose, or I will choose for you."

Aaron was going to complain further but found himself a bit frightened by whatever this voice was. The guy could totally snatch him up and make him a dungeon core, so who knew what else it could do to him if he ticked it off? Creepy voices in your head weren't things you should argue with.

"Sorry, man, I don't want to cause any problems. I just want the best start possible. Please, just give me a minute and I'll make a choice," Aaron whined, worried that the voice would be mad that he asked for more time. He didn't want it to stick him in some crappy starting location that would hamper his potential build.

"Very well. Take a moment and choose. Look upon your options and let your previous experience guide you," the voice said.

Aaron looked over the options. His memories of life as a human had continued to fade, but the gaming knowledge was still there. When he focused on each location or affinity, images of various creatures and how they functioned filled his mind. Draconic affinity with the fire mountain place sounded cool, but he knew that it would be a way long time before he could summon dragons. His starting creatures would be lame and weak stuff like kobolds or lizards.

The Varnham Wastes were a no-go as well. Reptilian and undead were overdone, and he had the sneaking suspicion that if he chose aberrations for his affinity, the place might become a water dungeon. Nobody wanted to clear a water dungeon; they were the worst. There was no way he was going to pick this place if there was even a small chance that he would be stuck becoming a water dungeon forever.

The Frost Peaks sounded cool. His mind was filled with images of raiders in longships attacking villages. Fierce barbarian warriors with swords and axes would be in his lineup of mobs, and having something sort of human was perfect. In the back of his mind, he got the feeling that the other classes might bleed over into the humanoid affinity, offering him frost creatures and even giants at some point. If he was going to be stuck in a dungeon his whole life, which was not a bad thing at all, this place would be where he wanted to live.

"I'll take the Frost Peaks of Ulmore and the humanoid affinity," Aaron said with confidence.

"Very well. I have an appropriate assistant created for you. Give me a moment or two to get things in order, and then you're off," the voice said.

As Aaron's vision faded, he wondered what the person's name was.

***

Time passed on this crazy Aerkon world, and Aaron Lavelle found the life of a dungeon core wasn't quite as easy as he had been led to believe. Even with all the skills of his previous life still available to him, Aaron had a few close calls. The creatures that inhabited the mountains were fierce, and his newly created dungeon seemed to attract everything around him. With his weak initial defenders, Aaron was barely able to hold off the various monsters and wildlife looking to consume his core. He had weathered the assaults, and now, the flow of monsters had slowed to a trickle. Instead of the denizens of these mountains feasting on his core, he fed upon them, and that feasting had allowed him to reach level 3.

His assistant, a scrawny, hairless frost hound called Qui, was of dubious assistance. Qui had promised that there would be adventurers flooding into the area as soon as they opened up. Apparently, new dungeons were rare, and adventurers should have been lined up at the entrance to test their steel and spells against his mobs and traps. Instead of a flood of adventurers, he got nothing. His location looked cool and all, with a spikey stone entryway accented with some glowing rune script that promised doom to anyone that entered. The problem was that his dungeon location turned out to be surrounded by fierce tribes of barbarians that drove away or killed any strangers, including any adventurers that happened to approach. His dungeon wasn't growing at the pace he had expected, and the frustration over it was mounting.

"Master, we have a visitor," Qui said. The wolf liked to sleep in his core room, and Aaron was glad he couldn't smell him. Qui looked kind of scuzzy.

Looking toward his entrance, Aaron saw a single traveler approaching, wrapped in a thick cloak and furs that hid his features. It looked like a humanoid of some sort but was too covered up for Aaron to tell exactly what race he belonged to. So far, he hadn't seen anything other than normal humans and a single dwarf, despite Qui insisting that there were a whole bunch of different races on this world. The man walked past the imposing spikes and dire warnings at the entrance without even glancing at them. It was like he didn't even care that a dungeon was about to kill him.

"Some fool nomad looking for a place to shelter from the storm, I'd wager," Aaron said. So far, the violent tribes that wandered the mountains had paid little attention to his dungeon. Qui said they were a superstitious people and wanted nothing to do with a dungeon, fearing the dungeon drained their souls when they went inside. Well, Aaron did drain their mana, but he didn't think his core did anything to their souls. He was glad enough to be left alone by the local tribes; they were pretty tough from what Qui had told him. When there were few victims to be found in the mountains, the tribes would often war among themselves or travel into the lowlands to raid the settlements there.

Aaron wished he could watch some of those battles, but being a core gem meant that his view was locked to his dungeon and its immediate surroundings. A single nomad or adventurer wasn't going to find his dungeon a hospitable place, and already, growls from the pack of wolves guarding the first chamber of his dungeon reverberated against the bare stone walls. Qui had tried to get him to decorate a bit, adding some things to make the dungeon more imposing, but Aaron hadn't become what he now was to waste his time and mana on creating window dressing.

As the three wolves in the entry chamber struck, the figure merely chuckled and waved his hand. A cloud of poisonous vapor filled the room, leaving the wolves choking to death on the cold stone floor. Instead of stopping to gather loot, the hooded figure pressed on. Aaron's dungeon wasn't very large yet, but Qui had assured him that his defenders were more powerful than their level would suggest, due mainly to the affinity bonus the location offered him. Room by room, the stranger progressed, and none of Aaron's defenders even laid a hand on the intruder.

Berserkers, wolves, a swarm of frost mephits, and even his champion, a warlord that would one day become a powerful giant, all failed to stop the intruder. Qui whined in fear and crouched behind the pillar that Aaron's core gem rested upon. This was what Qui had warned him of: a powerful adventurer that would destroy his core to gain a portion of his power.

"Hello there, little core. That wasn't a very friendly welcome. Sadly, it wasn't just unwelcoming. It was downright pathetic," the man said. His voice had an otherworldly timbre that Aaron found terrifying.

"Who are you?" Aaron asked. It felt strange to communicate with anyone other than Qui, whom he didn't really talk to since they could read each other's thoughts. In fact, this was the first time he had spoken aloud since becoming a core. At least Qui had taught him how to project his voice in the dungeon; otherwise, he would have just sat there without replying.

"Who am I? I am the one that has to decide whether to end your short life as a core or whether you might become my new best friend," the mysterious stranger told him.

"Woah, dude, since I don't want to be destroyed, what

exactly do I have to do to become your new best friend?" Aaron asked, trying to sound brave despite the terror starting to gnaw at his core.

"I'm here to make you an offer, one that should benefit us both," the figure said, finally pulling back his hood. Instead of the face of an adventurer, Aaron looked upon a skull covered in desiccated bits of flesh. This was the first undead creature he had seen, and the gamer in him put the pieces together quickly. This monster was powerful; it was a lich, and a lich was someone Aaron didn't want to mess with.

"What is this deal you mentioned, sir? Oh, and I didn't catch your name. I was once known as Aaron, but you can call me whatever." Aaron tried to put a friendly spin on their conversation.

"My name is Berikoz, and I can offer something very important to a newly created core. I can offer you a steady supply of victims for your dungeon to feast upon. You will grow powerful, despite the dearth of adventurers in this forlorn area. In return, I only require one little thing."

"What do you need?" Aaron asked.

"Why, all I require is your core for a new experiment. I should advise you that saying no to my offer is not an option. Oh, I should also inform you that your assistant's services will no longer be needed. I shall have a new advisor sent over to you soon." Berikoz pointed a finger at Qui, who shriveled up and died so quickly that only a small whimper escaped from Aaron's former assistant.

"What are you going to do to me?" Aaron asked, unable to mask the terror in his voice.

"Nothing much. I just need to make some small tweaks to your core gem. You, my new friend, will be providing me with temporary accommodations inside that shining little core of yours, accommodations I will enter when the time is right. Don't worry, my previous experiments have taught me much, and I'm nearly certain that you will survive completely intact, though I am afraid the process will be rather painful."

Qui might have only given a small whimper of pain when he died, but Aaron's screams lasted for much, much longer.

Afterword

Thank you for joining Florence and her cats for a second adventure. She's gone through a lot of changes, and deaths, but her most exciting and difficult task lies ahead. How will Florence and Doug liberate the cores under Berikoz's influence? Who will join them in their quest? Will they have enough time to do what they need to do? Most importantly, what will happen to Florence when the 199 days are up? We'll find out the answers to all these questions in Cat Core, Book 3: Road Trip, which should be out in early 2022.

If you've enjoyed your time in Florence's home, please leave a review on Amazon. Positive reviews greatly assist the author. As I write this, the audio for both books is being produced, and I think you'll be blown away with what the narrator, Andrea Parsneau, and the good folks at Podium Audio are creating. I want to also thank my readers, who contributed the names and a bit of the personality for all the cats featured in this series. I hope I've done your little monsters justice. More thanks to my editor, Bodie Dykstra, for his continued partnership in helping turn the ragged manuscripts I send him into something that is entertaining to read.

A special shout-out goes to the cover artist for Book 2. It was done by the legendary Erol Otus, whose work has graced the pages of gaming books for decades. The iconic images he created helped spark my imagination and have influenced my writing. I also need to thank my family for their unwavering support, and especially my daughter Sydney, whose love of cats spurred me to write such an unusual Dungeon Core story.

If you've enjoyed this book, you may also be interested in my LitRPG series *Limitless Lands*, as well as its spinoff *Limitless Seas*, or my space Dungeon Core series *Derelict*. You can find them all here on Amazon:

https://www.amazon.com/gp/product/B07G7GWFFL

https://www.amazon.com/dp/B08RNY2XQ2

https://www.amazon.com/dp/B087GH66WS

If you would like to support my work and get a peek at early chapter releases for my latest projects, consider supporting me on Patreon:

https://www.patreon.com/deanhenegar

To keep up with the latest news and new releases of my work (and to just maybe get a chance to see your cat's name in print), check out my Facebook author's page:

https://www.facebook.com/henegarauthor

Here are some great groups for readers of LitRPG, GameLit, and Dungeon Core:

https://www.facebook.com/groups/litrpgforum

https://www.facebook.com/groups/LitRPG.books

https://www.facebook.com/groups/Dungeonstories

https://www.facebook.com/groups/LitRPGReleases

https://www.facebook.com/groups/LitRPGsociety

Made in the USA
Monee, IL
11 October 2021